# Grid Zero

ANDREW DIAMOND

This is a work of fiction. Names, characters, and events
are the products of the author's imagination. Any
resemblance to actual people or events is purely
coincidental.

# Also by Andrew Diamond

Gate 76 (Freddy Ferguson #1)
Kill Romeo (Freddy Ferguson #2)
32 Minutes (Freddy Ferguson #3)

The Friday Cage (Claire Chastain #1)
The Reisman Case (Claire Chastain #2)

Impala
To Hell with Johnny Manic
Warren Lane
Wake Up, Wanda Wiley
The Sellout

# 1

## June 30

In the windowless supermarket on Monroe Avenue, they shopped by flashlight as the midday sun blazed outside. The shoppers moved in groups of four, each group accompanied by a clerk or security guard to prevent theft. They had shown cash to get in. Without electricity to run the payment terminals, credit cards were useless.

The store's diesel generator had run out of fuel on the third day of the blackout. By then, almost all the meat was gone, all the eggs, the dairy, anything that needed to be refrigerated or frozen. The ones who had bought meat while it was still available had to grill it right away because they had no working refrigerators to keep it cold.

What the store hadn't sold, they threw away. Minimum-wage workers tossed the last of the perishable food into dumpsters under a manager's supervision. The hungry onlookers who had been living on cereal and bread after throwing out their own spoiled meat looked angry. Why couldn't they have some?

"We can't give away food that might have gone bad," the manager explained. "There are liability laws."

Some in the crowd didn't like that answer. The manager wound up in the ER. Twelve stitches above the eye. Even though the hospital was depressing—all those elderly people being hauled in for heat stroke, and the accident victims, the ones who'd been out driving on chaotic streets where none of the traffic lights worked—the manager lingered an extra hour just to soak up the air-conditioning. The hospital's generator was still in service then, back on day four.

It had been on and off ever since, depending on when the diesel trucks could get through. Hospitals had priority. If there was any fuel to distribute, it went to them first. To them and to the police and fire departments, to the pumping stations that supplied the water, to the utility trucks repairing downed lines, and to the huge, power-hungry data centers in the northern part of the state.

People were angry about that. Was it really so important to keep the video streams running, to keep the memes flowing on social media, when people for two hundred miles in every direction had no lights, no air-conditioning, and no way to preserve or cook food? Were the entertainment needs of the South and Midwest and West, those parts of the country that still had power, more important than the physical needs of everyone who was suffering in the East?

The outage stretched from North Carolina through Virginia, Maryland, and DC into Delaware, Pennsylvania, and parts of New Jersey. The region had not even begun to recover from the first hurricane when the second hit. The first storm, a lazy, sprawling giant, had parked itself over the mid-Atlantic for two days and dumped over a foot of rain in some areas. The second was a tightly wound powerhouse that made landfall on the Virginia-Carolina border as a Category 5 before moving inland and racing north into Pennsylvania and New Jersey.

The rain from the first storm had flooded hundreds of counties and softened the ground. The wind from the second uprooted millions of trees, taking down power lines everywhere. It wasn't a single blow that had knocked out the grid; it was death by a thousand cuts. By a hundred thousand cuts. Trucks from the power companies prowled the streets— the streets that weren't blocked by fallen trees—to visually inspect lines, transformers, and substations one by one, making pen-and-paper inventories of what needed to be repaired.

Getting the components required to make the repairs was a whole other matter. Where do you find thousands of pole-top transformers on short notice? How do you get them into neighborhoods where the roads have washed out?

And what about the specialty equipment at the damaged substations? The switches, relays, breakers, and shunts? The big transformers that fed thousands of homes? Every day, as residents with chain saws cleared fallen trees from smaller roads, trucks from the electric utility pushed deeper into the neighborhoods to discover more damage.

Even now, nine days after the passing of the second storm, Empire Energy still couldn't make a full inventory of the problems. Their trucks were running out of fuel, and the gas stations, lacking electricity, couldn't pump any more.

Downed trees and flood-damaged roads hindered the progress of utility crews coming in from other states. Trucks from Ohio, Illinois, Kentucky, and Kansas brought fresh water, fruit, and snacks along with black-market gasoline, and sold it along their routes at thousand percent markups.

Sean Riggs knew from his brief stint with the electric utility how power would be restored in a scenario like this. First, fix the lines and equipment closest to the generation facilities—if you can get there. The power has to get onto the grid before it can be distributed. Then, Washington, DC, would be first in line. After that, the military bases, the shipyards in Newport News. Then Philadelphia and Baltimore and the large industrial customers. Then the suburbs. Then the medium-sized towns. Then the small towns, like his. The poor souls scattered along rural country roads would be last in line.

According to his AM radio, pockets around the gas-fired plants at Chalk Point and Doswell had come on line the previous morning. DC would start to light up that evening. He calculated that even with the crews that had rolled in from out of state, it would be four days before the lights came on again in his town of thirty-one thousand. Phone service was being restored piecemeal in the cities, but there still was no signal outside the metro areas.

In the dark, sweltering supermarket on Monroe Avenue, the shoppers and their flashlight-wielding chaperones moved in pools of bright white LED light along the middle aisles where the imperishables—cereal, chips, crackers—were in dwindling supply.

"That one," said an elderly woman, pointing to a box of cereal on a high shelf.

"Grape-Nuts?" asked the security guard.

"Yes, please."

He pulled it from the shelf and put it in her basket.

Danielle Duval and Sean Riggs reached for the last box of Raisin Bran at the same time.

"You take it," she said.

If the beam of the guard's flashlight had been on her face, instead of illuminating the floor behind her, Sean would have seen her smile.

They had run into each other a handful of times in the past year, at coffee shops, gas stations, supermarkets. She had flirted with him each time, but he hadn't picked up on it. If he had seen her in broad daylight, he would not have recognized her, would have sworn he had never seen her before.

She knew from a friend of a friend he was a software engineer. "Flirting with guys like that is pointless," her friend told her. "They don't get it. You have to be direct."

"Like, how?" Danielle asked.

"Like that show *Love on the Spectrum*. You say, 'Hello. I find you attractive, and I would like to spend some time with you. Would you like to join me for a drink?' Those computer programmers are socially clueless. And they're so damn literal about everything. What do you like about him anyway?"

"I don't know. He always has this look on his face like there's something really interesting going on inside his head. I want to find out what it is."

"Be careful what your wish for," her friend warned.

Danielle pushed the cereal box into Sean's basket. "Take it," she said, still smiling. "I don't have any milk anyway."

"I do," he said absently.

"Oh, yeah, and um, you're welcome, by the way."

"Right. Sorry. I mean, thank you."

"How do you still have milk?"

"You know those solar generators people use for RVs?"

She shook her head just as he turned his gaze toward the security guard's flashlight. The group was moving again, toward the rear of the store. She knew he'd missed her gesture, so she tapped his chest, the pectoral muscle next to his shoulder, and said, "No. How do they work?"

Would he get that? That she had tapped his chest with the palm of her hand instead of just touching his shoulder with her fingertip?

This is just day nine, Sean thought. People haven't turned on each other yet. They're not that desperate, but they're getting there. So far, the worst behaviors have been property crimes, people looting stores, stealing TVs they can't even turn on, stealing food, which isn't really even stealing in this situation. Wait another week, till people are really hungry and food is even scarcer than it is now. Then it will be the strong against the weak. I hope it doesn't come to that. I hope they get this sorted soon.

"You unfold the panels in the yard," he said, "and hook them up to this big battery."

His matter-of-fact tone told her that to him, their conversation was about exchanging information, not connecting. So, no, he didn't get that she was flirting.

"And you can run the fridge off that?" She tried to sound impressed.

"The fridge and the lights. The computer, the record player. And the air conditioner in the bedroom."

But I don't see how, Sean thought. I don't see how everything will be back to normal. The few trucks that have made it into the town, the big rigs delivering food and water, had mud stains on their tires from driving over washed-out roads. There are so many trees down, they're driving on dirt to get through.

Two days after the second storm had passed, Virginia had a confirmed death toll of twelve. Those people had died in floods. By day four, over forty deaths had been confirmed. He got the news from the AM station up in DC whose signal came through clearly at night.

The last report, from last night, put the number at over four hundred. The heat was killing people now. The brutal, sweltering heat that had settled in after the storm's passing had already dried the flooded fields, the parking lots, and schoolyards that had looked like lakes only nine days prior.

The death count will go up, Sean thought. All those people out in the county, the ones who couldn't get into town for food on days four and five and six. They're sweltering in their little cinder-block houses. The floods polluted their wells. They have no clean water, and they're sweating to death. The older ones can't take this round-the-clock heat. Watch, they'll find couples in bed together, both of them dead. The ones who have shown up at the hospital so far are just the tip of the iceberg.

And then the smaller towns that can't pump water. The diesel trucks run out of fuel before they get to the small-town pumping stations. People who are already dehydrated are drinking whatever water they can find, dirty water, getting diarrhea, getting even more dehydrated, and it's killing them.

He had been to the hospital twice since the outage began, trying to pitch in with his tech knowledge. The hospital's generators could power the computers at the nurses' stations, but the patient records and the databases that kept track of treatments were miles away, in the big data centers in Northern Virginia. And though the hospital and the data centers each had power, the internet service providers that were supposed to connect them did not.

So the nurses turned off their workstations and wrote everything out longhand on clipboards, like it was the nineteen forties. The younger ones couldn't read the older ones' cursive, so they had to remember to print. And no one could read the doctors' scrawl.

With the computers dark, the electricity went to the parts of the hospital that needed it most. To the respirators and heart monitors, to the dialysis machines, to the refrigerators that kept the medicines cool, and to the fridges in the basement morgue that kept the stench of the dead from rising up to the sick on the floors above.

The hospital morgue was designed as a temporary holding area. The bodies usually went to a funeral home within a day or so, but none of the local homes could take them now because they too lacked power. So, all twelve slots were full, and the hospital had ordered two refrigerated trucks to handle the overflow. While they waited for the trucks for to arrive, the bodies took turns in the refrigerated drawers. They had to stay just cool enough to stop the rot.

Again, Sean thought, we're only on day nine. How long can people stand this before they snap?

"Oh my God," Danielle said, "you have air-conditioning?" She grabbed his arm and turned him toward her. "You have air-conditioning, and that's the *last* thing you mention?"

Afternoon temperatures had been hovering in the high nineties for the past eight days. The bedroom in her apartment, with its west-facing windows, had reached a hundred five four days in a row. Sleeping was near impossible, as the room didn't dip below ninety until after midnight. When she wasn't lying in a pool of sweat, she was trying to cool off in a tepid shower in the dark.

When she was younger, Hitchcock's *Psycho* had left her terrified of showering. By the end of high school, the fear had diminished to a more specific scenario: showering in the dark in an empty house. Now, after nine days without power and nine sleepless nights, when she stood beneath the lukewarm spray, she fantasized about an intruder, just to break the tedium.

Why should he be a psychopath, she wondered as she rubbed shampoo into her hair. If he's going to be some one-in-a-million rando, he could just as well be one of those handsome models from the cover of a trashy romance novel, the kind who always wears his shirt unbuttoned to show off his six-pack abs.

Ooh, and wouldn't it be nice if he had an actual six-pack too? What she wouldn't give for an ice-cold beer in this heat!

She would hear him moving through the bedroom, bumping into furniture in the dark as he moved instinctively toward the sound of running water. She would call out, "I'm in here, Romeo. Check your clothes at the door and we can have some fun. God, I'm sooooo bored!"

"Yeah," said Sean in reply to her question about air-conditioning. "I—wait, have we met before?"

"I don't think so," she lied. She wanted to see if he'd correct her.

"Oh. I thought your voice sounded kind of familiar."

It should, she thought. Because I talked with you at the gas station two weeks ago when you were filling your tank. I talked with you twice at the coffee shop last spring. And once in the checkout line of this very store last fall. Am I that forgettable? Or are you just off in your own world all the time?

"Hey, um, if you want a bowl of cereal with some cold milk—" She tried to make out his figure in the dark as he spoke. The security guard's light shone ten feet behind him, making him a tall, thin silhouette. "You're welcome to come over. I'm just a few blocks down, if you don't mind walking."

*Finally,* she thought. Did he see my eye roll? Does he even know what an eye roll means?

Emerging from the dark of the store a few minutes later, he put his hand to his forehead to shield his eyes from the glare of the sun. He squinted at her as they passed the police car and the line of sweating shoppers waiting to be admitted.

"I think I *have* seen you before," he said.

He was tall and lean, with brown hair and intelligent brown eyes. He wore a dark blue T-shirt and khaki shorts, a regrettable mix of colors. She guessed he was in his early thirties, just a few years older than her.

She was average height, with a round face, full cheeks, full figure, fair skin, light brown hair, and hazel eyes. If the laundry machine at her apartment had been working, or if she had known she would run into someone worth talking to today, she would have worn something other than those paint-stained cutoffs and the white tank top and straitjacket torture bra that gouged red wire lines under her boobs. After sweating through everything else, she was down to the dregs of her wardrobe.

"Yeah, I think you have," she said in her friendliest tone. In case the tone didn't get through, she flashed a bright smile.

He eyed her for a moment, and she could see he was beginning to place her.

"Wait, have you lost weight?"

"God, what a question!" She laughed. "So, you remember me being fat? Yes. I lost weight. How can you not when you're living on crackers and old fruit and sweating twenty-four seven?"

Though she complained, she considered the loss of a few pounds as one of the benefits of the blackout. A diet forced by circumstance in which cheating was impossible.

Oh, and no work. That was another plus. No video calls. No annoying clients second-guessing the marketing tactics of the social media campaigns she managed. She didn't have to think about shilling for products and brands she didn't respect.

"Now, can I ask *you* a question?" she asked. They were walking side by side past the bus stop on Monroe Avenue, each carrying a plastic grocery bag filled with treasures they would have considered pathetic in normal times. Crackers, canned tuna, black beans, and a cellophane package of dried seaweed for her. Raisin Bran, tortilla chips, canned ravioli, and chili for him. She looked up at him with a curious side-eye, a playful smile forming on her lips.

"Shoot," he said.

They were approaching the piñata in the intersection of Monroe and Sumter. Piñata was one of the new words spawned by the blackout and repeated in the newscasts people listened to on battery-powered radios. With traffic lights out of commission throughout the mid-Atlantic, a number of trucks delivering food and water had been broadsided at unregulated intersections. Their trailers broke open and spilled their contents all over the streets. Hungry and thirsty passersby rushed in to scoop up all they could carry.

When the blackout entered its second week, people started hitting the trucks on purpose. Some of the drivers now carried guns.

"Wait," she said. "Do you mean *shoot* like 'Darn, look at that truck' or *shoot* like 'Go ahead and ask me a question'?"

"Go ahead and ask me a question."

The question she wanted to ask was, What the hell is going on in that mind of yours every time I run into you? Because, judging by the expressions on your face, it must be a hell of a lot more interesting than whatever's going on out here in the rest of the world. But you're not a big talker, are you? So, I guess I have to draw you out. I can already tell what kind of boyfriend you are. You're the kind who won't be drawn into a fight even when your girlfriend tries to pick one.

She decided to test her theory.

"Okay," she said. "When you ask a woman you just met if she's lost weight, is it because you're clueless about how that's going to make her feel, or you don't understand basic etiquette, or do you just not care?"

He screwed up his face as he considered the question.

"Oh, look at you!" She laughed again and playfully swatted his chest. "Thinking it through so you can give a well-reasoned answer. I'm teasing you."

He wasn't thinking it through. He was thinking of an inscrutable section of code he had run across two days before he was fired from his software security job at Empire Energy. It had disturbed him when he first saw it, though he couldn't explain why, and his mind had come back to it almost every hour since the power went out.

"Actually," he said, coming to a stop and finally looking her full in the face, "I've had a lot on my mind."

Any doubts she had had about whether this potentially frustrating pursuit was worth the effort were swept away by the butterflies she felt when he looked her in the eye.

"Sorry if I insulted you," he said.

She liked that he meant that. A wave of warmth swept over her, and she tried not to smile as broadly as she wanted to.

# 2

"How's it hanging there, Del?"

Ray Cooper had that smart-ass look that he always had when he ribbed his friend. At forty-one, Cooper was eight years younger than Delbert "Del" Wright. Cooper worked in the cool of the office, in a suit. Even now he looked clean and comfortable, his dark blond hair freshly washed and neatly trimmed.

Del, with his dark hair and beard, had sweat through his blue jumpsuit, and through the fiberglass cast that immobilized his left wrist and hand. The cast had been itching and stinking for days. He removed his cap, wiped his forehead against his sleeve, and said, "Whatcha got for me?" He nodded respectfully toward the third man in the room, who wore both a visitor badge and a government ID.

"It's still printing," Ray said.

Del could hear the printer whirring in the other room.

The lights, the printer, and the air-conditioning were powered by the big diesel generator behind the building. Empire Energy had to keep the central office running at all times.

"Read them through this time," Ray said. "Make sure you have orders for every crew. Distribute those first, then go on with your inspections."

Del had been hand delivering orders to crews in four different counties since the first day of the blackout. Yesterday, he'd missed one, drove fifty miles back to the office to get the paperwork and then fifty miles back to the idle crew. A huge waste of time.

Simple orders could be read over the radio. Fix the line break at mile thirty-six of Highway 29. That was easy enough. The workers would see where the line was down as soon as they rolled up. But out-of-state crews repairing buses in unfamiliar substations needed equipment ratings and wiring diagrams for everything they touched.

Del picked up the printouts, spent hours driving them around, then hours more inspecting lines and components in residential neighborhoods. His broken left hand prevented him from doing heavy repairs, so now he was saddled with the tedious work of mapping out downed lines and inventorying damaged equipment. He knew the roads better than anyone, and after twenty-five years on the job, he could visually identify every component on the grid.

If a pole-top transformer was damaged, if the glass or ceramic insulators on a line had shattered, he would note the exact items that needed to be repaired or replaced, and the utility would know whom to send where, with what tools and parts. He was doing useful work, but was frustrated at not being able to do the hands-on work he preferred. He had lived his whole life by his father's motto: If you see something broke, don't leave it for the next fella to fix. Take care of it yourself.

But for the past nine days, that was all he'd been doing, finding problems and leaving them for the next fellow to fix, cursing his broken hand, wishing he could be of more help. He'd started at four that morning. Now, at ten, he was six hours into his shift, and he knew he wouldn't knock off until midnight.

The out-of-state crews worked shorter shifts. Twelve hours, usually. And then they complained—justly, Del thought— about having to sleep in dark, hot motels.

"How are the crews holding up?" Ray asked.

Ray was a computer guy. Manager of software development in the transmission-and-distribution unit. His crew maintained the software that controlled the flow of electricity throughout the state.

In the course of a normal workday, these two would not have crossed paths. They had met four years earlier at a company picnic and found they had similar interests: hunting, fishing, four-wheeling in the mountains in the western part of the state.

Ray Cooper looked like an all-American boy grown up, the clean-cut, square-jawed high school football star who had kept in shape. He was a good shot with a rifle, shot pistols at the range as a hobby, could clean a fish, but could never cook it right. Always stopped at two beers, even when it was just him and the boys in the cabin after a hunt. Del once asked him why, and Ray said he liked to keep sharp.

"Keep sharp for what?" Del asked. "You think one of your hunting buddies is gonna jump you?"

He was kidding, but Ray wasn't when he answered, "You never know."

The answer bothered Del. What kind of person doesn't trust his own friends? But when he talked it through later with his wife, he saw it made sense. If a guy is going to be in charge of the software that runs the critical energy infrastructure that millions of people rely on day in and day out, he'd better be a little paranoid. What juicier target was there for the enemies and terrorists aiming to undo us?

Empire Energy's own training videos—required watching every six months—hammered home the need for caution. Don't click on links in emails from people you don't know. Don't divulge information electronically unless you're sure the person on the other end is who you think they are. Consider all company information to be confidential unless you're explicitly told otherwise. The bad guys are after us twenty-four seven. All it takes is one slip-up from one of our thousands of employees and the bad guys are in.

If a person wasn't already paranoid, the job of running and securing such an important system under such constant threat would make them so.

"You look haggard, Del." Ray was sitting on the edge of a cubicle desk, his arms crossed over his chest, shirt white and neatly pressed.

"Hell, I feel it." In the past nine days, when Del wasn't working, he was dreaming of work. The downed lines, the exhausted crews he'd been pushing past their limits, the heat and humidity and mosquito bites, the lack of fresh food—it was all a test of endurance, a living nightmare that he should have been able to escape in his sleep. But it followed him even there.

His wife was wearing down too, stuck day after day in a hot, dark house with four restless, cranky children. But she didn't complain. Not aloud, anyway. Del could see on her face the toll it was taking.

He had started late as a father in marriage number two. The first marriage was childless, "by the grace of God," he often thought, because Betsy was crazy.

The second time around, he found the right woman. Carrie was solid, stable, responsible, no-nonsense. His two boys, Teddy and Walt, were nine and seven. The girls, Marybeth and Annie, were five and three.

"I *feel* haggard," Del said. The long hours had inflamed every old injury in his body. His right shoulder, both knees, his lower back. "Who's your pal here? I don't believe we've met." Del pointed to the third man in the room, the stocky, brown-haired visitor in the gray suit with the government ID badge. He looked to be in his midthirties.

The man stepped forward and extended his hand. "Carlos Espinoza."

Del read the government badge as they shook hands. FBI.

"The Feds, huh? They questioning you about your excessive ammo purchases?" Del joked.

Ray Cooper frowned and shook his head gravely.

"Come on, Ray, I'm just giving you a hard time." You can have a sense of humor once in a while, Del thought. Can't you? Especially in days like these. If you can't have a laugh in all this misery, you're sunk.

"Not funny," Ray said. "We have a problem."

Del laughed. Ray and Carlos both winced as the smell of Del's sweat wafted over them.

"What's so funny?" Ray asked.

"Power's out to thirty million people in seven states and you tell me we have a problem."

"We have *another* problem," Ray clarified.

"Computers?" Del asked. He wiped his brow again and then turned his gaze to the right, toward the printer room. The whirring had stopped. His work orders were ready.

"You know what an advanced persistent threat is?" Ray asked. Espinoza shot him a sharp side-eye and shook his head.

"You mean, like, liberals?" Del asked. Another joke. Ray, who kept quiet on political matters inside the office, liked to tee off on the lefties once he got a beer in him up at the cabin. On his second beer, he'd really get going. And then when that one was empty, he'd clam up and stew. Del could see on his face all the dark thoughts running through his mind. Probably best he doesn't drink more than two, Del thought. He doesn't have the temperament for liquor. He'd be a mean drunk.

Del himself didn't care about politics one way or the other. As long as people were working and able to support their families, the world was right enough. In his mind, the country, even if it seemed to be perpetually on edge, had managed to balance itself out pretty well. While the extremists on both sides wasted their energy hating each other, the practical people in the middle, people like him, went about their work and kept the whole show running.

"No," Ray said. "I mean someone has gotten into our network. An advanced persistent threat is a kind of hack. They've been in here for weeks, exfiltrating data, sending it across the internet to God knows where."

Espinoza cut him off. "That's enough." And to Del, he added, "This information doesn't leave the room. Got it? This is an ongoing investigation."

Del zipped his lips to indicate he understood.

He went to the other room, pulled a warm stack of papers from the printer, and browsed the headings of each document, silently checking off the crew numbers in his mind. Sixteen. All present and accounted for.

On his way back through the main office, he heard Ray say with a sigh, "When it rains, it pours. If there's one bright spot to this outage, it's that the hackers can't pull any data from our systems."

Ray was a hard man, Del thought as he left the office. Right now, his hard edge came from the stress of the job. But he was like that anyway. There was something negative in him, something dark. When Del was a child, his father used to say that the truest measure of a man's character was the health of his wife. It took Del awhile to figure out what that meant. Back in the days when women didn't work, the man had absolute power at home, and no one to stop him from exercising it. How a person acts when they have absolute power, when they are accountable to no one and face no consequences for their actions—that will reveal their true character. And Ray's wife, Donna, always looked sad, worn, oppressed. They had money and a fine home and Florida vacations and a healthy twelve-year-old boy, but there was no light in her eyes. She always looked defeated.

That's the first thing you fix, Del thought as he settled himself into his truck. If the wife ain't right or the kid ain't right, you put everything on hold, and you fix that first. The rest can wait. There's a million people can fix things in the world outside. At home, it's on you. No one else is gonna do it for you.

He started the engine and cranked the air-conditioning. The radio came on softly, Waylon Jennings singing "Jole Blon." Where did they dig that one up, he wondered?

He sifted through the stack of papers and pulled out the instructions for the two closest crews, then shifted into gear.

Pulling out of the Empire lot, he thought, home is the inner circle. How are you going to fix the outer rings, friends and work, community and country, if you ain't got the core right? You ever think of that, Ray? You ever think maybe you ain't got your priorities straight?

# 3

Sean's house, a one-story brick rambler with a bay window in front, looked out on a dark green lawn shaded by two lush cherry trees. They had weathered the storms well enough. Better than the oak that had fallen at the north end of the block, or the sycamore that had fallen to the south. With two small bedrooms, attached garage, and an outdated kitchen and bath, it was what the real estate agents back in DC would have called a "starter home." Sean hadn't been thinking of staying when he came down here from the city, but he wasn't thinking of going back either.

When he arrived in town, the house was in foreclosure. He had enough in savings to cover the modest down payment, and he figured he could do some remodeling and make a profit on the sale when it was time to leave. His rough timeline was eighteen months. By then, he'd be too restless to stay in such a small town and would head back to the city. Not to DC, but to some other city.

In the year and three weeks since he'd arrived, he had already put in the bay window and refinished the main bathroom. The kitchen would be next, but for now that project was held up by a lack of funds. He had lost the job in DC after running afoul of corporate management. Then, after a contracting gig ended, he had gained and then lost a job with Empire Energy.

Now he was puttering along on contract jobs doled out by friends, earning a couple thousand here and there, with nothing steady. He had been applying for remote positions around the country, but his dismissal from Empire had hurt him, and it was blocking him from landing a meaningful full-time position.

"Wow! This place is nice," Danielle said as they stepped through the door.

It was no luxury mansion, but the wood floors looked bright and new because Sean had sanded them down and refinished them with a light blond stain. Daylight from the bay window and the sparse, neatly arranged furniture made the living room look more spacious than it was.

"Thanks," said Sean. "It's a work in progress."

The air in the living room was cooler and drier than the air outside. Not by much, but after nine days and nights in the stifling heat, it was enough for Danielle to notice.

The living room stretched from the front to the rear of the small house. Through the rear window she could see solar panels unfolded in the grass of the backyard. They were wired to two huge orange battery packs that looked like they might have weighed a hundred pounds each.

Sean explained he had four batteries in total, and used them in rotation. The two inside the house powered the fridge and the bedroom air conditioner. When they emptied out, he swapped them for the two in the yard.

"The kitchen's this way," he told her.

Scratching the mosquito bites on her arm, she followed him to the right, away from the bedroom. The kitchen side of the house was warmer. She could hear the AC humming through the bedroom door, which stood open a crack, and she realized that was the source of the living room's cool, dry air. She wanted to be on *that* side of the house, in *that* room, right in front of the AC. She wanted it blasting on her. Her skin hadn't been dry in days.

"Do you prefer milk or soy milk?" Sean asked as he set his bag on the counter.

What kind of question was that? Who offers a guest milk on her first visit?

She dropped her bag beside the sink.

Oh, right. The cereal. She had let him have the box of Raisin Bran in the store, and he said he had cold milk. He was actually going to feed her cereal.

When he opened the fridge, she saw a tall glass pitcher of lemonade and said, "I want that."

Her face was flushed from the seven-block walk in ninety-eight-degree heat. Her mouth watered at the thought of cool lemonade, and she almost cried with joy when she saw him pull the ice bucket from the freezer.

Ice, she thought! Honest to goodness, freezing cold ice! She listened to the cubes clink into the tall glass, then crack as the lemonade flowed over them. The sound of liquid flowing into the glass awakened something else in her. She had to pee. Bad.

She shifted gently from foot to foot. She didn't want to look like she was hopping. She was already self-conscious about how greedily she had eyed the lemonade, like a hungry dog watching its owner scrape food scraps into its bowl.

Now everything was catching up with her. The relentless heat. Nine nights without meaningful sleep. Nine days without a satisfying meal.

He turned to hand her the glass. She grabbed it with both hands, pulled it to her mouth, and drank as fast as she could. The glass was empty in seconds. Most of it went into her mouth, but some went down the front of her shirt, and an ice cube bounced off her foot and skipped across the floor.

She pushed the glass back at him and said breathlessly, "More!"

He thought she was funny. Against his quiet reserve, her forwardness and childlike earnestness were refreshing. She tried to down the second glass as fast as the first, but had to stop and catch her breath halfway through.

"Why are you laughing at me?" she asked as she pushed the glass back into his hands for thirds.

"I wasn't laughing."

"Smirking, then."

"Do you always act like this around new people?" He was trying to hold back a smile.

She shifted from foot to foot, clenching, even bending slightly at the waist. The front of her white tank top was yellow with sticky lemonade, and the back was soaked with sweat. She tried to remember when she had last put on deodorant.

"That way," Sean said, pointing toward the bedroom.

She looked over her shoulder and asked, "What? What's that way?"

"The bathroom."

She turned and made a beeline for the bedroom door. The bathroom was inside, attached. "Don't laugh at me," she called over her shoulder. "It's not polite to laugh at people." He couldn't tell from her tone if she was serious.

Inside the door, the bedroom air felt impossibly cool. She knelt and planted herself in front of the window AC unit, spread her arms, and tilted her head back. Sean could see her from the kitchen. The pose reminded him of a scene from an old black-and-white movie in which a woman abandons herself to a vampire.

"You have to pee, remember?"

"Dammit!"

She turned and skittered to the bathroom. Sean laughed. He finished his lemonade, set the glass on the counter, and looked through the windows of the kitchen door at the solar panels outside.

"Okay," Danielle said to herself on the toilet. "So far, you've invited yourself over, teased the guy on a long, hot walk, abused his hospitality, sweated and spilled all over yourself, performed a toddler's pee dance in the kitchen, attempted to seduce the air conditioner, and now you've unleashed a torrent in the bathroom that would make a Thoroughbred blush. God, I hope he can't hear me from the kitchen."

She leaned forward, curled and uncurled her toes, kneaded the wad of toilet paper in her left hand, and wondered how much more her bladder could possibly release.

The stream finally ended. "If he heard that and he still wants to talk to me, he either really likes me or he has no standards. And I'm fine either way at this point. Just give me a break from the crushing solitude of my dark, sweltering apartment."

She flushed and went to the sink.

"Oh my God," she thought. "The water here is twenty degrees cooler than at my place."

She kept her hands under the stream, not wanting to lose the coolness, but the stream went lukewarm after a few seconds. The cold stuff must have been sitting in the pipes in the air-conditioned wall between the bedroom and the bathroom. When it ran out, it felt like the water in her apartment.

She checked herself in the mirror. Puffy bags under both eyes. A few dry strands of hair had escaped her ponytail. The hair along her forehead was matted with sweat. Now that the heat rash on her face was subsiding, she thought she lacked color. She hadn't worn makeup in days, and her natural skin seemed pale. Too many sleepless nights. Not enough nourishing food.

Though her cheeks had lost the extra padding they had carried for so many years, and though her jawline was now sharp and distinct, she still saw in her reflection the chubby, bell-cheeked girl who everyone had assumed was a tomboy, even though she wasn't. She had played the role because that was the role people expected.

She shook the water from her hands and returned to the living room.

Where was Sean?

She checked the kitchen. Not there. Outside? Yes. She could see him through the windows in the top half of the door that led from the kitchen to the backyard.

He was checking the batteries attached to the solar panels. She liked his posture, even as he knelt to read the display on the battery pack. A straight back. Nice. And he can fix things. Double bonus!

She turned and opened the freezer, slid out the rectangular bucket of ice.

No, she thought.

Then—yes, why not? You've already gone this far.

Oh, you're crazy, she told herself.

Yes, I am, she agreed. It's the heat. I'm crazy, and so what? You only live once.

She slid the bucket out of the freezer and shut the door.

Kneeling in the yard, Sean read the numbers on the LCD display. The larger of the two batteries showed a ninety percent charge. It would be full in another hour or two. That was the workhorse that powered the bedroom air conditioner. Before dinner, he'd swap it out for the one that had been chugging along for the past day and a half.

The second battery, at sixty pounds, was smaller. It powered the fridge and the record player, charged the laptop and other odd devices. He knelt and checked the display. Sixty-five percent charged. It should have been full.

As he stood to check the wire leading to the panel, he caught a glimpse of Danielle in the kitchen, looking into the open freezer. If that screwy woman drinks any more lemonade, he thought, her bladder is going to explode.

He knelt at the solar panel and tightened the wire that delivered power to the battery. He must have jarred it loose when he positioned the panels that morning.

The ground, he noted, was firm and dry. Surprisingly dry, given the rain from the storms. But nine straight days of cloudless sun and extreme heat—that would do it. That would dry out anything.

Shadows from the tall bamboo stand at the rear of the yard were beginning to encroach on the panels. In an hour, he would have to move them closer to the house and farther toward the left edge of the yard, where the sun would be direct and unobstructed.

Why wait, he thought? I'm already hot and sweaty. Do I really want to come out here in an hour and sweat all over again?

He unplugged the wire from the larger battery and began the process of folding and moving the first set of panels. Once he had those set up, he lugged the heavier of the two batteries into a spot of shade and plugged it in. Then he repeated the process with the second set of panels and the smaller battery.

All that lifting in the hot sun left him soaked with sweat. When he reentered the kitchen fifteen minutes later, he poured the last of the lemonade into the glass of melting ice he had left on the counter and drank it all down at once.

Then he stood and listened. Except for the gentle hum of the air conditioner, the house was silent.

Where had she gone?

He walked into the living room and checked the coffee table. His heart skipped a beat when he saw that his wallet was gone.

He checked his back pocket. The wallet was there. He had never taken it out.

"Danielle?" He said it softly, tentatively, and got no response.

He turned and looked at the front door. It was shut. That didn't mean anything. It could have stayed shut because she was still in the house, or she could have shut it when she left. But her bag of groceries was still in the kitchen, by the sink. She wouldn't leave that, would she?

He walked into the bedroom, half expecting to find her on the bed, reading a magazine. He nudged the door open and felt the cool air wash over him. The bed was empty. The room was empty.

Had she left, then? With no goodbye? Just used him for his lemonade, wham-bam-thank-you-sir, and walked out without a word?

Screw her, her thought angrily. Because he liked her. He was already working on the needling questions he'd pepper her with at their next gas station or grocery store run-in. What kind of person invites herself to someone's house, chugs all their lemonade, and then walks out without so much as a thank-you?

He sat on the edge of the bed, kicked off his sandals, and scratched at the itchy bites on his ankles. He'd shower, pick out a record, and...

Wait. Why was the bathroom door shut?

He stepped quietly forward and put his ear to the door. At first, he heard only the sound of blood rushing through his ears. And then a breath, a deep inhalation followed by a long exhale.

"Danielle?"

"Yeah?"

"Are you okay in there?"

"I'm wonderful!" Her voice rang with delight.

"What are you doing?"

"Taking a bath!"

Oh my God, he thought. She's completely nuts.

"I heard that," she called. The sound of tinkling water told him she was moving in the tub.

"Heard what?"

"You think I'm crazy."

"I didn't say that," he called. "Did I?" He actually wasn't sure if he had muttered the words or just thought them.

"You thought it," she said. "Just like I would. Because I am. I'm absolutely batshit crazy. *You* try not sleeping for nine nights and living on crackers and hot, wrinkled grapes and stewing in your own filth in a dark, stuffy apartment and—sorry. TMI. Scratch that part about filth." He heard a splash as she moved in the water. "I actually have great hygiene. I was an Olympic finalist for bathing and dental care. But yes, I'm crazy and I don't care anymore, and I hope you don't either, but even if you do, I don't care about that either. By the way, sorry about the ice."

"What ice?" he asked.

"I dumped it into the bath."

"The whole bucket?"

"All of it!" The extravagant pleasure in her voice made him smile.

In all the dozens of times he had imagined a large-scale extended blackout, his biggest fear was the breakdown of the social order. The abandonment of social rules and basic civility, in his mind, always ended in chaos and violence. The strong would terrorize the weak, and the desperate would lash out at anyone who stood between them and survival. After the collapse of the social order, the world would become a dystopian hellscape of destruction and waste.

But what about the little things? The basic comforts we take for granted? What about just wanting to feel clean again? Wanting a decent night's sleep? Wanting to sit in a cool, dry place where you didn't stick to your clothes? How did social norms weigh against those humble needs? Deprive anyone of basic comforts long enough and their values will shift.

Yeah, he thought, I'd want to take a cold bath too if I'd been soaked in sweat for nine days and nights.

Am I making excuses for her, he wondered? Because she's cute? Because I like her?

Then his mind turned to more practical matters. She's not going to want to put on that stained tank top again. Or those sweaty shorts.

He heard her stand, heard the water dripping from her arms into the tub, pictured her reaching for the towel.

He opened the dresser and found a dark green cotton T-shirt. From the third drawer, he pulled a pair of khaki shorts and thought for a moment. Probably not very comfortable with all those pockets and seams. And what will she do for underwear? From the top drawer, he grabbed a pair of boxer shorts still wrapped in its original package.

She pulled the plug, and he could hear the water swirling down the drain.

Which will she want to wear, he wondered? A normal woman in this situation would choose the khakis because they're less revealing. But a normal woman wouldn't be in this situation in the first place. She'll pick the boxers. Watch.

She opened the bathroom door wrapped in a white towel and said, "Hey, do you have any—"

He pushed the clothes at her before she could finish her question. "Oh!"

She took the shirt, looked at the khakis, and then chose the boxers instead and shut the door. He was beginning to understand her.

He listened to her from outside, heard the towel drop and clothes go on, her mouth running all the while. "Oh my God, it feels so good to be clean and cool! To not care! If I knew being crazy felt this good, I would have lost my mind years ago. It's so liberating! Why do men always have such scratchy towels?"

His linear, disciplined mind was still trying to catch up with the whirlwind of hers when the door popped open.

"I'm hungry!" she announced with a big, beaming smile.

# 4

"Now fix her in right there," Del said as he pulled the line taut with his good hand. "She ain't gonna get no tighter."

The pale twenty-four-year-old standing opposite him in the bucket of the truck's boom lift looked ill as he began to fasten the line. The second-to-last crew to which Del had delivered instructions asked him to take the guy away. Ben Wood. Del hadn't met him before, but he had heard about him. He was one of the gang that went out bowling with Ray Cooper, went out to Thursday dinners and listened to guru Ray talk about whatever the hell Ray liked to talk about. The kid was abrasive, like Ray, and full of himself. None of the crews liked him.

"He's worthless today," the crew chief had said. To the young man, he added with disgust, "Get outta here, Ben." And then to Del, "Take him home."

"Come on, kid," Del said. "I'll take you back."

The kid, as Del now called him, was wilting when he got into the truck. He was worse now, after thirty minutes in the hot sun.

Del had taken a detour on the way back to the utility offices, left the highway to inspect some little-traveled residential roads that had been impassable the past few days due to fallen trees. Someone had come with a chain saw and cleared the road that led to this line, which was the one he wanted to see.

A branch had knocked the line from the pole-top transformer that served half a dozen homes along the narrow road on the other side of the trees. Those homes would remain without power when the grid came back up, and because there were only six of them, they would be near last in line for repair. The utility would start with outages that affected thousands of homes, then repair lines that affected hundreds, then dozens, and finally, the little lost sheep like this one.

Del's niece, seven months pregnant with twins, lived in the last house down this line. He remembered his own wife's misery during the two pregnancies—two of her four—that stretched into late summer. A back sleeper forced to sleep on her side, always hot, sweating, tired, getting up to pee every hour. If he left this line to the utility, it might not be repaired until three weeks after the rest of the county had power. His niece would be sweating in misery the whole time.

Like so many others he had talked to, she didn't understand that the newly installed solar panels on her roof wouldn't supply power in an outage. Those panels were attached to the grid, and when the grid was down, the panels sat idle.

"Why?" she asked. "What's the point of that?"

"If power's out, you got crews trying to fix it. They're working on lines they expect to be dead. If your panels are pushing juice back onto the grid, you'll kill the linemen."

She's got two inside her, Del thought. And that makes a body miserable even *with* air-conditioning and a fridge full of food and a stove to cook it on. I ain't gonna let her go without.

Technically, he wasn't supposed to be doing any repairs. Technically, he wasn't supposed to touch a line without the okay of the central office. But technicalities went out the window nine days ago. There were crews crawling over every line in the state, and no one even had a full picture of where they all were.

"All right, that's a wrap," Del said to the kid who stood opposite him in the bucket. "You look like crap."

The young man groaned.

In the truck, with the AC on high, Del said, "Why the hell'd you go out partying last night?"

The kid looked loopy, his muscles slack and his movements uncoordinated, like a punch-drunk boxer. He rubbed his chin and said, "'Cause I ain't done nothing but work twenty hours a day for the past... How long's it been?"

"I don't know." Del put the truck in gear and headed back toward the highway. "But you don't need to go blowing off steam when the work's like this. You need to sleep. Alcohol dehydrates you. Speaking of..." He reached down to the cup holder in the door beside him and pulled up an unopened bottle of orange Gatorade. When he offered it, the young man shook his head weakly.

"You need to drink something."

"Can't," Ben said weakly. His head was beginning to droop.

Del slowed the truck and looked closely at him. The young man's face was dry. The skin on the backs of his hands was dry.

"When'd you stop sweating?"

The young man's eyes were closed. He shook his head without opening them and whispered, "Dunno."

Del hit the gas. "You stopped sweating 'cause your body ain't got nothing left to sweat out. You're too sick to drink Gatorade and—" He turned the truck hard to the left. Forget the highway, there was a hospital in town four miles down. The kid needs an IV, like all those old folks who keep showing up at the ER. One liter, or maybe two, of that saline solution to get him back on his feet, and then go home and sleep. The kid would be worthless for the next two days at least. And that was if the hospital had any saline left. *If.*

He jammed the gas and brought the truck up to fifteen miles an hour over the speed limit on a long, straight stretch of road.

"You hang in there, buddy," he said, eyes fixed on the pavement ahead. "I know you don't want to hear a lecture now, but I'm gonna give you one anyway. Don't roll into work like this, son. You got a crew depending on you. I know you can do good work when you put your mind to it, because them boys told me so. There's two parts to success in life. One is doing good work, and the other is doing it consistently. You hear me, kid? Show up, do good work. It's as simple as that."

He took his eyes off the road for a quick glance at his passenger. The kid might have heard, but he didn't understand. His mouth was half-open, his eyes half-closed, and he looked like he was trying hard to hold on to consciousness.

"I was your age once," Del muttered softly as he studied the debris in the road ahead. "Had my share of days like you're having now." He shook his head, steered the truck around a large, leafy branch. "Glad to be done with all that."

# 5

"The malware hides in the computer's memory." Carlos Espinoza, the FBI agent, was explaining the virus that had infiltrated Empire's network to a woman wearing jeans and a white button-down shirt whose badge said Homeland Security.

"I know," Anya Lakhani replied. "I'm not new at this."

The two agents sat at an oval conference table beneath fluorescent lights inside Empire's headquarters, with Software Development Manager Ray Cooper and Cy Madhi, head of the utility's transmission-and-distribution control center. Through the walls, they could hear the growl of the giant diesel generator that powered the building. Ray and Cy stared into their laptops as the other two talked.

"By hiding in memory," Espinoza said, "and never writing itself to disk, the virus evades detection by virus scanners. Do you always dress like that?"

Anya looked down at her jeans. She had long since run out of the pantsuits she preferred. They sat in a pile by the lifeless washing machine back home near DC. "You mean in clean, fresh clothing?" she asked. "Yes. I do."

In the two previous cases she had worked with the FBI, she had received the same kind of treatment, at least from the male agents. She had a high regard for the agency, but not for all its representatives. Some of them, she noted, liked to take credit for the work of others. Some didn't like getting their hands dirty. It was too early to judge Espinoza, but if he wanted her esteem, he would have to earn it.

"Any idea how this got onto the network?" Espinoza asked.

"Probably phishing," Ray Cooper replied without looking up from his laptop. "We get those kinds of attacks twenty-four seven. Some project manager gets an email that looks like it came from a contractor. She clicks a link that looks legit, and then we have a problem. We train them to watch out for these scams, but it only takes one slipup."

"This is a bad one," Cy added, turning his laptop toward Espinoza. He pointed to an on-screen map of the company's computer network, a mesh of intersecting lines in which employee laptops and workstations appeared as small circles and important servers appeared as large ones. "We don't know which machine was affected first, but this shows all the machines from which it has exfiltrated data." He pointed to a number of red, glowing circles. "See, it sits in memory on some developer's laptop, attaches to the shared network drives, and starts harvesting files. Word documents, Excel sheets, source code, emails, anything. Sends it out to servers all over the place. We don't even know where the data is going.

"The developer shuts down his laptop, and suddenly the virus starts sending out files from a workstation in the transmission control center. We can't find this thing. It skips from computer to computer, and we're always a step behind."

This was the advanced persistent threat. Advanced because the virus's ability to hide itself and steal data was unusually sophisticated. Persistent because as soon as you rooted it out of one machine, it popped up on another. A threat because it had unfettered access to the internal network. It could and would steal anything.

"It's not sending anything out now," Anya said. "It can't, because the internet service providers in Virginia are offline."

"It can," Cy Madhi said. "This building has power from the diesel generators." He pointed up toward the ceiling. "And a satellite dish on the roof. The malware sends data through the satellite link to just anywhere it wants."

"Huh," Ray grunted. "I forgot about the satellite dish."

"This looks like a nation-state attack," Espinoza said. "This isn't the work of script kiddies. Someone spent a lot of time engineering this."

"Or someone just stole work that was already out there," Anya said. "And repurposed it for their own ends."

"Unlikely," Espinoza said. "Utilities are hard targets to crack."

Ray Cooper, leaning back in his chair and cupping his hands around the back of his head, added, "And what's the payoff? You're not going to steal electricity. If you're China, you want internal documents, emails, technical diagrams of system topology, any kind of intelligence you can gather."

Anya didn't like the way Ray looked at her. She felt his eyes were always probing for weakness. But only in her. He wouldn't look at another man that way. A man would read that brazen, domineering stare as an act of aggression. A man might call him out, ask him if he had a problem. Why didn't the other men in the room say anything about the way he looked at her? Did they not notice? Did they not have the moral backbone to speak up? Or did they not want her there either?

"If you're Russia," Ray continued, "you want access to transmission control, so you can disrupt power distribution, shut down the grid, and cause chaos. If you're North Korea, you want anything you can get. Encrypt all the hard drives and demand a ransom to unlock them. They're always looking for ways to generate cash over there."

"So, what kind of activity are you seeing?" Anya asked.

She had directed her question to Cy Madhi, director of the transmission-and-distribution operations center, but Ray Cooper answered. "Mainly information theft," he said. "Data exfiltration. There's been some probing of the control systems, but that doesn't seem to be the main area of interest."

"So, you're thinking China?" Anya asked.

Without answering her, Ray looked at the other two and asked, "Anyone else hungry?" He turned back to Anya and said, "Why don't you go out and get us some sandwiches?"

"That's not my job." She tried with some success to keep an even tone and to not look as irritated as she felt, and then regretted it. Ray Cooper was measuring her to see if she would acquiesce. She should have responded more firmly. Ray leaned back farther in his chair, hands still cupped behind his head, legs spread in that arrogant fashion that always annoyed her, like he was positioning himself to receive a sexual favor. "Go rustle something up from the cafeteria."

"Are your legs not working today, Mr. Cooper?" She returned his steady, even gaze. "You can't walk there yourself?"

"All right, you two," said Espinoza.

"All right, what?" asked Anya.

"Let's get some lunch and try to keep focused on the task at hand," Espinoza replied.

A few minutes later, when she pulled Espinoza aside on the way to the company cafeteria and told him he had missed an opportunity to step up and do the right thing, he told her not to take Ray's remarks personally, that the storms and the blackout and the hack had made everyone tense.

"I do take them personally when they're directed at me. And you *will* do the right thing next time, Agent Espinoza. I know you will."

It wasn't a question. It was an assertion. His smile and simple nod told her he understood.

# 6

Sean Riggs finished watering the plants in his neighbor's house, locked the door, and walked to the curbside mailbox. The Millers had left for Arkansas four days before the first storm hit, and were supposed to have returned on the day of the second storm. Whether they had tried to drive home, he had no way of knowing. There were no lines of communication into or out of town. So he continued to go in every other day to check their plants, and each afternoon, he peeked into the mailbox he knew would be empty.

The street was quiet now, after forty minutes of whining chain-saw noise. Two guys in a blue pickup had cut and dragged sections of trees from either end of the block, making it a through road once again.

Sean watched a boom truck from the electric utility thread its way through the cut sections of fallen tree at the south end of the block. The truck barely fit through, bouncing over a mound of fresh sawdust between branches.

They couldn't be fixing the lines here so soon, he thought. Maybe in a day or two if we're lucky, but Richmond doesn't even have power yet.

The driver, Del Wright, slowed the truck and rolled down his window as he approached.

"Hospital?" He pointed his finger left, then right, with a questioning look.

"Left," Sean said, noting that the young man in the passenger seat looked ill. "He okay?"

"I hope so. I got a little discombobulated on all these side streets. There ain't a direct way to get anywhere. Thanks for the tip."

The engine revved, and Sean watched the truck chug toward the intersection.

Crossing his lawn on his way back to the house, he could see Danielle moving in the guest bedroom that he had converted into an office. In the fifteen minutes since he'd left, she had found the wine. She held a generously poured glass of red in her left hand as she scanned the desk and the adjacent bookcase. He watched her lift a glass ornament from one of the shelves. She turned it in her right hand, examined the colors as she sipped her wine, then replaced it carefully on the shelf.

He watched her repeat the act with other items: a book, a broken handheld radio, a brand-new hard drive, still in its box.

He entered the house to the sound of Frank Sinatra singing "Fly Me to the Moon." So, she had found the phonograph as well. He turned right toward the office, stopped in the doorway, leaned against the frame, and watched her. She had moved on to the far bookcase, pulling paperbacks from the shelves, studying the covers, turning them over, skimming the summaries.

She turned to take advantage of the window light as she read the rear cover of a book, her weight on her right leg. She silently mouthed the words of the song as her left leg moved rhythmically to the tick-ticka-tick-ticka-tick of the music. So, this is who she is when no one's watching, he thought. Curious, maybe even a little nosy. At ease with herself. For the first time, he felt a strong physical attraction.

He second-guessed himself when she turned to look at him. Maybe she knew he'd been watching. The timing of her look was uncanny. He wondered if some instinct had alerted her the moment he felt that attraction. She smiled and her teeth were purple with wine, and he thought, it's impossible to take this woman seriously.

"I poured you a glass," she said. "It's in the kitchen."

She was playing his records, pouring his wine, examining his belongings. "Go ahead and make yourself at home," he joked.

"I already did."

She wondered if spending the night in his air-conditioned bedroom meant she would have to have sex with him. Not that she'd mind. But what would *he* think?

She didn't mind him thinking she was crazy, but she didn't want him to think she slept around. For all her flirting bravado, she was always shy in her first intimate encounter with a new man. Her personality was bright and lively enough to keep a man's attention. But her body, however womanly it looked now, was in her mind still the body of the chubby girl who, until a year ago, didn't have a discernible waist. She did have that now, but in the dark, between the sheets, her perception was a year behind and twenty-five pounds above what Sean Riggs saw before him.

For a moment, she felt threatened by his admiring glance. She feared she would have to live up to whatever it was he found so attractive. There was only one way for her to know whether they would hit it off. That was what made her nervous about the first time with someone new.

She didn't want to spend another night staring at the ceiling in her hot, stuffy apartment. She did want to sleep with him, partly because she liked him, partly because after nine days and nights of horrendous boredom, it was something to do. But she would like to hold off, take things slowly, because he was easygoing, good company, fun to poke at and explore. When the power came back and life returned to normal, she didn't want to be his midnight booty call or his daytime left-on-read.

Mostly, right now, she wanted the air-conditioning. Was that so bad? Was it so hard to understand, given the circumstances? Would he be offended if she just came out and said it?

They drifted from the office to the kitchen. When he lifted his wineglass from the counter and took a sip, he touched the small of her back, sending a thrill through her that straightened her spine.

"Can I sleep here?" she blurted.

Oh, God, Danielle! What is wrong with you? She clapped her hand over her mouth. He was looking at her half-amused, half-amazed.

"I mean, just for the air-conditioning," she added awkwardly through the fingers that still covered her mouth. And immediately, she thought, Nope. Wrong again, Danielle.

What was he thinking now? That she'd ask him for money? Charge him for the pleasure of her company? The way she'd been coming on to him, such thoughts might not be off base. She pleaded with her eyes. Forgive me. I haven't slept in—

"Sure," he said. "You're welcome to stay."

He could see she was embarrassed.

"I'm going to shut my mouth now."

He pulled her hand gently from her lips and said, "Say whatever you want."

He was laughing at her. No, he was smiling. No, he was laughing. She was too agitated to read his mind.

"Sometimes, I have no impulse control," she confessed.

"I can see that."

He felt her whole body relax when he kissed her.

# 7

Del parked the big bucket truck across three spaces in the hospital lot, then walked to the entrance to get a wheelchair. He lifted his slumping coworker out of the truck, lowered him into the chair and wheeled him across the hot asphalt lot into the waiting room of the emergency department. He didn't hear the question that the woman at the intake desk had asked. He assumed she was asking about Ben.

"Kid needs water," Del mumbled. He rubbed his temples, felt lightheaded, took two steps back, and collapsed into a chair.

When he had arrived home the night before, the kids were asleep. He left this morning before they woke up. In the four hours between arriving home and leaving again, he had eaten leftovers in the living room by the light of a battery-powered camping lantern. When his wife, Carrie, asked about his day, he said, "You first."

He fell asleep in the chair as she tried to tell him about the kids.

At 3:45, his phone alarm woke him. He checked to see if it had a cell signal yet. No. The battery was low too. He would have to remember to plug it in to the charger in the truck.

He stood slowly, hips and knees popping, every joint in his body reluctant to move. Once on his feet, he struggled to straighten his back. "So, this is what eighty is gonna feel like," he mumbled.

He turned on his phone light, saw the jumpsuit Carrie had hand-washed and folded over the couch, and decided to shower. At 4:05, he was back in his truck.

Wait, was that today, he wondered? Hunched in a chair by the emergency department intake desk, his elbows on his knees, head in hands, he stared down at the gray tile of the waiting room floor. Or was that yesterday?

What was he working on now? Was he supposed to be distributing orders to other crews? Or actually fixing something?

The days were all one, he decided. There was nothing to delineate them. His field of vision began to narrow. The edges of the world grew dark as a wave of weakness and nausea swept over him.

Like today and yesterday and every day he could remember, tomorrow would be another day of not seeing his kids' faces, not connecting with Carrie, who needed his support.

Tomorrow would be another eighteen, nineteen hours in the heat. Hot before the sun came up, hot after it went down, and hotter in between.

"Sir?"

Someone was trying to get someone's attention. A woman. It was a woman speaking. She sounded concerned.

The dark edges of the world closed in, crowding out what little light remained in the center.

"Sir?"

The voices around him faded in and out, like someone was turning the volume up and down on a radio.

And then Carrie's hand was on his shoulder. Her slim hand with the clear nail polish.

"Sir?"

He put his hand on hers. She's young again, he thought. Her skin is smooth. He felt for her ring. It wasn't there. Where had it gone? He wanted to ask her, but the words wouldn't come.

"Oh God," the nurse said, as he fell forward.

The world went black.

# 8

The table in the Empire conference room was littered with sandwich wrappers and empty potato chip bags. The cafeteria, it turned out, was well stocked for outages. In an emergency, the employees responsible for getting things running again would have to be fed.

"Okay, we have a unit where the virus is active," Cy said. He turned his laptop to show Ray Cooper and the new woman in the room, who knelt and squinted at the monitor. Mei Chen had arrived during lunch, a representative from the cybersecurity firm that all the big corporations called in when they had a mess like this. Anya had worked with her before.

"The network gateway shows data coming out of this machine—" Cy tapped a red dot on the network map on his monitor. "A desktop up on the third floor."

"Are there people working up there?" Mei asked.

"No," Cy replied. "I booted a couple of desktops up there this morning. I've been monitoring them, waiting to see if the virus copies itself. This one"—he tapped the monitor—"has it."

"It will be in memory only," Mei said. "So, we'll have to scan that."

"Right," said Cy. "This one's tricky. It knows the only way to catch it is to scan the memory. And it knows only an account with full admin privileges can do a memory scan, so it deletes itself when an admin logs in. It flees to another machine. But the virus has a bug."

"What's that?" Anya asked.

"It checks to see if an admin logs in, but if the logged-in user is already an admin, it doesn't check for that. When I booted that machine, I logged in as administrator. The virus copied itself onto the machine about twenty minutes ago. It doesn't seem to know it's running on a box where we can spy on it."

"We can scan that one?" Mei asked.

Cy nodded. "There's a USB drive with the scanning software already plugged in."

"Let's go," Mei said.

# 9

The question of whether they would sleep together had been settled within thirty minutes of the kiss. It happened too fast, and Danielle was too caught up in the excitement to be nervous.

Afterward, still trying to catch her breath, she said with a smile she couldn't have wiped away if she tried, "Okay, I *really* enjoyed that."

"I could tell," Sean said. "It's the first time since I met you you stopped talking."

She laughed at that, aloud at first, and then quietly, her body shaking gently under the caress of cool air blowing across the bed. For the first time in nine days, sweat felt good and welcome and right.

He turned to look at her. "Were you stalking me?"

"What do you mean?"

"I remember now running into you at the gas station and the coffee shop."

"*Now* you remember?" she joked. "This is what I have to do to get you to remember me?"

"And you cut in line outside the grocery store today so you'd be in my group when we went in to shop."

"Aw, you noticed!" she teased. He hadn't at the time, she recalled. He'd been off in his own world, thinking about God-knows-what.

"I admire your initiative," he said. "Why me?"

She rolled onto her stomach, propped herself up on her elbows, and said, "What in the world goes through your mind all day? Every time I see you, it's like you're floating around in some fantasy world."

"What do you think goes through my mind?"

She frowned and shook her head.

"It's a lot less interesting than you imagine," he said.

"Really? Okay, what were you thinking about in line outside the grocery store a few hours ago? You were staring at the ground, but there was nothing down there."

"You really want to know?"

"I'm asking, aren't I?"

"All right." He rolled over, lifted his phone from the bedside table, scrolled through some photos, and then turned the screen toward her.

The image made no sense. It was a photo of a computer monitor displaying some inscrutable software code.

"What's that?" she asked.

He zoomed in and pointed toward a line of gibberish. "See that? That one nonsense word in double quotes at the end of the line?"

"What is it?"

"It's encrypted."

"And?"

"This line of code says, if I encrypt the value passed into the current function and it matches this value in quotes, then I'm going to issue some commands to an external system."

"That's what you think about? I thought you were pondering the meaning of life. Or looking for change on the pavement. I almost threw a penny down there just so you'd have something to find. Why is that interesting?"

"Because it doesn't make sense."

"That's why *you're* interesting," she said, touching the tip of his nose. She threw her leg over his hip and sat on top of him. "When you read code like that, do you want to make out with it?"

"No, it's just—" She interrupted his response with a kiss.

"Stop," he said, laughing. "It's just, code like this has no place in a system as important as the electric grid."

"That's where you found it?"

He had come across it back in March, during his brief stint with Empire Energy. The laptop they had given him was so tightly secured, he couldn't copy files from it, so he had snapped a photo of the code with his phone.

What was the meaning of the encrypted value? What was the meaning of the external commands the code invoked when the values matched? To what external system were the commands issued, and what was the ultimate effect? And why was this strange function buried in the company's test code, where it would have no effect? It wasn't even testing anything. Test code was supposed to run functions from the main code base and then check outputs to make sure they were correct. This code didn't check anything. It simply issued a set of commands and then quit.

"Why do you care?" Danielle asked.

"Why do people go to escape rooms or read mystery novels?" he asked. "Puzzles beg to be solved. I want to solve this one."

His curiosity had gotten him in trouble before. Four weeks into a job in the suburbs of DC, he found some problems in the company's flagship product. The company sold routers and firewalls to secure corporate computer networks. Much of their source code, he discovered, had been stolen from another company, brought in by a former employee of one of their competitors. Other code had come from open-source products and was being used illegally, with the public licenses stripped out and replaced by bogus copyright notices. Critical sections of the test code had been deactivated, and when he reactivated them, the tests failed.

The company's thousands of customers, he realized, had staked their security on a shoddy product riddled with flaws. The product's flaws had potentially serious consequences. This was how companies got hacked. This was how people's personal data was stolen, their medical records, their financial information. This affected the day-to-day lives of millions of people who had no idea of the ways in which the companies they depended on were putting them at risk. When he raised his concerns to management, they fired him.

When he reported his former employer to the government, he was supposed to get whistleblower protection. What he got instead was retaliation and intimidation. The federal investigator assigned to the matter told him the incriminating source code he had copied onto his personal laptop didn't exist in the company's code repositories.

"You think I made all this up?" Sean asked incredulously. "You think I typed thousands of lines of code by myself and then filed a false report with the government? What would I have to gain from that?"

The company managed to cover up what he had unearthed. The government closed the case after a few weeks, due to "unsubstantiated allegations from an unreliable source." He was, they said, a disgruntled former employee. The report also noted he had violated company policy by making unauthorized copies of proprietary source code. That's what galled him the most. First, they said the incriminating code he had shown them was fake, that it didn't exist in the company's code repositories. Then they said he had stolen it. Well, which was it?

He left DC in disgust and found this town, this house. For seven months, he worked as a remote contractor for a company in California. When that gig ended, he went to Empire, where he worked on interesting code under a grating boss. Ray Cooper fired him after six weeks.

"You didn't tell us you'd been fired for cause from that company up in DC," Ray said.

"You didn't ask."

"I'm pretty sure it's a standard question on the job application."

"It's not," Sean said. "Why are you bringing this up now?"

Because, during the hiring process, when HR called his former employer to verify that he had worked there, they got a grunting yes from a harried supervisor who said he was too busy for a full conversation. "Give me your number, I'll call you back," he said.

Six weeks into the new job, the old supervisor called back and told Empire's HR department that Sean had been fired for stealing source code. The phrasing rankled Sean. The company had stolen the source code. Sean had merely called them out on it.

"Get out of here," Ray Cooper said. "Give me your laptop and leave your badge at the desk."

Sean's face showed a tinge of anger as he relived the scene in his mind.

"See, there you go again," Danielle said. "Living inside your mind. What are you thinking about that makes you look so sour?"

"A guy I used to work for," Sean said. "A real asshole."

Empire ran all of its critical systems internally. Its data and its industrial control systems were too sensitive to outsource to the big cloud providers in the northern part of the state. It secured its closely guarded systems with the routers and firewalls whose vulnerabilities Sean Riggs knew all too well.

Ray Cooper liked to brag that his system was locked down, that every machine his developers worked on met the most stringent federal security requirements for critical energy infrastructure. But what did that matter, Sean thought, when the digital vault that was supposed to protect the whole network was built with a faulty lock?

# 10

## July 1

Danielle awoke at nine fifteen to the smell of bacon, eggs, and coffee. She rarely slept that late, even on weekends. That she had done so now, in the cool hum of the air-conditioning, was a testament to her fatigue, to the toll of the relentless summer heat and all those sleepless nights.

The smell of coffee made her tingle with excitement. Since the blackout, she had had only sweetened, creamed coffee from a can. It was neither bracingly hot nor refreshingly cold. She drank it at a tepid eighty-four degrees, the temperature of her apartment in the morning. Lukewarm, sticky, and unpleasantly sweet, she forced it down like a child drinking cough medicine.

She pushed away the crisp white sheets, put on the shirt and boxers her host had given her, used the toilet, said a quiet thank-you for the seat being cool and dry, then left the bedroom just in time to see Sean turning from the kitchen counter with a plate in either hand. "We'll eat in there," he said, nodding toward the bedroom.

She turned from the moist, sticky air of the kitchen with another quiet "thank you."

They ate on the bed. She sat cross-legged, he with his back against the pillows. He asked her where she lived. On the opposite end of town, in the newish apartment building with the pool that no one was supposed to use because the pump stopped working when the power went out. People were using it anyway. It was stagnant and gross, the surface covered with a sheen of oil from the sunscreen that washed off the bathers who defied the "Closed" sign.

What did she do for work? Plastered social media with text and images approved by the marketing team to convince people that the convenience store chain, which also happened to be one of the East Coast's major gas station chains, was green and eco-friendly.

"I also reply to the comments," she said.

"People comment on those ads?"

"Believe it or not."

She had finished her breakfast before he was half-done. He, after all, had been eating cooked meals these past ten days, not scavenging stale, room-temperature scraps.

She wiped her mouth and then asked the question she had been putting off. She had already overthought it and was nervous about sounding too forward.

"You don't, um, have an extra toothbrush, do you?"

How easy would it be for him to assume she was moving in? Especially given the way she had acted the day before. It was an honest question with no ulterior motive. Her mouth felt dirty when she awoke, and coffee and hot bacon only made it worse.

"I don't," he said simply. He showed no suspicion of an ulterior motive, no worry about her encroaching on his bachelor pad. "What do you say we go to your place and get one?"

"Really?"

"You ever been on the back of a motorcycle?"

Ugh, she thought. Not that! Her ex rode a crotch rocket when he wasn't doing doughnuts in his Chevy pickup or shooting empty beer cans in the woods. What a refreshing change to be with someone so different, someone whose mind was active and focused. And now here he was pulling a page from Ronnie's playbook, putting her on the back of his bike. She hoped the motorcycle wasn't a whining racer with a stiff rear seat.

"No," she lied. "Don't you have a car?"

She knew he did. A dark blue Honda Civic. She had talked to with him twice at the gas station as he filled it.

"I do," he replied, setting his plate on the bedside table. "Did you know there's a cut through the woods that goes all the way across the north end of town?"

She shook her head.

"Almost from my place to yours. There's a path under the power lines. I've taken the bike out there a few times. Wanna do a little adventure ride?"

She would rather have gone in the air-conditioned Honda.

"Sure."

# 11

"This is a variant of well-known Chinese attack," Mei Chen said.

She dressed like a man, Ray thought. Or a wannabe man. All these women from the high-priced cybersecurity consultancies dressed like men. Some women's suits at least made an attempt to acknowledge the waist and hips. Not to accentuate them, but they didn't smooth them over. But this woman, in this suit... She looks like a boy, Ray thought. Like a little boy who wants to be a man.

"It's been modified by the attacker to shore up some known weaknesses," she continued. "And it's been customized specifically to target your environment."

"How do you know that?" Ray asked. His unfriendly tone told her he wasn't merely seeking information. He was challenging her. If she was going to dress up like a man, she should be able to defend her ideas like one.

"We ran it through a decompiler, turned the machine code back into semi-readable source code. The source still contains Chinese symbols, but some sections of the canonical code base have been replaced."

Ray turned to her coworker, the nerdy-looking man in the rumpled suit with the enormous belly who handwrote notes on a yellow legal pad.

"Who do you think is behind this?"

Ray read the man's name tag for the third time. Phil Rudolph. A fat, soft man with a doughy, pasty face. Weak, Ray thought. Probably got beat up a lot as a kid. Probably deserved it. A guy who doesn't learn to stand up for himself is basically just asking for it.

Phil Rudolph pointed his pencil toward Mei, who replied, "Symbols in the new code sections are in English, and they're not misspelled. So, we don't know. Maybe Russia. Maybe North Korea. Maybe they have a fluent English speaker."

"Or they ran their code through spell-check," said the fat man. A weak attempt at a joke.

Ray fixed his eyes on the woman. "Shouldn't you know?"

"We're still looking into it," she replied.

"You? Or your experts?"

He was beginning to grate on her.

"Our security engineers," she said coolly.

"So, not you?" Ray replied. It was more of a statement than a question.

He turned to the big man and said, "Look, I can tell you who this is. It's either China or North Korea. If it was Russia or any of its proxies, they'd be digging into our control systems, figuring out how to take down the grid. This intruder doesn't care about any of that. Aside from a few weak pokes at transmission and distribution, they've focused almost entirely on corporate espionage and intellectual property theft."

He stood and slid his hands into his pockets and began to pace. "They've gone after our emails, the documents on our shared drives, our source code, our databases."

He paced too near the woman—deliberately, she thought, looming over her, glaring down at her.

"This is either China wanting to vacuum up our internal knowledge, or North Korea preparing to leak our dirty laundry all over the internet if we don't pay them a ransom."

The Yellow Peril, Ray thought. And who needs them when we have enemies like you already inside our gates, dressing like men, acting like men, trying to upend our way of life?

He imagined his thoughts were private, that no one could read his mind. But he had stewed over his resentments for so long that they had begun to show on his face. His bitterness had become such an habitual state of mind, he no longer recognized the thoughts that stoked it, or that the negativity could leak out in the hard, unfriendly gaze he cast on the objects of his hatred.

Mei looked uneasily to her coworker, as if to say, *He's threatening me. He is making me physically uncomfortable. Do you see this?*

She wanted acknowledgment, not protection. If her coworker didn't say something to this man, she would.

The fat man stood. "All right," he said, placing himself smoothly between Ray Cooper and Mei Chen. "We've said what we have to say here. We'll get back to you when we know more from the forensics team."

He gently grasped his coworker's elbow, nodded subtly for her to gather her belongings, then turned to Ray.

"I hear you hunt," he said with a friendly smile.

"Deer," said Ray. "And bears, if I can find them."

"Are there bears around here?"

"Not in Richmond. In West Virginia."

The big man kept his ears tuned in to what was going on behind him. He'd stall Ray for half a minute after his coworker's exit, give her time to round the corner of the corridor and get out of sight.

"What kind of gun do you shoot?"

Ray shrugged. The alertness his body had shown a minute earlier, the muscular tension of a cat in sight of prey, had slackened. His eyes seemed to lose interest in his surroundings. "Depends on the day," he said indifferently. "And the target."

# 12

The lines that ran through this stretch of woods should have been fine, since Empire Energy's contractors had cleared a twelve-foot swath of brush and trees on either side less than two months ago. Del Wright took it upon himself to check them anyway. No one else would do it, he reasoned, unless the customers along the lines reported outages after the power came back on for everyone else.

He had left the hospital at four thirty that morning after nearly nine and a half hours of uninterrupted sleep. The nurse told him he couldn't leave until he peed.

"We gave you two liters of lactated Ringer's," she explained. "We can't be sure your kidneys are functioning properly until you pee."

Lactated Ringer's. That's what had dripped from the clear plastic bag into his arm, bringing him back from what had felt like the brink of death. The nurse now encouraged him to go into the bathroom and "Give it a shot."

Her standing just outside the bathroom door, which was still cracked open, made him nervous. Did she not trust him? He felt like a felon whose urine test required a witness.

"How's Ben?" he asked.

"Worse than you," she said.

He pushed the door shut, not wanting her to hear.

"He won't be leaving till late afternoon at the earliest," she added. "You're not going back to work, are you?"

"If I don't, who will?"

"All those workers who drove in from out of state."

"They won't know what to do," Del said. "Until I get their orders to them."

He flushed and went out to the hall.

"You could at least wait till daylight."

"If I wait till daylight, some of those teams will be sitting idle. That adds hours to the outage. People are dying."

"Be careful," she said. "The body doesn't recover from dehydration quickly. It'll creep up on you. You'll feel fine one minute and wiped out the next."

"Thanks for your concern."

He had pulled on his cap, jumped in the truck, and driven to Richmond to pick up the day's work orders. The boom truck was running on fumes when he reached the office. They told him to leave it for another crew. He left the lot in a white pickup with an ATV loaded in the bed. After distributing orders to the crews, he could run the ATV through the forest cuts, inspect some of the backcountry lines.

He drove a hundred-twenty-mile meandering route from substation to substation, crew to crew, line to line, locating the teams, handing out orders, and answering questions.

At ten, he had an hour to kill before he had to head back to Richmond. Make use of the time, he thought. Unload the ATV, the four-wheel Kawasaki, and run down that cut in the woods. Check the line for breaks. You never know. Even with no branches in striking distance of the wire, there could be problems. The second storm had blasted the region with hurricane-force winds for hours, sending debris smashing into houses, cars, everything.

His inspection paid off. The transformer atop the pole halfway down the cut had been hit by something—a tree branch, perhaps, that had blown in from twenty or a hundred yards away. The transformer hung almost upside down from the pole where the woodland cut split in two. The line it served forked left, through a narrower cut, to a cluster of a dozen homes.

Who knows, Del thought, maybe someone's pregnant in one of those houses too. Or maybe someone's old, dying in this heat.

One of the crew chiefs told him that morning that the death toll in the state had officially passed a thousand. From four hundred to over a thousand in just twenty-four hours. Not that they were dying faster now. It was just that as the rural roads cleared, the people who had died days ago in their homes were starting to be found. The elderly, the poor, the sick in isolated areas who couldn't get help. They died from heat, dehydration, lack of clean drinking water. How many more were waiting to be found? How many were within days or even hours of the dehydration that had nearly killed him?

If I was twenty years older, I might not have made it, Del thought. If I had blacked out on one of the back roads instead of right there in the hospital, I might not have made it.

Del looked up at the work that needed to be done. The transformer would be an easy fix, if he could make it up the pole. But he couldn't. With the cast on his left hand, he could barely manage the clutch of the ATV. He'd been puttering along in first gear.

He rummaged through the tools on the back of the Kawasaki until he found a pair of hand shears. He cut first through the narrow fiberglass band between his left thumb and index finger, then slowly up along the side of his wrist toward his elbow. When he was able to pry the hard shell off at last, the stink of pasty dead skin almost made him gag.

He began to scrape off the dead skin with a stick, and then kept going, scratching the itch that had been driving him crazy for the past week and a half. His arm felt twenty degrees cooler.

He put on his tool belt and climbing belt and a pair of spikes and made his way slowly up the pole. The hardest part was raising the belt after each two steps. The muscles of his left hand moved reluctantly, the wrist sore and stiff, and when he gripped the belt handles tightly, pain shot forward into his fingertips and backward up to his elbow.

The climb up with the heavy tool belt took more out of him than he had expected. The nurse was right about the aftereffects of dehydration. You feel okay one minute, and then after a little exertion, you're wiped out.

The transformer itself didn't appear to be damaged. It needed to be righted and refastened to the pole. The low-voltage outgoing lines were fine. They had enough slack to be unaffected when the unit was knocked out of place. Del reattached the incoming lines, checked that the unit was securely mounted, and then began the slow, careful descent. He was exhausted and short of breath, but there wouldn't be much exertion the rest of the day. He'd be driving around, checking on the progress of various crews, checking in with the office, relaying instructions.

He was back on the ground, dropping the belts onto the rear of the ATV, when he heard the sputtering of an approaching motorbike. He looked up expecting to see a rider and was surprised to see a pair instead. A man on the front, a woman on the back. A couple out joyriding on the trail the utility company had cleared. The woman on the back wasn't wearing a proper helmet. That was a bicycle helmet.

The shield on the driver's helmet was open. The driver made eye contact as he approached. Del shook his head reproachfully and said, "Y'all ain't supposed to be out here."

Sean couldn't hear him over the noise of the engine. He stopped a few feet in front of the ATV, dropped the engine to an idle, and said, "You guys are all the way down to the small lines? Does that mean you fixed the big stuff already?" If so, he thought eagerly, power might return that day.

Del shook his head. "I'm just out here fixing what I see. Did you hear me when I said you ain't supposed to be out here?"

Sean cut the engine and removed his helmet. Danielle, with her arms around his waist, peeked out from behind his shoulder. Del noted that she tried to put her feet down when Sean turned off the ignition. Tried, but couldn't, because the bike was too high. She's cute, he thought. Nice, bright smile.

"What'd you say?" Sean asked.

"I said this trail is off-limits to unauthorized vehicles."

"Thanks for working on the lines." Sean had seen him descend the pole as he approached.

"You're welcome," Del replied. "Didn't I see you yesterday?"

"You were in the Empire truck, asking which way to the hospital."

"That's right."

"Everything okay?" Sean asked.

"With me," Del said. "I don't know about my buddy. Guy stays up all night drinking vodka after a twenty-hour workday's got a few things to learn. Best way to learn is the hard way, and he's on it. How are you two holding up?"

"Well enough," said Sean. Danielle gave a thumbs-up.

"You been feeding that bike ethanol," Del said. "That's why she runs rough."

"Is that the reason?"

"Gums up the carbs, especially if you let it sit all winter with the petcock open. Try running a tank of ethanol-free gas through it."

They talked for a few minutes about the bike. "The Bush Pig," as Del called it, was a classic. One of the few carbureted bikes still in production. It was easy to repair, had no electronics, and would probably survive the apocalypse.

"I've owned two of them," Del said. "They're supposed to be indestructible, but I managed to destroy the first one by accidentally burning down the garage it was stored in. Second one runs about like yours. Carbs need to be cleaned and rejetted."

"You know how to do that?"

Del nodded. "Ain't hard. Just takes patience."

"It's hot out here," Danielle said. "Can we please get going? At least with the breeze, it's not so bad." She pinched Sean's side to urge him to get a move on.

"Here," said Del, handing Sean a card. "In case you can't figure out the jetting from the YouTube videos, give me a call. I mean, when the phones come back on."

Sean pocketed the card. Del wished them both a good day and stepped out of the way as Sean started the bike.

# 13

"The virus reaches out to a command-and-control end point, a 'C and C server,' to request its next set of instructions," Mei Chen, the security consultant, told the team gathered around the conference table. Her colleague from the private security firm, Phil Rudolph, wrote on his notepad as she spoke. Carlos Espinoza and Anya Lakhani tapped notes into their government-issued laptops. The head of Empire's transmission-and-distribution control center, Cy Madhi, listened attentively while Ray Cooper drummed his fingers softly on the surface of the table. His expression showed a mix of concern about the intrusion and annoyance at having to waste time talking about it. The utility still had a statewide outage to clean up. That was, or should have been, the company's primary focus.

"Where is the C and C server?" Cy asked. "In China?"

"In the US," said Mei Chen. "But the instructions it's giving"—she turned and looked uncertainly at Phil—"are in Chinese."

"Chinese code?" asked Cy.

"Chinese, um... written Chinese. Not computer language. Human language."

"What's that about?" Ray asked.

"We don't know yet," said Mei. "They may be using a codebook. The virus asks for a command to execute. Instead of sending back instructions like 'Copy these files' or 'Get all the data from the database,' it sends back simple words like 'tiger' or 'teacup.'"

"And what does the virus do with those instructions?" Ray's impatience with the speaker came through in his condescending tone.

Again, Mei looked uncertainly at Phil Rudolph. Not wanting her to take the brunt of Ray's hostility, he answered the question himself. "We don't know. It appears to the throw the instructions away without doing anything."

"Well, what's the point of that?" Ray asked.

"We're not sure yet," Phil replied.

"There is a separate section of code," Mei offered, "that does receive and execute computer-readable instructions, but so far, we haven't seen it in action. None of the responses from the C and C server we've seen so far include executable code."

"Do you have the IP address of that server?" Cy asked. "Can't we add a rule to the firewall to block it?"

"We'd like to keep it open," Mei said. "So we can record the information coming in."

"And let this hack continue?" Cy asked. "So they can finish stealing what they haven't already stolen?"

"As I said," Mei replied, "the C and C server doesn't appear to be sending actionable instructions. At least, not that we can understand. The more information we can gather, the better chance we'll have at cracking its secrets. In the meantime..." She nodded toward the FBI agent, Carlos Espinoza.

"The C and C server is inside the US," Espinoza said. "We traced its IP address to a suburb of Lexington, Kentucky. We have a team ready to move in as soon as the warrant clears, which may not be till morning. Once we seize it, we cut off the head of the command-and-control unit. We can open it up and look inside, see what we have there."

"What about you?" Ray asked Anya. "What is Homeland Security contributing to this?"

"Carlos's team has the lead on this at the moment," Anya said.

"So, you just sit here and take notes?"

"Homeland Security is working with other utilities around the country to scan for similar intrusions."

"I asked what you're doing for *us*," Ray said.

"The virus sat in your network for weeks before you detected it," Anya replied.

"Don't make this about us. I'm asking about you. What are *you* doing?"

"I just told you," she said. "If this is part of a broader campaign, other utilities may be infected and not know. Just like you didn't know."

"And you tapping on your keyboard is going to fix that?"

"Ray," Cy said sharply. "That's enough."

"No, this bugs me."

"What bugs you, Ray?" Cy asked. He sounded worn out, like a man who was tired of coming to work every day and having to deal with the unpleasantness of Ray Cooper.

"The government sending two people to do the job of one. That kind of waste sucks the life out of our country."

"Moving forward," Mei said. Her assertive tone was meant to preempt further discussion on this fruitless topic. "The plan is to follow the usual playbook for an advanced persistent threat. We'll keep a couple of infected computers running, so we can monitor communications with the C and C server and observe the malware in action. We'll isolate those infected machines from the rest of the network, so they can't do any harm.

"Then we'll shut down every other computer in the system. Every desktop, every laptop, every server. Wipe the disks clean, reinstall the operating system on every device, then the software, user accounts, everything."

Cy shook his head. "No way that will ever happen. You can turn off the desktops and laptops, but the servers that control and monitor transmission and distribution?" He shook his head. "No."

"We wouldn't do it all at once," Mei said. "We can go sector by sector. Isolate each office from the rest of the network. Replace everything there. Put in guards against the virus, then bring that sector back online. Repeat for every unit of the business."

"You'll still have to deal with transmission and distribution at some point," Cy said. "You can't just take those servers offline. They control the flow of electricity throughout the state. Shut them down and you'll wind up with what we're trying to fix right now. A blackout."

"For those systems," Mei replied, "you bring up new servers first. Brand new machines that we know are clean. You switch control of the transmission-and-distribution systems over to the new servers, then you kill the old ones. There's no downtime."

"Do you understand what it takes to certify new servers?" Cy protested. "To ensure that the hardware and software and configuration all meet federal standards for critical energy infrastructure? You don't just flip a switch and turn the thing on."

"I understand," Mei said.

"We just bought new servers this year," Cy said. "And you expect us to shell out again? To replace units that are four months old?"

"We're not selling you hardware," Mei said. "We don't profit from this. But the answer is yes. For those systems that cannot have downtime, you'll have to buy new servers."

"That's going to be expensive as hell," Cy said. "Not just the hardware, but the people to manage it. Reinstalling and reconfiguring operating systems across all those devices? Reinstalling all that software?"

"Welcome to the reality of large-scale cyber breaches," Mei said. "And, by the way, this is why you have insurance."

# 14

The smell of musty sweat overwhelmed Danielle when she pushed open the door of her apartment. She had meant to wash her sheets the day the power went out. It had been a week since their last wash. Then out went the power and in came the heat, and the sheets and pillowcases soaked up nine nights of perspiration.

By the third day of the blackout, she had established a system for sorting her clothes. The dirty stuff went on the floor. Anything folded in the dresser drawers or hanging in the closet was clean. With seven days of preblackout clothing in the hamper, and three days of postblackout clothes on the floor, she had run out of decent things to wear. What remained in the closet and dresser were leftovers from college and even high school, T-shirts and jeans and slacks that fit her old body but were now too big, blouses that could never have been in fashion, the kinds of things friends didn't let friends buy when they were sober.

"Sorry about the smell," she said to Sean as she flipped the light switch. The lights stayed off, and she said under her breath, "Oh, right."

"It's hot in here," Sean said as he followed her into the semidark.

"Not as hot as it gets," she replied. "Wait till afternoon, when the sun comes through those windows. Even if you shut the blinds, the whole wall gets hot. And watch where you step," she said. "I left some clothes on the floor."

Sean made his way to the window and opened the blind to let in more light. Danielle went toward the bedroom to search the hamper for the clothing she preferred.

"I'll be right back," she said.

Sean opened a second blind, and though the sunlight at this hour wasn't direct, it was more than enough to see by. When he scanned the apartment, he saw a cheap, black IKEA couch, the kind that flattens into a bed. A glass coffee table, a cheap rug with a fake, faded Persian pattern, a black end table, also IKEA, and two free-standing shelf units with metal frames and wood shelving. Those held a few books and magazines, a stack of mail, a crystal ball, some photos, and various other knickknacks. There was no order to the mess. It looked like anything that didn't have a home elsewhere had been parked on the shelves with the vague idea that someday its owner would get around to straightening it all out.

Her apartment is arranged about the same way as her mind, Sean thought. Stuff everywhere, in random order.

He walked to one of the shelving units and examined its contents. A toy pickup truck, orange with yellow flames painted on the sides. Beside it, a framed photo, face down. He turned it upright and saw Danielle, her face rounder and fatter, pressed against the face of a light-haired young man with a scruffy beard. His baseball cap said Chevy, and in the background sat a life-size version of the orange-and-yellow toy truck.

Behind him, Danielle returned from the bedroom saying, "I need a backpack to put my laundry in. Hey!" That last syllable sounded angry. She reached around his elbow, took the photo, and laid it face down again on the shelf. "Don't go through my stuff."

"What? It was sitting right there!"

"Yeah, but I didn't *know* it was there. Do you know where my backpack is?"

"How would I know that?"

"Okay, that's my ex, in case you're wondering, and no, I don't still have a thing for him."

"I didn't ask. And I wasn't wondering."

"Yeah, well, I don't. Have a thing for him. Ronnie has a new girlfriend. I give them three months. She's not very bright."

"How do you know that?"

"Duh! Because she's with Ronnie. Anyone who dates him has a screw loose."

"How long were you with him?"

"Eight months."

"And how bright does that make you?"

"Okay, nice one," she said. "You got me. Now, if you were my backpack, where would you be?"

"On the floor."

"That's not helpful," Danielle said. "You look here and in the kitchen. I'll check the bedroom and bathroom and closet."

Sean found the backpack on the kitchen counter. He removed from it the tangerines, soft with blue mold from the relentless heat, and dropped them into the garbage can.

On the motorcycle ride back through the cut in the woods, he kept a low speed, just over ten miles an hour. Danielle sat behind him with a backpack full of clothing and, he hoped, the toothbrush whose retrieval was the purpose of this expedition. She kept her feet on the pegs and leaned with the bike when they turned, which made Sean think she had lied about not riding on a motorcycle before. She talked over his left shoulder as they puttered along.

"I'm not seeing him anymore," she said.

"Okay."

"I just want you to know that, so you know I wasn't cheating on anyone with you."

"You don't have to shout. I can hear you."

"I don't do that sort of thing. And I've never slept with a guy an hour after meeting him."

"Me either."

The problem with Ronnie, she thought, was that he was as impulsive and unfocused as she was. Worse, actually. One of them had to be the adult in the relationship, and she got sick of it being her.

What did Ronnie do anyway? Float from job to job, quitting every time he had a dispute with his boss. He was never sober, but usually not quite drunk either. He'd take her out to McDonald's because that was all he could afford after pouring all his cash into twelve-packs of beer and mods on his truck. If she wanted a decent date, she had to pay for it herself. Not that she minded once in a while, but she did start to mind when it was all the time.

Now, as they reached a smoother section of path beneath the power lines, Sean shifted the bike into second gear. The breeze from the increased speed cooled her off. She squeezed her arms around Sean's waist and noted how lean he was. Ronnie had a gut and a big spare tire around his middle from all the beer he drank. Ronnie was rarely troubled by a thought of any kind. Sean seemed to think all the time. The pendulum had swung, she thought, from one extreme to the other.

Ronnie could be insecure and judgmental. Sean showed neither of those traits. Not yet, anyway. Ronnie took her out to the woods in his truck and taught her to shoot. After a few months, when she could outshoot him, he acted resentful and sullen. She lined up all his empty beer cans and shot the red center out of the Miller Lite logos from thirty feet.

"You think you're cool?" Ronnie asked.

"If you didn't drink so much, you could hit those marks too."

"If I didn't drink so much, you'd have no cans to shoot at."

She would shoot through all his ammo, and the next time they went out, he'd have more. Beer, truck, ammo. His three big expenditures.

On their six-month anniversary, he gave her his least favorite pistol, the .22-caliber revolver she had mastered.

"Why this one?" she asked. "Why not the Glock?"

"You don't want a semiautomatic," he said.

"Why not?"

"If they jam or hit a dead round, they fail. You die."

She turned and looked toward the bullet-riddled beer cans at the foot of the muddy embankment. "The beer cans are going to kill me?"

"You know what I'm saying."

Ronnie's anniversary gift was the gun he didn't want, she mused. Sean cooks me breakfast in bed. I'll take bachelor number two, thank you.

Where is that gun, anyway, she wondered? It's the kind of thing a girl should keep track of. This is why she needed to date a guy like Sean, someone who had his feet planted firmly on the ground and his house in order. Let *him* keep track of the gun. Then she would be free to follow her mind wherever it liked to wander. Lean in to the joy of thinking about eight things at once, she told herself, of getting nothing done, not caring that I can't remember why I opened the fridge. Attention deficit disorder isn't a disorder when you're having fun. You just have to learn to embrace it.

As they neared the road at the end of the forest cut, the engine began to sputter. Sean slowed the bike and thought, She's awfully quiet back there. I wonder what's going through her mind? Do I even want to know?

He stopped at the edge of the pavement, put his feet down, and switched the petcock to run off the reserve tank. Part of the so-called charm of the old Suzuki was its bare-bones simplicity. Who needed a fuel gauge? When the bike was out of gas, the engine just sputtered and stalled. Switch to reserve and then start looking for a gas station.

Danielle kept her feet on the pegs as he revved the engine to prevent a stall. She tapped his shoulder to get his attention, then raised her phone in front of his face. The battery indicator was red.

"Dead battery?" he said.

"No, this." She pointed to the signal indicator. "Five bars!"

Cell service had been restored.

# 15

"You look awful, Del! What happened to your cast?"

For the first time in ten days, he was at home during daylight hours. Eight twenty-two, and the sun was hovering on the western horizon. His wife, Carrie, had left the back door and several windows open—anything that was protected by a screen—to try to rid the house of hot, stuffy air.

She had come from the kitchen when he entered, a roll of paper towels in her hand.

"I cut it off," Del said. "Couldn't do a damn thing with it on. Where are the kids?"

"Next door. Couldn't you hear them?"

Del shook his head.

Carrie told him the neighbors had picked up two big watermelons that morning from a food distribution truck in the Walmart parking lot. The kids—their four plus the neighbors' two—had put the them in a wagon before lunch and rolled it down to the edge of the woods. They left the melons to cool in the deep part of the shaded stream and had just hauled them back before Del arrived.

"We cut them open a few minutes ago," she said. "They feel almost cold in this heat. Come join."

He washed his hands at the kitchen sink, then followed Carrie into the neighbors' backyard, where he was greeted with shrieks from his four children. The nine-year-old, Teddy, had his mother's straight dark hair and freckles. He was the fastest of the gang and the first to give his dad a hug. Behind him trailed Walt, the clumsy, goofy seven-year-old who was always smiling and whose limbs flailed wildly when he ran.

The girls, Marybeth and Annie, five and three, brought up the rear. For a moment, they were all stuck to him at once, the kids who hadn't seen their dad for so many days. The boys held him around the waist, while Marybeth clung to a knee and the little one wrapped her arms around his shins. Del greeted them warmly and did his best to pry Annie from his legs, so he wouldn't fall. Walt asked if his daddy would get a medal for fixing the blackout, and Marybeth told him he smelled bad.

Hank Bruns, the neighbor, handed him a can of beer that felt cool. Maybe it had been in the creek with the watermelons.

"Thanks," Del said.

As happy as he was to see his family, Del wanted most of all to sit. The neighbors obliged him with a chair on the patio. He sat heavily and shut his eyes and listened to the shouts of the kids chasing one another around the yard.

Carrie sat beside him and gripped his hand.

"You notice how hard the ground is?" Del asked, eyes still shut.

"Del, you need a rest."

"I'm taking one now," he mumbled. "Did you notice the ground?"

"No."

"And how thin the grass is getting?" He opened his eyes to look at her just long enough to register her expression of concern, then closed them again. "First, we get a biblical rain, and the whole state looks like a mud pit that'll never dry out. Then ten days of heat, not a cloud in the sky, and the plants that were drowning are starting to wither."

"Del?" His wife's tone told him she had something more pressing on her mind.

"I see it everywhere. You know, I'm driving five, six counties a day. Everything's drying up. Be nice if nature could give us some balance. Maybe parcel out the rain a little more evenly."

"You worked five days in a row before the outage," Carrie said. "Plus ten since puts you at fifteen straight without a day off. They can't kill you."

Del chuckled. "I'm starting to think they can."

"I'm starting to think *you* can," Carrie said. "You're not much good to them with that cast—"

"That's why I cut it off."

"Let me finish. You're not much good to them with a broken hand. I know you don't like to sit around while the crews are out working, but the injury and your exhaustion are legitimate reasons to take a break."

"I'll lay down when I'm dead," Del said with a grin. His eyes were still closed and his belly went up and down as he breathed deeply. He still hadn't opened the beer.

"I talked to Donna today," Carrie said.

"Ray's wife? She come by?"

"Cell service came back a few hours ago."

"Oh, yeah," he said with a heavy sigh of relaxation. "With all the stuff going wrong, I lost track of what's right."

"She says Ray is taking a couple days off. Tomorrow and the third. He's going to his cabin in West Virginia."

"Good for Ray," Del said softly.

"You should go with him."

"I'll take a break when the power's back."

"When the power's back where? Here? That could be tomorrow."

"Could be tonight," Del said. "I passed Ty Wilson and Rosa Salazar's crew on the way home. They were at the substation off sixty four. Looked like they were wrapping up."

"Then you should go. Take a break up in the mountains."

"We still got the rest of the state to fix."

"And that's going to take awhile. Del, you're no good to the company when you're exhausted. You might even crash your truck."

That gave him a jolt. He had almost fallen asleep at the wheel twice in the past two days. He had resolved not to tell Carrie about that. His solution to the problem was more caffeine, iced tea to stay awake. Never complain about a problem you can fix.

"Go up to the cabin with Ray," Carrie said.

"Ray sometimes ain't the most pleasant guy to be around."

"Because he's stressed. This whole situation has him stressed out. An outage and then this hack."

Del's eyes shot open. "You heard about that?"

"Donna told me the computer systems were hacked. She said it's bad."

"Whew." Del breathed a sigh of relief. "I thought maybe I let it slip. We ain't supposed to tell nobody about that."

"Go to West Virginia."

"If I went up there, all I'd do is sleep."

"Which is fine," Carrie said, squeezing his hand. "You need rest. It's fifteen degrees cooler up there, and the air is fresh and clean. You can take your fly rod, sit on a rock in the river, and doze off. You never catch anything anyway."

"Now, that ain't true."

"Will you go?"

"Will you stop nagging me if I say yes?"

"Yes."

"Then yes, I'll go. How's Donna?"

Carrie was quiet for so long he opened his eyes to see if she had heard him.

"The usual," Carrie said with a note of resignation in her tone. Or was it sorrow?

He pictured "the usual" Donna. Tired, defeated. To him, her dark eyes always seemed to ask, Doesn't anybody see me in here?

The sun dipped below the horizon, leaving a soft orange glow. Del closed his eyes again. He didn't realize he had fallen asleep until the simultaneous shriek of children and parents jolted him awake. He opened his eyes to see the decorative lights strung above the patio glow with color. A second later, the heat pump beside the house sprang to life with a rattling buzz.

He smiled and cracked open his semi-cool beer and said to himself, "Ty and Rosa, I owe you two a drink. You and your whole crew."

# 16

"Why didn't you call me?" Ray asked his wife, Donna, in the foyer just inside the front door. Power hadn't yet returned to their neighborhood.

"Because the phones weren't working yet." There was an edge of fear in her voice, as there always was when she had to explain to her husband a decision she had made without his approval.

"The car was making a noise. It was so loud, I couldn't ignore it."

"So, you went by his house?" *His* being the mechanic from the dealership where the Yukon was under warranty. He lived two miles away.

"I was worried. I drive Martin and his friends in that car. Do you want your son riding around in an unsafe vehicle?" She didn't bother to ask whether he cared about her own safety.

"You realize that work done outside the dealership could void the warranty?" His face and tone had that edge that warned her to tread carefully. He wasn't angry enough yet to strike, but things could be headed that way if she didn't manage the conversation right.

"No," she said, "but Lenny is the same mechanic the dealer would have assigned—"

"I'm not done," Ray said. "Don't interrupt me. How much did he charge you?"

"Nothing. It was just a loose belt. It took him five minutes."

"I didn't ask for a diagnosis. Did he give you any paperwork?"

"No." She watched him anxiously, not sure if no was a good answer or a bad one.

He rubbed his chin and thought. "Okay. So as far as the records go, this never happened. The warranty's intact. What else did you do today?"

It was time for the full account. He demanded it every day when he got home. Where did she go? Who did she talk to? When did all this happen? If she talked to certain people—a man he didn't trust, a woman he thought was a gossip—she would have to recount the conversation, careful to ensure that none of it could be interpreted as flirting, and that she didn't divulge too much information to a loose-lipped friend who would turn around and tell the neighbors.

"Carrie Wright?" Ray asked. "Del's wife? What did you talk to her about?"

"I told her you were going to the cabin—"

Ray cut her off. "You went to her house?"

"No. We talked on the phone."

"You said the phones weren't working."

"They weren't working this morning, when I had trouble with the car. They came on around lunchtime, and I called Carrie."

"Why her?"

"Ray, will you let me finish?"

"Okay," Ray sighed. "Finish."

"I told her you were going to the cabin, and I suggested Del might like to join you."

"You invited Del to my cabin?"

"He needs a break, Ray. I saw him the other day, and he looked exhausted. You two could go hunting together."

"Deer season isn't till winter."

"Fishing, then. Please, Ray. Give the man a break." And give me a break too, she thought. With you out of the house for a few days, I'll be able to breathe.

Ray thought about her proposal. He had been meaning to talk with Del. Del was a capable, all-around handyman. He wasn't too bright, in Ray's flawed estimation, but he did follow orders, and obedience was more important than intelligence. He could be useful for general maintenance work.

Del attended church too, another plus. His pastor preached the wrong flavor of the right religion—too much mercy, not enough justice—but Ray might be able to bring him over to a more sensible point of view. Del wasn't *that* stupid. He could see what the world was coming to. Some evil actor hacks the electric utility, puts the whole state in peril, and who does the company bring in to fix the problem? That skinny Mei Chen girl from the land of the Wuhan flu. And then the Feds send Anya, who claimed to be Indian but was probably Pakistani, probably a Muslim, maybe in cahoots with the hackers themselves.

The state is in peril, and the company brings in a couple of DEI hires to try to fix things. This is why America is going to fail.

In the few seconds these thoughts took to cross her husband's mind, Donna watched him closely. He's angry, she thought, but not at me. She felt her muscles relax as her alert level dropped from danger to the usual high wariness she was accustomed to feeling in his presence.

Del would be a good asset, Ray thought. He had considered this before. Maybe now was the time to make the move.

The tension in Donna's body dropped another notch as she read her husband's face. Whatever he was thinking about now must have been a pleasant thought, or at least a not-too-bad one. For the moment, he didn't look angry.

"We have a couple cans of chili," she said, wanting to slip in mention of dinner before his ill temper returned. "I can  heat them up," she added. "I found a can of Sterno with the camping gear in the garage. When's the last time we had a hot meal?" She smiled warmly, hoping he would too.

"Why the hell would I want to eat hot chili when it's ninety degrees in the house?" Ray asked angrily.

As Donna braced herself for a smack, the lights came on.

Oh, thank God, she said inwardly. Thank God! She turned before he could raise his hand and said, "Why don't I fix you a drink?"

That was always a risky proposition. A drink could calm him, or it could make him more irritable. This evening, her main concern was to distract him, get his mind off that track of anger directed at her.

She went to the kitchen without awaiting his response, listening closely all the while for his movements. He's going to his office, she thought. That's good. He'll turn on the Wi-Fi, turn on his computer. Watch those videos and hopefully sit there all night. The videos of the church of the apocalypse, or whatever it was called, stoked his bitter feelings. How long had it been since he'd watched one? Ten, eleven, twelve days? He would miss them. He would return to them like a mistress, giving them the attention and passion he had once given her.

She opened the fridge, knowing it was empty. She just wanted the reassurance of seeing the light come on.

From the cabinet above, she withdrew the whiskey bottle. In the side cabinet, she found the syrup. On the counter was half a lemon that she had cut the day before to make a glass of lemonade for their son, Martin.

She mixed the whiskey sour in a tumbler, then instinctively opened the freezer for ice, forgetting there was none. Would Ray be angry at having to take his drink warm?

She left the glass on the counter, walked through the living room, opened the sliding glass doors, and stepped onto the back patio. Thank God, she thought. Thank God the power is back.

When he goes, I'll pack two bags, put Martin in the Yukon, and where we go, he'll never find us. The plans are made. Get cash from the bank. Keep a thousand in bills for emergencies. Buy prepaid credit cards he can't trace. Ditch the phones so he can't see our location. Drive west, thirty-five hours. If he spends two days at the cabin, we'll have reached our destination before he returns.

She hadn't discussed the plan with Martin yet. Martin wasn't good at hiding his thoughts. He was visibly anxious whenever he held on to secrets. Ray might beat it out of him.

But Martin had tried to broach the topic many times. He never got much further than, "Mom..." She could see in his eyes what he wanted to talk about. *What's wrong with Dad? Why are we living like this?*

But they couldn't talk in this house. Ray's presence was so strong, even when he wasn't there, they felt that anything the walls heard, he heard too, and he would make them pay. She was scared to even think a thought he disapproved of, and she knew their son felt the same way.

Ray might read it in their minds, see it in their eyes. He punished them even for things they didn't do, thoughts they didn't dare think, because he thought they might have thought them, and that was enough. His paranoid mind projected onto them its own crimes, its own dark motives, and for this, they were the bad guys, and he made them pay.

She would tell Martin tomorrow. After the Yukon was fueled and packed and he was buckled in, she would say it as plainly as possible. *We are leaving, and we are never coming back.*

This was supposed to happen weeks ago, before the storms knocked down the trees and blocked the roads. Only now were the roads clear enough to make the attempt.

She took a deep breath, wiped her eyes, and tried to suppress the rising panic in her chest as she watched the last fiery wisp of orange sun sink below the horizon. This is the way this chapter of our lives ends, she thought. The whole sky on fire. And then comes the darkness, the not knowing what's next. Hoping it will be better than this. It has to be better than this.

She took another minute to quell her panic, get her breathing under control. The grass in the yard was thinning and drying out, withering in the heat. A funny thing to notice, she thought. Then she returned to the kitchen and picked up the drink, trying to remember the last time it had rained, the last time she had even seen a cloud in the sky.

She carried the whiskey sour into the office, where Ray sat with his back to her, listening to the preacher talk as the world burned in the background.

"Sorry it's warm," she said, as she set the tumbler on the desk in front of him.

He waved her off with his left hand, his eyes fixed on the monitor.

She turned and left him to his brooding indulgence, the one that lulled and soothed him by affirming his dark view of the world. The preacher absolved him of responsibility for society's ills and put the blame for all that pained him squarely on the shoulders of the damned. Unlike the church she grew up in, the one he rejected and forced her to leave, this one made no demands on him to fix a broken world. This world was doomed to burn. The enlightened ones could see the signs of the day of justice coming. Their duty was to be prepared, so they could survive the culling of the human species and found civilization anew once the scourge of the disbelievers had been wiped out.

On her way up the stairs, she made a mental inventory of what to pack. She wanted to start now. But she didn't dare even locate the suitcases for fear that he would see.

# 17

At ten p.m., power had been back on for about an hour and a half, enough time for the central air-conditioning to cool Sean's house to a comfortable seventy degrees. He removed the window unit from the bedroom and put it back in the garage.

Danielle lounged on the living room sofa, catching up on texts and social media. Her friends in Maryland, Virginia, and North Carolina shared survival stories of the outage. The ones who lived in smaller towns, farther from urban areas, and the ones who lived near the battered coast weren't yet back online.

Was it too early to share that she was seeing someone new? Were she and Sean even "seeing each other"? They had met only yesterday, but after spending the past thirty-two hours together, many of them in bed, she felt like they had been together for weeks.

This kind of tired, she thought, is so much better than the kind of tired she felt before. In the heat, lacking food and sleep, she had felt drained. Now her body felt relaxed and at peace.

She wouldn't tell anyone about Sean yet, she decided. Keeping such a happy secret filled her with a delicious sense of joy. If things continued to go well, she looked forward to springing the news on her friends. In the meantime, she scrolled, reacted to photos of storm damage, checked in with friends, and sank into the black hole of digital distraction that she had cursed before the blackout and had missed terribly during.

Sean sat at his desk in the adjacent office, puzzling over the lines of code that had baffled him for weeks. Again, he ran through the logic in his mind. Some part of this computer program passed a bit of data into this function. If the encrypted value of the data matched the encrypted string of text, then the function issued some commands to an external system.

What was it all about?

The first thing he wanted to know was what external system the code was reaching out to. If the laptop that Empire Energy had issued him had not been so tightly locked down, if he could have plugged in a hard drive and copied all the source code, he would have done it. But as things stood, he had only the photo he had snapped with his phone, showing just the text of that one curious function.

He would have liked to see more. He would have liked to scroll up to the top of the file to see which other code libraries were included. Some of those libraries would point to external systems, and that would give him his first clue about which systems this code was trying to manipulate.

Now that internet service was back, he could connect to his drop servers. These were the machines to which his malware sent their data. He had thirty-six servers in all, all hacked, and most of them decoys. The decoys received data from Empire's internal network and then deleted it. The investigators, once they found the decoy servers, would waste days puzzling over where the data might have gone, and what data might have been stolen in the first place.

He had no interest in the company's emails, Word documents, spreadsheets, or design documents. His malware exfiltrated them merely as a feint. The inscrutable Chinese characters that his command-and-control servers sent back to the virus lurking inside Empire's internal network were another feint, a red herring to lead investigators down blind alleys.

He had borrowed an old malware created by a unit of the Chinese military. It had been captured years ago inside a number of US corporate networks and had been thoroughly dissected by government and private security experts. Its source code was studied in cybersecurity courses around the country as an example of advanced design. It could hide itself in memory. It could inject itself into the kernel of the operating system, into code that virus scanners didn't scan. It could copy itself silently from machine to machine across a network, surviving reboots and even full reinstallations.

Its tricks were all known. This particular variant could no longer escape modern antivirus scanners. But its basic architecture was still sound, still a model for other malware creators.

Sean had studied it for years, fascinated by its cleverness. From the dark web and from public malware archives, he had retrieved examples of North Korean, Russian, and Israeli viruses. Those performed similar tricks in different ways. As with human viruses, they lost their potency over time. Commercial virus scanners grew wise to them and figured out how to inoculate the systems they protected.

But, also like human viruses, computer viruses could mutate—at least, under the guidance of a clever hand. Inject some of the Russian and North Korean tricks into the framework of the old Chinese malware, and you could build something dangerous, a virus with real potency. Like the human immune system that scans for certain proteins to identify biological viruses, computer protection systems looked for certain code signatures to identify malware. A minor change to the proteins on a biological virus's outer shell could help it evade the body's immune system. A minor change to the digital patterns of a malware exploit could keep the virus scanners from recognizing it for weeks or months, until the security researchers had time to catch up. But in those precious weeks or months, it could inflict tremendous damage.

Most of the data his virus sent out from Empire's network—the documents and emails that his drop servers deleted—looked like data the Chinese would steal. They were interested in gathering information, technology, and intellectual property. The combination of the malware used and the data it appeared to be stealing would point the finger at the People's Liberation Army. Empire and its security consultants would be looking east for the source of the hack.

While they were thus distracted, Sean could dig into the material that really interested him: the source code that ran Empire's transmission-and-distribution system, the code that controlled how power flowed through the grid. That code would be on a drop server in central Missouri, an unpatched computer belonging to a corporation with a lax security policy, the kind of machine that automated bots scanned for constantly on behalf of hackers looking for an easy target. His drop server was probably infected with thirty other viruses as well, probably used as a soldier by script kiddies in distributed denial-of-service attacks.

He leaned forward toward his computer, checked his connection to the Tor network, and from there issued the command to connect to the drop server. Once connected, he found what he was after: the entire source-code repository for all of Empire's transmission-and-distribution systems. It would take about thirty minutes to download through the sluggish Tor connection.

As he waited, he checked to see which of his other thirty-five drop servers were still online. All but one. The one outside Lexington, Kentucky, had disappeared. Most likely, that meant the Feds had confiscated it. Empire would know by now it had been compromised. The external security consultants would be onsite, isolating, decompiling, and disassembling his malware. To root it out, they would force the company to wipe out and cleanly reinstall the operating system on each of its thousands of computers, a process that would take weeks.

The Feds would be on-site too. Empire would have seen traffic going out through its firewall to the drop servers. The Feds would track down the servers' IP addresses, locate and seize each machine, extract their hard drives, and analyze the contents.

And that, to them, Sean thought, would be the most baffling part of all. Thirty-five of the thirty-six compromised machines deleted the data his malware stole as soon as it arrived. The Feds would find nothing on the hard drives. What would they make of that?

The thirty-sixth drop server, the one to which he was now connected, did contain stolen data, the source code he was after. He would delete that as soon as the download completed. And because he had connected to that computer through the untraceable Tor network, there would be no record of a connection that could be traced back to him. Everywhere they turned in their investigation, the Feds would run into dead ends.

He wouldn't even be a suspect. The target of the hack, the repurposed Chinese malware, the data that was exfiltrated—everything pointed toward China.

When the download completed, he checked the files on his computer. As far as he could tell, all the code was there.

He sent a command to the drop server to delete all the source code, the only bit of evidence that existed anywhere outside Empire's network.

From the kitchen, he could hear Danielle opening the fridge.

"You hungry?" she called.

"Not really."

"I am. Wanna watch a movie?"

"Sure. Just let me wrap up."

He plugged an external drive into his computer and typed the command to back up all the files he had just downloaded:

```
cp /home/sriggs/downloads/empire.tar.gz
/mnt/usb1/backup/
```

The computer replied:

```
/home/sriggs/downloads/empire.tar.gz: no
such file or directory
```

He puzzled over the message for a moment. How could there be no such file or directory? He had just been examining its contents. He blinked uncomprehendingly at the screen for a moment, and then an even more alarming message appeared.

```
Remote host disconnected.
```

A flash of panic shot through him. The two black terminal windows on his monitor, one commanding his own computer and the other commanding the remote drop server, looked identical. He had typed his backup command into the wrong window, and it had gone to the remote server.

He tried to reconnect. The message said:

```
No route to remote host.
```

What did that mean?

The drop server was no longer online. Had the Feds gotten to it that very minute? While he was connected?

He tried again and got the same message.

"Whatcha doing?" Danielle asked. He startled when she laid her hand on his shoulder. How had she crept in without him hearing?

"Work," he replied curtly.

"Ooh, you're tense! Everything going okay?"

"No."

"All right, you don't have to snap at me. Are you almost done?"

"Almost," he said.

"We can watch a movie on the iPad. In bed. You up for that?"

"Yeah, I'll be there in a minute."

Twenty minutes later, when the film had passed its opening credits, he lay beside her, rigid with anxiety. Her hand was on his chest.

"Your heart is racing," she said playfully. She slid her hand down past his stomach, and then said with surprise and disappointment, "Oh. I thought you were excited."

She sat up and looked at him with alarm. "Is everything okay, Sean?"

"I screwed up," he said.

"At work?"

"Yeah."

"Maybe you shouldn't work so late at night."

Thinking it through now, he saw he had made two mistakes. The first was in planning, the second in execution. The planning mistake was the way in which he had chosen his drop servers. He found a nationwide chain of coffee shops with a network of poorly secured kiosks and exploited the same flaw in thirty-six different machines across their system. That was a bad choice. As soon as the Feds found one drop server, they'd find all the rest because they all belonged to the same company.

That would not have been a problem if it weren't for his second mistake, the mistake of typing a command meant for his local machine into the remote host. And at the worst possible moment! The moment before the machine went offline and likely into the custody of the federal government.

Now the Feds had one clue, the name of the directory he had typed included his username: sriggs. There might be ten thousand people named S. Riggs in the world, but how many of them had worked at Empire? How long would it take the Feds to figure this one out?

"Sean?" Danielle looked worried. "Do you want me to leave?"

"No. Stay."

"Are you sure? I feel bad, hauling my laundry over here without even asking. I don't want to impose."

"You're not imposing," he said, his throat dry with anxiety and dread.

"Have you..." She looked down at him with compassion as she rubbed his chest. "Have you ever had a panic attack?"

"I think I'm having one now."

"Okay," she said calmly, "we're going to start with our breathing. Take a deep breath in and follow my lead..."

# 18

July 2

"Can I help you guys?"

The woman behind the counter with the cat eye mascara and impossibly long nails couldn't have been more than nineteen. At five thirty a.m., still sleepy-eyed and yawning, she was the only employee in the coffee shop.

"Can we speak to the manager?"

"Yeah, um—" She put her hand to her mouth to cover a yawn. "She's like, not here right now? If you, like, want to order? You can just punch it into the kiosk over there and I'll get right on it."

The man in front, the biggest of the four, handed her a piece of paper.

She looked at it for a second without taking it from his hand and said, "Yeah, we don't take written orders. You have to use the kiosk or the app. Do you have the app?"

"This is a warrant, ma'am."

She looked at the letters printed on the front of the man's jacket. FBI. The other three wore the same jacket. Two of the men had pistols on their belts. Two did not.

"Okay, if this is about Joey? You should totally go to his house. I'm not, like, seeing him anymore. He started, like, giving me the ick. Serious pervy vibes."

"This isn't about Joey, ma'am. We have a warrant to seize those kiosks."

She looked down the counter to her right at the two touch screens. "Both of them?"

"Both of them."

"Yeah, well, I don't think you can, like, do that? People use those to order."

"We can, ma'am. The warrant says any and all computing devices on premises."

"Even my phone?"

"Please read the warrant, ma'am."

She finally took the paper and glanced at it. The man in front signaled the others to begin work. One of the two without guns traced his finger along a wire that ran from the touch screen through a hole in the counter. He nodded to his friend, who walked behind the counter and knelt.

"Both screens run into a single unit," he said.

"Take it," said the big man in front.

# 19

"You make sure to fill the tank this morning," Ray Cooper told his wife in the driveway in front of their home. He opened the door of his pickup and flung a backpack onto the passenger seat.

The red-orange sun was just peeking over the horizon. The air that was normally thick with humidity this time of year was dry and clear. It would be hot by nine thirty. Donna stood in her white floral-print nightgown, arms folded across her chest, to see him off.

"I will," she said.

"I left a grocery list on the counter," Ray said, his hand still leaning on the edge of the truck door.

"I saw it. The stores aren't restocked yet. They won't have most of that stuff."

"Your problem," he said. "If it's not at the first store, drive till you find it. I want steak when I get back."

"When will you be back?"

"On the fifth. I'll call you when I'm an hour out, so you can start getting the food ready. And then we're going to have a talk about Martin's school."

Three days, she thought. He's going for three days, not two. Nice of him to tell me now. It doesn't matter. I'll be gone either way before he gets back.

"What about Martin's school?" she asked.

"We're moving him out of public."

"You couldn't tell me this before?"

"I'm telling you now."

"Where are we going to send him? We can't afford private school." Because you spend all our money on that stupid cabin, she thought. The only benefit of that place is that it gets you out of the house for days at a time.

"Like I said, we'll talk when I get back."

"What's wrong with the public school?"

"Goddammit, what did I just say?" He slammed the door of the truck and came toward her with that angry look that sometimes preceded a lecture, sometimes a blow. "Did I say we were going to discuss this now? Or did I say we'd discuss when I get back? Answer me!"

"When you get back," she said, trying not to cringe, trying to stand tall.

"All right," he said. "When Martin wakes up, tell him I said bye." He reopened the door and climbed into the driver's seat. "And tell him next time I go up there, he's coming with me. And so are you."

"I'll tell him," Donna said.

She watched him start the truck, stood with her arms crossed, and watched the truck until it was out of sight.

Then, even though she feared he would return, feared he would catch her in the act, she summoned all her resolve as she entered the house. She marched up the stairs, arms still folded tightly as if guarding her heart, and moved like a machine on autopilot toward the guest room closet that held the suitcases and the big duffel bag.

She told herself all she had to do was keep this resolve till late afternoon. By then, she and Martin would have passed through West Virginia into Kentucky, where her sister would be waiting. Her sister would drive the next leg, and much of the way to Colorado, and this house and everything that had happened in it would be eighteen hundred miles behind her.

If Ray ever managed to find the remote home of the cousin he didn't know she had, both her cousin and her cousin's husband vowed to shoot him on sight.

She pulled the two large suitcases from the closet, one blue, one black, and went through her mental checklist. Warm-weather clothes, pullovers for cold weather because nighttime in the Rockies would be cool, even in summer. One extra pair of shoes for her, one for Martin. Socks, plenty of underwear, toothbrushes, toothpaste, deodorant. And that was all. Travel light.

The bank would open at eight thirty. She would get cash from two different branches. Then to Walmart to buy prepaid credit cards. Fill the tank, come back home, wake Martin. Don't tell him anything until they hit the highway. Best-case scenario, that would be ten o'clock. She would be four hours behind Ray on the same highway. She prayed she wouldn't run into him.

# 20

Del chose not to leave until the kids were awake. On the one hand, he would be sorry to leave them, having seen so little of them over the past couple of weeks. On the other hand, he knew he'd be tired and cranky all day, not much good to anyone. And while his wife understood that, the kids, at least the girls, didn't so much.

On his way to the grocery store to pick up breakfast, he reminded himself that even the Lord Almighty gave himself one day off out of every seven, and it had now been sixteen since Del had had a break.

I'll drive the five and a half hours into the mountains, pull in to the cabin, and have a couple of cold brews. If we go out fishing, I'll shut my eyes for a while, soak up some of that West Virginia sun. It's fifteen degrees cooler up there, and quiet. So quiet!

The shelves of the grocery were mostly bare. He managed to find a box of pancake mix and a bag of chocolate chips that had melted into a solid lump during the blackout. There was no milk to be had, but he did find a box of soy milk, the kind that didn't need to be refrigerated, so he tossed that into the basket and wondered if he could make pancakes with it.

Not good ones, he discovered half an hour later at the kitchen stove. Passable, but not as good as with real milk. The kids, however, were delighted. Since the chocolate chips had all glommed together, Del had chiseled off big chunks from the block into each pancake. The vanilla in the soy milk added an extra sweetness to the mix.

They ate together, Mom and Dad and all four kids. Either the sugar hit the children faster than usual, or they were excited to see Dad. They peppered him with questions. Would he bring home some fish to fry? Were there moose in West Virginia? What about giraffes? That one came from the youngest, Annie. "You wouldn't shoot a giraffe, would you, Daddy?"

Del wiped a bit of chocolate from his mouth and said, "I'm not shooting anything this trip. Might do some fishing, though. I'll see if I can catch you a hammerhead or a great white." The three youngest kids took his words as fact, while Teddy, the nine-year-old, smiled at the joke.

At ten, after cleaning up from breakfast, he tied a fly rod and a freshwater rod into the bed of the truck and tossed his backpack into the passenger seat.

"That's all you're taking?" Carrie asked.

"That's it," he said. The children hugged him in turn and said their goodbyes. Annie, the youngest, clung to his leg as he gave Carrie a kiss and reminded her he'd be back in two days, in time to celebrate the Fourth.

In fifteen minutes, the old blue Ford was heading west on the interstate. Despite doing his best to restore it, it still ran rough and burned too much gas. But it looked good. The paint job was solid, the seats had been reupholstered with classic late-seventies-style blue vinyl, the steering wheel was the original, and the chrome mirrors were upgrades.

The forty-six-year-old truck had black Virginia antique tags. An antique that's three years younger than me, Del thought. He wondered if there was some service out there that did restorations on middle-aged men. Yeah, Doc, he said to himself, I'd like a new shoulder over here on the right. This one's shot. And maybe take in that belly a little bit. Put a little more hair back on top. And, ow! The left hand. I broke it and I took off the cast, and now I'm thinking maybe that wasn't such a good idea.

# 21

"I have to go to work," Danielle said. She had finished her toast and coffee and was putting her dishes into the dishwasher.

"You can work from here if you want," Sean replied. He was already onto his second coffee, looking less anxious than he had the night before.

"I want," she said. The strange closeness they had felt after spending so many hours together had intensified last night. He had let her see him in a state of deep distress. He had accepted her help, and she had calmed him. His openness during that period of vulnerability made their growing intimacy feel more real to her. It even put a little fear into her, finding someone whom she could relate to both physically and emotionally. Things don't go this smoothly, she thought. They never do. You need to be on guard, at least a little bit, so you don't get stung if things take a turn for the worse.

During his panic attack, he hadn't told her the reason for his fear. He had simply followed her breathing, kept eye contact, and entered into her mood, which was calm and soothing.

In his eyes, she had seen fear and uncertainty. Sean, she thought, must carry a lot of anxiety. Maybe every now and then, it flares up, as it does with me. Maybe he's falling for me and it scares him. I don't know. This is all so weird. You don't spend two days with a person and feel like you've been friends since childhood. It's never that easy. But there's something interesting in there, inside him, and I want to explore it.

"I'd love to work here today," she said. "But today is an in-office day, so I have to go to Richmond."

And it will do me good to get some distance, she thought. Take a look at this from an outside perspective, when he's not right here in front of me, when I'm not enclosed in his space and this weird little bubble world that's grown up around us in the past two days.

Two days? God, why does it feel like it's been weeks?

"Sure," Sean said. "It'll be good to get a change of scene. For you, I mean. Be back in the office around other people. Maybe even go out to eat."

"If the restaurants have any food. It hasn't even been twelve hours since the power returned."

After he drove her home—in the car this time, not on the motorcycle—and kissed her goodbye, he returned and sat at his computer, thinking.

Let's say the Feds find a record of that command he typed in. They see the username, "sriggs." They see that Empire once had an employee named Sean Riggs. A software security engineer, no less, who completed high-level cyber-forensics courses back in the DC area, reverse engineering some of the more sophisticated malware created by China, Russia, Israel. They'll come and ask questions. They'll want to look at his computer. What should he do?

Answer the questions as innocently as possible, he told himself. Delete the source code he had exfiltrated from Empire and downloaded from the drop server. Delete it from his personal computer, but keep the backup on an external drive, and stash that somewhere outside the house. Delete the virus he had altered from the Chinese original. Remove that source code, for sure. Then wipe the drive. Do a full military-grade wipe, overwriting every sector of the drive seven times, so the old data would be unrecoverable.

But they would be able to spot that. The Feds' forensics team would see the telltale signs of a military-grade erasure. The disk would have junk data written into thousands of sectors that should have been empty. They would ask him why he wiped it. What did he have to hide?

Okay, he thought, next plan. Back up only the essential, non-incriminating files, then destroy his laptop's internal hard drive. Drill a hole through it and then drop it off with the trash at the transfer station. It would be in landfill by the end of the day.

After that, install a new drive. But don't go out and buy one, because they'll ask why he went to Best Buy and bought a new hard drive the day before they arrived.

He lingered on that thought for a moment. *The day before they arrived.* Could they be here as soon as tomorrow? Maybe, maybe not.

But he wouldn't have to buy a new drive. He had another drive on the shelf behind him, still in its original box, a larger drive he had bought as an upgrade but hadn't got around to installing. He could put that one into the laptop and he'd be clean. The package would go into landfill with the old drive.

Then what evidence would the Feds have against him? They had seized at least one and possibly all of the drop servers as well as the C and C server, but those were almost all clean. They never stored the data that was sent to them, and he didn't connect to most of those machines, only to one.

So, again, the only clue they had was that username, sriggs, who could be anyone. That was on the machine he had connected to through the untraceable Tor network, so there was no way they could know that the computer on the other end of that connection belonged to him. He made a mental note to omit Tor when he set up his new disk drive. He didn't want them to find that on his computer, since it was a favorite tool of hackers around the world.

Okay, he thought. So, if there's no evidence on the remote machines, and no evidence on my machine, and nothing with my fingerprints on it inside Empire's network, then they'll really have to do some thinking. The first thing they'll want is a motive. Why would I want to hack into Empire?

For financial gain? They'll examine all my accounts and find no recent big deposits. No major debts either. They'll examine my devices for evidence of cryptocurrency holdings and they'll find nothing, because I don't have any. They'll look into my recent past to see if I've had contacts with foreign agents, and they'll find I haven't.

What's my motive, then? Hating Ray Cooper? Lots of people hate Ray Cooper. Or at least, nobody likes him. And even if I hated Ray, why would I go after Empire? Why not go after Ray on social media, or slash his tires, or put sugar in his gas tank, or steal his phone? Why would I risk breaking into the network of such a powerful company to take revenge on a single person?

Because that's not what it's about, he thought. Ray is dangerous, with his end-of-the-world hellfire resentment and his little club of think-alike doomers and preppers. He tried to pull me into that group, those guys who used to meet for lunch outside the office, and for Thursday-night dinners at that burger place in Glen Allen. What made him think I'd want to join his cult? I don't know. Maybe because I asked so many questions about everything that went on in the company, he assumed I was looking for the same "truth" he saw. The same paranoid vision of conspiracy, which was the only "truth" he seemed capable of comprehending. His mind accepted only facts that agreed with his bitter temperament.

His group of acolytes included some field technicians, young guys, clean-cut, who seemed lost, like wayward soldiers in search of a commander, people who couldn't tolerate uncertainty and gravitated toward a mind that seemed sure, uncompromising, that could simplify the baffling complexities of the world into a reassuring black and white. The more they listened to him, the more confident they became. He was making sense of a world that vexed and frightened them, confirming their fears that whatever was beyond their comprehension was evil, that the good life the world owed them had been ruined by others, and that those others needed to pay.

That one young guy, what was his name? Ben? Ben Wood. He would have been trouble without Ray. Bad attitude, full of resentment. A human weapon just waiting for someone to point him in the right direction. A little Ray junior.

Two meetings were all Sean could endure with that crew, and when he dropped out, Ray turned on him with the venom of a spurned lover. Harassment from the minute Sean walked into the office till the minute he left. Taking him off projects, writing him up again and again for minor infractions he hadn't even committed. Bad-mouthing him to his coworkers.

And meanwhile, Ray was up to something. He kept asking the security team for access to the transmission-and-distribution control center. "It's my damn software that runs the place. Why can't I get in?"

They told him what he already knew. The first rule of security in a large organization is that everyone gets access to the minimum resources required to do their job. For Ray, that was the code that runs the system and the tools to write and test it. Nothing more. Access restrictions limited how much damage a single person could inflict on the system. Usually, that was unintentional damage, a person making a mistake.

But you, Ray... Sean rubbed his chin as he sat musing at his desk. You, with your God complex, or prophet complex, or whatever it is. Something is wrong with you. The way you manipulate your eager acolytes, the way you puff up as they worship you in that cult of personality. I would have reported you, but the security officer who takes those reports is a member of your group. Charles Lehrman. Another paranoid. Somehow, you managed to stack the key positions with loyal followers. Or you just knew who to recruit.

Sean had tried to take his concerns higher up in the organization, told Ray's boss about his little group, and the way Ray harassed him. The boss told him that, from what he understood, Sean was the problem. Sean had eleven write-ups in twelve days. Ray had been in good standing for years. Ray could be abrasive, for sure, but he got things done.

"If you have security concerns," he said, "take them to Charles Lehrman. But frankly, meeting coworkers for lunch and dinner isn't a crime, if that's what you're accusing Ray of doing. Neither is writing up an employee for dereliction of duty. That's part of a manager's job."

Sean had thought about taking his complaints to an outside regulator. The Federal Energy Regulatory Commission or the

FBI. But what would he tell them? That he found some funny-looking test code and his boss was an asshole?

The last time Sean went to the Feds, at his DC job, the corporate brass brought the hammer down on him. He had no idea they'd come down that hard. And that time, he had real evidence of a problem, not just suspicions. And still, the investigators didn't believe him. Try to get a big corporation to do the right thing, and it'll drag its feet, tell you it doesn't have the resources to clean up every little mess. Then go to the Feds, put the company in a situation where it has to cover up wrongdoing, and you'll see just how fast it can act.

The company had resources to wipe out years of evidence in just a few days. It had resources to threaten and harass a whistleblower, to make Sean's life so miserable he left the city for good. What credibility did he have with the Feds after that fiasco? His name was probably on a list of false accusers, wackos, disgruntled troublemakers.

So, I'm stuck, he thought for the hundredth time. Stuck with questions and suspicions that he could neither prove nor explain. He had run across a puzzling bit of code that smelled of malice. Why was it hidden there in the tests, where it would have no effect? People didn't write code to do nothing. In the two days between when he found the code and when they fired him, he traced the entire code base, and found no reference to this strange code anywhere. No other functions invoked this strange bit of code so, because it seemed pointless, he deleted it. Ray, his manager, had to approve the deletion, but he rejected it.

Sean deleted it again. Again, Ray rejected the deletion and the code remained.

When he went to talk to Ray about it, Ray got so angry, Sean feared a physical attack. Ray raged and blustered about what a bad coder Sean was, how Sean was insubordinate, how he was poison to the software group because he wasn't a "team player." A team player for Ray was one who blindly, unquestioningly followed his commands.

"Ray," Sean said, "can we just stick to the issue at hand? Why is this code here? What does it do? It's dangerous to have code you don't understand inside a system that runs the grid, that affects the daily lives of millions of people. But it can't even reach the actual grid, because it's part of the test code. So, what's the point?"

Ray's nostrils flared, and there was murder in his eyes.

"You're fired," he said.

"You can't fire me. There's a process. You have to go through HR."

"HR?" he sneered. "HR just talked with your former employer. You didn't tell us when you applied that you'd been fired for cause. That you stole code."

"Because I didn't," Sean said. "I didn't steal anything. That company had some serious problems and—"

"Get out!" Ray commanded. "Give me your laptop and leave your badge at the security desk."

So, Sean left. He used his phone to take a snapshot of the code on his computer monitor, walked out the door, and never went back. HR called the next day and told him to stay home until they resolved his case. Two weeks later, he was officially unemployed. Fired for cause, the cause being what Ray said, that Sean hadn't explicitly told them during the hiring process that he had been fired from his DC job.

And now, he thought, the Feds are probably already on-site at Empire. They'll see the record of complaints and write-ups from Ray. They'll peg me as a disgruntled employee, he told himself. Still, once he destroyed the hard drive and removed the external drive from the house, they'd find no evidence anywhere to connect him to the breach.

Eventually, prudence would tell the investigators to turn their attention back to the bigger threat, to China. If he had strewn his clues well enough—and he thought he had—China would look like the most likely culprit. And the Chinese government was a scarier adversary than some lone hacker in a modest house thirty miles west of town. China was an adversary they couldn't ignore.

If he could play it cool for a week or two when the Feds brought the pressure, he could come out unscathed on the other side of this.

"They have no evidence" became his mantra, what he told himself to keep calm.

But what about Ray? Why had he been so insistent on keeping that code in place? What was he up to?

Sean turned to the computer monitor on the desk in front of him. He opened the file explorer and dove into the Empire source code he had downloaded the night before.

The first thing to check was the logs of the source-control repository. The logs recorded who added each bit of code, and when. He searched for records of the curious test file, and in a few minutes, he found what he was looking for. But it was not what he expected. The strange code had been added to the repository by a woman named Drishti Singh back in January. Sean had seen her name elsewhere in the code base during his time at Empire, but he had never met her.

He opened a browser, went to LinkedIn and looked up her profile. She had left Empire at the beginning of the year. Now she was working for a company in India.

He clicked the Message button on her profile and began to type.

> Hey, Drishti, Sean Riggs. I worked on your code at Empire after you left. I guess we just missed each other. I wanted to ask you about some code you committed back in January. Do you have time to chat?

He sent the message, then wondered what time it was in Mumbai. The search engine told him it was 6:30 p.m. Would she still be working? Did software developers work in offices over there, or at home, like they did here?

A message popped up on screen.

> Happy to talk. Number?

He sent his number.

I'll call you in twenty. Just wrapping up some work
here.

Sean loaded the Empire source code into his development environment and again read through the bit that puzzled him, starting with the first four lines inside the "if" statement.

"Okay," he said under his breath, "if the encrypted input matches this weird string of gibberish, then we execute the following instructions."

```
STRCAP ALL TRUE
SLEEP 900
STRTERM ALL
STRREW 0
STRPUSH MASTER LOOP
```

He had no idea what STRCAP, STRREW, or STRPUSH meant. Those commands were sent to some external system, probably an industrial control system that managed equipment outside the computer itself. Sean's background was in pure computing—operating systems, compilers, databases. Industrial control systems were a whole other realm.

The SLEEP 900 command told the program to pause for nine hundred seconds—fifteen minutes—and do nothing.

He searched the code base for other mentions of STRCAP. He found one match, embedded in a comment from another developer.

```
/*
STRCAP sensorid - Capture input from field sensor.
STRCAP ALL - Capture input from all field sensors.
*/
```

Okay, so this code told some external system to capture input from all of its sensors. STR probably meant "stream," since this data would flow in as a stream of electronic bits.

Capture the data, then wait fifteen minutes. Then call STRTERM ALL. What did that mean? Again, he searched the code for other instances of that command, this time with no luck. He could make a guess, though. STRTERM probably meant terminate the stream. Cut it off.

STRREW 0 looked a lot like the file seek command commonly found in other programming languages. It meant rewind the stream to the beginning.

And then STRREAD probably meant "read the stream." Read it in a loop, going back to the beginning each time it ended. Why would you want a system to do that?

His phone rang. Drishti Singh. After introductions, he explained the code in question, to give her some context.

"It compares its input to an encrypted value—"

"What does the encrypted value mean?" she asked.

"I don't know. But then it starts sending commands to an external system."

"I didn't write that," she said.

"Are you sure? Can I read you a few lines?"

"Go ahead. But I'm sure I didn't write that code."

As he read the code line by line, he could hear her mumbling on the other end, "Nope. Nope. No!"

"You're sure?" he asked.

"A hundred percent."

"But your name is on the commit in the code repository."

"I never wrote that," she said. "Those commands, STRCAP and all that, those go out to the system that controls and monitors the grid, software from that giant German conglomerate. I would never put code like that in production."

"It's not in production. It's in the test code."

"Well, that's pointless. Why would code like that be in with the tests? What's it even testing?"

"Nothing," said Sean. "It doesn't test anything at all. But you committed this code on January fifth of this year."

"I left on December thirtieth, last year. I turned in my laptop that afternoon and flew back to India the next day."

Sean paused for a moment and thought.

"Is there a problem?" Drishti asked. "Did the code mess something up?"

"Not yet," he said. "When you left," he asked slowly, "who did you give your laptop to?"

"To my supervisor."

"Ray?"

"Yes, Ray. Why?"

Why, Sean thought? Because if Ray could get into your computer, he could commit the code from there. Then it would look like you did it, and his fingerprints wouldn't be on the evidence. Too bad it took him five days to figure that out. Too bad he couldn't have committed the code before you left the country.

Sean pulled a notebook from the shelf and wrote in the dates.

- Dec. 30 - Drishti gives laptop to Ray
- Dec. 31 - Drishti leaves US
- Jan. 5 - Code committed to source repo under Drishti's name

"Just curious," he said. "Maybe I'll ask Ray about it."

That last part was a lie.

After the call, he continued to puzzle over the meaning of the other commands. There were dozens of them spanning fifty more lines. He knew now, though, which system those commands were manipulating. The system that controlled the flow of electricity on the grid. Ray Cooper had repeatedly requested, and had repeatedly been denied, access to the operations center that would have given him hands-on access to that system. If he couldn't get physical access to Empire's grid-control center, he could get electronic access through his code.

But once again, Sean was stumped. This was test code, something the developers ran locally on their laptops as they worked, to ensure their changes didn't break things. Test code never went into production systems. It ran in separate, isolated systems that could never reach the grid. So why would Ray bother putting his commands here?

He plugged a thumb drive into the USB port and began copying the code so he'd still be able to access it after destroying and disposing of his incriminating hard drive. Then he sat back and thought, his mind going in circles.

# 22

A few minutes past noon, FBI Special Agent Carlos Espinoza and Homeland Security Investigator Anya Lakhani sat before a monitor in a conference room at Empire headquarters. On-screen, a woman from the Bureau's digital forensics team summarized what they had found so far.

"The drop servers and the command-and-control servers belong to a coffee-store chain that was negligent in applying security patches."

The woman on screen wore a gray suit with a white blouse, open at the collar. Her dark hair was cut short. She enunciated clearly and spoke with conviction and self-assurance. Anya guessed she was Korean. Probably second-generation American, like her.

"These machines were easy targets. Our Chinese friends, or whoever is behind this breach, weren't the only ones taking advantage. The kiosks had dozens of viruses. Mainly, they were being used for denial-of-service attacks.

"We were able to isolate the malware related to the Empire breach because we knew that traffic coming out of Empire was going to port forty-four-forty-eight. The service listening on that port was receiving the stolen data.

"The strange thing is, the malware receiving the data seems to have just discarded it all."

"All of it?" asked Carlos Espinoza.

The woman nodded. "As far as we can tell."

"Are you sure that's not a ruse? Like, the malware wants you to think it threw away the data to throw you off?"

"Could be," said the woman. "We're still digging in. But the disks show no sign of the data ever having been saved."

"Who was connecting to those machines?" Anya asked. "Was anyone trying to download the stolen data the machines were receiving?"

"There were lots of connections coming in," the woman said. "We pulled the routers that connected those kiosks to the internet. The router logs show incoming connections from Tor exit nodes. That usually means hackers and other bad actors. Unfortunately, because it's Tor, the exit node is a dead end. We can't follow the traffic back to its origin.

"Another problem," she said, "is that, except for one instance, none of that traffic appears to have connected to the malware receiving the stolen data. All the incoming connections were aimed at manipulating the other malware, which was script-kiddie-level work compared to the sophistication of what we've seen inside the Empire network."

"What about outgoing connections?" Anya asked. "Were the drop servers reaching out across the net? Trying to connect to other machines?"

The woman shook her head. "There were outgoing connections from the other malware, but not from the one we're investigating."

"So, what's the point, then?" asked Agent Espinoza. "Why steal data and then throw it away? Why make no effort to retrieve it from the drop servers?"

The woman shrugged. "We're as baffled as you are. But we expect to find more as we dig. Oh, and by the way, that one instance I mentioned—the hacker or hackers appeared to have an open connection to one of the drop servers when we seized it. So that server does seem to have had some importance. The hacker was actively logged in, typing commands when we took the machine offline."

"What were they doing?" Anya asked.

"We're still analyzing that. The router in front of that kiosk shows a large download had just completed."

"Going where?" Espinoza asked.

"Tor. Where else?"

"So that's untraceable too," Anya said.

"Untraceable. But the hacker did leave us a clue."

"What's that?" Espinoza asked.

"A command that was probably meant for his or her own machine," the woman replied. "It looks like they typed it into the wrong terminal window by mistake. I'll paste it into chat."

Espinoza and Anya Lakhani stared quietly at the first clue they had so far as to who was behind the hack.

```
cp   /home/sriggs/downloads/empire.tar.gz
/mnt/usb1/backup/
```

Both knew the language of the command line well enough to understand the command's meaning. Copy the file called "empire.tar.gz" to an external drive. The name of the file suggested where its contents had come from. It was data stolen from Empire Energy. The name after the word "home" was the name of the user's personal directory, and also their username. Someone who logged into his or her own computer as "sriggs" had downloaded a cache of stolen files from a hacked coffee-store kiosk a few blocks away from the state university in Columbia, Missouri.

# 23

If the mystery code was issuing commands to the transmission-control system, Sean thought, the system that moves electricity through the grid, it would help to know what the commands meant. A programming manual would be useful, but the software from the big German conglomerate was used on power grids around the world, and for that very reason, the company didn't publish its manuals on the open market. Why give hackers the information they would need to cause trouble?

If you wanted the manual, you had to shell out hundreds of thousands of dollars for the software, and the company wouldn't sell you the software unless you had a grid to run it on.

Leaning back at his desk, Sean told himself there were probably discussion forums online where programmers who worked on grid-control software traded questions. He could poke around in those, search out the commands he had seen in the code. But he knew he needed to be careful. When the Feds followed the obvious lead pointing to user "sriggs," who was most likely the disgruntled former Empire employee Sean Riggs, they would dig up all his internet activity. They wouldn't find anything incriminating, but if they saw someone from his IP address had been asking questions about power-system commands related to the specific software that Empire used to run their grid, that wouldn't look good. He wondered whether there was a way to get the info anonymously. Maybe. He could connect to the message boards through Tor. But he'd still have to engage in back-and-forth with other software engineers in the forums, and it could take days or weeks to get the answers he needed.

Was there a faster way?

He opened a Tor browser and searched for a used version of the printed manual. To his surprise, he found dozens of results. And why not, he thought? What did people do with those precious manuals when the software conglomerate released a new version and the old manuals became obsolete?

Amazon showed a number of used copies, but when he clicked on one of the results, a page informed him his access was blocked. Probably because his request was coming from a Tor exit node. That made sense. Amazon wouldn't want competitors or anyone else anonymously scraping product data from its site. A Tor exit node was, by default, not to be trusted by a commercial entity.

He could reach the same page through a normal browser, but even in private mode, he feared Amazon would be able to identify him. From the drawer of his desk, he pulled an old Android phone and checked its charge. Twenty-five percent was good enough. He slid the phone into his pocket. Then he picked up the thumb drive onto which he had copied the stolen source code and put that in his pocket as well. To his faithful laptop he said, "See you later, old friend."

He shut it down, then rebooted it from an external drive. From the options list, he chose "Format Disk Drive." He selected the computer's internal drive, and chose the "Full Secure Reformat" option. The computer warned him that all data on the disk would be lost forever and asked if he was sure he wanted to do this. He clicked Yes, then watched the bright green progress bar begin its crawl from left to right. The machine had begun its work.

From the kitchen, he grabbed the keys to the Millers' house next door. He stopped and checked their mailbox, which was still empty, then went inside. The house was freezing. The Millers had set the thermostat high when they left, but after the power outage, it had lost the setting and the air-conditioning had come on full blast.

He turned the thermostat up to seventy-six and then walked down the hall from the living room to Sid Miller's office, passing three dozen photos along the way. Miller taught history and coached girls' volleyball and boys' basketball at the local high school. The photos documented three decades of success, smiling students, and shiny trophies.

In the office, the flashing blue lights on the small black tower unit told him the Wi-Fi had come back on with the power. He looked for a piece of paper taped to the back of the tower with a password. Finding none, he checked the bottom of the unit. Nothing there either.

He pulled the old phone from his pocket and checked the Wi-Fi settings, where he saw a strong signal from "TheMillers," with no lock on the Wi-Fi icon. The network had no password. He clicked Connect. An alert said, "Unsecured network. Are you sure you want to connect?"

He clicked Yes and left the box that said "Automatically connect to this network" unchecked.

He sat in the chair at Sid Miller's desk, opened his phone's browser, and went to Amazon, where he typed in the title of the software manual. The results showed twelve used copies available from bookstores around the country. The first result he tapped was from a store in California. The second was in Ohio; the third, in Washington state.

Something clicked. Each of these bookshops was in the same city as the state's power utility. That made sense. Who else besides software engineers working on the grid would have a reason to own such a book?

He went back and looked at the editions. The manuals covered versions of the software from four and five years ago. They might be a little out of date, but software for mission-critical systems changed much more slowly than consumer apps and web-based software, because introducing change to complex systems was dangerous. A slightly out-of-date manual would still be helpful.

He continued clicking through results until he came to a copy belonging to a used bookseller in Richmond. Bringing up a map, he saw it was less than four miles from Empire's transmission-control office. Some engineer, or possibly even a janitor coming across the book in the trash, had cashed it in for a few bucks. This particular edition was three years old. Not bad.

He would go the store and buy the book with cash. Like Tor, cash was untraceable. It left no digital record.

He slid the old phone back into his pocket and walked to the kitchen. He listened to the Millers' landline phone ring as he filled the watering pail at the sink. It had been two days since he had last watered the plants and, in that time, the unusually dry air had hardened the soil in the pots.

After six rings, the water pail was half-full. He twisted the tap shut, opened a high cabinet, and hid the tiny thumb drive with the stolen source code inside as the answering machine began its recorded greeting. "You've reached Sid and Martha Miller. We can't come to the phone right now, but if you leave your name, number, and a good time to reach you, we'll get back to you just as soon as we can."

Sean hadn't seen an answering machine since he was a kid. His parents had one. The Millers were about the same age as his mother and father, in their late sixties, and like his parents, they clung to technologies they understood.

He left the pail on the counter and walked to the small table in the corner of the kitchen. The machine looked just like the one his parents had, black with four buttons and a little red light that shone solid when it was recording and that flashed when it had new messages to replay.

The unfamiliar voice that came through the speaker said, "Hey, Sid, it's Jerry. I know we had an outage here, but you were supposed to pick up this Mustang two weeks ago. I told you I ain't got much room on my lot, and usually I charge if you leave a car more than seventy-two hours. Please come get this thing. I'm overflowing here. Oh, and I hope you all are doing well. And hi to Martha."

Where the Millers were now was anyone's guess. They had left to visit family before the first of the two storms arrived. They were supposed to have returned from Arkansas more than a week ago. Obviously, they would have known about the power outage, the downed trees, and all that went with those: impassable roads, lack of food and fuel, hot days and nights in a stuffy house. It made sense they stayed where they were. Life in the Ozarks, or wherever they had gone, had to be better than here.

A cordless landline phone sat beside the answering machine. Beside that was a sticky note with a handful of numbers, including Sid Miller's cell. Good. He could call the man from here. He didn't want to leave a record of their conversation on his own phone. Not the conversation he was about to have.

He picked up the landline and punched in the number. Sid Miller answered cheerfully on the second ring.

"Hey, Sid, it's Sean."

"Sean!" Sid was usually overenthusiastic in his greetings. He had the outgoing nature of a high school teacher and coach who loved his jobs. "How are you? Is power back on there?"

"I'm good. And yeah, it came back last night."

"How many days was it?"

"Eleven, I think."

"And the news here says nine million people are still in the dark up and down the East Coast."

"I feel for them," Sean said.

"You guys got lucky, getting it back sooner than so many others."

"I know. Hey, listen. Some mechanic just called to tell you to pick up your Mustang. It's taking up space on his lot. He's going to start charging you."

"You ever drive a sixty-seven Mustang, Sean?"

"No." He had seen the car parked in front of the Millers' house. Sid drove it on errands and took it out into the country on weekends. It was shiny and well kept, but to Sean, it sounded like a rumbling junker, and the exhaust smelled bad.

"You want to try it?" Sid asked.

That's what Sean was hoping to hear. He already had a plan for it. If the mystery code did what he feared it might do, he would need the Feds' help at some point. But he wouldn't be able to get their help until he could show them a solid case—he had learned this the hard way the last time he had tried to report trouble to them—and his case wasn't solid yet. If he were to prove anything, he would need more time to review the code, the system manual from the big German conglomerate, and parts of the stolen source repository he hadn't even dug into yet. He would not be able to do any of that in a federal detention facility.

That they would come for him was now a foregone conclusion. Plan as if it's going to happen, he told himself. They would ask questions and he would play innocent. They would threaten him with evidence they didn't have, because there was no evidence. They'd probably back off after a few days and go back to the China angle. Still, he had to give himself every chance. And an extra car that the Feds didn't know about would be a solid asset. It could allow him to move around unnoticed, buy him a few days' time, and that might be all he needed.

"I mean," Sid Miller said, "I don't want to impose or anything. I'm just saying, if you can get to the shop, I'll tell Jerry to give you the key. It's ten miles out. You have a way of getting there?"

"You're not imposing," Sean said. "I'll pick it up."

"I'll tell Jerry you're coming."

After hanging up, he watered the plants in the living room. Then he went outside and checked the potted flowers on the back deck. They hung their heads in weariness from the heat, languishing in dry soil hard as concrete. He refilled the pail and watered them too. The whole lawn could have used a watering, he thought, but he'd leave that task to the Millers.

He returned the pail to its place on the kitchen counter and rechecked the Amazon page on his old phone. The page listed the bookseller as Gatsby's. He knew where that was, near the corner of West Broad and North Belvidere. He had passed it dozens of times, though he had never been in.

He returned to his house and pulled the new hard drive he'd been meaning to install from the office shelf. It was still in its box, sealed in cellophane. He turned off the laptop, flipped it over, and opened it up with a tiny screwdriver. He unfastened the clips that held the old solid-state drive in place—the one he had just erased—snapped it out of the socket, and slid the new one in.

He closed up the laptop, plugged in a USB stick, rebooted the computer, and installed a new operating system. Then he took the old hard drive to the garage and drilled four holes through it with an electric drill. He returned to the office and grabbed the packaging of the drive he'd just installed.

Using his regular phone, he called an Uber. The Feds would probably track the Uber ride, he thought. Track it after the fact, once they got a warrant for his phone. He picked an address a mile from the auto repair shop so the Feds wouldn't know exactly where he had gone. The driver would drop him there and he'd walk the rest of the way. When the Uber arrived, he left the regular phone on his desk and slid his old phone, the one he had used at the Millers' house, into his pocket.

Fifty minutes later, he was cruising east on Interstate 64 toward Richmond in the 1967 Mustang. He left the highway at Short Pump and drove to a cluster of office buildings. The parking garages behind the offices were unrestricted. He entered one and drove up to the third level, where two thirds of the spaces were empty.

He killed the engine, then glanced back at the load of sports equipment in the rear seat. New basketballs and volleyballs, stacks of jerseys and shorts with the high school logo. Did coach Miller store this stuff in his car? Or had he been out shopping when the car broke down and had to go in for repairs?

Maybe I should put that stuff in the trunk, he thought. So no one steals it.

He got out and popped the trunk, only to find it stuffed to the brim with more sports equipment. Bats, baseballs, softballs, gloves. Sid Miller didn't even coach those sports. He must have been out on a buying spree for the school athletic department when the car broke down. He closed the trunk and went back to the driver's door, slid the keys under the driver's seat, turned, and headed for the stairs.

It was now almost four thirty in the afternoon. Danielle's office was a mile or so away. He could walk and meet her, surprise her, take her out to dinner, and get a ride home to boot.

When he reached the sidewalk, he pulled the old phone from his pocket and opened the map. The phone had no SIM card and couldn't connect to the cell network. It would leave no trace of his journey. What was the name of the agency Danielle worked for? He was going to look it up, but with no SIM card, and no service, he wouldn't be able to do a search or load a map until he found a coffee shop with free Wi-Fi.

He headed south past a row of shops, dropping the old hard drive and the packaging from the new one into a garbage can. On the next block, he found a Starbucks.

There, alone at a table for two, he typed in what he thought was the name of Danielle's employer. The map corrected him and showed him the right place. One point four miles. A thirty-minute walk under a hot July sun. He would be sweaty when he arrived.

The walk was a straight shot, with only one left turn a block before his destination. He slid the phone back into his pocket and thought of Danielle and how the scent of her skin lingered in his sheets.

He was excited to see her, excited to take her out. Would she like that he showed up unannounced for a surprise date? Or would she be put off? He decided she would be excited. From what he had seen of her so far, he couldn't imagine anything putting her off.

As he walked, he became uneasy without knowing why. He felt he had missed something, but he didn't know what. He ran through a quick mental checklist—he had his keys, he had his wallet, he had locked the house, the computer disk was erased and disposed of, and the thumb drive was hidden in a cabinet in the Millers' kitchen, where no one would look for it. What was there to worry about? What besides the knowledge that the Feds would soon question him, knowledge that he had already accepted?

He couldn't explain why he was uneasy, but he couldn't shake the feeling either. The sun felt unusually strong in the clear, dry air. His lips felt dry and chapped. His mouth and throat became dry as well. Whether that was from the weather or his anxiety, he couldn't tell.

When he made the final turn, hot and sweaty, he saw the name of Danielle's firm on the building ahead. And just beneath it, there she was behind the big glass window, nodding attentively in the ground-floor conference room as a young woman in blue slacks and white blouse explained something.

A tingling thrill ran through him at the sight of her. He remembered all at once how much her enjoyed her company, the lightness of her spirit, her playfulness, her body, the scent of her hair. From this view, he saw her in profile, and though her attention was on the woman speaking in front her, she turned as if by instinct to look at him. Her face lit with delight, she leapt from her seat and waved her hand excitedly toward the building's main entrance, motioning him to go there.

How could anyone *not* respond to her, he wondered? How could such a delightful person be single? He thanked his luck as he watched her speak to the woman inside. Danielle was saying something about him. The woman looked at him, looked back at Danielle and smiled. Her happiness was contagious.

Danielle closed her laptop and rushed outside and hugged him.

"Oh my God, did you come to take me out? Are we going to dinner? You're sweaty and gross. It's so good to see you!"

As she wiped his sweat from her hands onto her pants, he said, "I love the way all your thoughts tumble out at once. It's like watching The Three Stooges all try to go through a door at the same time."

"Okay, I'll take that as a compliment. Can you give me a minute to get my stuff? You want to come in and use the bathroom?"

"Yeah, actually."

Her eyes narrowed. "What's wrong?"

"Nothing. I'm happy to see you. And yes, we'll go out to dinner."

"Cool." Still, she eyed him, unconvinced. "You sure nothing's bothering you?"

Now it hit him. He sucked in a sharp breath all at once, alarming her.

"What?" she asked.

The phone, he thought. The old Android phone he used at the Millers' house. Before he left, he looked again at the book listing on the Amazon page. But the first time, when he connected to their Wi-Fi, he didn't check the box that said "automatically connect to this network." That was consistent with his security-minded habits. Never automatically connect to insecure networks.

So what network was he on when he looked at the book for the second time? His home network. The old phone connected to his home Wi-Fi automatically. And the signal was strong enough to reach the kitchen side of the Millers' house next door. Their kitchen was less than twenty feet from his bedroom.

So now there was a record of an Amazon search for an obscure and incriminating software manual coming from his Wi-Fi, from his IP address. Would the Feds see that when they requested his search history from Amazon? They absolutely would.

Sean pulled the old phone from his pocket and looked at it.

"What is it?" Danielle asked, grasping his shoulder tightly. "You look so worried!"

"I brought the wrong phone," he said.

She looked at him wide eyed. "That's it? You get that worked up about your phone?" Her bright smile returned. "You have got to loosen up, Sean. How about a Margarita?"

"How about two?"

"Sounds good," she said. Somehow, her good cheer prevailed over even his gloomiest fears. "Come inside. I'll get my stuff and you can use the bathroom. Do you want to drive, or should I?"

"You drive," he said.

He would tell her to drive down West Broad toward North Belvidere. He would tell her he had to run into the drugstore. He would give her fifty dollars in cash and ask her to go into Gatsby's used bookstore and pick up the software manual while he was on his errand. That way, there would be nothing tying him to the purchase. Nothing but her.

# 24

Del was surprised at how much had changed since he had last visited Ray's cabin, twelve months prior. It was no longer the only structure on the two-mile stretch of dirt-and-gravel road along the mountainside. Now, it was the last of four. Del knew Ray loved the solitude of the place. When he asked later whether Ray minded having neighbors, his friend responded, "Not at all. As long as they're the right kind."

Del had run into one of those neighbors along the road. The man had stopped to secure the large steel tank in his pickup bed. Del stopped to ask if he needed a hand, and the man responded by asking curtly what business Del had out here.

"Visiting Ray Cooper down at the end of the road."

"Oh, you're Ray's friend. Welcome, then. Name's Carl."

Carl was tall, middle aged, with thinning blond hair and a sunburned face. The upside-down American flag patch printed on his shirt matched the sticker on the rear window of his truck, which sported Michigan license plates. The silver stenciled lettering on the big tank in the bed of the pickup, Del noted, said the interior was glass lined. The tank was for drinking water. Its owner said he didn't need any help, but thanks for asking.

The trucks parked in front of the next two houses along the road were from Michigan and Ohio. Their respective owners were unloading cardboard boxes from the beds.

Ascending the gravel drive to Ray's cabin, Del saw that the roof was newly covered with solar panels. An eight-by-twelve-foot patch of raised red earth beside the house probably covered a recently buried tank even larger than the one Del had just seen.

Ray met him truck-side and gave him a tour. The solar panels fed into a bank of batteries in the basement. "Lithium iron phosphate," Ray said. "The kind that doesn't catch fire. Otherwise, I wouldn't have them inside."

Del noted the capacity of the batteries. Forty kilowatt-hours was much more than a person needed to run a home for twenty-four hours. Was Ray planning on riding out a long outage?

"That's a lot of money," Del said.

"Money well spent," Ray replied.

Del also noted that while there didn't seem to be much food in the kitchen, the basement was heavily stocked with canned meats, canned beans, canned vegetables, and sacks of rice, cornmeal, and flour.

They went out hunting for rabbits near dusk, bagging two before the sound of gunfire forced the remaining creatures back into hiding. Del skinned them as twilight fell, and Ray lit a fire in the outdoor fire pit to roast them.

"Did you know the Indians had a word that meant rabbit starvation?" Ray asked.

"I never heard that," Del replied.

"Sometimes, in winter, rabbits were all they could find. But if all you eat is rabbits for two or three months, you'll die. They have almost no fat. Your body can't handle the imbalance of a pure protein, no fat diet for very long."

Del decided he would look that up when he got home. Up here, there was no cell service, no internet of any kind, unless you had a satellite dish. The nearest town was sixteen miles away, and half those miles were unpaved. The town, if you wanted to call it that, had a post office, a gas station, a tiny grocery, and a shop that sold tools and hardware.

"Good thing you got all that food in the basement," Del said. "Keep you from rabbit-starving in a cold winter."

"Yeah," Ray muttered. "Good thing. You know, I've been meaning to talk to you about something, Del."

I had a feeling, Del thought, when I saw that neighbor, the one you say is "the right kind." He had a sour look, kinda like you, Ray. Like he spends a lot of time stewing about things that make him unhappy.

"What'd you want to talk about, Ray?"

Ray pulled a spit from the fire. The rabbit was charred on one side and not quite done on the other. He rotated the spit and put it back over the flame.

"You read the Bible, Del?"

"'Course."

"The last chapter?"

"I try to stay away from that one."

Del found Revelation to be the darkest of the books, and the least comprehensible. His pastor had told him that John of Patmos wrote it in a sort of code that other Christians of the day would understand, but that looked like nonsense to censors and authorities trying to suppress the church. Del agreed with his pastor about the main takeaway, that the world as we know it would someday end. He didn't like to think about how, or the suffering of the people who had to live through the end times.

"That's the one you should be reading," Ray said. "Look around you. You see where the world is heading."

"The world is running about the same as it ever was," Del said. "Just a little louder and faster. Everyone's trying to hold their lives together. Some are doing better than others."

"That's all you see?" Ray asked.

"That's all I concern myself with." Del pulled a beer from the cooler.

"Grab me one of those," Ray said.

"You sure? You already had two. Ain't that your limit?"

"Was," Ray said. "Toss me one?"

Del tossed him a can of beer. Ray popped it open and took a sip. He withdrew the spit from the flame, checked the rabbit, and put it back, deciding it needed another minute.

Maybe that's what made the other fella look so sour, Del thought as he recalled the unfriendly face of Ray's neighbor. Thinking on the end times. That'll bring anyone down.

"I like your truck," Ray said, nodding toward the side of the house. "You rebuilt that yourself, right?"

"I did," Del said. "After it sat in the yard for a year. Carrie wasn't too happy about that. She said I made that old redneck joke come true and the neighbors were telling it about us."

"What old redneck joke?"

"What happens when a redneck cuts his grass?"

"I don't know. What?"

"He finds his truck." Del chuckled and took a sip of his beer. "How's Donna doing, by the way?" He wanted to steer the conversation away from religion. As his daddy used to say, it was one of those topics where people had to agree to disagree.

"Donna's fine. Why do you ask?"

"Because she's your wife. Why else would I ask?"

"You're getting a little testy, Del."

"I admit I am. Seems you got an agenda here. I don't mind hearing it if you'll just lay it on the line. Let's out with it and get it over with."

Ray withdrew the spit from the flame and pushed the rabbit off the end using the side of a broad knife. The carcass landed on a wood cutting board on the ground, and Ray began to carve it up.

"All right, Del, I'll put it to you straight. I don't see this society going much further, and I think most of the people in it aren't fit to survive in the world that follows."

"Which world are you talking about, Ray? Earth? Or the world above?"

"Earth, for now." He laid a pile of meat and bones on a plate and passed it to Del, along with a fork and napkin.

"By survive, I mean the basics of keeping house, keeping fed, keeping safe."

"Looks like you set yourself up pretty good here. Got yourself a big water tank and laid back a year's worth of food."

Ray nodded. "More than a year's worth. What I'm saying, Del, is that there aren't a lot of people who can hunt like you, fish like you, fix things like you. You can rebuild a truck from the ground up. You can repair an air conditioner, a transformer, a refrigerator. The master panel in the basement there, you could have wired that yourself without even looking at a diagram."

"Right. So, what's your point?"

"My point is that most people today can't do much more than swipe at their phone screens or diddle with numbers in a spreadsheet. As far as they know, food is something that comes from the supermarket. They don't know how to grow or kill. They don't know how to feed themselves from the earth. They don't know how to repair and maintain the things their lives depend on—their cars, their stoves, their heat pumps.

"They've bought into this devil's bargain where, in exchange for comfort and ease, they've given up control of their own lives. And you know how the devil runs his bargains. You win in the short term, but he takes everything in the end. Once he's got your feet firmly planted on his rug, he pulls it out from under you.

"Now, look at what happened with this power outage. It was, what, eleven days in our part of the state? I was listening to the radio on the drive out here. They're still pulling bodies from city apartment buildings and far-out country houses. Old people who died in the heat, fat diabetics, all the weak ones who weren't meant to live. The official toll was four hundred before the power returned. Then it jumped past a thousand the next day as searchers started going house to house. You hear the latest?"

Del shook his head.

"Twenty-six hundred. That's in just eleven days, Del. Twenty-six hundred dead in one state in eleven days."

"There was a lot of flooding," Del said. "People drinking contaminated water, or no water at all. And it's been a hot eleven days since, with no air-conditioning."

"Yeah, and next summer will be hot too. And the summer after that. Hell, this summer isn't even over yet. But look what else happened. The food supply basically collapsed. In eleven days."

"Yeah, I saw it." He had seen the bare shelves when he went to buy pancake mix. Carrie had told him about the neighbors scrounging the dregs of the pantry, making a meal of pickles and ramen noodles. "My neck of the woods, after that second storm, you couldn't go a quarter mile without running into a fallen tree blocking your way. How's anyone supposed to deliver food through that?"

"And then look at how people behaved," Ray said. "In the Walmart parking lots where the few trucks that could get through were handing out food and water like a damn communist mess hall, people were fighting, mothers against mothers. And then there were the piñatas, people broadsiding those big rigs to break them open, and all the looters descending like rats to steal what the commie government was going to give them anyway."

"I didn't see none of that where I live," Del said.

"Doesn't mean it didn't happen."

"Where I live, folks pitched in and helped each other out. The kids were down putting watermelons in the stream to cool off. Life handed them a bad situation, and they turned it into a picnic. That's the most time we've spent with neighbors all year."

"All right," Ray said. "But that was eleven days in. How do you think this would play out if the days stretched into months?"

"Now that would be a problem," Del conceded. "People's patience gets stretched, and their tempers start flaring."

"And then they have to look out for themselves," Ray said. "For themselves first. That's what I'm getting at here. That's why I asked you up here. You're a sensible man, Del. That's plain enough for anyone to see. You also have a lot of skills. When the world gets to the point where we have to rely on ourselves, when there's no one else to turn to and we have only our own hands to keep it going, then guys like you are valuable."

"You want me to join your little commune?" Del asked.

"That's what I'm saying."

"What's the rush? You really think the world's going to end tomorrow?"

"Tomorrow, next week. It's hard to tell."

"All right, Ray, for shooting straight with me, I'll shoot straight with you."

Del put his plate on the ground and took a sip of his beer.

"I don't agree one bit with your take on where things stand. All that stuff we got now, what you call the devil's bargain, we made with our own hands. People made the cars and the lights and the stoves and the air conditioners. It's the work of many minds, and people keep it all running. People working together, not in isolation.

"And you're right that society might fall apart, but it won't be from technology failing us. Not solely from that. It'll be from people reacting to trouble with the kind of attitude you're showing. With that me-first and screw-the-rest-of-you mindset. You know what holds a ship together? A captain who's willing to go down with it. That's where I stand, Ray. When trouble comes, I stick with my people. I ain't off in the mountains looking down on the suffering from on high."

Across the flickering fire, a dark look clouded Ray Cooper's face.

"You have some nerve, Del. Coming up here and accepting my hospitality and then talking to your host like that."

"I said we'd shoot straight," Del replied. "You said your piece, and I said mine. I'm sorry if I offended you. Like my daddy used to say, there's no seeing eye to eye on religion or any of the big-picture stuff that people can only guess at but never know. So, when arguing is pointless, we agree to disagree."

Ray shook his head slowly, his angry eyes fixed on Del. "No," he said. "This isn't a matter of debate. This is the word of God. Go back and read the last chapter of the Bible again. See what he has in store for the addicts and the fags and the trannies and the whores, for the doubters and defiers and idol worshippers. It's been twenty centuries, Del. A hundred generations of humanity, and they're still not listening. Time's up."

"I don't know how you get outta bed with that kind of mindset." Del licked a smudge of charred meat from his fingers. "I'd be so damn depressed, I'd shoot myself. How 'bout I give you a little reading assignment? Go back to some of the earlier chapters in that book. A man came down here and gave everything he had, including his life, because he believed in us. It wasn't an easy road, but it was the right road. He asked one thing of us. Love thy neighbor. I been trying my whole life, and I ain't been able to master that one yet. Some of my neighbors I can barely stand. But I *will* stand by them. Maybe it's a matter of temperament, Ray, but I like His example better than yours. I'd rather die with my brothers and sisters than survive without them."

The darkness in Ray's eyes intensified and deepened. His mouth set in a hard angry line.

"You're trying to make me the bad guy," he said. "You're talking like you have the moral high ground."

"You ever talk to a doctor, Ray? A psychologist?"

"Don't change the subject."

"I don't even know what the subject is anymore."

"The subject is your superiority complex."

Del narrowed his eyes to better see the man across the fire. "Listen, Ray. My grandmother suffered from depression—"

"Who gives a fuck about your grandmother?"

"Well, I did. I'm just saying, the way she described it, when the sickness came on, it was like falling. That's what she said. Like falling into a black, bottomless pit. She'd fall for weeks and weeks into this darkness filled with threatening shadows. Every way she turned, there was something to fear."

Ray got to his feet. "Shut up, Del."

"You got that same look on your face. Same look she used to get. And this ain't the first time I've seen it, Ray."

"Get out of here."

Del stood. "All right, Ray. I'll go. But you worry me."

"You don't need to worry about me."

"Think about talking to a doctor."

"Go fuck yourself, Del."

Ray watched him brush the dirt from his jeans. Del turned and walked toward the house, saying as he walked, "A doctor, Ray. Because the world you're in ain't a happy one. But you can get to a better place with a little help."

A few minutes later, Del started down the gravel drive in his old blue pickup. The fishing rods were back in the bed, and the backpack sat on the passenger seat. Del's phone said ten thirty-five. He wouldn't make it home till four in the morning. One of the benefits of the power being back was that the brightly lit gas stations along the highway would have hot coffee ready around the clock.

# 25

## July 3

"Sean Riggs," said Anya Lakhani, staring into her laptop monitor. "Security engineer, worked here for a total of six weeks earlier in the year. Was written up a number of times by his supervisor."

"Sounds like he got on his manager's bad side," Agent Espinoza said.

"Where is that manager? Ray Cooper?"

"On vacation."

"I want to call and ask him about Sean Riggs," Anya said.

"We've already tried. His cell is out of range."

"Do we know where he is?"

"We called his wife. No answer there either."

"Damn. What would you think about approaching Riggs directly?"

"I've been thinking about that," Espinoza said. "I'd like to talk to someone close to him first, get a better sense of what he's like, who we're dealing with. His manager, Cooper, obviously had some vendetta against him with all those nasty write-ups. I wouldn't call him an objective source. Let's see if we can talk to someone else first."

"Who?"

"Does he have a crew? Drinking buddies? Gaming buddies? A girlfriend?"

"I don't know."

"Well, find out. To be honest, I don't see him as a player here."

"No?"

"No," said Espinoza. "A lone individual doesn't choose a target like this. It's much easier for a solo hacker to steal money from someone's crypto wallet. What's he got to gain from hacking critical energy infrastructure?"

"Maybe a ransomware attack," Anya said. "He steals all those documents and threatens to dump them on the dark web unless Empire pays him ten million dollars."

Espinoza shook his head. "If he wanted money, a Fortune 1000 company would be easier to hack, more likely to pay, and would bring a lot less heat from federal investigators. Besides, the drop servers routed all the data to '/dev/null.' That's the equivalent of a digital black hole. Permanent deletion. Forensics checked the hard drives and found the data was never even written to disk. So, the hacker has nothing to ransom. This entire case is one of feints and misdirection. I have a feeling user 'sriggs' is just one more red herring to send us down a blind alley. But we do have to follow the lead, if only to rule it out. You want to take this one?"

"Sure," said Anya.

"Get a warrant for his online activity. Google, Meta, Amazon, all the big players who keep search records. While you're waiting on them to respond, see if you can find some of his friends, do a little probing, find out what they think of him."

"Should he know we're asking? Do we want him to feel the pressure?"

Espinoza thought for a moment. "No," he said slowly. "At this point, we have possession of all the drop servers and the command-and-control server. There's nothing left out there to receive stolen data. The malware isn't trying to connect to new IP addresses, so it's effectively neutralized. For now, let's let Mr. Riggs think he's in the clear. We'll see how he behaves when he thinks no one is watching him."

# 26

Ray Cooper paced the pavement beside the gas pump with his phone to his ear, looking angry. His tank was full, as were all six five-gallon gas cans in the truck bed. On the passenger seat inside sat a dozen cans of fuel stabilizer that would help preserve the gas for long-term storage.

As he listened to the phone ring on the other end of the line, a rusty old Lincoln Mark VII pulled up behind him, its front end bouncing over a trough in the pavement. The driver, a young, heavyset man with a dark beard and ruddy face beneath a baseball cap that looked too tight, looked to Ray like a younger version of Del.

The remembrance of his conversation with Del the night before added bitterness to the anger that was already burning inside him. It was hard enough to be right in a world where everyone else was wrong. The task of trying to bring good people over to the right side was a thankless one. Even seemingly sensible people like Del could be immune to truth. Ray's words by the fire last night were seeds falling on stony ground.

He wondered if his judgment was off, his judgment about who he could convert. That Riggs kid, Sean, the pesky programmer, had also seemed like a good candidate for the cause. One of the few who actually questioned the status quo. Ray had sensed Riggs's feelers extending in the right direction, seeking deeper truth. They just needed something solid to grab on to. Ray brought him into the fold, but the kid turned his back on salvation after just two weeks.

He never bought in, Ray thought. He only pretended to be interested, like one of those barroom whores who teases you till your dick is hard and then walks off with a smirk.

His phone pressed to his ear, he listened again to the unanswered ring on the other end of the line. Ray took two steps past the side of the truck, spun on his heel, and paced back toward the pump. The man in the Lincoln tapped his horn lightly, and when Ray looked, the man motioned with his fingers as if to say "Move your truck!"

Ray pointed to the phone at his ear. The man in the Lincoln put his hands up as if to say "So what?"

Ray's call went to voicemail. "This is Donna. Leave me a message and I'll call you right back."

The chipper tone of her voice further stoked his rage. How could she be so nonchalant, so flippant as to take that tone at a time like this? And what was this bullshit about calling right back? She hadn't returned either of his calls from yesterday.

He began to shake with rage. When his wife's recorded greeting ended, he said through clenched teeth, "Listen, you, this is call number three. Number three, and I haven't heard back from you yet! I don't know what the hell you're doing that's so goddamn important, but you know the rule about answering when I call."

The man in the Lincoln watched him pace, watched his face grow red with fury. He laid on his horn, and when Ray turned to look at him, the man saw murder in his eyes.

Ray turned away and growled into the phone, "I'll be in cell range for about ten more minutes. Call me. And when I get back, we're going to have a little talk about respect. We're going to have a refresher course on rules and consequences. Understand?"

Again, the horn blared. "Move your goddamn truck," the man yelled.

Ray slowly lowered the phone from his ear. He walked to the open driver's window of the car, his eyes fixed on the face of the big young man. The driver's eyes looked as hard and angry as Ray's. He wasn't going to budge. Before Ray could say a word, the man said to him, "Do not fuck with me today. Do *not* fuck with me, because—"

Ray pulled his gun from his pocket and put it to the man's head.

"You know what you're going to do, Gomer? You're going to turn this piece of shit around and find another gas station, understand?"

"Yes, sir," said the man, wide eyed.

"Now, get out of here."

As the Lincoln backed away, Ray kept the gun pointed through the windshield at the man's face, in case the driver tried to run him over. The muzzle of the gun followed the rear end of the Lincoln as it chugged out of the lot and down the road.

Ray put the pistol back in his pocket and turned his mind back to thoughts that nursed the moral outrage that had become his emotional home. Goddamn scatterbrained wife is right there in the damn house and can't even pick up her phone. I know she's there, he told himself, because I can see her location! He jumped into the truck, started the engine, and gunned it angrily.

"Woman doesn't get anything done unless you're on her ass twenty-four seven," he growled. "And even then, you have to check up on her after. Walk through every minute of her day, because you know she screwed up somewhere along the line, and you have to make her see it."

He continued talking aloud to no one as the truck swung out onto the road. "What's wrong with public school, she asks? Look at your damn kid, lady. Those sad, girly eyes. He's turning into a fag. You think the public school's going to turn him around? Hell, they'll push him further down that road."

His mind, that swirling vortex of victimhood and outrage, had already lined up the next target of its scorn.

"Del Wright, my ass," he muttered. "Del Wrong is more like it. Del's gonna die with the rest of them when the world burns. What kind of ass stands on the deck of a sinking ship and says no to a spot on the lifeboat? What damn Bible is he reading?"

He pressed the gas pedal to the floor and listened to the roar of the engine as the burst of acceleration pressed him back into his seat. He had been coming to West Virginia more often in the past year, twice a month at least, because here he could let off some of the pressure that built up at work, where he had to sit through pointless meetings listening to women who dressed like men tell him things he already knew.

And most of the men were no better. They had been neutered by their wives, by the stultifying jobs that provided neither physical nor mental challenges, by the sterility of the office environment that was designed to suppress all of their animal instincts. They had been brainwashed by the media, by the crap that Hollywood fed into their brains, crap that passed for entertainment. They had been duped into chasing careers, money, and comfort, lulled to sleep by the promises of dead-end capitalism whose only real goal was to make people consume and conform while they waited for their purposeless existence to end.

Every aspect of their lives depended on technology, gasoline, electricity—things beyond their control—and they didn't realize how easily it could all be taken away.

It should have happened already. It should have happened on day two of the first of those back-to-back hurricanes, but the storms threw the schedule off. In a twist of irony, God himself had intervened and performed the work he had assigned to his agent, Ray Cooper. God flooded the land and washed out the roads and knocked down the trees and took out the power.

It was an act of mercy, Ray thought. A dress rehearsal for the real end-of-days, a final wake-up call for those who might listen, a warning saying "This is what awaits." And who had heeded it? If not Del Wright, consummate man of sense, then who?

In all those days of rain, when the rivers spilled their banks and put so much land underwater, did people not get the reference of the Flood? Did they not remember God's promise of what would be in store for round two? Not water this time, but fire.

No, Ray thought as his truck sped along the country road at twenty miles an hour over the speed limit. No one was paying attention. No one noticed that in this extreme and increasingly dry summer heat, the state was on its twelfth day without rain, without so much as a cloud in the sky, that the forests were drying, preparing to burn.

Did people not look at the forecast, at the heat dome building over the Midwest that would arrive in a day or two? Could they not see that it was all going to burn down? That their phones and their spreadsheets and drag balls and pride marches wouldn't save them when the fire came?

They don't believe in hell, he thought. They think it's some mythological underground dystopia populated by exotic demons. But it's right here on Earth, and they're the demons building it. They're already in it, but they're too blind to see that.

The rear end of the truck fishtailed as he swung the vehicle left onto a dusty gravel road. The gas cans toppled over and slid across the bed.

Bastard! Ray thought. That stupid fat redneck at the gas station got me so angry, I forgot to tie down the cans.

Even me, he mused. Even I am sometimes blind. Stupid people like that guy in the Lincoln are the devil's agents. Their purpose is to get you off track, make you forget what you're supposed to be doing. You should have seen that, Ray, when he was egging you on. You should have recognized he's just the devil playing tricks, to get you off track, make you lose focus.

He hit the gas hard, and the truck kicked up a cloud of gray-white dust. His eyes seemed to sink with his spirits, to retreat into their sockets. Dark hollows had grown below them in the hours since his talk with Del, and his face began to look old, tired, deprived of sleep and rest and peace. This was the look his wife watched out for, the one that preceded his worst explosions, that made her leave the house on some sudden errand, always with Martin, always with the boy.

Del had seen it too. That dark, sullen look that came over Ray as he sipped his third beer by the fire the night before. It was as if his mind had vacated his body and a darker, more volatile spirit arose from the depths to take the reins.

"What was I thinking about?" Ray shouted as he gripped the wheel. "Goddammit!" He smacked the wheel. "I lost my train of thought!"

"Oh yeah," he said. "Hell. All those people going to hell because the trees are dry and the heat dome is coming and the power lines sag in the heat. They'll sag if you overload them. They'll melt and burn, but people don't know that because there's a lot of things they don't know. Like, God himself can whip up a couple of storms, delay the end by a couple of weeks, if it's His will, but the end is still going to come. It'll all burn down, and they'll be kicking themselves for not heeding the warning of the last outage. They'll be kicking themselves when they're not killing each  one another, when they're not waking up to the fact it's too late and throwing themselves on His mercy. They had their chance and they blew it, and there's nothing left to do but kill and rape, or wait to be killed, wait to be raped."

The truck slid around another turn at dangerous speed and began the climb into the hills.

"You just have to hold on till the fire," he said softly. "Keep your nice face on at work. Take it one day at a time. It won't be long now." He was almost whispering now, as if to soothe himself.

"Don't let them see that you know. They'll find out for themselves soon enough. They'll find out hell is a swirling descent into a bottomless pit that has no exit. You keep thinking it can't any get darker, you can't go any lower. But then you do. You just keep falling forever and ever and ever. It's like... Wait."

He hit the brakes and brought the truck down to a sane speed.

"Wait. How did Del know that? How did he know what it felt like? The darkness and the falling?"

His face blanked for a moment, then he smacked the steering wheel and shouted, "Dammit, Del, you're one of us! You just don't see it."

He looked at the road ahead, bewildered. Was this the way back to the cabin? What road was he on? Did it matter?

"I gave you your chance and you wouldn't take it," he said aloud. "I did my duty by the Lord. That puts me in the clear. The penalty is yours to pay. At the end of the day, we're all on our own. Even the Messiah himself. Even Jesus was alone on his cross. What were his last words? 'My God, my God! Why hast thou forsaken me?'"

He drove on blindly, the gray-brown road blurred by tears he cursed but couldn't stop.

# 27

"Why'd you leave early?" Carrie asked.

Del stretched his legs across the couch and groaned before accepting the mug of coffee his wife held out to him.

"Ray was in one of his moods. Thinks the whole world is going to hell. Wanted to know if I'd like to join his gang, play in his treehouse. I told him no thanks. He don't take rejection well."

"What time did you get home?"

"Dunno. Four, four thirty?"

"Why didn't you come to bed?"

"Didn't want to wake you." Del sat up carefully, trying not to spill the coffee.

"Was Donna up there?"

"At the cabin? Ray don't take her there. That's his boys' club. Why do you ask?"

"I keep calling and she doesn't answer. The cabin is out of cell range, so I thought maybe she was up there. I've been worried about her, Del."

"I'd worry about anyone who has to share a house with Ray. The man's in a bad place, only he don't know it. He thinks it's everyone else got the problem. You can't reason with a fella like that."

"Donna's been sinking."

"Listen," Del said as he stretched his arms. "You been with the kids going on three weeks now, and I ain't hardly seen them at all. How 'bout you take a break today? I'll take them to the pool, maybe out to lunch, maybe to a movie if the theaters are back in business."

"Oh, sure," she joked. "After weeks in the house with angry Mama, Sugar Daddy comes home and treats them to a day of fun."

"I'm just saying, take a break. Give yourself a rest."

"I'd actually like to hang out with you. How about I take a couple hours to run some errands? You take care of breakfast. You get the kids ready for the pool."

"Sounds good."

Carrie had her itinerary all mapped out. To the grocery store for whatever food she could find. And shampoo and soap and toilet paper. Gas up the van. Do it all at a slow, easy pace. No kids begging for candy in the checkout line. No fighting in the back seat. Nothing to listen to but her own thoughts.

And then she'd stop by Donna's to check in.

# 28

"Wait," said Danielle, turning her head on the pillow to face Sean. "We drove home from Richmond in my car."

"Yeah?"

"What happened to your car?"

"It's in the garage."

"How did you get to Richmond, then?"

"I rode with a friend."

"Ooh! You have friends," she teased. "Do tell!"

"How about some breakfast first?"

"And then we'll go out!"

"Out where?"

"When's the last time you went canoeing?" she asked.

"When I was a kid."

"We'll hit the James. We just have to get some bug spray."

Over a breakfast of waffles and coffee, Danielle asked him about the friend who had driven him to Richmond.

"A guy named Ali."

"How do you know him?"

"His name popped up when I requested the Uber."

"You said he was your friend."

"We had a good rapport on the drive."

"Smart-ass! Do you actually have any friends?"

Sean rattled off a few names that sounded like the screen names of online gamers.

"Any *real* friends?"

"They are real friends."

"I mean, people you go out with. People who come over to your house."

He realized then to his surprise that he didn't. Not here. Since he'd bought the house, he spent all his time working, coding on the computer, sanding floors, putting in windows, removing and replacing drywall, adding insulation.

He told her about friends from high school in DC, friends from college in New York.

"Those are all from years ago," Danielle said. "Do you really keep in touch with them?"

"Online," he replied. "On road trips. I'll go up to DC or New York. Sometimes we meet up for a getaway. A bunch of us went to New Orleans last year."

"But you don't hang out with anyone around here?"

"Not really."

No wonder she ran into him so infrequently.

"What about you?" he asked.

"Mmm... I had a boyfriend. I kind of hung out with his crew. Until we broke up. Usually, I go to Richmond when I want to go out. There's more to do there, and the people from work are more..." She screwed up her eyes, trying to think of the right way to phrase it.

"More what?"

"Well, I can go out to clubs with them. I can go to restaurants that serve more than beer and pizza."

"You're talking about your ex here? Not too adventurous when it came to food?"

"No, but adventurous in other ways."

She told him how Ronnie taught her to shoot, taught her to fish and camp, took her canoeing and hunting. Every date seemed to take place in the woods.

"It was exciting at first," she said. "I even got used to the bugs. But I think the woods were just an excuse for Ronnie to drink all day."

"Did you actually hunt?"

"Of course."

"Did you shoot anything?"

"Cans with a pistol. Ronnie got mad when I became a better shot than him. I could hit a target pretty consistently. But in answer to your question, no, I never killed anything."

"But he did?"

A wave of revulsion swept over her as she remembered that day.

"What?" Sean looked with concern at her stricken face. "Bad memory?"

"It was awful," she said. "Ronnie had been drinking all afternoon and... No. Never mind. Not while we're eating."

Ronnie's first misaimed shot hit the buck in its right rear flank. He chased the animal through the bare trees of the winter forest as it lurched on three legs. Danielle was horrified by the creature's distress. Ronnie fired a shot midrun into the buck's shoulder as it zagged left. As the deer staggered, trying not to topple, it watched its killer run toward it to deliver the final blow. Its nostrils flared a second before Ronnie sent a bullet through its head.

Danielle was crying when the buck went down. "What the hell is wrong with you? What kind of barbarity was that?"

"It ain't supposed to go that way. A good shot will drop them all at once. They don't feel it. They don't even know they're dead."

"You're a fucking drunk, Ronnie. You're a drunk, and that was disgusting."

Instead of admitting he had screwed up, he got defensive. He repeated what he had told her on an earlier trip, the day she had a deer in her sights and refused to fire. "As soon as you put that gun in your hands, you've made the decision to kill. If you're not ready to kill, don't pick up the gun." Then he added, "It was a messy one. Sorry. I had to finish the job."

That was their last trip to the woods and their last date. He had taught her a number of things in addition to shooting, chief among them, how to stalk prey from downwind, to move through the forest without being seen or heard. When she got good at it, she used to sneak up behind him, pinch his sides, and watch him jump with fright. She could do it every time, creep up and scare the daylights out of him, even when he was sober.

"Dammit, woman! Don't do that!"

The one lasting gift he had given her was an appreciation of the outdoors. She loved hiking the woods and paddling the rivers. If she had a tent and a willing companion, she'd go camping again in the mountains, where the air was cooler.

"So," she said to Sean, "today I'm going to teach you how to paddle a canoe."

"I already know how." He picked up their plates from the table and carried them to the dishwasher.

"You said you haven't gone since you were a kid."

"Which means I've done it before. Which means I know how to do it."

"Okay. I'll let you paddle in front."

Sean slid the dishes into the bottom rack of the washer. "You're trying to trick me," he said. "The front person just pulls the boat along. The person in back actually guides it."

Danielle clapped and smiled. "So, you do understand!"

"That you'll be running the show out there on the river? Yeah, I get it."

Ronnie wouldn't have let her steer. Ronnie would have filled the cooler with beer. Sean filled it with food from the fridge—cheese, hard-boiled eggs, lemonade. He apologized for not adding fresh fruit, but there was none to be had. Danielle bumped his boyfriend score up a notch for even thinking to say that.

Sean paused to remember where he had put the software book Danielle had picked up for him in Richmond the day before. It was on the desk in his office. He would have a look at it when they returned.

# 29

Anya Lakhani was about to leave Ray Cooper's doorstep when a gray Toyota van pulled into the driveway. She watched as the driver, a woman of forty or so, cut the engine and opened the door. Carrie Wright eyed her with a curious but friendly look.

"Mrs. Cooper?" Anya asked as Carrie approached.

"No. A friend." Carrie extended her hand and introduced herself.

Anya responded with a business card. Carrie read the name of the organization. Homeland Security.

"I'm looking for Ray Cooper," Anya said. She noted with interest how Carrie's posture stiffened at the name.

"Is Ray in trouble?"

That's where your mind goes, Anya wondered? *Should* he be in trouble?

"No trouble," she said. "I came to ask him about one of his former coworkers."

"Have you rung yet?" Carrie put the card into the pocket of her shorts.

"I rang a few times, but no one answered."

Carrie turned and checked the driveway and the curb. "Donna's car's not here. Ray is in West Virginia."

"I heard. I was hoping he'd be back by now."

"He should be back in a day or two. But I'm pretty sure Donna didn't go with him. She would have told me."

"Good to know." Anya noted the look of puzzlement and concern on Carrie's face as she stepped toward the door and rang the bell. "Everything all right?"

"I don't know," Carrie said slowly. She pulled her phone from her pocket and called Donna. "It's strange she hasn't answered her phone for days."

"You sure she didn't go to West Virginia with her husband? She might be in a place with no cell service." That would explain why Anya's own calls to Ray went unanswered.

Carrie shook her head. "She's not in West Virginia. My husband was just out there."

"With Ray?"

"Yeah." Carrie moved the phone away from her ear and said, "Listen." She pointed through the narrow column of windows beside the front door. "Do you hear that? The ringing inside?"

Anya nodded.

"That's her ringtone." Carrie ended the call and looked puzzled. "Why would she leave her phone? That's not like her."

This was frustrating, Anya thought. If Ray's wife was home, she could tell Anya where the cabin in West Virginia was. All Anya wanted, for now, was to talk to the man and get a little more info about Sean Riggs.

From her conversations with Sean's other coworkers back at Empire Energy, Anya had heard nothing but good things. Sean was good natured and easy to talk to. He occasionally had a beer or went bowling with the other developers. He got along with everyone except Ray, his boss. He didn't seem to hold grudges or show bitterness toward anyone or anything.

Politically, he was middle-of-the-road and not very engaged. Nothing about what she had heard so far pegged him as the type of disgruntled loner who would launch an attack on a major component of America's critical energy infrastructure.

He had no ties to radical groups. He was not in debt, nor did he spend lavishly. He lacked the money motive to steal or sell secrets, or to demand ransom for pilfered documents.

She wanted to rule him out as a potential suspect so that the joint FBI-Homeland Security task force could focus its resources on a more likely culprit, a hostile nation. She wanted to talk to Ray, probe his bitterness, and write him off as an unreliable source, a prickly man whose negative write-ups were fueled by a personal grudge against an otherwise blameless employee.

But why would Ray hold a grudge against Sean? What about him set the man off?

"How well do you know Ray?" Anya asked. She knew from Carrie's hesitation that she was trying to restrain a negative comment and craft a diplomatic response.

"Um, kind of" was all she could come up with.

"You said he's in West Virginia. And your husband was with him? Do you know the address of the house? Or the town?"

"It's not even in a town. It's up on a hillside. I don't know where. Ray's poured a lot of money into that place." Much to his wife's distress, Carrie thought.

Anya nodded. "Thank you," she said as she turned to leave. "Enjoy the rest of your day."

Anya checked her watch on the way to the white Ford Escape parked at the curb. Eleven twenty-two. If Ray's West Virginia house was within five hours, that would make a ten-hour round trip, plus at least an hour interview. She would find the address through public records and make the drive tomorrow, leaving first thing in the morning. If he had gone to the mountains for the long holiday weekend, he would almost certainly be up there tomorrow, on the Fourth.

She would complete her interview and make her write-up. Better to get it done than wait "a few days," as Carrie Wright said, for Ray to return. A few days might be five or ten, for all she knew, with Ray out of cell range the whole time. She needed to close out the Sean Riggs avenue of investigation so the task force could move on.

In the meantime, she'd have a look at Sean's house and take some time to dig through his internet history. The big tech companies had indicated they would respond to Homeland Security's warrant within twenty-four hours. For them, it was merely a matter of querying the digital logs for one user's recent activity and sending the results across the internet.

# 30

July 4

A few minutes after eight a.m., near the town of Covington, Virginia, Ray Cooper's white GMC Sierra pickup heading east on Interstate 64 passed Anya Lakhani's white Ford Escape heading west.

Two hours later, the Sierra pulled into the Coopers' driveway in a suburb just west of Richmond. Ray noted that his wife's Yukon was absent. The paranoia and resentment he had felt the day before had metastasized into a seething rage, and it was all directed at one person.

That car better be in the garage, he thought. Or she's really going to get it.

He had called ten times on the drive, and each call went to voicemail, to that flippant, mocking voice telling him she wasn't there. Well, where the hell was she?

He dug his thumb so hard into the garage door opener, the button cracked. The door was opening too damn slowly, so he ducked under it to get inside. Even before he was in, he could see the Yukon wasn't there.

"Donna!" he yelled. He dashed to the door that led into the house and rattled the knob. "Donna, you stupid bitch, get down here and unlock this door!"

Who was he shouting at? He knew she wasn't there. He pulled his keys from his pocket, but his hands shook so much, he couldn't get the key into the lock.

"Donna, goddammit!"

Does she think this is funny, he wondered? Does she think she can explain her way out of this? She's only making it worse. She's going to get it this time. She is *really* going to get it!

At last, he got the key into the lock. He twisted it open, bolted into the house, and screamed again for his wife.

He knew she wasn't there, but in his rage, he wanted to count each unanswered call as another offense, another justification for the punishment he would inflict on her when she finally turned up. He would make her pay for the insults and disrespect she had heaped on him these past few days. No, not just these past few days. For all the frustration she had heaped on him during all the years of their marriage. For her stupidity and disobedience, for her weakness and childishness and irresponsibility.

"Donna!" He flew up the stairs in a fury, barged into the bedroom, the bathroom, the closet. No Donna. He flung open the door to his son's room. No Martin.

If he had taken the time to open the dresser drawers she had so carefully closed, he would have seen that they were emptier than usual. If he had thought to open the closet of the guest bedroom, he would have noticed the missing suitcases.

Or he might not have. Things in the house that didn't belong exclusively to him were beneath his notice. He knew where his guns were, his clothes, his whiskey. It was Donna's job to keep track of the rest.

"Donna!" Ray barreled down the stairs so fast he nearly fell. He rounded the corner, past the front door, through the living room, and then froze at the sight that awaited him on the kitchen counter.

There, to the right of the sink sat Donna's phone. Beside it, the two GPS trackers he had hidden in the Yukon to keep tabs on her in case she ever turned off location sharing. How had she found those? She couldn't have done it herself. She was too stupid, too inept. She must have had help. From whom?

That mechanic guy, he decided. The one who fixed the screeching belt on the Yukon, who did the work outside of the dealership, the work that might have voided the warranty because his stupid wife was so goddamn clueless.

I'm going to put a bullet through his head, Ray thought.

But what was this? A piece of paper folded beneath the phone. He picked it up, unfolded it, saw the ragged line of holes at the top where it had been torn from a spiral notepad.

Who gave her a notepad, he wondered? I'll kill him too.

His hands were shaking so much he had to flatten the note against the counter to read it.

Ray, you're a sick man and I hate you. You don't deserve me or your son. Please get help. —Donna

Who the hell wrote that? It couldn't have been his wife. She didn't speak like that. If she even dared to think such thoughts, he would have beat them out of her.

Ray pulled his phone from his pocket and dialed 911.

"What's your emergency?"

"Someone stole my car."

"Okay, sir. I'll give you the non-emergency number."

"This *is* a goddamn emergency," he insisted angrily. "Do you understand?"

The operator gave him the number for the police department and hung up.

Ray was too angry to remember the number, so he looked it up. A woman answered on the second ring.

"Police, how may I help you?"

"Someone stole my car."

"I'm sorry to hear that, sir. Can you give me the make, model, and license plate number and tell me where you last saw the vehicle?"

"It's a 2022 white GMC Yukon. It was in my driveway." He was shaking less now, trying to get the information across to the police, who were going to help him. They would pull Donna from the car, maybe beat her Rodney King style, right in front of their son. Teach them both a lesson. "My wife took it," he added.

"I'm sorry, sir, did you say your wife took the car?"

"Did I stutter? That's what I said."

"All right, sir, I understand you're upset. Is your wife's name on the car's title or registration?"

"Of course it is." Because Ray couldn't be bothered to fill out the paperwork at the Department of Motor Vehicles. That was her job, so she put her name on the registration.

"Sir, if the car is being driven by its registered owner, it's not stolen."

"Okay then, I want to report a kidnapping," Ray blurted.

"A kidnapping?"

"Goddammit, are you a fucking parrot? Yes. I said a kidnapping."

"Sir, if you can't be civil, I'm going to end this call."

"Do your job," he commanded. "I'm reporting a crime!"

"Who is the victim?"

"My son."

"Do you know when this kidnapping occurred?"

"No. My wife took him. Maybe two days ago."

"Your wife took him?"

There she went again, parroting his words. Ray took a breath to calm himself. "Yes," he said as evenly as possible. "My wife kidnapped my son."

"Is your son a minor?"

"He's twelve."

"And your wife is his legal guardian?"

"What kind of fucking question is that? Are you a retard? Do you want me to spell it out for you? My wife is his biological mother and legal guardian."

"Sir, it's not a crime for a mother to have custody of her son."

"Okay, I'm done. Put a man on the phone, will you?"

"Excuse me?"

"You heard me."

"Sir, a male officer is going to tell you the same things I'm telling you now. The law is the law."

"What's your name?" Ray asked impatiently.

"My name is Officer Shelley McBride."

"When I find you, Shelley McBride, I'm going to beat your fucking face in."

He ended the call.

When the patrol cars arrived at the house a few minutes later, Ray was back out on the road in his truck. He would check the grocery store first, then the pharmacy, then the other grocery. He would drive by each of the gas stations she visited, then the church and the bank. If he didn't find her in any of those places, he would look for the Yukon outside Del's house. Sooner or later, he would find her and inflict on her a punishment terrifying enough to ensure she never disobeyed him again.

# 31

Sean and Danielle returned from their canoe trip smiling, tired, sunburned, and bug bitten. They stopped by her apartment to pick up a change of clothes, then drove to his place to shower and change before dinner.

While Danielle showered, Sean stood at his desk looking down at the technical manual she had picked up from the bookstore in Richmond the day before. It was a large paperback with fifteen hundred eight-by-eleven-inch pages. He picked it up and thumbed through the first few chapters, which gave an overview of the software used to control large distributed power grids. The remaining thirteen hundred pages described all of the system's commands, how to use them, and what they did.

The mystery code that had puzzled him these last few weeks was safely stored on a thumb drive in the Millers' house next door. He would have to retrieve that and look at the code again to see which commands it issued to the grid-control system. He would look them up one by one in the manual and get a sense of what the strange code was trying to accomplish.

How soon could he get started on that? Not this evening. Not while Danielle was here. She was a bundle of energy. After dinner, she would want to take a walk, be outside in the evening air. She might want to take him back to her place. They had yet to spend the night there.

Wherever they wound up, they would spend a good chunk of time in bed. She's impossible to resist, he thought. Her lightness and playfulness is so damn attractive. She makes you forget your worries.

They had twice pulled the canoe to the side of the river, once for a bathroom break, and once to eat. Both times, she had disappeared and then crept up silently behind him and scared the daylights out of him with a simple "Boo!" She wasn't just light in spirit, she was light on her feet too. She told him her ex taught her how to stalk.

"I think you already knew how," he said. "You stalked me across town, remember?"

"Uh-huh," she replied with a laugh. "And you didn't notice me then either."

Sean put the book down on the desk and looked out the window, scanning the street for unfamiliar cars. A black Chevy Malibu idled in front of a house across the way. Exhaust from the muffler told him someone was probably inside. Why would they just be sitting there like that? Did the Feds drive those? Had he seen a black Malibu in the parking lot outside Danielle's apartment when they stopped to pick up her clothes? Had it followed him here?

He couldn't remember. It didn't matter anyway. He knew it would start soon. Someone would come to surveil him. Or they would just come right to the door and say, "Sean Riggs?"

They would show their badges, ask to come in. He would answer their questions, offer as much help as he could. If they pointed out that he seemed nervous, he would say it wasn't every day the FBI showed up at his door. Or maybe it wouldn't be the FBI. Whichever agency came for him, it didn't matter. He had never even had a visit from the local cops before. They would understand how their showing up could make a person nervous.

He went through the checklist in his mind. His computer, with the new hard drive, was clean. He had destroyed the old hard drive and dumped it in a garbage can in Short Pump. By now, it was in a landfill. The external drives in his office, the backup drives, held no incriminating evidence.

The Feds could get records from his internet service provider showing everywhere he had been online, but they'd find nothing there either. Or, almost nothing. The Tor connections he had used to download Empire's source code were all encrypted and could not be traced back to him. And using Tor was no longer the automatic red flag it once was. It was now built into some consumer web browsers.

I have no motive, he thought. Not as far as they know. There's no evidence here for them to find, except this book. The evidence is in the neighbors' house, and they don't know to look there. I should move the software manual over there as well, to be safe.

He watched the Malibu pull away from the curb.

They'll ask me questions, do their search, and turn their attention back to the more likely culprit. The bigger, scarier one. I wonder who they're thinking. China? Or North Korea? Maybe even Iran.

At least, I hope that's how it goes. But who knows what information they really have? Who knows what pressure they can bring to force the truth out of me? Who knows how much pressure I can take?

Nothing has happened yet, and I'm already racked with fear. I see a strange car, and my chest tightens. I try to guess what will happen tomorrow, when they might show up, and my mouth goes dry, my throat starts closing up. I'm getting paranoid. Every stranger now is a threat.

And whose fault is that, he asked bitterly as he focused on the pale outline of his reflection in the window. You did this to yourself, Sean Riggs, on your relentless quest for knowledge. You just can't stand to see a mystery unsolved. It provokes you. You need to know when to turn away, when to leave other people's problems to other people. But you haven't figured that out yet. When will you?

He felt a sudden pinch at his sides, jumped at the surprise, then turned to see Danielle smiling playfully.

"Gotcha!" she said.

"How the hell do you do that?"

Her eyes lit up like a child's when she laughed. Life was a game to her, reflecting back on her the joy she brought to it. I want to live in her world, he thought. Not this mess. But how do I get from here to there? Is there some secret to being happy, to not taking life so seriously?

When he kissed her, his thoughts were all mixed up. She's delightful. She's a distraction. She brings me back to earth when my worries start to swirl. I'll never get my research done, never solve this problem. We'll be up past midnight, and I won't want to be away from her.

Why now, he asked? Of all the times in my life, why does someone I really like come along when I'm not even looking? When I'm in the middle of so much trouble? I don't want to drag her into this. She doesn't belong in a mess like this. I don't deserve her.

# 32

The sun was dipping below the horizon behind her white Ford Escape as Anya made her way back to Richmond on Interstate 64. She felt she couldn't reach the city soon enough. The trip to West Virginia that had begun as a relaxing drive early that morning had taken a strange and frightening turn.

After some misdirection from the GPS, she had found the road that led to Ray's cabin. The Escape rattled along the washboard surface of the dirt road, kicking up dry, gray dust beneath the hot sun.

Having lived in crowded cities all her life, she found the silence and isolation of the mountains otherworldly. Halfway down the two-mile road, she stopped to watch a group of deer creep cautiously onto the road, their heads turning sideways as they stopped to look at her. She lifted her phone from the passenger seat and turned on the video camera to record them. The youngest of the animals, a fawn that still had its spots, stared curiously at her before raising its tail and dashing off into the woods.

Anya kept the camera rolling as she resumed her drive, panning left to take in the newly built houses, each with a solar-paneled roof. The truck in front of the first house had Ohio tags. The truck in front of the second was from Michigan. The driveways of the third and fourth houses stood empty.

Too bad, she thought. The last one on the road was Ray's, and it looked as if he may have stepped out. Maybe he went into the town she'd passed through half an hour earlier.

If she had driven into the wilderness to interview a person she didn't know, she would not have come alone. But she had met Ray Cooper more than once at Empire's offices. He wasn't the most friendly or approachable man, but he was a responsible professional managing a team of software engineers. He showed up regularly for work, had a wife and child in one of the nicer suburbs, and was respected, if not particularly liked, by his coworkers.

She pulled into the gravel drive and decided to wait. After coming this far, she wasn't ready to turn around and go home empty-handed.

She parked beside the house, killed the engine, and got out to stretch her legs. The air was hot and dry, though not nearly as hot as the air back in Richmond. She glanced at the side of the house as she arched her back. If she had to describe the style, she would call it a modern rustic survivalist compound. Two stories, wood exterior, stone chimney, expensive thermal-efficient windows, and a pair of video cameras hanging from the two corners of the roof that were within her view.

Between the car and the house, a large patch of raised red earth looked like a freshly covered, oversize grave. A scar of soil one foot wide and six feet long ran from the patch to the house. Pipes, she thought. There's a tank buried here, and pipes from the tank go into the house.

Two more scars originating from the bottom of the downspouts ran from the corners of the house to the tank. A cistern, she realized. He's capturing rainwater from the roof.

She walked around the rear of the house and saw the remains of the fire beside which Ray and Del had eaten supper two nights earlier. Beyond that, a cloud of flies swarmed around a pair of brown rabbit skins drying in the sun. The skins hung from six feet of rope strung between two short wooden posts.

Strange he would hang flesh out like that, she thought. Seems like it would attract bears. But maybe that's what he wants. Maybe he waits in the house with his rifle hoping some creature big enough to fill his freezer will come lumbering into the yard.

Beside the rear wall of the house sat an open garbage bag. Inside it, she found shallow cardboard boxes imprinted with rows of circles. She pulled one out and read the side. Black beans, twenty-four cans. Then another. Canned chili. And another, canned salmon. All in bulk. Was Ray stocking up for a long winter? In July?

She walked up to one of the rear windows, put her hand over her forehead to block out the sun, and peeked in. The interior was clean and well furnished. Ray kept an orderly house. That didn't surprise her. In person, he came off as a controlling type. In his scathing reports of Sean Riggs's job performance, he sounded overly particular, impossible to please, resentful, and somewhat vindictive.

Behind her, she heard footsteps approaching steadily, purposefully, crunching twigs and stones beneath heavy boots. Dropping her hand from her forehead and moving her face back from the glass, she saw the reflection of a man too tall to be Ray. She turned to face him, an unfriendly man with a gun on his belt and something bulky beneath his jacket.

Why a jacket in this heat, she wondered? And what was under it? A bulletproof vest? Did the rabbits here shoot back?

"What the hell do you think you're doing?" he asked. The tall, thin man had thinning, dirty-blond hair, blue eyes, and a sunburned face.

"Looking for Ray Cooper," she said.

"What business do you have with Ray?" His tone was hostile. Before she could answer, he said, "He give you permission to be on his property?"

"I know Ray from Richmond. From Empire Energy, where he works."

"You don't work at Empire," the man said.

"I didn't say I did."

"What's your business?"

Her heart beat furiously, and her stomach began to churn. This man clearly didn't like her. He had a gun on his belt and she literally had her back against a wall. If it came to a fight, there was no way past him. She would have to use her gun, and she sensed from the look in his eye that if she reached for it, he would get his first. He seemed to be anticipating it, the way his right arm hung at his side, elbow slightly crooked. If he shot her here, who could help her? Who would even know?

She realized it had been a mistake to come alone. She knew the man she was coming to see, but she hadn't considered the neighbors.

"I told you," she said, looking around in vain for a way out. "I came to ask him some questions."

"What's the government want with Ray Cooper?" the man asked.

How did he know she was from the government? The gun on her belt. The license plates on her car.

"We don't comment on ongoing investigations. All I'll say is it's work related, and Ray is not in any trouble."

"Tell you what," the man said slowly. "Why don't you hop in your car and go back to where you came from?"

"I'd like to speak to Ray," she said. "I came a long way."

"Get out." The man's look threatened imminent violence.

Refusing to be cowed, she said, "I'm going to give you my card."

"Keep it."

She reached with her left hand into her pocket, away from the gun side of her belt, so he wouldn't think she was drawing.

"I said I don't want it." He stepped back out of her way. "Get in your car."

She let out a sigh of frustration and defeat. As she walked past him, she kept an eye on him, wary of his every move. He stood with his feet planted, his hand near his gun, quietly watching her retreat.

When she got into the car and started the engine, he stood at her front bumper, eyes fixed on her with an intimidating glare. She thought for a moment of putting the car in drive and running him over. No one was there to help him either. No one would know if he was killed.

Except those cameras hanging from the corners of Ray's house.

She put the car in reverse, and as she backed down the drive, he walked slowly after her. She turned the car around on the road at the end of the driveway and took off in a cloud of dust.

Later, she told herself, she would review the video she had made on the drive in, see if she could read the license plates on those two trucks, do a lookup, and find the owners. A man like the one she had just encountered had no business roaming free in society. Maybe that's why he took himself out of it, she thought. Self-isolated in this wilderness with bears and deer and trees and ticks.

The man seemed to be a friend of Ray's. What did it say of Ray if this was the company he kept? Her negative opinion of Ray Cooper grew a little darker.

When she reached the first paved roads, miles from the hillside cabin, she had a realization. If Ray wasn't at the house, he may be in town, or driving along a road that had cell service. She slowed the car, found his name in her contacts, and tapped the phone icon.

On the fourth ring, he answered with an angry "What?"

"Ray, this is Anya Lakhani, Homeland Security."

"This is not a good time," Ray said. He sounded agitated and angry.

"Are you still in West Virginia?"

"I'm at home," he growled.

The echo she heard after his words made her picture an empty room. He was in a bathroom or a kitchen, some place with tiled walls that made an empty, lonely-sounding echo.

"I wanted to ask you about Sean Riggs."

"He's a whiny little prick."

"Okay," she said. "Maybe you're right. Maybe this isn't a good time. Will you be in the office tomorrow?"

"Where else am I going to go?" She heard him take a shuddering breath, and his voice seemed to break in desperation as he repeated, "Where the hell else am I supposed to go?"

"Ray?"

He hung up.

That was the first half of her day. The five-hour drive followed by the altercation at the cabin left her feeling drained.

She was hungry and wanted food, but she was also rattled. She didn't stop for lunch until well past two.

She parked herself at a booth in a cafe in Lewisburg, had a long lunch, and reviewed the materials that had come in from Google, Amazon, and the other tech companies that had responded to warrants for Sean Riggs's internet search records.

Among a sea of innocuous activity—checking the weather, reading the news, looking up videos about how to unclog motorcycle carburetors—there were two items of interest. The first was a message he had sent through LinkedIn to a former software developer at Empire. Sean Riggs had joined the company a few weeks after Drishti Singh left, so their paths could not have crossed at work. What would he want to talk with her about? Probably something harmless, but it was worth an inquiry. Anya sent Singh a LinkedIn message asking if they could chat.

The second item of interest was dated two days prior. Sean had gone to Amazon in search of a technical manual describing the inner workings of the software that controlled electric power grids.

What would he want with a book like that?

She went back to LinkedIn and saw that since leaving Empire a few months ago, he had been building websites and databases on short contract jobs. A technical manual about power-grid control systems had no relevance to that kind of work? So... why?

According to Amazon's logs, he had viewed almost a dozen listings for the same book. She followed each of the links in the report. All of the copies available had been listed by used bookstores spread across the country. The prices they charged ranged from thirty-five to fifty-nine dollars. Pricey for a used book, but technical manuals could be invaluable to the workers who needed them. When she clicked the last link in the list, the page said, "This item is no longer available."

Had Sean bought that one? Someone had.

She checked the order history that Amazon had sent in response to her warrant. He had *not* bought the book. His last

Amazon purchase had been four weeks earlier, a vinyl LP record of Frank Sinatra's greatest hits.

It seems too much of a coincidence, she thought, that he would search for such an obscure book just a few days ago and that the book displayed on the last listing he viewed would have been purchased.

She reviewed the other listings again, noting this time the locations of the used bookshops that sold the manual. On a hunch, she began looking up the office locations of major electric utilities throughout the country. The cities began to match up. That made sense. Where else would those books be needed? They were valuable only to people who worked in the power industry.

What if, she wondered, that one missing copy had come from a bookseller in Richmond? It was plausible there could be a copy of the book floating around used bookstores in the city where Empire had its headquarters. What if Sean had gone in person to pick it up?

Before she left the cafe at nearly four in the afternoon, she made two calls. The first was to Empire's director of transmission and distribution, Cy Madhi. She wanted to know whether Empire used the grid-control software described by the book. It did.

The second call was to a woman at Amazon whose name and contact information had been included in the digital information packet the company sent in response to the federal warrant.

"Can you tell me the name and location of the third-party seller who listed this book?" She pasted the link to the no-longer-available title into the email.

Now, closing in on Richmond's western flank along a wooded stretch of I-64, with the orange glow of dusk behind her, she thought over what a long day it had been. Her sense this morning had been that after talking with Ray, she would be able to write off his complaints about Sean Riggs. Ray was just a bitter man with a grudge. The positive picture Sean's former coworkers had painted was the more accurate one.

Sean had neither the motive nor the inclination to hack his former employer.

She had imagined that, by the end of the day, with Sean crossed off the list of suspects, the task force would be able to focus on the actual perpetrators, whoever they turned out to be.

She was passing the junction of the two major interstates, I-64 and I-295, when her phone chimed with a response from the woman at Amazon. She pulled the car onto the shoulder and rolled to a stop.

She read the message once, and then again. The seller of the software manual Sean had been searching for was in downtown Richmond, near the intersection of West Broad and North Belvidere.

# 33

Dusk was falling on Dogwood Dell, along the north bank of the James River in Richmond. Children chased fireflies between blankets spread by families across the field of drying grass. Del and Carrie Wright watched as their boys wrestled over a last piece of gum while the girls finished their snow cones.

"I forgot to tell you," Carrie said. "I stopped by Donna's today."

"How's she doing?" Del's face looked pained as he rubbed his left hand, which was splinted and wrapped in a fresh cotton-elastic bandage.

"You really shouldn't have taken that cast off," Carrie said.

"I know it now. I'll go back to the doc and get a new one."

"And then we'll get a bill for three hundred dollars. Was it worth it, Del?"

"Yeah, all right, you don't have to rub it in. I'm the one living with the consequences. You were saying about Donna?"

"It's the strangest thing. She hasn't been answering her phone. When I was at her house, I called her, and I could hear her phone ringing inside."

"That is strange." Del watched the girls get up from the blanket to coo over a neighboring family's puppy.

"Do you think Ray would ever hurt her?" Carrie asked.

"I think Ray would be a hard man to live with."

"And while I was there, a woman showed up. From Homeland Security. She wanted to talk to Ray. What do you think that could be about?"

"The company got hacked," Del said carelessly. "Remember? Donna told you that the other day. If Homeland Security is involved, that's what it's about."

"Why would they go to his house?"

"'Cause that's where he lives."

"No, I mean, if it's about work, why not talk to him in the office? Oh, never mind."

The first firework of the evening shot up with a hiss, leaving a snaking trail of bright golden sparks before bursting into a massive ball of red and blue. Del watched as the five-year-old Marybeth clapped her hands over her ears and smiled with delight. Funny how she can be so scared and so pleased at the same time, he thought.

"The woman gave me her card," Carrie said. "You want it?"

"Yeah, sure." Del watched as a series of red rockets exploded across the sky. "I'll take it."

# 34

## July 5

"Bye, sweetie!" Danielle, leaving for work at eight o'clock, kissed Sean and told him she'd be working late and then going back to her place at the end of the day. "Text me if you want to meet up."

On her way out the door, she thought about how she was already calling him sweetie after just a few days. Were they getting too familiar too fast? Well, she had slept with him less than two hours after they'd met, she thought. The amazing thing was that they had spent this much time together without driving each other crazy.

She noted the white Ford Escape parked across the street. The woman in the driver's seat seemed to be staring into her lap. Probably at her phone. A salesperson, Danielle thought. Psyching herself up for a house call. What do people sell door-to-door anymore? Cleaning services? Solar panels? New gutters?

Danielle opened the door of her car, tossed her shoulder bag onto the passenger seat, and got inside. She would work in the Richmond office until six, due to a late meeting with a client. And then maybe she'd stay in town for dinner, go out with a coworker, give the Sean-and-Danielle show a break for a few hours.

From the office window, Sean watched her pull away from the curb. He watched the white Ford Escape that had first appeared twenty minutes earlier follow. The Ford was too far away for him to read the license plate, but close enough for him to see it wasn't a Virginia tag.

Is that them, he wondered? Is today the day? He felt his chest tighten as a wave of fear swept through him. Oh, God! Am I really up for this? Can I really pull this off?

Part of him wanted to flee, pick up the Millers' Mustang from the garage in Short Pump, and run. The cops wouldn't know where to find him. They wouldn't even know what kind of car to look for.

But how long would that last? Two, three days? He would need to live on cash or prepaid credit cards, something the cops couldn't trace. He would have to ditch his phone, use a burner. And then he'd be sneaking around all the time, looking over his shoulder, paranoid that every customer in every diner he ate at was secretly a cop or an informer.

He was already beginning to think that way. What reason had he to suspect the white Escape?

A guilty conscience, he told himself, perceives threats everywhere. Every person, every event, is invested with the awareness of his guilt and the threat of punishment he expected the world to deliver at any moment.

If he told the Feds what was happening, then he wouldn't be in trouble. If he told them what he had found in the code... But he still didn't know what the code did. And the last time he went to the Feds, he regretted it. They wouldn't believe him this time unless he could prove his case, and he wasn't even sure he had a case. "Oh, God," he groaned. "Why did I do this to myself?"

He looked again to make sure the white Escape hadn't returned. Then he picked up a few items from his desk: the laptop, the software manual, the keys to the Millers' house next door.

# 35

"Looking for something in particular?" asked the man behind the counter of the cluttered bookstore near West Broad and North Belvidere. With a long white beard and long, thinning white hair, he looked like an old hippie who lived with his nose in a book, one to whom customers and the world at large were annoying distractions from his treasured reading time.

"Yes," said Anya. "I'm looking for a book about software that controls electric power grids."

The man smiled. "When it rains it pours!"

"Sorry?" Anya asked, not catching on.

"That one sat on the shelf for a year and half. Not a lick of interest. Then two people in two days want to buy it."

"Someone bought it already?" Anya phrased it halfway between a question and a statement, hoping he would pick up and elaborate.

"She did," the man replied.

"She?" Anya hadn't expected that. "A woman?"

"A cute one!"

Anya showed the man her government ID. He put on his glasses, read it skeptically, his eyes narrowing with distrust.

"Can you describe the woman who bought the book? And when did she come in?"

The man leaned back away from her and suddenly looked less friendly. "What's this now? The government's going after people for reading books? Is this part of the governor's censorship agenda?"

"I don't work for the governor. I'm federal. Did the woman use a credit card to buy the book?" If she did, Anya would be able to find the name of the buyer through the card company's transaction records. But the fact that a woman had bought it left her deflated. She was trying to tie the purchase to Sean. The only thread she had to hang on to now was that the man had said the woman was cute.

The woman she saw leaving Sean's house that morning was cute. Not beautiful, but cute, with her bright smile and bright eyes and friendly round face.

"I'm not sure I should be talking to you about this," the man said.

"This is part of a larger investigation."

"About what people read?"

"Sir, I don't care what anyone reads. I do care about why some rando woman wandering in off the street has an interest in power-grid control systems. That's not beach reading."

"No, it sure isn't," the man replied. "Now, if this is really part of a larger investigation, as you say, then you'll be able to get a warrant to compel me to turn over information I'd rather not give out. I'm not a snitch."

He seemed to puff up with self-importance as he spoke.

"Is that what you want me to do?" Anya asked. "Get a warrant?"

"And I'll tell you what else," the man continued. "I hope she takes that book right over to Empire, because they could learn a thing or two about running a power grid. I had a full fridge when the electricity cut off, and I had to chuck almost two hundred dollars' worth of food."

Oh boy, Anya thought. Here come the old-man gripes. Take a deep breath and we'll give this one more try.

"This woman," she began patiently, "you said she was cute. Would you say she was about five foot five with shoulder-length, sandy-brown hair? Late twenties? Full-figured?"

"And chatty!" the man replied. "A little sprite, full of spunk!"

"All right," Anya said. "Thank you."

She had followed Danielle from Sean's house to the office of an online marketing company. Outside the bookstore, she typed the company name into the browser on her phone and navigated to the About Us page. There she was, Danielle Duval, marketing associate.

As she considered paying Danielle an in-person visit, a text arrived from Agent Espinoza.

Ray Cooper is here at the office. You want to talk to him? Because I don't. Guy's a damn grouch.

Anya texted back.

Be there in twenty.

# 36

Sean sat at Sid Miller's desk in the neighbors' house. He had pulled the blinds down, but didn't shut them all the way. He watched the street through narrow slits that allowed him to see out without others seeing in. His laptop stood open, the thumb drive containing the source code plugged into the USB port on the side. He held the software manual in his lap.

The commands in the book were grouped by function into thirty chapters. Diagnostic commands for relays and breakers were in one chapter, control commands for transformers in another. Other chapters described the queries that could tell you which capacitors and inductors were attached to a bus, the voltage required to trip digitally controlled relays, and a hundred other things Sean Riggs never had much interest in knowing.

Because he was unfamiliar with the commands in the mystery code he had stolen, it would been more helpful if the book had just listed them in alphabetical order. Then he wouldn't have to try to guess whether the words he was looking at on-screen pertained to buses or shunts or inductors or what.

After a few minutes of flipping through pages, he had an aha moment. Use the index! The index at the back of the book was alphabetized.

Over the next hour, he figured out what the first set of cryptic commands was doing.

```
STRCAP ALL TRUE
SLEEP 900
STRTERM ALL
STRREW 0
STRPUSH MASTER LOOP
```

The first command, STRCAP, meant "stream capture." STRCAP ALL told the system to capture all incoming data streams from all of the electronically monitored devices on the grid. Okay, he thought. All of those transformers and breakers and switches and whatnot sent a constant stream of information about their status to the control center. The variable-voltage transformers sent info about how much voltage they took in and put out. The breakers told you whether they were open or closed. The technicians monitored all that information in real time, looking for outages, anomalies, and other signs of trouble.

Sean had never been inside Empire's operations center, but he had seen photos. The room was arranged like NASA's mission control center, with technicians sitting in concentric rows before curved consoles, all facing the giant monitors at the front of the room that displayed an overview of the entire grid. Trouble spots, when they appeared, were highlighted in yellow and red.

So, Sean muttered, STRCAP ALL means capture all data streams coming in from all monitored equipment. That's hundreds of thousands of components spread throughout the state. The last word in the command, TRUE, according to the manual, meant to save all the data to disk in addition to sending it to the monitors.

The next line, he already understood. SLEEP 900 meant do nothing for nine hundred seconds, or fifteen minutes.

He went back to the manual for an explanation of the next command. STRTERM ALL meant "terminate all streams." Effectively, that put an end to the data-capturing process that STRCAP had started.

So, the code thus far recorded fifteen minutes of sensor data from every item on the grid and saved it to a file. Then what?

STRREW 0 meant rewind the stream to position zero. That is, go all the way back to the beginning of the recorded data. Just as he had guessed earlier.

The next command, STRPUSH MASTER LOOP, meant push all the data from the recorded stream back to the master control system, and keep playing it over and over in an infinite loop.

What would be the effect of that, Sean wondered? The technicians in the operations center would keep seeing the same view of the grid played over and over on their monitors.

Why in the world would anyone want to do that? To give the operators a false view of a correctly functioning grid? To hide trouble as it was brewing?

Sean leaned back in Sid Miller's old swivel chair and rubbed his chin as he looked out through the blinds. The vague malice he had instinctively perceived when he first saw this code was taking on a more solid and definite form.

# 37

Danielle sat outside the glass-walled conference room that the Empire employees had nicknamed "The Fishbowl." When the call came into her office on the company line, she assumed it was a client or a prospective client. The woman on the other end of the line asked if she was Danielle Duval. Something in the tone of her question seemed off. This wasn't going to be a normal business call.

"Yes?" Danielle replied.

The woman introduced herself as an investigator from Homeland Security. She said her name, but Danielle could not now remember it.

"Can I ask you a few questions?"

"Sure."

"In person?"

"Um, let me see. I may have some time the day after tomorrow."

"Today?"

"Hmm." The calendar on the computer monitor in front of her showed one remaining morning meeting, followed by a long lunch with coworkers, and then back-to-back meetings all afternoon.

"Where are you?" Danielle asked. "Would you be coming here?"

"I'm at the offices of Empire Energy. I'm afraid I can't get out of here until at least six. Any chance you could drop by during lunch? I'm about fifteen minutes away."

Danielle sighed. She had been planning on telling her friends about Sean over lunch. They'd been teasing her about her unusually good mood, her happy glow. Was she holding on to some secret, they asked? Did she have a new boyfriend? She'd been coy, but today she was going to spring it on them. She wanted to hear what they thought. Was she crazy for getting so wrapped up so quickly? Was it too good to be true?

Would this guy turn out to be a closet psycho? A narcissist? A player with another woman or two on the side?

"I guess," she said. "Can I ask what this is about?"

"We'll talk when you get here."

Well, now she was here, watching through the glass as the woman who had called her interviewed a sour, angry-looking man who seemed to carry a cloud of darkness about him. Dark hollows beneath his red-rimmed eyes spoke of sleeplessness. His mouth was set in a tight, bitter frown. His body was tense to the point of rigidness. His chest and shoulders rose with each slow breath, and then collapsed again as the air went out of him. He clenched and unclenched his fists on the table as the woman inside asked him questions he didn't seem to want to answer. The man's eyes fixed on the woman from time to time with a look of aggression and resentment. And then the look faded as the man seemed to lose himself in thought. Lost in a world of dark, unhappy thoughts, Danielle imagined.

When the man turned and glared at her, she felt a rush of primal fear. She flushed and felt herself squirm in her chair. She turned her eyes away, looked at the floor, at the clock on the far wall, at her fingernails. When she glanced back up, he was still watching her, eyes boring in with a kind of hatred that was chilling because it was so cold.

If looks could kill, she thought.

The man continued to stare. She stared back, wondering what dark thoughts flashed behind those eyes. She felt for a moment like a tourist at a zoo watching a tiger in a cage.

Inside the room, Anya Lakhani said, "Ray? Is today not a good day?"

"Today is not a good day." His tone conveyed a seething undercurrent of anger.

Anya picked up her notepad and said, "I've been through all of your write-ups of Sean Riggs."

"Well, la-di-da," Ray muttered sarcastically.

"Did Sean ever talk about politics? Any strong political beliefs?"

Fourteen years, Ray thought. I gave that woman fourteen years and she threw it all away. Threw *me* away. I gave her a house and a kid, put food in her mouth, clothes on her back. Brought her out of the darkness of that stupid, wrong-headed church. Taught her obedience. Took her to task when she got out of line. Checked her worst impulses, kept her on the straight and narrow, acceptable in the sight of God, and all that time she was plotting against me. A good little wife on the outside. Dishonest, disloyal, disobedient dissembler on the inside. God sees that black heart of yours, you nasty bitch. He has a place for you when all is said and done.

"Ray?"

"Sean never talked about politics," he said.

And there's another one right out there, Ray thought, sitting on the other side of the glass with her round, cutesy face and her black female heart. How old is she? Twenty-five? Proud. In glowing health. She hasn't been broken yet. It's just a question of finding the right man. She doesn't even know it's coming. She'll know when it happens. She won't be a little girl anymore.

Look how she returns my stare. That kind of insolence can only come from ignorance. She doesn't know yet. Do you think I'd tolerate such arrogance from you if you were my wife? Do you really think I'd let you look at me like that in my own house?

"Did any of Sean's interactions with coworkers raise any red flags with you?" Anya asked.

She has hips, Ray thought, still staring at Danielle. And boobs that could nourish a brood. She was built to breed. Not like Donna. The Lord put Donna here for one purpose, and she was deficient at that. One kid in fourteen years of marriage. And it wasn't for lack of trying.

"Ray?"

"No," he said. "No red flags." He tore his eyes and thoughts from the woman on the other side of the glass. "I didn't really socialize with Sean. Kid was a punk."

"Did any of Sean's work, his coding, ever raise security concerns?"

"His work was shit."

"Can you be a little more specific? Was the quality poor? Actually, never mind. How were his skills?"

Ray leaned forward, his red-rimmed eyes boring into Anya's face.

Brown skinned, he thought. Like the earth. It's like they come out of the ground over there. Their country is overflowing, so they come here to pollute ours.

"Don't look at me that way," Anya said sternly. "Just answer the question."

"His skills were fine," Ray said. "He just didn't follow directions. He was always poking around where he shouldn't have been. And I didn't like his attitude."

"What do you mean, poking around where he shouldn't have been?"

"Why are you asking me about Sean?"

"Please answer my question."

"Answer mine."

Anya pursed her lips and let out a long breath. "Okay, Ray, we're done here. Thank you for your time. I may want to follow up tomorrow with a few more questions."

"We're done here?" Ray asked. "You're dismissing me? Like you're the teacher and I'm the student? Let me remind you that I work here. This is *my* office. My country. You're the outsider."

Anya picked up her phone, tapped the screen, and put it to her ear. In a second, she said, "Carlos? Can you come in here?"

"Are you calling your boyfriend?" Ray mocked. "To take me away?"

"I do not want to deal with this person," she said into the phone. And then after a pause, "In the fishbowl, yes."

In the half minute between the end of the call and the arrival of Agent Carlos Espinoza, Ray glared at her. He was lost so deeply in his thoughts, she felt he wasn't seeing her at all.

When Espinoza arrived, Ray rose from his seat without being asked, and the two men left together.

Danielle watched through the glass as Anya let out a sigh and slumped onto the conference table. Danielle could hear her frustrated words through the open door. "Oh. My. God!"

Danielle entered the conference room silently and touched Anya's shoulder, startling her. Anya straightened up and said, "Sorry. I didn't hear you come in. You're Danielle?"

"And you're having a rough day." Danielle smiled.

"Tough customer," Anya said. "Have a seat. Would you like some coffee? Water?"

"I'm good, thanks." She took a seat to Anya's left.

Anya composed herself and said, "Forgive me for getting straight to the point, but how long have you known Sean Riggs?"

The question sent a jolt of fear through Danielle. This was supposed to be the lunch where she told her coworkers she was seeing someone new, someone who had brought out the glow of happiness they had noticed with curiosity and, she thought, a touch of envy. This was supposed to be the time when they peppered her with questions and she would listen to her own answers as attentively as they would. Hearing herself answer would help her know where she thought things stood in this unexpected fling that had moved more quickly and smoothly than she could ever have hoped.

Her friends would ask the tough questions, expose the friction points, the doubts, maybe help her put the brakes on this freefall romance and suggest she move forward a little more prudently. Because it should never be this easy.

Now, instead of her friends and coworkers stoking doubts, it was a stranger, a federal investigator from Homeland Security wanting to get right to the point. About Sean! What kind of trouble could he be in? Danielle felt her throat tighten.

"Um. Just a few days."

Her face flushed at the words. Just a few days, and she had slept with him how many times? Just a few days and she had spent how many hours at his house? How few hours without him?

"Pardon me for asking, and you don't have to answer, but are you two intimate?"

Before Danielle could even consider whether she wanted to respond to that question, a huge, beaming smile lit her face.

"Okay, so things are good," Anya said. "Does Sean ever talk about work?"

"Not really." She tried to control her smile, tone it down at least. "He writes software. He doesn't talk too much about boring things."

She noticed her fingers drawing nervously, aimlessly on the table. She stopped, pulled her hand back closer to her body, and saw that Anya was as aware as she was of her involuntary movements and her attempts to control them.

"Has Sean ever expressed any kind of extremist political views?"

"Oh, no!" She shook her head vigorously. "Nothing like that. We haven't talked about politics. I don't even know if he's a Democrat or a Republican or an independent. Or—wait. He did once talk about something he was working on."

She told Anya what she remembered—lying beside him in bed, in the air-conditioning. She had asked what he had been thinking of earlier in the day, when they first met. He said he had been thinking about some computer code that didn't make sense. He showed it to her.

"Like, on his laptop?" Anya asked. "He had his laptop in bed?"

"No. It was on his phone. It was a photo of a computer monitor with some code."

Anya sat back and tapped a pencil to her lips as she thought. "Why would he take a photo of computer code and carry it around on his phone?"

"I don't know," Danielle said helplessly. She felt she had to justify his strange behavior. For a second, she felt foolish, as if the investigator had pointed out an obvious red flag that she had missed. As if Anya had said, *Can't you see you've fallen in with a code fetishist? Get out while you still can!*

"Do you remember anything else about the code? Did he say why it was important?"

He did, Danielle thought with a start that did not escape Anya's notice. He had said, "Code like this has no place in a system as important as the electric grid." Now it all fell into place, why she was here, why the investigator from Homeland Security was asking about Sean.

Danielle shook her head. "No. I mean, I don't remember."

"Are you sure?" Anya gave her a lingering look of disappointment. "You looked like you just remembered *something.*"

Danielle knew that the investigator knew she was hiding something. But you don't understand, she pleaded internally. I've just been drifting along for months, trying to keep my chin up, trying to pretend that I like my job and my friends don't bore me. And I take this one big chance, I take a *huge* chance with a guy I have this crush on, and I make a fool of myself in every possible way, and after all that, he actually likes me! He likes me, even when I'm acting stupid! And I like him. And we can talk. The respect is just there. It was there from the beginning—acceptance and respect—and it's never wavered. Please don't take him away from me. I am *so* enjoying this. Please don't tell me it's an illusion, that I've been let down again.

"Do you feel safe around him?" Anya asked.

That question made her angry. "Do you think I'd waste my time with him if I didn't?"

"Okay. It's just something I ask as a law enforcement agent. Would you feel safe telling us if you saw him doing anything suspicious?"

"Suspicious, like what? You want me to spy on him?"

"No. And I don't mean to turn you against him either. I'm just saying, as a citizen, would you be willing to assist your government if your country was under threat?"

"My country?" Danielle asked incredulously. "Sean is, like, an average guy. I couldn't see him even shoplifting. How is he going to threaten a country?"

"Did you buy a book for him the other day? A book about power-grid control systems?"

That question hit her like a blow. How in hell did she know that, Danielle wondered?

"From a used bookstore near West Broad and North Belvidere? Yes, or no?"

"Yes," Danielle said bitterly. "Now I have to get back to work." She rose on shaky legs. This was all too much at once, federal investigators following her, her too-good-to-be-true boyfriend a threat to national security. She was going to cry, but she didn't want to do it here. Not in front of this woman, not in this building.

"Let me give you my card," Anya said.

"I don't want it." She struggled to hold back her tears.

"Please," Anya said. "Take it."

Danielle took the card reluctantly, without looking at Anya. She didn't want to argue. After being blindsided by this interview, by these questions and all they insinuated, she had no fight left in her.

Anya stood. "I'll escort you out," she said.

"Don't bother."

"I have to. It's policy. No unescorted visitors. And by the way, I need your mobile number."

"I don't want to talk to you."

They were walking quickly now through the hall, Anya a step behind.

"But I need it."

Without slowing or turning to look at her, Danielle reluctantly gave her the number. Anya scribbled it on the back of one of her own business cards.

When they reached the building exit, Danielle walked fast toward the parking lot. She would drive away from the building, round a corner, park, and cry where no one could see her, cry for the loss of this new friend and lover that had come to her so unexpectedly, only to be taken away so rudely.

Anya watched. From behind, she couldn't see that Danielle's tears were already flowing. She watched her walk almost right into Ray Cooper, the dark, angry man standing beside his big white truck with the door open.

Ray said something to her. She said something back, put her hand to her face, and continued, walking briskly, tensely, in a hurry.

Anya was about to go back inside when she saw a police cruiser pull into the lot. More trouble, she thought. Everywhere is trouble.

She watched as the cop pulled his car up behind Ray's truck, blocking its exit. Ray was inside the truck. Now he got out. He was angry.

Anya let go of the building door, let it close behind her. She walked toward Ray and the cop. The cop bolted from his car toward Ray, club in hand. What was this about?

The body language of both men showed aggression. Anya picked up her pace. She was almost to them now. She saw the cop poke the end of his club into Ray's chest, pushing him back. She was close enough to hear his words.

"You don't ever talk to an officer of the law like that, Ray Cooper."

"She was a bitch and she wasn't helpful."

Do they know each other, Anya wondered? They seem to.

"That's assault," the cop replied hotly. "You don't tell a cop you're going to beat her face in! Who did you think you were talking to? Who do you think you are?"

"She left me, Tom." Ray's shoulders slackened; his back hunched and began to heave.

Was he sobbing, Anya wondered? Was Ray Cooper crying? It appeared he was.

"I understand you spoke in anger, Ray. But you don't talk like that to a cop. Ever. Understand?"

"Why can't you people do your damn job? Bring her back?" He sounded pathetic now, helpless and wounded.

"That's not our job. Your job as a citizen is to obey the law. That means you don't threaten cops. You talk like that again, Ray, you're in for a world of hurt."

Anya turned and walked quietly back toward the building. She had heard enough to understand that the man had lost his wife. Enough to make sense of Ray's dark state of mind, his sleepless, tortured appearance.

I was right, she thought. Trouble. Trouble everywhere.

# 38

Wiping the sweat from his brow in the heat of the afternoon sun, Del thought back to this morning's meeting. Attended by more than four hundred other field technicians in a warehouse that usually stocked replacement components to repair the grid, it was more of a pep rally than a meeting. Del noted the warehouse was empty of goods. Not only were the transformers and switches gone, so were the spools of conductor wire. Even the porcelain and glass insulators had been depleted. With nothing left to load onto the fleet of trucks outside, the warehouse's yellow forklifts sat idle against a side wall. They probably hadn't moved in days, he thought.

Almost half the four hundred workers standing on the bare concrete floor had come from out of state. Their shirts and helmets bore the logos of energy companies from Ohio, Illinois, Missouri, Arkansas, even Kansas. Their eyes and ears were fixed on the man in the white collared shirt standing before them. In one hand, he held a microphone. In the other, a printed paper with talking points.

"First of all," he began, "I want to thank all of you for the hard work you've put in these past two weeks. For the overtime, the time away from family, for working in extreme heat and less than ideal conditions. A week ago, more than ninety percent of our customers were without power. Today, that's down to twelve percent. How about a round of applause for yourselves and your coworkers?"

He nodded and smiled as the crews began to clap and cheer.

"We still have a long way to go," he continued. "Twelve percent of our customer base represents almost a million people. A million people still suffering in the heat, who can't run a refrigerator, can't get a cold drink, can't use the microwave or the toaster oven.

"I don't mean to pressure you folks, but in case you need motivation when you're toiling under that hot sun, I want you to keep in mind that the work you're doing is saving lives."

Another cheer went up from the crowd.

"Last night the governor announced a grim milestone. Three thousand confirmed deaths. Almost all of those were from the heat. Most of you guys—and gals—are young and in good shape. You know how hard it is to spend hour after hour, day after day in this heat. Now imagine what it's like for a person who is seventy, eighty, ninety years old. Imagine what it's like for a person with a chronic disease. Their bodies get depleted quicker. They don't bounce back as fast.

"Most of the dead have been elderly. Think grandma, granddad. Think of that family member who has diabetes, asthma, who depends on daily medication. These are the people you're going to be working for in the coming days. Three thousand of them have already lost their lives, despite everyone's best efforts. How many more are out there among our million customers who are still in the dark?

"The difficult, uncomfortable work you are doing is deeply appreciated by many people, by families throughout our communities. For some of them, the twelve-hour day you put in today is literally a lifesaver.

"But I want you all to keep in mind that while the roads are more passable now that the trees and flood debris have been cleared, the weeks ahead may be harder in some ways than the ones we've just been through. When we initiated repairs, we were seeing big wins. We would fix one substation and watch the lights come on in thousands of homes.

"The people without power now are living in more sparsely populated areas. The wins we get going forward may be just a few hundred homes at a time. In some cases, just a few dozen. And we'll have to work just as hard for those as we did for the big ones. Maybe even harder.

"Look around this warehouse and you'll see that we have no stock left to replace damaged equipment. North Carolina, Maryland, Pennsylvania, New Jersey, they're in the same predicament. These storms used up all our reserves and, I'm sorry to say, with all the orders flooding in to manufacturers from all over the East Coast, the components we need may be back-ordered for months.

"When you all go out on your respective assignments, your orders are to repair what you can, to make an inventory of components that are beyond your skill to repair, and bring us those lists at the end of each day. We have technicians coming in from the manufacturers who may be able to fix some of this stuff, but they have to know where to go first. We're going to triage your lists based on the likelihood of the equipment being fixable and the number of customers whose power will be restored.

"I also want to let you guys know that we're now on day thirteen without rain. The national parks all over Virginia have their red flag warnings up. The fire risk is high, particularly in the parched forests. When you're out there driving around, take a look at how many of our lines run through cuts in pine woods, through cuts in the deciduous forests.

"We do our best to keep those cuts clear. In most places, there's an air gap between the lines and the branches. But the rains from the two hurricanes fed the underbrush. In many places you'll see it's grown up thick beneath the lines, and then it dried out. This is a dangerous situation. Add to that the number of trees that fell into areas along the lines that we had previously cleared, the branches that broke off in hurricane-force winds. Those too have dried out.

"What we have now is thousands of miles of power lines running through a tinderbox. Many of those lines, especially in the more remote areas, are still down, felled by the storms. If we send power through a grounded line, we get a forest fire. That's the last thing we need right now.

"So, your orders, in addition to fixing components, in addition to repairing substations, in addition to cataloging equipment that our manufacturers' technicians should look at, in addition to restoring power to a million suffering people—your orders are to find and either repair or neutralize every downed line you see. Trace the line back to the breaker. Make sure the circuit is open. If you can't locate the breaker, call the office.

"How's that for a job, folks? Enough to keep you busy?" He smiled as a murmur arose from the crowd.

"Now, lastly, because you all don't have enough on your minds already, keep in mind the weather. One hundred one degrees today. One hundred four tomorrow. Above a hundred for each of the next seven days. That means we've stepped down the voltage on the transmission lines. They're simply running too hot. We're struggling to meet demand, and if we have to, we're going to shed some load. That means a rolling blackout.

"People are going to be mad. After what they've just been through, no one wants their power taken away. But that might have to happen. You might run into some angry customers. Tell them to call customer service. We'll take the complaints so you can focus on work.

"Most of all, keep in mind that for each of you, this heat is dangerous. We don't want anyone getting sick out there. We're sending you out with extra water, extra ice, with electrolyte mix. If you start to feel lightheaded, go back to the truck. Sit in the air-conditioning and drink lots of water. Hydrate, hydrate, hydrate, people! Don't go back to work until you feel strong again. And if you don't feel strong, if you still feel weak or lightheaded, don't go back at all. Rest up, and hopefully you can come back and be productive tomorrow.

"Keep an eye on your coworkers. If you see your crewmate acting confused, responding slowly to questions, if you see them having trouble maintaining balance, swaying on their feet, if you see them stop sweating, get help! Heatstroke is a dangerous thing, people! It can be fatal, even to the young, even to the strong. The person suffering it doesn't always recognize that it's happening. That's what's so insidious about it. It takes away your cognitive abilities. You don't know what bad shape you're in until it's too late. So, every single one of you out there"—he pointed a finger at the crowd, moving his arm from left to right to include them all—"I want all of you to look out for one another. Now let's get out there and be heroes!"

Another cheer went up. Del nodded quietly in agreement with the speaker, then turned, adjusted his cap, and headed out to his truck in the lot.

That was eight hours ago. It seemed like days. Del was weakening under the heat of the burning sun. He could feel it.

He wiped his brow again and told himself that as long as he kept sweating, he wasn't too dehydrated to work.

# 39

Hungry?

The text was from Sean. It was seven thirty in the evening, and Danielle had just walked into her apartment.

Not really.

She felt exhausted and deflated. The one good thing that had happened in her life in the past few months was now potentially a bad thing. A dangerous thing. She wished that that Anya lady had never called her. She would rather have remained ignorant and happy than have her bubble of joy popped so cruelly.

Want to hang out? My place or yours. Either way.

No, Sean, I don't want to hang out, she thought. I want to ask you point-blank what the hell this is all about. I want you tell me unequivocally that none of this is real, that there's nothing to worry about. That you're the guy I thought you were, a decent person who's nice to me, who's easy to get along with, who felt like an old friend after just two hours of knowing you. I knew this was too good to be true. People don't just click like this. It doesn't happen. And I'm stupid, stupid, stupid for letting myself believe it could.

Not tonight.

Who am I supposed to turn to for comfort on this awful, terrible, horrible, day, she asked herself? I want *you*, Sean, because you put me at ease. Or you used to. Now that investigator has taken away my trust in you.

Bad day?

Yeah, she thought. Thanks for getting me. She texted back:

Bad. Yes. Exhausting. I need some rest.

Besides, she thought, it's about time we spent a night apart. I've been too caught up in you. In us. How can I think clearly when I'm so wrapped up? When I keep seeing you and the sight of you makes me so happy? When your presence makes me feel warm inside?

I miss you! I miss your scent. I want to believe you're not a horrible person, that you're not going to prison. That you won't be leaving me all alone after giving me a taste of something so good.

And my place is a mess. I've been putting off cleaning since before the blackout.

He texted back a winking emoji blowing a red-heart kiss. She responded in kind, then set the phone to Do Not Disturb and put it on the nightstand beside the bed.

You just have to rip the bandage off all at once, she told herself. It'll hurt, but the sooner you detach, the better. The pain will end more quickly.

She stood, picked up a pillow, and shook it out of its case. Then the second pillow. Then she removed the thin summer blanket, the top sheet, the fitted sheet, the mattress pad she had sweat through during the blackout. They all went into the hamper.

The clothing strewn across the floor filled the second hamper ten inches past the top. She couldn't carry them both down the stairs at once, so she took the bedding first. The basement laundry room was hot and smelled like mildew. Water had leaked in during the hurricanes, and when the power went out, no air flowed through. It was dry now, but the smell remained.

The washers and dryers were full, though not all were still running. The other tenants, like her, were catching up on the laundry of the past two weeks. Through the window of one idle washer, she recognized a neighbor's T-shirt.

He won't mind if I take his stuff out, she thought. She removed damp clothing by the handful, placed it atop another machine, then loaded her bedding into the washer and added detergent. She moved the neighbor's clothes into her hamper, which she left on the empty folding table.

On her way back upstairs, she stopped on the second floor, knocked on a door, and told the young guy in two thirteen his clothes were in her hamper. "Two of the dryers are done," she added. "If you want to kick out someone else's clothes and dry yours, go for it." The man thanked her.

When she returned to her apartment on the fourth floor, she recoiled at the smell. It wasn't as bad as it had been when she first returned with Sean, but her apartment shouldn't smell at all. She went to the kitchen, pulled the bag from the garbage can, and cinched it shut. She put in a new bag, took the old one to the bathroom, and picked up the garbage can there. Back down the stairs, to the dumpster out back, and she was rid of two sources of odor.

Four flights up to the apartment, and now she was hungry. She opened the fridge, expecting to see yogurt, vegetables, sliced turkey, cheese. The reality of the past two weeks had slipped her mind. The fridge was empty. And spotless. She had thrown out the food on day two of the blackout. On day six, she was so bored, she picked up a sponge and paper towels and disinfectant spray and gave both fridge and freezer a thorough cleaning.

Okay, what now, she wondered? I'm starving.

She picked up her phone, looked at the menus of a few restaurants in town. The Thai place sounded like the best option. A light curry with rice sounded good. Bold red text at the top of the menu said, "We're sorry. Delivery not available yet. Pickup only."

She ordered green curry with chicken and vegetables. Then she put her phone in the pocket of her slacks, the slacks she had put on that morning before work, the ones she was wearing when Sean kissed her goodbye. She slid on a pair of flip-flops, grabbed her keys, and headed out to the car.

She pulled up to the restaurant just in time to see him walking in, his blue Honda Civic parked in front of her.

Are we *that* alike, she wondered? We crave the same food at the same time?

She couldn't go inside. The thought of running into him made her feel sick, like her body was physically rejecting something it knew would harm it. She backed up, left the lot, and drove home, her mind bouncing back and forth between thoughts she couldn't reconcile.

He's a good person. He's kind and attentive. He gets me.

He's a terrorist. We just went through a horrible outage that killed three thousand people, and he hacks into the electric utility? He buys a book about how to control the grid, so he can make this happen again? Is that what he's doing? He sends *me* into the bookshop to get it, makes *me* buy the book, so now I'm part of this too? What the hell, Sean? How could you drag me into this?

Her face burned with shame at the thought of having slept with him, at the thought of giving herself up so easily, on the day they met.

She was starting to cry when she remembered the comment he had made after sex that first day. He could tell she enjoyed it because for the first time since he had met her, she had stopped talking. Now she was laughing and crying at the same time.

A truck to her left screeched to a stop and blasted its horn because she had just run a stop sign.

Pay attention, she told herself. Get a grip!

She leaned forward, tightened her hands on the wheel, and muttered a curse as she realized she had run another stop.

Back in her apartment alone, she thought, well, at least I haven't told my friends. I won't have to backtrack on all my praise, on telling them all what a great guy he is.

She pictured herself at a bar with her coworkers a year from now, telling the story. "You know that guy who was in the news for hacking the electric company? The one who just got sentenced to twenty years in prison? Yeah, well, I actually dated him. *While* he was doing it! You would never in a million years have suspected him. He was that good at dissembling. He hid it *that* well."

She pictured her friends' wonder and amazement, and then her heart sank even further.

I don't want to think of him that way, she told herself. Ever. I want him to be the person I thought he was. Please be that person, Sean.

She lay on her bed, watching the walls as the apartment darkened around her. What was the point of turning on the lights? What was the point of doing anything this evening?

She twirled her hair around her finger as she had done in childhood when no one was around to comfort her. She cursed him. Cursed herself for making such a blunder. Then she asked what signs she had missed. Signs of deception, manipulation, secrecy, dishonesty. She thought and thought and came up with nothing.

An hour past dark, she told herself she wouldn't go on like this. She would confront him tomorrow, ask him point-blank if he was involved in this illegal activity. She would tell him the Feds were onto him. The Homeland Security investigator never said she *couldn't* do that.

She would tell him he had done something stupid at best, possibly evil, and he would have to pay for it. And then she would watch him squirm. Then it would be *him* suffering for his actions, not her. That would be justice.

And if he denied it, said this was all a misunderstanding, would she believe him? If she did believe him, would it be because she desperately wanted to? Would it be because he was a good liar?

What if he got angry? What if he truly was dangerous? Dangerous enough to warrant a federal investigation?

She thought again about the gun, the old .22 caliber her ex, Ronnie, had given her. Where had she put it?

She got up from the bed, turned on the lights, searched the closet. There it was, beneath the rack of shoes. The old revolver she had used to shoot the logos out of empty beer cans Ronnie chugged on their dates in the woods. It had a long barrel for better aim. She popped open the cylinder and counted six rounds.

Pointing the gun toward an empty Sprite can on the nightstand, she said to herself, "Now I'm truly crazy. Now I've really lost it."

# 40

In her hotel room at ten o'clock that night, Anya sat at a desk in front of her laptop, amending the administrative warrant request she had drafted a few hours earlier. Agent Espinoza had reviewed it and emailed some good feedback.

> You need to show more of a motive as to why Sean Riggs may have committed this hack. I know it's thin, but mention the apparent bad blood between Riggs and Ray Cooper. Good catch on the girlfriend and the book purchase, and that detail about him having a photo of the company's internal source code on his phone. It doesn't totally mesh with the grudge-against-ex-boss motive, but it does show he's in possession of confidential internal info and may be planning to cause problems with the grid software. Anything else you can add, add it. We don't want this one sent back for lack of probable cause. Submit it tonight. HQ is awaiting your request and will have admin judges reviewing first thing in the a.m.

Anya had revised the request and was about to submit it when a lead she had reached out to earlier finally responded. The alert that popped up on her screen said, "Hey, sorry I didn't get back to you. We're nine and half hours ahead in Mumbai. It's morning here. You wanted to talk?"

Anya clicked through the alert and was now looking at LinkedIn's messaging page. "I can talk now," she typed. She added her cell number, clicked Send and then waited.

When her phone rang a moment later, she told Drishti Singh, the woman on the other end, that she was with Homeland Security, gathering background information for an investigation.

"Sean Riggs recently reached out to you."

"Yes," said Drishti.

"Did you work with him?" Anya knew she didn't. Sean had joined Empire after Drishti left.

"No. I was gone before he came on."

"That's what I thought. So, I'm wondering what you two had to talk about."

"He asked me about some code."

"About Empire code?"

"Yes."

"Did you know he stopped working at Empire three and a half months ago?"

"I didn't know that. And I wasn't familiar with the code he asked about. He said it was mine, but I didn't write it."

"What was in the code?"

"I don't know. Part of it was encrypted. That's what he was confused about. But I couldn't help him. I had never seen that code before."

"Why did he think you wrote it?"

"He said it was committed to the source control repository under my username."

"But you didn't commit it?"

"No."

Anya thought for a moment. "You turned in your laptop when you left?"

"I had to."

"When you turned it in, did the machine contain any uncommitted code? Anything you had worked on but not pushed to the central code repository? I'm wondering if the person you gave the laptop to could have pushed your code before the IT department wiped the hard drive."

"There was no uncommitted code. I had pushed everything more than a week before. My last week at the company was offboarding and packing for India."

"So why did Sean think the code was yours? Did he say?"

"He said it had my name on it, but that's impossible. It was committed a week after I left the US. The laptop wasn't even in my possession."

"Okay," Anya said. "Who did you give your laptop to when you left?"

"My supervisor. Ray Cooper."

Him again, Anya thought. It keeps coming back to those two, Sean and Ray.

"Hello? You still there?" asked Drishti.

"I'm here. Just making some mental notes. Listen, thank you for taking the time to speak with me."

"Am I in any trouble?"

"No. I don't think so."

After the call, Anya added a paragraph to her warrant request noting that Sean's conversation with a former Empire software engineer, one he didn't even know, pertained to some computer code he wasn't supposed to have. Since Sean himself no longer worked for Empire at the time, he could have no valid reason for needing to know about the code. She noted that possession of code pertaining to critical energy infrastructure on an unsecured personal device violated federal regulations. One more red flag warranting a search of the home and computer systems of Sean Riggs.

At eleven p.m., Anya laid her head on the pillow of the hotel bed and reflected on the end of a very long day. Tomorrow would be different. Equally long, perhaps, but she wouldn't spend it sitting around a conference room interviewing people. She would likely be in Sean Riggs's house, helping supervise the seizure of computers and other electronic equipment.

She closed her eyes and saw again the lively young woman with the bright smile in the Empire conference room, the one whose day she had ruined. She saw again the sour, angry face of Ray Cooper, heard his rude, insulting tone, felt the menacing aura of his seething hostility. That man needs help, she thought.

She turned on her side, switched off the lamp on the night table, and told herself to put that awful man out of her head.

But she couldn't, and she couldn't sleep either.

# 41

"What are you doing in the kitchen, Del?" Carrie fastened the belt around her blue terry cloth robe. "It's past midnight."

"Writing a report." He sat hunched over the kitchen table, pecking awkwardly at the laptop keyboard.

"For work? You got out of bed for that?"

"It was bugging me."

"What's bugging you?" She leaned down toward the chair and hugged him from behind. "You have to let it go, Del. The grid is working again, but you're going to break down if you don't stop and get some rest. You want some tea?"

"Yeah." Del squinted at the keyboard and tapped out a few words with his index fingers.

"Sleepytime?" Carrie asked as she filled a kettle.

"That'll do."

"What's so important that you have write a report on your field computer at midnight?"

"These outsider crews don't know what the hell they're doing."

"The crews from out of state?"

"Yeah, them. They mean well, but I don't know what kinda standards they got. I was out doing follow-up inspections today. I go to one substation, they got this old mechanical relay. Supposed to trip when too much current comes through, send it off to a shunt. It tripped during the storm. Crew went in there the other day to reset it. They reset it, only some jackass dropped a plastic screwdriver handle behind the armature. Next time that relay is supposed to trip, it won't be able to. The plastic will prevent the armature from hitting the contact. You know what that means?"

"I have no idea, Del. Does it mean you have to stay up all night working?"

"Well, yeah. It means next time too much current runs through that line, the switch won't trip. The juice will run right through and fry everything the switch is supposed to protect. We don't have replacements for those components, and we can't get any. Everything's back-ordered now."

"Why didn't you just fix the problem?"

"I did. And now I'm writing it up. You know why? 'Cause in the next substation, I found a newer relay, electronically controlled. Someone tried to jam something into one of the control ports and scorched it.

"Technician's report said that station was all fixed. Well, it wasn't fixed right. Whoever messed up that relay had to have been inside the station. And you know what else? You know those sensors they're putting on everything now?"

"No, Del. And I don't think this tea is going to do it for you. I think maybe you need a sleeping pill. Or a shot of bourbon."

"Wait till I'm done typing."

"It takes you ten minutes to type your name using one finger at a time like that."

Del gave her a sharp this-is-not-a-joke look. "Someone went in and jammed a screwdriver up into some of those sensors. That's what it looked like to me."

"Why would someone do that?"

"That's my question. We got sensors all over the place now, telling the central control system what's happening on the grid. The controller gets bad data, it'll make bad decisions. Cause another outage. And I sure as hell don't want to work no more twenty-hour days."

"You want sugar in your tea?" Carried pulled the electric kettle from its base and poured his tea.

"It'll keep me up."

"Who do you send the report to?"

"Security and the field operations office. I want to know who the hell's doing this stuff."

"You think it's one of the out-of-state crews?"

"It couldn't be one of our folks. Least, I hope not."

# 42

July 6

"Hey, babe!"

"Hi, Sean." Danielle's voice was flat, devoid of its usual enthusiasm.

"You okay?" Sean sounded surprised and concerned. He had never heard her sound down or defeated.

"I didn't sleep well."

"Everything all right?"

"I don't know."

"I was wondering if you were working from home today. I thought maybe we could grab lunch."

"No." She sat on the edge of the bed, trying to rub the sleep from her eyes. "I have to go in to the office." That was a lie. She wanted to go to the office because then she'd be farther from him. She wouldn't run into him when she did go to lunch.

"Did something happen?"

"No. Just, um, bad sleep, you know? And I was up late cleaning. And I have a full schedule today."

"Maybe I'll catch you after work, then?"

"Maybe." She didn't sound eager to see him.

"Are you sure you're okay?"

"No, Sean! No, I'm not. Are you sure *you're* okay?"

Before he could respond to that, she hung up. When he called her back, she didn't answer.

What had gotten into her, he wondered?

Looking out through his office window, he saw a black SUV roll past for the third time. Either it had been circling the block, or there were three identical black SUVs in the neighborhood.

Maybe that's what had gotten into her. Maybe someone had questioned her about him. Who?

He thought back to the white Ford Escape parked in front of his house the day before. He had watched it follow

Danielle's car out of the neighborhood. Maybe that was who questioned her. If so, what would they have asked? And what information would she have to offer?

The book! He had sent her into the store to buy the software book because he didn't want to leave a digital trail by buying it online, and he didn't want the store clerk or anyone else to be able to describe him. But in covering his own tracks, he had put her at risk.

A wave of remorse washed over him, settling in his stomach as a leaden weight. He sat on the edge of his desk and thought, Oh, God, Danielle, I'm sorry! I never should have dragged you into this. I should never have gotten *myself* into this. So what if Ray is evil? This was none of my business. I should have turned it over to Empire security, or to the auditor, or to the Feds.

But he had already worked through those options. The security officer at Empire was one of Ray's buddies. A member of the doom-and-gloom, end-of-the-world cult that went out to dinner on Thursday nights. Reporting to him would have no effect except to tip Ray off that someone was onto him.

And he *did* tell the auditors, the ones whose task was to make sure Empire abided by federal safety standards for critical energy infrastructure. The auditor responded with indifference.

"The code you're objecting to is part of the test suite. It never touches the production system, so what's the problem?"

"Code like that shouldn't be anywhere in the code base," Sean told him.

The auditor agreed the code looked strange, but said it could pose no immediate threat from its location in the test suite. He flagged it for further review, marked the ticket as low priority, and queued it at the end of a list of issues that would take months to wade through.

Sean tried to delete the code himself and then was fired.

Now his inability to let go of the problem had drawn him into a world of trouble. Worse yet, he had dragged Danielle into it, into a matter in which she was entirely innocent. He had betrayed her trust, and she was justifiably upset.

If the person who followed her in the Ford Escape yesterday really did question her, it must have blindsided her. That would explain her sudden coldness.

You can't do this to her, Sean told himself. You can't.

And you can't undo it either.

Outside the window, the white Ford Escape he had seen the day before rolled into view. Behind it, two black SUVs.

They have their warrant, he thought. And I have that damn thumb drive with all the source code in my pocket.

He picked up a pencil from his desk and wrote on a slip of paper:

Username: sriggs
Password: a-just-w0rld!

He dropped the paper onto the laptop and picked up his keys and the old Android phone, just as the men and women began to exit the SUVs. They weren't dressed in raid gear. That meant they weren't expecting him to resist.

He put the old phone in his pocket, grabbed his backpack from under the desk, and slid the heavy software manual inside. He pushed his arms through the straps, walked back through the kitchen and out the rear door, leaving his regular phone on the desk. Outside, he fired up the old Suzuki and swung the bike around the corner of the house just in time to pass two agents making their way around to cover the back door.

He hit the street in second gear and turned hard right. The Escape and two SUVs were pointed in the same direction. The agents, including Anya, got back into their vehicles to give chase. As he reached the end of the following block, he could see them in his rearview mirror. The SUVs had flashing lights above their dashboards. The white Escape was in front, leading the charge.

The pursuers gained on him even as he gunned the engine. It didn't matter. In a few seconds, he would reach the entrance to the wooded trail. Approaching the T and the end of the street, he slowed the bike. The big knobbies and tough front shocks of the Suzuki rolled over the curb onto the narrow dirt path beneath the power lines. The low-riding Escape behind him hit the curb hard enough to bend the steering rods, rolled forward a few dozen yards, swaying back and forth, and then blocked the SUVs from entering the cut.

Sean watched them shrink in the rearview as he headed for the right turn ahead, the one that led into a narrower cut where the SUVs would not have been able to follow, even if the white Escape hadn't blocked them.

Ninety seconds later, he emerged into a cul-de-sac with a house on either side. He gunned the bike two blocks east, then turned left and headed for the interstate.

# 43

"Where the hell are you, Ray?"

Ray Cooper, sitting in a leather chair in his semidark basement, pressed the phone to his ear. "Why do you care?"

Why did anyone care about anything?

"Are you coming in today?" Cy Madhi asked.

"Why should I?"

Ray pointed the gun at the sewing mannequin he had dressed in his wife's favorite orange sundress. The first shot he had put through its heart had knocked it down. After standing it back up against the wall, he had switched from the .45 to the nine millimeter. The less powerful Glock could pump five or six bullets into her abdomen before she began to swivel and fall. She would feel those. She would feel them and she would know she was going to die, and then he could watch her be scared and he could ask her if her betrayal was worth it. He wanted her to understand why she was dying. He wanted her to feel the pain of remorse.

But Cy Madhi, the stupid ass, wanted to talk about work.

"If you're not coming in, you should call," Cy said.

"Who are you?" Ray asked bitterly. "My mother?"

Ray sent a bullet through the mannequin's right breast, the first shot he had fired since answering Cy's call.

"What the hell was that?" Cy asked, alarmed.

"Car backfired."

"That wasn't a car. What are you doing, Ray?"

"Why are you calling me, Cy?"

"I wanted to tell you the investigators have a lead on the breach."

"Well, whoop-de-do!" He squeezed the trigger again and the gun clicked. Had he not fully loaded the magazine? He slid it out to check.

"They're looking at a software developer who used to report to you. A guy named Sean Riggs."

"He's a little shit."

"You don't sound good, Ray."

"I don't feel good. I'm not coming in today. Tell the boss I'm sick."

"You are the boss, Ray."

"That's right," he said slowly. "Thank you for recognizing that."

He hung up, picked up the box of ammo from the table beside him, reloaded the magazine, and slid it back into the grip.

He walked to the mannequin and said, "Do you remember when you met me, Donna?"

He shot it through the left shoulder. The mannequin spun and fell at his feet.

"You were pretty young, pretty clueless about the world."

He pointed the gun at the mannequin's belly.

"You didn't know then that you were looking for a guide. A master, of sorts. But you found me. That's how the Lord works. He guides you to what you need. You look up to me, and I look up to Him. That's the chain of command. It took you awhile to learn that. A hard lesson, I guess. But you bore my corrections well. Like the Lord himself does to all of us, I took you to your limit, but not beyond. You learned your lessons well, and you fell into line eventually. Only, it was all a lie."

He pumped four bullets into the belly of the prostrate mannequin. The shots sent fragments of concrete flying through the room. Some of them came up through the cuff of his pants and cut into his shins. One nicked his face beneath the chin, and one left a thin trail of blood beside his right eye.

"You were lying all this time, deceiving me. Making a mockery of your vows, of what God had joined together, of all the work I put into you. You were waiting for your moment to spring it on me. The big betrayal.

"Well, it's okay, Donna. I admit, it hurts, but in the end, the Lord squares all accounts. You'll pay your penalty, and you're not going to like it."

He shot twice more. Two bullets in the waist, and a spray of concrete pocked his right arm with little bloody holes.

"You'll have plenty of time to think about it then. An eternity of time. And remember, the boy's soul is on your account too. As his mother, you're supposed to look out for him. Not take him away from God and master. Did you think about that when you packed the car?"

Another bullet. Another spray of concrete.

He walked back to the chair, laid the gun on the table, and sat thinking, scratching his chin, not noticing he was smearing blood from the cuts the concrete had inflicted.

"In a way, I almost can't blame you," he said. "Being a woman, your mind is susceptible to many influences. And look at the world we live in. People worship everything *but* God. They worship money. They worship power. They worship comfort and luxury and movie stars and glamour. They're mesmerized by movies of men screwing their friend's wives, watching little college whores in bars prostitute themselves to half-wit athletes. And no one ever stops to think, is this right? Is this really how we should be living? Is it right in the eyes of the Almighty?"

He paused and looked indifferently at his bloodied arm.

"No," he said. "It isn't right. The Lord gave us the freedom to act as we please and a set of rules to act as would please Him. He threw us out on the stony path, and He left it up to us to make our mistakes and find our way back home.

"We've all made mistakes, Donna. Even me. I freely admit it. The difference between the ones headed for the fire and ones bound for glory is that the glorious do the hard work of discovering and correcting their errors. Meanwhile, the great mass of humanity plods on, indifferent to their eternal fate, looking only for the next thrill.

"Eventually time runs out. It runs out on us all, Donna. We don't think it will, but it does. On whole civilizations, time runs out. Rome fell to dust, and a hundred civilizations after them, countries that lost track of what was important, forgot who they should be grateful to, who was worthy of their worship.

"Time's up, Donna, and not just for you. It was actually supposed to be up two weeks ago. The time bomb was set to go off, but then the Lord himself intervened. He has a way of doing that when the stakes are high. The little project that would have detonated the time bomb, at the substation not too many miles from here, was put on hold because of the hurricanes. Two of them, back-to-back, Donna. In late June, no less. What are the odds of that? Huh? In a normal year, hurricane season doesn't ramp up until September.

"But God doesn't care about odds. He makes them. Did you know that the law calls hurricanes 'acts of God'? It's true. Read your insurance policies.

"He sent those storms as a final warning. He took away power from millions of people. Made them suffer in the heat. Made them scrounge for food. Why?

"To remind them that they're dependent on Him. To remind them from whence all blessings flow. That should have been a wake-up call to the millions of people affected. They should have flocked back to church as soon as the lights came on.

"But did they? I didn't see it.

"And where are we now? The situation now, my sweet, is that if this happens again—*when* this happens again—the utilities won't have the equipment they need to fix what's about to break. They used it all up after the hurricanes, and they won't be able to get more for months. Years, maybe.

"Think about that for a moment. An eleven-day outage in high heat killed three thousand people. People looted and stole. In some places, they fought each other for food.

"That's what eleven days did. Peeled away the veneer of civilization. Showed what animals we are underneath.

"Now, imagine those eleven days stretching into months on a grid that can't be repaired because the parts are no longer available. Imagine how people will act then.

"And think about this, Donna. Think how perfectly God set this up. After two weeks of dry heat, the state is parched. The forests are ready to burn. When the transmission lines overheat—and they will in this heat wave, believe me! I've seen to it that they will! When the molten wires hit the kindling of the underlying brush, it will all go up in flames.

"How are the firefighters going to stop that, Donna? Did you think about that when you ran away? When you stole my son? They can't pump water without electricity, so how are they going to put out the fires?

"They can't, Donna. The Bible says so. The fires of hell cannot be quenched.

"And what about all the people living in that heat? Over a hundred degrees for each of the next seven days. We were only in the high nineties when three thousand geezers kicked off. If the elderly and infirm couldn't handle ninety-five, they're not going to survive a hundred four.

"Think of the stench, Donna, the stench of all those bodies rotting under an indifferent sun. The gas stations will run dry, and the ambulances won't be able to haul them all off. Where would they put them anyway?

"How do you think people will behave when the world around them is burning and the bodies of their family members are rotting, stinking to high heaven, and there's nothing to eat? That's when people will understand that hell is right here on earth.

"And I know what you're thinking, Donna. That help will come in from other states. That the Feds will rush in and save everyone."

Ray shook his head and stroked his chin.

"No. This last outage depleted the Feds, trying to serve tens of millions of people across so many states. They haven't had time to restock. And the other states, the ones everyone thinks will be able to help, they won't. I've seen to that too, Donna. God gave me the foresight and the connections to cover that. Ohio will be just as bad off as Virginia. Illinois, Michigan, they'll be dark too.

"Too bad you'll never meet those connections. I was going to take you up to the cabin and introduce you. If you had stuck around, I had a little paradise laid out for us out up there.

Quiet, peaceful, loaded with everything we'd need to ride out the terror unfolding below.

"All that, I laid out for you. And all that, you rejected."

He paused and thought awhile, his eyes glistening in the semidark.

"Sometimes I wonder if your leaving wasn't for the best. The Lord does everything for a reason. You just have to trust and know it's so.

"I saw a little woman at the office yesterday, young and firm and fertile, and I started thinking, who's going to populate this new world? After the idolators starve and kill each other off, after diseases wipe them out, how will the elect replenish the earth?

"Funny, isn't it? That that's what I started thinking about just as this plump little fertility goddess appears in front of me. And still, I don't put two and two together till the next day: my wife left, and a new woman was shown to me, one who could bear more children for His glory. This is what I mean, Donna, when I say that none of us is perfect. God was talking to me yesterday, but still, I didn't hear. Devoted and loyal as I am, I didn't get the message till it was too late."

He pushed himself up from the chair and walked to the stairs, leaving the gun on the table. It wasn't the right gun for the job he had to do next, the job of supervising the launch of his grand project.

"Tomorrow will be the day," he said as his foot landed with a thud on the first wooden step. "It's in the ticket system, in Empire's work queue. I just have to nudge them to make it a priority, to make sure it happens tomorrow."

At the top of the stairs, he stopped and turned around. "I'm not leaving this one to chance either. Not even with my loyal boy assigned to the task. I'll be there to supervise from afar, the way God himself does. I'll make sure it goes down right."

He put his hand on the edge of the door and, peering down the steps, he concluded, "Goodbye, Donna. Sorry it didn't work out. You'll get used to the dark down there. In a million years, it'll feel like home."

He shut the door gently and went up to second floor to find his rifle.

# 44

Sean parked the motorcycle on the ground level of a public parking garage and walked a quarter mile to the garage where he'd left his neighbor's Mustang. He retrieved the keys from beneath the seat and cranked the old engine to life. It was half past eight when he hit the street. He headed straight for Danielle's office.

Was she in yet? If he had had his regular phone with him, he could have called. But the regular phone was on his desk at home. Her number wasn't in the backup, and without a SIM card, the backup couldn't make calls anyway.

When he reached the block she worked on, he slowed the car and scanned the street for police cruisers, black SUVs, white Ford Escapes, any vehicles sitting at the curb with drivers still inside. After a minute or so, he decided it was impossible to identify all potential threats. The more he looked for danger, the more he stoked his paranoia.

They don't know where to look for me, he reminded himself, or what kind of car I'm driving. Their only chance is if they see my face. I'll steer clear of cop cars and focus on Danielle.

Rolling slowly past her office, he looked through the window of the first-floor conference room. She had been sitting there last time he came by. Now the room was empty. That made sense at eight thirty-five a.m.

He turned left, rounded the block, and was approaching the office again when he wondered whether it was worth the risk of pulling into an open spot on the street and waiting. If he wanted to catch her on her way into the office, his best chance would be to watch the office door. That was the only place she would be certain to pass.

There was no sign of her on this go-round, so he turned right and looped around again. What if I missed her, he wondered? What if she walked in while I was on another street?

He decided to pull into a spot across the street, then regretted it almost instantly when he saw a patrol car approaching in his side mirror. He pulled out before the cop reached him, drove to the intersection, and turned right. He watched in the rearview as the cop went straight through the intersection behind him and disappeared.

Then, half a block down, he saw her white Mazda turn right into a lot. He drove to the end of the block and made a U-turn in the intersection. When he returned, he saw her walking out of the lot, dressed in jeans and a white V-neck T-shirt with a backpack slung over her shoulder. Why the backpack? He had seen her go to work before with only a shoulder bag.

Her hair was down. Big smoke-colored sunglasses covered her eyes. She was frowning, walking toward him, not recognizing the Mustang, not knowing he was there.

She turned onto the sidewalk and now she was in front of him, walking away. His left hand went to the armrest on the driver's door in search of the switch to open the passenger window. When his fingers couldn't find it, he looked.

Right. 1967 Mustang. You had to crank the windows down by hand. That meant leaning across the passenger seat and—screw it.

He hit the gas to catch up. She turned at the sound of the growling engine, her face still frowning.

He passed her, shifted into park, left the engine running, jumped out, and ran to her.

"Danielle, I need your help!"

Her frown turned into a big, warm smile, then faded back to sadness and anger.

"For what? To blow up the electric grid?"

"I'm in trouble."

"I'll say." She tried to walk past him, but he grabbed her shoulder and turned her to him.

"Look, I'm sorry I dragged you into this, but I'm kind of freaking out right now, and I need your help."

"How could I possibly help you?" she asked coldly.

"I think I have this almost cracked—"

"Blowing up the grid?" she asked sarcastically.

"Hear me out, okay. I'm sorry if I hurt your feelings, but there's something bigger going on here."

"You're crazy." Again, she tried to push past him. Again, he stopped her. He saw her face harden, her anger rising.

"What the hell do you want from me, Sean?"

"Ten minutes of your time. Will you get in the car and give me ten minutes to explain?"

She turned and looked at the Mustang. "Where did you get that?"

"It's the neighbor's car."

"You stole it?"

"I didn't steal it."

"So, they said you could take it?"

"No. Well, kind of."

Her eyes narrowed, and in her angry, determined expression he could see that when faced with the choice to fight or flee, she was the type who would fight.

"You know, I really liked you, Sean Riggs." She punched the heel of her hand so hard into his chest, it knocked him backward. She took a step forward to stay right on top of him. "I *really* liked you, and now I just feel stupid for spending all that time with you. I've never felt so stupid and humiliated and ashamed in my life. I thought by now I had learned enough to spot the red flags, but I guess I'm not as smart as I thought. I still don't see them. Except for you. Your whole face is a red flag to me now. Your whole stupid face and you stalking me on the street in a stolen car. How could I be so fucking stupid? I hate you!"

She marched past him, frowning in anger and disgust, her eyes pained. He grabbed her again and didn't let go.

"Let go of me!"

"Please get in the car. Please talk to me. Give me ten minutes."

"Talk out here."

Sean looked down the street, then back at her. "I can't talk out here. I'm on the run. The cops will be looking for me."

"What the hell did you do, Sean?"

"That's what I want to talk to you about."

She saw the fear and doubt in his eyes, the same feelings that had tormented her through the night, the same feelings that had attacked her the moment she awoke. Only he looked worse. She pitied him. In his eyes she still saw everything she liked about him: intelligence, kindness, decency, warmth. Against reason and her better judgment, she wanted to give him a chance.

"Five minutes, Sean. And then you drop me in front of the office."

"Thank you!" He let go of her arm.

On the way to the car, she said, "And by the way, I have a gun."

He would have laughed if he wasn't so tense. Why would she say something as ridiculous as that? Did she really feel she needed a weapon to protect herself from him?

When they got inside, she gave the interior a quick inspection. "Cool seats! I like the leather. And that dash! The old-fashioned speedometer. What's all that in the back?"

"My neighbor coaches high school sports."

He put the car in gear and headed north. Danielle pulled her hair back with both hands to cool the matted sweat, then let it fall again to her shoulders.

"Okay, Sean, spill it."

"It's a long story. I don't know if I can tell it all in five minutes."

"You hacked into the electric company. Start there. Why'd you do that?"

"Turn off your phone."

"What?"

"Turn your phone off, so the cops can't track us."

"No! Why did you hack the electric company?"

"Because I think someone is trying to sabotage the grid."

"Who? You?"

"A guy I used to work with."

"Uh-huh." Her tone told him she wasn't buying any of this. "So instead of going to security or blowing the whistle, you take it on yourself to hack in?"

"I tried to go to security, and I did blow the whistle. I brought it to the attention of the auditors."

"So, why didn't they fix it? Four minutes, Sean. That's how much time you have left."

"Because it's too subtle. The attack is too subtle. They couldn't put the pieces together."

"But you could?" She still wasn't buying it.

"Almost. I think I know what the code does now."

"You think?" she mocked.

"I mean, I think I might be starting to get it."

"Because I got you that book? You took advantage of me for sex and then you dragged me into this stupid mess by sending me to the bookstore on the most innocent-looking errand. That's who you are, isn't it, Sean? All innocence on the surface, all rotten at the core. A liar, and a convincing one too."

"Excuse me? I took advantage of you for sex? You threw yourself at me!"

"Is that really what you want to argue about right now? Three minutes."

Seeing a police car approaching in the other lane, Sean turned the Mustang right and headed into a residential neighborhood.

He took a deep breath and said, "Okay, yes. The book helped me figure it out. Long story short, this code will take over the grid-control system and raise the voltage on the lines until they melt."

"Ugh!" She rolled her eyes, not believing a word of it.

"And it does more than that. I can't explain it all in three minutes."

"Two and a half."

"And I still can't figure out how it actually gets access to the control systems. It's in the test code, not in the production code."

"So, you want me to look at it? You want me to figure it out? Because I'm the software expert?"

He hit the brakes, and she jolted forward. "No! No, Danielle. I'm freaking out because something really bad is going to happen. I'm within an inch of figuring it out, and now the cops want to lock me up."

"You should have thought of that before you started playing hacker."

"I told you, I tried to go through the proper channels, but without being able to describe how it all worked, no one would listen to me."

"You're whining, do you know that? I can't stand guys who whine. The reason I was attracted to you in the first place was because whenever I saw you out in public, you seemed confident and decisive, like you had a purpose. And now you're just whiny and pathetic. But thank you for showing me this side of you. It makes it a lot easier for me to walk away."

Sean pressed his forehead against the steering wheel and cupped his hands over his face. He began to sob.

"Oh, God, don't do that." Danielle was exasperated, beyond done. She turned and looked away from him, through the passenger window at the quiet houses where people who lived ordinary lives were spared the drama of flash romances with closet psychopaths.

She made no effort to comfort him, checking the time on her phone every few seconds until his sobbing stopped.

When he was calm, he turned the car around and headed back to her office. They drove in silence for several minutes until at last he said, "Thank you for listening. Thank you for hearing me out."

She nodded and said softly, "Sure."

A minute later, as they rolled up in front of her building, she turned to take one last look at the man who had brought a few days of unexpected joy into her hot, boring summer.

"It was nice knowing you, Sean."

"Yeah. You take care." His voice was flat, his eyes fixed on the road ahead to avoid looking at her. She could see he was holding back emotion. She could feel his sadness and his fear.

She held the door handle for a moment, not yet ready to open it. "So, what are you going to do now?" she asked softly.

He shrugged. "I don't know. Turn myself in? Try to get the Feds to understand what's going on here. But I don't think I could bring anyone up to speed on this in time for them to work it all out."

He turned and looked at her. "When I took this to the auditor at Empire, they put it on the back burner, at the end of a queue of tickets that will take months to resolve. The Feds' first concern will be to lock me up. They're focused on the breach, not on the bigger threat I'm looking at. They may begin to understand it in a week, a month, six months. By then I think it will be too late."

She watched him quietly, as pity and true compassion contended in her heart. "You're really wrapped up in this, huh?"

"How can I not be? Look at what the state just went through. Now imagine that happening again, lasting for months this time, with even more damage."

She thought quietly for a moment, then in a soft voice, she said, "What did you come here to ask me, Sean? What was it you wanted?"

"First, to apologize. I'm sorry I got you involved in this. I'm sorry for the worry and fear I caused. I'm sorry I gave you reason to doubt me. I'm sorry I made you doubt yourself. I never wanted to hurt you."

"Apology accepted."

"And I wanted you to come with me."

"Where?"

"I don't know. Away from here. Away from the pressure of the Feds—"

The sincerity of his words and the desperation in his eyes still had the power to move her. She turned her head away, looked at the entrance to the office, to avoid having to see him and to avoid letting him see that she was wavering. Part of her wanted to shut her ears to his entreaties; part of her wanted to help him. She leaned forward to gather her backpack from the floor, and as she straightened, her eyes caught a glimpse of the passenger-side mirror. What she saw there sparked fear in her heart. She was scared for him, though she didn't want to be.

What to do, she asked herself? What to do, Danielle? Do you really want to trust this person? Do you really want him to be the person you thought he was in the few days of happiness you shared? Her heart and body answered the question before her mind could weigh in.

"Put the car in gear," she said.

"What?"

"That SUV coming toward us—if they're looking for you, they'd start with me, wouldn't they? Why else would they come by my office?" She turned her phone off.

He put the car in gear and pulled into the driving lane.

"Continue," she said. "Why did you want me to go with you?"

"Because I'm on the verge of cracking this. Because when I can lay it all out to the investigators—how this whole thing works, from beginning to end—then they'll have to take action. They'll see there's a real, imminent threat, a time bomb with dire consequences, and they'll have to do something."

Danielle nodded. Her face was blank, too exhausted from the emotions of yesterday, last night, this morning, to register much of anything anymore.

"And how do I help in that picture?" Sean could hear the exhaustion in her voice.

"As an extra pair of eyes." Sean looked up into the rearview, watched the SUV stop at the curb in front of Danielle's office. "Like you did just now. And as an anchor of sanity. I start to freak out when I'm alone. This is all overwhelming, and I'm barely keeping myself together. You're like a balm. A soothing balm of sanity."

"Funny you say that," she said softly. "I've thought the same of you. You have that effect on me."

"So, what I'm asking is for twenty-four hours. If I can't figure this out by lunch tomorrow, then I'll turn myself in. Let the Feds figure it out."

She turned to look at him. "You mean that? You'll turn yourself in?"

"I mean it," he said.

They drove in silence for a moment. As they approached a sign for the interstate, Danielle pointed left.

"What?" Sean asked.

"The highway."

"You want me to get on?"

"Go west. To the mountains."

Sean put on his turn signal. On the way up the ramp, he said, "Does this mean you're in?"

"It means I'm thinking, and I don't want you to get caught before I've decided."

"You can say I kidnapped you. That would clear you of being an accomplice."

"You'd go to prison for that."

"I'm going to prison anyway."

"I hope not. I'd miss you."

"I'd miss you too."

"Besides, the kidnapping excuse wouldn't stick. I'm the one with the gun."

"What's all this about a gun?" Sean asked impatiently. "What makes you think you need to bluff? Do you honestly think I'd hurt you?"

She pulled the revolver from the backpack between her feet and pointed it at him.

He had to turn his head and look to be sure what he saw was right. "Jesus! Don't point that thing at me!"

"It's not a bluff, Sean. It's an actual twenty-two. And why do you look so scared? Do you honestly think I'd hurt you?"

"Put it down!"

"Uh-huh," she said, to prove her point. "It's different when you're worrying about your own safety, isn't it? The Feds had me scared you were a psychopath. So yeah, I brought my gun.

Just in case you did something crazy, like, you know... stole a car and stalked me on my way to work. You have to learn to think like a woman, Sean."

She slid the gun back into the backpack. "Twenty-four hours, Sean. I'll take your word that you're not going to assault me, and you'll take my word that I won't shoot you. You mind if I ask a few more questions?"

"Go ahead. It's not like I have anything else to do."

They looked ahead at the long expanse of highway running west toward the hills and mountains.

"What put you on this quest to save the world?"

"If you asked my mom, she would say my disposition. According to her, I was born for trouble and always too curious. If you ask me, I'd say a code smell."

"A code smell?"

"That's what programmers call code that gives you a gut feeling that something isn't right. This code looked malicious."

"Uh-huh," she said coldly. "Did you ever think you were just being paranoid?"

"Of course. But then I learned a little something that made the paranoia go away."

"And what was that?"

"That the code was written by a malicious person who tried to cover his tracks."

"And who is this bad guy, Sean?"

"A guy named Ray Cooper."

Her eyes widened and a chill went down her spine at the mention of the name. She had seen Ray in the conference room less than twenty-four hours ago glaring at her with unmistakable malice. She could see the dark thoughts roiling behind his sunken, red-rimmed eyes, like magma churning in the crater of a rumbling volcano. His presence oozed psychosis, malevolence, and hatred.

"Ray Cooper," she said, turning to Sean. "Dirty blond hair? Blue eyes? About forty years old?"

"Yeah. How did you know that?"

"I saw him yesterday."

"Sounds like he made an impression."

"He did."

"Where'd you see him?"

"In the office at Empire. He was glaring at me. He was—honestly, if I was walking alone at night and he was behind me, I'd fear for my life."

"I don't know if he's that bad. He's definitely an asshole."

"You don't know if he's that bad, but you think he's bad enough to want to destroy the power grid? You're not a woman, Sean. You wouldn't catch the same vibe from him that a woman does. I think he's unhinged. There is something very, very dark in him."

"What makes you say that?"

"When I was leaving the Empire offices yesterday, a police car pulled up. The cop got out angry, ready for a fight. He pushed Ray with his club, and the two of them yelled at each other."

"What was that about?"

"I don't know. I was too upset to process the words. But what had Ray done to make the cop so angry? And why didn't he back down when the cop shouted at him? There's something violent in that man. It's deep and it's powerful, and it seems like he's ready to explode. I could sense it. On a primal, animal level, I could sense it, and it scared me."

# 45

"So, he got away?" said Agent Espinoza. He was standing in the door of Anya's temporary office in Empire's headquarters, part of the suite the company had opened up to members of the investigative task force.

"For now," Anya said. "He won't get far. We issued a bulletin. The State Patrol is looking for him."

"Looking for him where?" Espinoza sipped his coffee. "In what vehicle? With whom?"

"Unknown vehicle. Unknown location. Possibly with Danielle Duval. Her phone is turned off, but according to her cell provider, its last known location was at her office. Her coworkers say she never entered the building."

"You think she's colluding?"

"I don't know. She was pretty upset when I questioned her yesterday. She obviously has feelings for the guy. It's a shame to see a young woman get into a situation like that. Sometimes they want to protect the guy they should be running from."

"So, you think Riggs is your man?"

"Why else would he run?"

"Panic. Guy's thirty-two years old. Never been arrested. It's kind of scary when the Feds show up at your house."

"Not if you have nothing to hide."

"Okay, what's his motive? Understand, I'm playing devil's advocate here. I know what you wrote in the warrant request. I'm just asking you to clarify. He doesn't seem to be after money. He's doing okay on that front. He doesn't adhere to any radical ideology. No association with extremist groups. We traced his contacts. No known foreign agents. What's he after, then?"

"I don't know." The undertone of frustration in her voice was unmistakable.

"You get his computer?"

"Yeah. He actually wrote his username and password on a note before he left. Made it easy for us. We're still digging into the laptop and the backup drives."

Espinoza nodded. "You fill out the forms yet on that Ford you wrecked?"

"I didn't wreck it. I just hit a curb too fast. It's fixable."

"Those forms suck," Espinoza said as he turned to leave. "Give yourself a good forty-five minutes to plow through them."

When he left, Anya turned her attention back to her computer. What could she do now but wait? She had sent a message to a coworker asking where to find the form for the damaged car. Now she was waiting for a response. She had watched members of the task force seize Sean's computer equipment. Now she was waiting for forensics to analyze it. She had put out the bulletin on Sean Riggs. Thirty-two-year-old white male. Tall, thin, dark brown hair. Unknown location, possibly riding a motorcycle, possibly not. Possibly accompanied by a twenty-eight-year-old white female. Five foot five, one hundred forty-five pounds? Ish? Light brown hair, hazel eyes. Now what?

Just wait. Just sit here and... Wasn't there *something* she could do?

She leaned back in her chair and thought back to yesterday's interview with Ray Cooper. Ray was struggling to hold himself together as dark thoughts possessed his mind. She thought back to the cop in the parking lot. He yelled at Ray because Ray had threatened another cop.

Ray's wife had left him. He was angry, wounded. He looked like he was disintegrating. It sounded like he had unloaded some of that anger on the cop's fellow officer. The cop gave him a pass because it was a domestic dispute. Those are always messy. Emotions are high. A man loses his wife, he's hurting. She could feel it during the interview, rage and hurt and hostility radiating like heat from the skin above an angry, swollen wound.

I don't wonder why she left, Anya thought. How could anyone live with a man like that?

She thought back to the nasty write-ups Ray had given Sean Riggs. Those were the work of a vengeful, ill-tempered person, the words dripping with venom. HR should have recognized the bias in those write-ups, the unprofessional language. They should have taken a look at Ray. His reports showed the hostility of a spurned lover. What could Sean Riggs have done to provoke such bitterness?

Maybe Ray always had this streak of malice in him. Maybe it wasn't just his wife's leaving that brought it out. Maybe it was why she left. Spouses don't abandon a marriage without provocation or enticement.

Anya thought of the cabin in West Virginia. Ray had poured a lot of work and money into his little retreat from the world. He had added solar panels and stocked it with canned food, as if anticipating a long stay.

And that neighbor! That hostile, aggressive neighbor! He had threatened her both verbally and physically when she had her back against the wall there at the cabin, when he followed her as she backed out of the gravel drive, his hand hovering by his gun.

Anya picked up her phone. She pulled up the video she had taken when she drove in along the unpaved mountain road and watched it for the first time. She fast-forwarded past the deer. There, in the first drive, sat one pickup truck with Ohio plates. In the second drive, a truck from Michigan.

She rewound the video, paused on a still of the first truck and zoomed in. The letters and numbers on the tag were blurry but after pausing and unpausing the video, moving to different stills, she could make them out. She pulled a notepad from the edge of the desk and wrote down the plate number. Then she did the same with the Michigan tags.

Why, she wondered, had they all installed solar panels? Why did the neighbor feel he had to defend Ray's property? Why had he specifically called her out for representing the US government?

*What business do you have with Ray?* That's what the man had asked her. Now that she thought of it, it was an excellent question, one she could just as well have posed to the man who had threatened her. What business do *you* have with Ray?

She typed her password into her laptop and clicked through to the database that would give her the information she wanted. She typed in the number of the first license plate, then wrote the name and address of the registered owner onto her notepad. She did the same with the second.

She opened a second database and looked up the names. Neither man had a criminal record. Both had passed the background checks that allowed them to buy firearms. That was as much as the government's system could tell her.

What about social media? The man who had confronted her outside Ray's cabin didn't seem very social. Not the type to post selfies on Instagram. But if he worked, he might be on LinkedIn.

In a minute, she had found his profile. Oddly, he too worked in the energy industry, as a supervisor in the transmission-and-distribution center of a major electric utility in Ohio. In his photo, he looked friendly and professional. An engineering type in a white short-sleeve button-down with a pen in the breast pocket.

She wasn't alarmed until she found the Michigan man's profile. He too worked in energy, he too in the operations center that controlled a state power grid.

And the three of them happened to have houses on the same remote road in rural West Virginia, houses with solar panels to survive off the grid. If the two houses she didn't examine were like Ray's, they had cisterns to capture rainwater. They were stocked with canned food for a long stay. They were occupied by hostile, defensive, armed men.

# 46

"Okay," Danielle said. "So, explain it to me again. What does the code do?"

They were now over an hour west of Richmond, in view of the Blue Ridge mountains. Sean had turned south off the interstate onto rural Route 29.

"It waits for an input. It encrypts the input, and if the encrypted input matches a certain value, then it starts issuing commands to the grid-control system."

"Why would it encrypt the value?"

"To make it hard for people reading the code to understand what value it's waiting for."

"Why would the person who wrote the code want to make it hard to understand?"

"Exactly," Sean said. "Why? The encrypted value is some kind of key. It's the trigger that sets the whole thing in motion. If it's encrypted, if no one can read it, then no one knows what will set this thing off."

They were rumbling along now at sixty miles an hour through horse pastures, woods, and rolling hills. The air outside was a few degrees cooler than the air in Richmond, but still hot.

"All right, so this code receives some input that matches the encrypted secret. Then what?"

"Then it records the entire state of the grid for fifteen minutes. All the data coming in from all the sensors on every component throughout the state of Virginia. It records the temperature on the transmission wires, whether each breaker is open or closed, which relays have been tripped, the input and output voltage of all the transformers."

"What's the point of that?"

"Once it captures the data, it feeds it back into the main control center. At that point, the operators in the control center are seeing a recording of a stable electrical grid."

"Why? What's the point?"

"To set up for the next step," Sean said. "In the next step, it issues commands to all the variable-rate transformers, telling them to jump the voltage to one hundred percent."

"Is that bad?"

"Normally not. The big lines are rated to carry half a million volts. They have no problem with that in cold weather. In hot weather, the lines are derated, meaning the amount of voltage they can safely carry is dialed down. You ever look at an old Edison bulb? Or an electric stove?"

"I have an electric stove."

"What happens when you turn it on?"

"It gets hot."

"Right. Electricity running through metal makes the metal hot. The filament in a bulb gets so hot it glows white. A stove turns red. The bulb is running at a hundred twenty volts. The stove runs at two hundred twenty. The big power lines on those high metal towers run at five hundred thousand. That's a lot of voltage and a lot of heat. In winter, the utility company can run them at full throttle. The air is cold enough to dissipate the heat. In summer, they can't. The hotter the weather, the further they have to dial down the volts."

"Or what?"

"Or the lines start to sag and melt. If they sag, they'll touch a tree branch or something else to ground them out. The sparks from that are enough to cause a fire. If the lines melt, they'll literally turn to molten metal and drip to the ground. Imagine that happening today. It hasn't rained in two weeks, and it's been roasting hot. The whole state is dry as a bone."

He pointed to the tall electrical towers whose lines crossed the road ahead. "Look where those go. Through the woods, over the mountains. There are thousands of miles of those lines across the state. Now imagine them all dripping molten metal into parched underbrush. Imagine every fire department in the state having to go on call at once to try to put that stuff out. It would be impossible."

He looked at her to see if she understood what he was saying. Her thoughtful look told him she was picturing it all in her mind.

"But there's something else in the code," he continued. "I wasn't able to figure out all the commands until you got me that book. Most of the important circuit breakers on the grid are now software controlled. The software constantly monitors the amount of current coming through. If voltage gets too high, the breakers trip and cut the power to everything downstream. They do that so the downstream equipment doesn't get damaged.

"This code I've been looking at opens all the breakers and instructs them to stay open, no matter how much current runs through. That's a deliberate act of sabotage. It means all the components the breakers are supposed to protect will get fried. This code was engineered to inflict maximum damage."

He turned again to look at her. Her focused expression told him she was taking it all in. He turned his eyes back to the road.

"When did you figure all this out?"

"Last night. When you said you didn't want to hang out, I stayed up late with the software manual, piecing it all together.

"Look at the state we're in now. Empire is struggling to clean up from these hurricanes. After all the damage the storms inflicted, how many spare components could they have left to repair the next catastrophe? Right now, they're probably depleted. And I imagine the surrounding states are too. Carolina, Maryland, Pennsylvania.

"This code will cause much more destruction than the storms because it was explicitly designed to do so. And Empire won't be able to fix it. Not for months. Maybe years.

"Think about what we just went through, all the people who just died. Think about having no job to go to for the next six months, not having a fridge or a stove, or a paycheck, going to the Walmart parking lot to get government handouts from the back of a truck. And you'll be walking there, by the way, because the gas station pumps won't work.

"How long do you think it will be before people are at each other's throats? Where will all the people go who were displaced by fires? It's going to be bad, and I have a feeling that whatever sets all this in motion is going to happen soon, because the whole attack depends on the heat. It depends on those lines being overvolted and sagging in hot weather. You could probably pick any day in an East Coast summer to launch this attack, but you couldn't pick a better day than one this week. The state is dry and ready to burn. We have a heat wave coming, and it's going to be a long one."

Danielle tried to calm her racing heart. Either Sean was insane or life for everyone was about to get really bad.

"So, if this is the case," she said, "why not alert the company now? Alert the investigators, or whoever."

"I'm going to soon. They're going to arrest me, you know. I think I'm the person in the best position to unravel this, but when they arrest me, I won't be able to do anything. I can spell it out for them, but it will take time for them to catch up, and by then it may be too late."

"But what's left to do? For you, I mean? You seem to have it figured out already."

"I don't. I still need to figure out how this code accesses the production systems. It's test code, remember? It's meant to do some sanity checks in a controlled test environment, and it never leaves that environment. It can't touch the actual grid, but it's written as if it can. If it can, I want to know how. Second, I want to figure what the secret input is that triggers the mayhem."

He took his eyes off the road for a second to gauge her reaction.

"You look scared," he said.

She hesitated, then slowly shook her head. "I don't know what to believe."

He put his hand on her knee to soothe her.

"Like I said. Give me twenty-four hours. If I can't figure it out by tomorrow morning, I give up. I turn myself in, hope they believe me, hope they look into it."

Danielle closed her eyes and hung her head and let out a sigh. "I don't know," she whispered. "I just don't know." And then, too softly for him to hear, she added, "Why did we have to come to this?"

# 47

Anya rewatched the videos of her interviews with Sean's coworkers, lingering on a single comment from a software tester who had worked with both Ray and Sean.

"Ray has, like, this group of followers. This little clique that looks up to him. Sean went out with those guys a few times, and then he stopped. After that, Ray started hating on him hard."

Could that have been the trigger that turned Ray against Sean? Had Ray tried to pull him into some trusted inner circle that Sean had then rejected?

She thought again of the cabins along the road in West Virginia. They belonged to survivalists. Could Ray's "little clique" within Empire Energy be a group of like-minded preppers? Was that the group Sean had rejected?

Anya pulled up her notes, found the name and phone number of the young man who had told her about Sean dropping out of Ray's group. She called him, reminded him who she was, and asked if he knew the names of the people Ray had surrounded himself with.

He gave her two: Charles Lehrman in IT security. And Kenny something. He worked on the dispatch team that assigned work crews to jobs out in the field. And then there were some field technicians, mostly younger guys. He remembered them, because it was unusual for the field guys to have much personal interaction with the office tech staff.

"All of them were men?" Anya asked.

"Come to think of it, yeah."

"But you don't know their names?"

"No. I mean, I think maybe one of the field techs was named Ben. I think? I don't know."

"Thank you."

After ending the call, Anya leaned forward and poked around on her laptop until she found the document she was looking for, Empire's internal report on Sean Riggs's employment activities. There wasn't much there. He had completed all his mandatory trainings. All of the code he had written had been approved and merged into the main code base. Some of his code-removal requests were rejected. Rejected by Ray Cooper.

After those rejections, Sean had opened a ticket in the IT request system about a security concern in some test code. Charles Lehrman in IT security closed the ticket without comment an hour later.

Sean then requested the code be reviewed by the company's external compliance auditor. The comments on the ticket showed the auditor had marked it as low priority and kicked it back to the internal security team, where Charles Lehrman had flagged it as invalid and closed it again.

She looked at the time stamp on the auditor's comments. He had marked the ticket as "investigating" at ten twelve a.m. on a Thursday, about three and a half months ago, just days before Sean was fired. At ten twenty-four that same day, the auditor added his second comment. "Strange code. Contains encrypted variables. Not suitable for production, but it's not in production. This is test code, so harmless. Remanding to internal security for follow-up with recommendation that developers should remove. Low priority because there's no risk of this code touching production systems."

It took her forty-five minutes to track down the auditor who had written those comments. When she had him on the line, she asked about the ticket. He couldn't remember it, so she read his comments back to him to refresh his memory.

"Oh, yeah. That one shouldn't have come to me. That one belonged to internal IT. I sent it back to them. Maybe you should check in there."

"IT closed it the day you remanded it."

"With no action?"

"With no action," she said.

"Yeah, well, it's test code. Not a big deal. Just needs to be cleaned up."

"Why would someone put encrypted data in test code?" she asked.

"I don't know. But it's out of my hands."

"Wait. One more question. Does test code get audited regularly?"

"Not so much," the man said. "Production code gets audited. Mistakes in production have consequences. Test code runs in an isolated environment against a simulated grid. It doesn't touch anything in the real world."

# 48

Mike Malinowski, the maintenance coordinator, looked up from his computer monitor when he heard the knock at the door.

"Come in," he called through a mouthful of ham sandwich. Then, recognizing the face, he added, "Hey, Ray. Cy told me you weren't coming in today."

"I changed my mind."

"Everything all right?" He laid his sandwich gently on the paper plate on his desk and wiped his hands with a paper napkin. "You look a little sleep deprived."

"I'm fine," Ray said. His dry skin and the bags beneath his bloodshot eyes said otherwise. "I wanted to ask you about this work order."

"Which one?"

"The one for Collier's Ridge. We were supposed to replace components on the C-bus in that substation. We were getting bad readings from some of the sensors. Remember? That work was supposed to start a few weeks ago, around the time the first storm hit."

"Yeah, a couple of hurricanes will throw a wrench in the works." He smiled. "Dozens of tickets got put on hold. The best-laid plans of mice and men, right?"

"Kenny had put together a team to work on that one."

"Kenny? Oh, your buddy in dispatch. Right, I remember. He's out this week."

"He's up at his cabin in the mountains. This bus needs to get fixed."

"A lot of things need to get fixed. We'll get to it."

"Soon. Like, today."

"You know I can't schedule anything today. The crews are already out. What's your rush?"

"My rush is that it's hot as fuck out there and—"

"Watch your mouth, Ray."

"You watch—" Ray almost exploded. His face turned red, but he checked his anger and started over. "It's hot out there, and I'm worried that if the readings on that bus are wrong, it puts all the downstream equipment at risk. The last thing we need is another outage."

"Okay, Ray. I'll bump it up. When do you want it done?"

"Tomorrow. I already said that."

"You said today. But no worries. I'll see what I can do."

"And make sure Ben Wood is on that crew."

"You said Kenny already set up the crews."

"Oh, yeah." Ray scratched his head.

"You sure you're okay, Ray?"

"Just a little tired."

"I'll try to bump up the ticket."

"Ben's a good kid," Ray said. "Trying to build his skills. Collier's Ridge has some of the newer equipment. If he starts getting experience on those components, he can move up, advance his career."

"Nice of you to look out for him. You know, I've heard a few complaints about him. Some people don't like his attitude. They don't want him on their team."

"Kid has passion, that's all."

"I'll do what I can," he repeated.

"Thank you."

"You're welcome, Ray. The kid's lucky to have a sponsor like you looking out for him."

"Yeah." Ray turned to leave. "A good sponsor can be like a savior to some people."

Malinowski sank his teeth into his sandwich as he watched Ray leave.

In the hall outside, Ray pulled his phone from his pocket and called Ben Wood.

"What's up, boss?"

"Just a heads-up. We might be on for tomorrow. Don't go out drinking tonight. I need you on your toes."

"Where's the gig?"

"Collier's Ridge. If they don't assign you to that crew, find a truck that's going and get in it."

"That's west of Richmond. Past Goochland. They got me working east now. The west-of-Richmond crews started bad-mouthing me to the supervisors."

"Doesn't matter. Get on that crew however you can. I don't want this falling through a second time."

"Will do, Ray."

"I'll be there too."

"In the substation? They won't let you in."

"Not in the substation. More as a guardian angel, making sure things stay on track."

"See you there, then."

Ray ended the call, pressed the down button for the elevator and muttered, "Maybe you will. Maybe you won't."

# 49

"How does that sound?" Sean asked, pointing to a road sign ahead.

"Nellysford?"

"The turnoff is six miles ahead. Seems like a remote little town. Not somewhere the Feds or the Richmond cops would be looking."

Not somewhere anyone would be looking for a young man on the run in a possibly stolen car with his possibly kidnapped girlfriend. Danielle swallowed uneasily, her hand gripping the armrest on the passenger door. In the ninety minutes they'd been driving, she had had plenty of time to think and overthink their situation.

"Why so far away?" she asked. "I mean..." Her throat began to tighten. I mean, I've known this guy for what? Like, five days?

"It's up there." Sean pointed west, toward the Blue Ridge. "Nellysford."

She turned and looked through the window to her right. "In the mountains?"

"Yeah." He smiled. "Fresh air."

"Okay, wait. Explain something to me." She was second-guessing everything now. Why had she gotten into the car with him? She should have been at work, in the calm, cool office, where life was orderly, predictable, and worry free.

Why had she obeyed when he asked her to turn off her phone? She was protecting him at the expense of her own safety. No one knew where she dwas. If one of her own friends had called her with this dilemma, called and said, "Hey, this guy I've been dating for a few days is on the run from the cops and wants me to jump in his car—actually, his neighbor's car, he stole it—but I have to turn off my phone and disappear... What do you say? Should I do it?"

She would have said, "Are you crazy? Are you drunk?"

"Yeah?" Sean urged her on after her long pause. "You have a question?"

Her mouth was dry, and she tried to keep the fear out of her voice. "Why, um..." She struggled to formulate the question. "Why, if this guy wants to damage the grid—"

"Ray."

"Whatever. If Ray wants to commit this terrorist act, why doesn't he just walk into the control center and turn all the dials to ten or shut off all the computers or whatever? Why not just do it directly?"

Her chest tightened and her heart beat fast and hard. The start of a panic attack. What was she doing in the middle of nowhere with this guy? How could she know if anything he said was true? He talked convincingly about computer code, but how could she verify any of it?

"Because he can't get in there. Security is incredibly tight at Empire. If access to a facility isn't absolutely required for you to do your job, you can't get in. Period. No exceptions. That applies to the control centers, the data centers, the substations, everything."

She swallowed hard again, swallowed nothing from her dry mouth, glanced at him quickly, and then looked away. Deep breath, she told herself. The voice inside her head urging her not to panic was itself panicked. She couldn't command her feelings to disappear.

"You nervous?" He put his hand on her knee to reassure her.

She brushed it off. "Don't."

"I'm just trying to—"

"Just don't, okay?" She turned away and looked out the window.

He fixed his eyes on the road, and for a minute, they drove in silence. He turned and looked at her once, twice, three times.

"You're having second thoughts, aren't you?"

"Yeah, well, this counts as what? Like, our third date?"

"You said you liked adventure."

She slid her hand down to the backpack at her feet and felt the outline of the gun.

"Can we stop at that place up there?" she asked. "I need to use the bathroom. And I need something to drink."

"Sure."

She remembered the card Anya Lakhani had given her after their interview in the Empire conference room.

# 50

Anya scrolled through the report from the FBI's digital forensics unit. The compromised computers receiving stolen data exfiltrated from Empire—all those hacked coffee-shop kiosks—showed no trace of the pilfered documents. A full recovery scan of the hard drives showed the data had never been written to disk. During a normal deletion operation, the file names would have been deleted, but the actual bits would remain. Though hidden from the average user, forensics experts would still be able to recover them.

But there was nothing here to recover. They reverse engineered the code that received the stolen documents and found that it discarded all data as soon as it arrived. Access logs from the kiosks and from the routers that connected them to the internet showed no one had ever tried to retrieve the stolen data.

What was this, then? Another feint? The malware was mimicking the behavior of other known malwares, acting like what investigators called "an advanced persistent threat," but it wasn't actually stealing anything.

So, what was the point?

The next section of the report detailed the one exception to this baffling pattern. A kiosk in central Missouri, the one into which user "sriggs" had accidentally typed a command meant for his own machine, showed traces of deleted files. Forensic recovery found that the files contained the source code of Empire's power-transmission-control software. Network logs on the router showed someone had recently connected and downloaded the data before deleting it. The connection had come in through a Tor exit node and was untraceable.

The final section of the report recommended that Russia and its allies not be ruled out as a source of the attack. The theft of documents, spreadsheets, emails, and employee records—all that data that had been thrown away on the other kiosks—was a feint designed to make the attack look like it came from China. It made the malware appear to follow the Chinese pattern of "steal all available information" rather than the Russian pattern of "give us control of a vitally important system."

The fact that the hacker *did* seem to want the code suggested they may be interested in compromising or sabotaging the distribution of electricity.

Anya leaned back in her chair, swiveled away from the monitor, and thought to herself, That's not what it is. It's not China and it's not Russia. I know it looks like a state actor, but that's not what this is.

She picked up her phone, called the other forensics lab, the one looking into Sean's laptop and backup drives.

"Any news on those?"

"No smoking gun yet," said the woman on the other end of the line. "And I don't think we'll find one."

"What makes you so sure?"

"This isn't the laptop's original drive. This model of Lenovo never shipped with a one-terabyte Seagate drive. My guess is the owner destroyed the original and did a fresh installation of the operating system on this new drive. One way we can tell is that a well-used drive will have fragments of deleted files strewn all over it. The user can't see them, but we can. This drive, outside of where the system files are stored, is completely clean. I wouldn't be surprised if it was installed in the past few days."

Anya thanked the woman and thought, Well, Sean Riggs is thorough. He knows what he's doing.

Then her mind wandered back to Ray, his hostility toward Sean, his survivalist neighbors up in the West Virginia mountains who happened to work in the electric power companies of Ohio and Michigan.

She swiveled back to her laptop and pulled up Empire Energy's website. She browsed through the public information pages, stopping on one that gave a layman's explanation of Empire's grid. She clicked on the video and watched an animation of electricity flowing from generation facilities through transformers and wires into people's homes.

"The bulk electrical system, also known as the grid, must maintain a constant balance between supply and demand," the narrator said. "If demand is too high, power transmission collapses. If supply is too high, transmission lines and other equipment can be damaged."

She fast-forwarded the video until a map appeared. She watched as, in fast motion, the view zoomed out from Virginia to include a dozen other states. Connections between the grids in different states appeared as glowing yellow bars. She stopped the video and backed it up. The narrator explained that all of the state grids in the eastern US were connected. The glowing yellow bars were called interconnects. If demand was too high in one state, power flowed in from other states to meet it.

She paused the video and traced the interconnects from Virginia to Maryland and Pennsylvania, west to Ohio and north to Michigan.

If the connections between the grids allow them to support each other, she reasoned, they must also allow them to drag each other down. If the grid in one state collapses, what happens to the grids in connected states?

She thought again of the houses she had seen in West Virginia. The two she had passed on the road to Ray's house both had trucks in the drive. Why were the owners there now, during this particular week, and not at their jobs in the Ohio and Michigan power companies? Were they simply taking advantage of the long Fourth of July weekend? Had they too installed cisterns to capture rainwater, as Ray had done? Had they too been stockpiling canned food?

Perhaps. But her mind kept returning to the question of timing. Why now? Why did they all choose this particular week to be there?

If you wanted to know exactly when a disaster would occur, the type of disaster that would drive survivalists into the hills, the best way to know would be to make it happen. Choose the date yourself.

But how could they cause a disaster if they weren't at work? If they wanted to burn down the grid, wouldn't it be best to be in the control center, sabotaging things directly?

Maybe. But what if you could do it without being there? What if you installed a time bomb? Let the system destroy itself while you're tucked safely away in the mountains, living off the grid on solar power, watching the chaos from on high?

She thought back to the ticket Sean had sent to the auditor, the ticket that complained of unusual and dangerous code. The auditor had passed it off to the security reviewer of Empire's internal IT department, and he had done nothing. The code that Sean Riggs had flagged as potentially dangerous was still there, still lurking in the system.

Who was in charge of the security section of the internal IT department? She looked it up on the org chart that Empire had given to the Feds and the private consulting firms who were helping them sort out the security breach. Charles Lehrman. Wasn't that one of the names the programmer had given her? One of the members of Ray's group of followers within the company? Why had Charles Lehrman dismissed Sean's concerns? Why had he closed out that ticket without a full investigation and write-up? She looked up Lehrman's name in the company directory. His office was on the third floor.

When she got there a few minutes later, it was empty.

"Looking for Charles?" Anya turned to see a young Asian woman holding a paper coffee cup. "He'll be back next week."

"Is he on vacation?"

The woman nodded as she sipped her coffee. "Went to his cabin in West Virginia."

Alarm bells! Was his the other house on the road to Ray's? The only one that hadn't been occupied when she visited?

"Damn!" She turned on her heel and headed back to the auditor's office in the basement. On her way, she stopped by her temporary office and opened the tracking app on her laptop. Danielle Duval's phone was still offline. Last known location, the street outside her office earlier that morning.

She dug into her purse, found the business card on which she had written Danielle's mobile number and tapped out a quick text.

# 51

"I really have to pee," Danielle said as she got out of the car. "Can you get me an iced tea?"

"Yeah, sure." Sean looked at her backpack. For a moment she feared he would ask why she needed to take that with her if she was just going pee. If he asked, she'd say her tampons were in there—a lie—and that would shut down further inquiry.

But he didn't ask. He turned and said he'd meet her back at the car in a minute.

He didn't ask where her phone was. She had turned it off, as he had requested back in Richmond, to make them untraceable. No one knew she was here beneath the sweltering sun, in this dirty, decaying gas station on the side of a rural highway.

The restroom door was on the outside of the building. To reach it, she had to step through a field of broken glass and around a puddle of what looked like drying puke. The doorknob required a key, but the door wasn't shut all the way. She pulled it open and recoiled at the smell. Whoever had recently puked outside the door had done something even worse inside.

She flushed the toilet twice, lined the rim with paper and sat. She didn't want to put her backpack on the wet, putrid floor, so she held it in her lap.

She unzipped the big compartment, pulled the revolver from inside, checked the safety—on—and the cylinder—loaded.

She would never actually fire it, but if she wound up in a situation she had to get out of, she could use it as a threat. Having it in hand reassured her and took the edge off the worst of her fears. She slid the pistol back into the bag, zipped the big compartment shut, and opened the smaller one. She pulled out her wallet, opened it, and searched for the card Anya

Lakhani had given her. When she found it, she read the name and title. The Homeland Security logo reassured her. Not as much as the gun, because they weren't here and it was, but it reminded her that someone on the outside had an interest in her safety.

Anya seemed like a sensible, no-nonsense person, a counterbalance to Sean's paranoia. If there really was some plot going on, as Sean insisted, then the federal investigators would surely be onto it. They were right inside Empire's offices, after all. Right in the center of things. Anya seemed to have an even temper. She didn't act rashly, or speak wildly of the world burning down, the way Sean had done throughout their drive. Anya didn't hack into corporate networks. She probably didn't gaslight people either.

As Danielle reached back into the bag for her phone, a shadow blocked the sunlight coming through the crack in the door that wouldn't fully close. Anyone could walk in here, she thought. And that's a big someone out there, almost certainly a man. She could hear the glass grind beneath his feet.

She held the dark phone in one hand, the bag in the other, frozen.

If that's Sean, she thought, I can't make this call. He'll hear me. If it's someone else, I'm better off with the gun in my hand.

She thought of calling out, saying hello? Is that you, Sean?

But what if it was someone else? A stranger? Why signal her presence? Why let him know she was alone in that filthy little room with her pants down?

She waited, her heart racing. Say something, she thought. Why are you just standing there?

She heard glass grind beneath the man's feet as the shadow shifted.

Screw it, she thought. I have to choose.

With the side of her index finger pinning Anya's card against the black phone screen, she pressed the power button with her thumb. The phone made its start-up noise, loud enough for the person outside to hear.

If that's Sean, she thought, he knows what I'm doing. If it's some psycho rapist, he knows I'm in here.

She watched as the glow of the phone's logo illuminated the card from behind.

When the phone is fully booted, she told herself, it will connect to the network. They'll know where I am.

She was going to tell Anya she had made a mistake when she agreed to get in Sean's car. She felt for him in his distress, but then she had a long time to rethink that decision as they drove. Sean said some lunatic wanted to set the world on fire. But maybe Sean was the lunatic. She couldn't tell. She was too close to him to see clearly. But ultimately, this was his mess. He got himself into it, and he would have to get himself out. Anya would understand all this, would understand her predicament, and send someone to pick her up. Sean could explain himself to the Feds. He's crazy, she thought. He's reckless and crazy.

The voice that liked to criticize her said, You're crazy, Danielle. Pushing yourself on him, following him home, sleeping with him. All because you were bored. Are you bored now?

"Shut up," she muttered under her breath.

The home screen lit up. She looped her left arm through the strap of the backpack to keep it from falling while she used both hands. Anya's card was in her left hand, the phone in her right.

The number she was about to dial, the one on Anya's card, appeared unexpectedly on screen. The text in the alert beneath it said, "I know you're with him. Did he say this is about computer code?"

She blinked uncomprehendingly at the text. Before she could fully digest the message, her thumbs typed, "Yes."

How did Anya know to text her? How did she know this was about code?

"Danielle?" It was Sean standing outside the door. "You okay in there?"

"I'm fine," she said. "I'll be right out."

The phone chimed loudly with Anya's response. Danielle winced, knowing he must have heard it.

She read the text and then replied.

> Are you safe?

> I'm not sure.

> Do you want me to send help?

> I don't know. Why did you mention code?

> Because that's what this is about. I think something very bad is going on, and I think he's way ahead of us in figuring it out.

Danielle reread the message three times, not knowing what to think. Finally, she responded.

> He doesn't trust you. He thinks you'll lock him in a cell and not believe what he has to say.

"Danielle?" Sean called.

"What?"

"You sure you're okay?"

"I'm fine."

"I got your lemonade."

"Okay. I said iced tea. Go back to the car."

"Are you trying to get rid of me?"

Anya replied:

> He may be right. By the time I can persuade my higher-ups to listen to him, it might be too late. They all think this is a nation-state attack.

"I'm on the toilet, Sean. Leave me alone!"

She heard him groan, heard the grinding glass as he turned and his shadow disappeared.

> What should I do?

Panic now flooded in from another direction. I don't know this woman either, she thought. I'm in a mess I don't know how to get out of, how I even got into it. I'm half-scared for my life, and I'm asking for advice from a woman I don't even know. She could be as crazy as he is.

Calm down, she told herself. Calm down!

Again, the nagging inner voice mocked her. *Are you bored now, Danielle?*

"Shut up!" she said aloud.

Does he have the code with him? Is he still studying it?

Yes. And yes.

And you feel safe?

I don't know. What should I do? I don't know what to do.

Stick with him. Don't tell him we've communicated. He might stop trusting you. Let him dig through the code. Your boyfriend is incredibly smart and way ahead of us. He's in a position to figure this out before we can. Report to me if you can. If you ever feel in danger, call. I can see where you are. You're in a gas station on Route 29, south of Charlottesville.

She began typing her response: We're going to Nellysford. Then she second-guessed herself. What if Anya sent the local cops to watch them? Sean was already worried. How would he be able to concentrate if he knew or even suspected the cops were watching him?

She erased the message and replied instead,

Will do.

When she exited the restroom a minute later, the bright sun stung her eyes. She put her hand up to shield them as she walked to the car.

When she got in, Sean handed her a bottle of lemonade and reminded her to buckle up. The engine growled when he turned the key, but instead of putting it in gear, he let out a long breath, rested his head against the steering wheel, and shut his eyes.

"Everything okay?" Danielle asked. She twisted the top off the lemonade bottle with a loud pop.

"Please turn your phone off." He sounded weary. He didn't move or open his eyes.

"My phone?" she asked in a tone of surprise, playing dumb.

He turned and looked her in the eye. Not with the anger she expected, the anger that would be at least partly justified by her turning on the phone and giving away their location and then lying about it.

His look was soft and gentle, though strained by the stress of circumstances.

"I asked you to trust me," he said softly, "and you did. I'm going to return the favor and trust you too. I'm not going to ask you whom you called or texted. I'm pretty sure I already know.

"I know you feel scared. I would too if I was in your situation. I'm scared too.

"If you want an out, you got it. If you want me to drop you off somewhere, I will. Just please don't give me away until tomorrow. Will you promise me that?"

She nodded, watching him closely, appreciating his honesty and openness. He might be crazy and he might be incredibly smart, but he definitely wasn't boring. This was one hell of a third date.

She wouldn't have stayed with him if it weren't for the texts from Anya, if it weren't for the fact that a seasoned professional investigator looking into the case had come to the same conclusion as her crazy-ass boyfriend.

Boyfriend?

Sure, why not?

And now Danielle's job was to keep tabs on him. To let him do his work. To report his progress if there was any.

Better yet, she thought, I'll make him report it himself. When the time is right, I'll tell him that Anya suspects what he suspects. If he starts to waver, if he starts to doubt or lose confidence, I'll tell him she's on his side. It will give him a boost.

"Sorry, Sean." She pulled her phone from the backpack and made a show of turning it off.

He looked surprised at how quickly she had given in. He searched her face for signs that she was holding out, keeping some secret. Maybe she had already told the cops where they were headed, what kind of car they were driving.

She met his questioning gaze without flinching. Her look was as open as his. Neither hid anything from the other. Each understood in that moment that the other had extended a deep and binding trust. Whatever happened from here on out, they were in it together.

Hell of a third date, Danielle thought as the Mustang rolled onto the highway. This is all going way too fast.

Delight overwhelmed the voice of prudence that at any other time would have told her to back off, to be cautious. Sean noted her smile—the bright, happy smile that he could only respond to with a smile of his own. He didn't ask what it was about.

# 52

Ray Cooper sat on his living room couch, cleaning a pistol and half watching the local news on TV. Across the coffee table and ottoman in front of him lay a buffet of guns and ammunition. All but one of the rifles would be packed up. The Winchester 70 with the worn walnut stock would go on the rack behind the seat of his truck. He liked that one for its accuracy. The magazine held three cartridges, but as he liked to tell people, he never needed more than one to fell his prey. The other two were for celebrating.

For a sidearm, he chose the Sig Sauer .45 semiautomatic. Its powerful kick gave beginners fits, but once you mastered it, the recoil wasn't a problem. Besides, the target bore the brunt of its power. If your first shot didn't kill them, it disabled them long enough for you to finish the job.

He had recently tested it against the head of a local mechanic and found it to be more than satisfactory. The newscasters were talking about that now. An unusual execution-style killing in a Richmond suburb. Police were searching for a motive.

"Are they?" Ray muttered as he wiped down the Sig. "I mean, isn't it fucking obvious that when you help a woman disobey her husband, when you fix—I should put that in air quotes. When you 'fix' a Yukon outside the dealership—the dealership where you fucking work—you void the warranty. Did the cops not think that through? They're as dumb as she is."

Ray's train of thought continued internally. How about the fact that the guy helped Donna remove the GPS trackers from the Yukon? I know it was him, Ray thought. She couldn't have found them on her own. The guy basically stole a man's wife, and those dumbass cops are wondering what the motive is? How stupid are these people?

Stupid enough to tell the news they don't know who they're looking for.

He tried to remember, had the news stations reported that his wife had left him? Hadn't it been the lead story on every broadcast? Wasn't everyone making fun of him? Or had he just dreamed that?

When would he have dreamed it? He hadn't slept in days. His skin was pale and his face looked gaunt, hollowed out beneath his dry, red eyes. He wondered if the dry sting in his eyes would hinder his aim as he looked down the barrel of the polished Sig.

This whole thing was supposed to be done already. The switch at the substation was supposed to have been thrown weeks ago. But then God intervened. God called timeout, made some hurricanes, told Ray he had to wait. Ray was frustrated. He worked hard not to be angry with God.

He finished wiping down the pistol and laid it on the coffee table. He picked up a magazine and loaded it from a box of ammo. Ten cartridges. He wouldn't need that many under even the worst of circumstances. But they might come in handy if he encountered any rude drivers after he left the substation, on the long drive west. A forty-five to the head was a surprisingly effective remedy for the road rage of obnoxious motorists. A cure, in fact. One treatment, and they never misbehaved again.

He would supervise the process at the substation, supervise from afar, and make sure things went right. The work order would be assigned before daybreak. The crew would arrive around eleven in the morning, when it was already hot. The forecast said ninety-seven degrees by eleven a.m. His acolyte, Ben Wood, would be in one of the trucks. Ben would ensure the switch was thrown. If anyone tried to interfere, Ray would shoot them. They wouldn't even know he was there. They would never know what hit them.

Once the switch was thrown, the breaker would send the signal back to the central operations center, the signal saying it was going offline. The breaker's equipment ID would be passed into the poison function he had inserted into the code.

The function would encrypt the ID to see if it matched the magic value. It would.

That would trigger the series of commands, and the process would begin. Fifteen minutes of silent data capture, recording healthy, expected data from all over the grid. Then the code would start replaying those fifteen minutes of normalcy to all the monitors in the ops center.

Then the overvolting would quietly begin. His code would step up the voltage coming out of the big transformers, maxing out the lines, pushing them beyond their approved ratings in the heat. The ops center would never know. The loop of prerecorded data flowing into their monitors would make everything look fine to them.

Once the overvolting started, the lines would begin to sag and melt within minutes. He wondered if people would stop and gawk when the lines on the big steel towers began to glow like filaments in an old-style light bulb. Would the fools just stand there and watch? Watch molten metal fall into the parched underbrush? Watch the forests burn?

He hoped they would. He wanted them to know they were damned, to understand the price of their disobedience. He wanted to watch their terror as they fled one fire only to run into another. He liked to imagine the look of horror in their eyes as they realized there was no way out. He wanted to hear the moans of woe from the hungry, dehydrated people living in darkness without food, without any prospect of life returning to normal in the foreseeable future. Such are the wages of sin, he reflected. You made your bed, you evil bastards, now lie in it. It's not like no one warned you. You've had two thousand years to read the book. You know how it ends. It ends in fire.

That reminded him. There were lines running into the substation and lines running out. From his position on the hill above, on the stony outcrop that overlooked the Collier's Ridge substation, he would have a clear shot at most targets. As long as someone wasn't standing behind a piece of equipment, the Winchester could hit them.

But the lines. If he lingered too long, the incoming line that crossed the gravel entry road would set the woods ablaze and possibly block his escape. He should be out of there within fifteen minutes of his code being triggered. He should make his exit in that safe window before the overvolting began. But in case things went wrong, he would park a little farther up the road, behind where the lines crossed. The gate that guarded the substation itself would be locked anyway. Park a couple hundred yards back, and the truck would be out of the initial fire zone.

There was a spot near the trailhead. He had already scoped it out. A spot where the gravel road widened. He could pull the truck over there, park it, and enter the woods at the trailhead. Follow the narrow path up the ridge, then turn left, go thirty yards downhill, and set up on the rocky outcrop.

He picked up the Sig, removed the magazine, and tried to slide in the one he had just loaded. It didn't fit. His face turned red, and he began to shake with anger.

He jumped from the couch and screamed, "Donna!"

Where was she? He headed for the stairs.

Wait. She was gone. She was gone, and still she was messing things up. Making him try to slide a nine-millimeter Glock magazine into a Sig .45. Was that funny? Goddammit, who the hell was laughing?

He turned and looked back into the living room.

The woman on TV. The newscaster. She was laughing.

"You think that's funny?" Ray growled. He marched back to the coffee table and picked up the magazine belonging to the .45. "How funny is this?" He slid the magazine into the gun and pumped three rounds into the television.

"Is it funny now?" he shouted. "I don't hear you laughing now!" He looked at the flat-screen lying on the carpet, blasted and shattered and dark. "Yeah, I didn't think so."

Now, where was the tactical vest? It was supposed to be in the closet by the gun safe. Had he seen it when he took out the guns? He couldn't remember. He laid the pistol on the coffee table and headed for the stairs, his red-rimmed eyes straining at the edge of sanity.

If she moved it, he thought, I'll fucking kill her. He bounded up the stairs two at a time. That will be the last fucking straw. She's gone too far and she knows it. She's gone way too far.

# 53

## July 7

Sean hunched over a cheap round table behind the red curtain of a motel room window. Dried smears from the cleaner's rag marked the table's fake wood veneer. His chin rested on his hand as his tired eyes pored through lines of code on the tiny screen of his backup phone. The greasy pizza box in front of him was empty. The light of dawn crept through the narrow space between the curtains. Danielle lay in the bed behind him, her face turned toward the muted television she had been watching when she fell asleep.

"What the hell?" Sean muttered. "This is impossible."

Danielle's eyes opened slowly at the sound of his voice.

"Any progress?" she asked sleepily.

"I'm stumped." He stood from the table and sighed as he paced the room and stroked his chin.

"What time is it?"

"I don't know. Five thirty?"

"What is it you're trying to find again?"

"I'm trying to figure out how this code could connect to the grid-control system. There's no point in creating this time bomb if it can't reach the system it wants to destroy. What is the mysterious input that matches the encrypted value that sets all this in motion? Where does it come from? I can't figure it out."

He continued to pace, running his hand through his hair as he looked down at the motel's cheap patterned carpet.

"I wish I could help you," Danielle said. She sat up. "Do you want to take a break?"

"No."

"You're tense. It might help to relax."

"I wouldn't mind taking a walk, getting some air."

"You should."

"I don't want to."

"You just said you did."

"I think you gave away our location when you turned your phone on at the gas station."

"Sorry."

"It's okay. I would have done the same thing if some psycho I'd known for only a few days had kidnapped me in a stolen car."

She laughed.

"Okay, so tell me again why you think this code can't access the grid-control system."

"I don't feel like going through it again."

"Explain it like I'm five. If you make it clear to me, you might make it clear to yourself."

Sean frowned and shook his head. He continued pacing.

"Come on, Sean. Talk it through."

"All right, look. The code gets compiled into an actual program that can run. It's compiled in two parts. The program and the tests. Once the actual program is compiled, they put it on an isolated test system where the tests make it do all sorts of things to ensure it's working correctly. If the tests pass, the main program gets copied onto the production system where it can do its work."

"Running the grid?"

"Right."

"And what happens to the test code?"

"Nothing. It's done its job. It doesn't get copied to production."

"What if someone copies it onto the production system?"

"They don't."

"How do you know?"

"Because I checked. The whole deployment process is automated. It copies only the program itself. Nothing else. The test code never gets to a place where it can access the grid."

"Are you sure?"

"Dammit! I just told you!"

"Okay, Sean. Calm down. I'm just trying to make sure you look at every possibility."

He sighed, looked down at the ugly carpet and shook his head as if dismissing her useless ideas. He went into the bathroom, filled a glass of water, and drank it down.

He returned to the main room and resumed his pacing, sighing in frustration.

"Kind of tense in here," Danielle said. Her voice had that teasing quality that could usually lighten his mood.

"How can you smile at a time like this?" he asked.

"How can I not? Because what's the alternative? To be a nervous wreck like you?"

"How can I *not* smile? Are you seriously asking me that? When the world is literally about to go up in flames?"

"Don't be so dramatic. Besides, if it is going to end, I want to go out smiling. Don't you?"

He gave her a puzzled look. "Where the hell did you come from? I mean, how does a mind like yours and a mind like mine arise from the same world? Are we even perceiving the same reality?"

"It's all a question of attitude," she said, tapping her finger against her temple. "You can choose to let the world upset you, or you can choose not to."

She got up from the bed, walked to him with a wicked smile, and gave him a playful shove.

"Don't push me."

"Why not?" She smiled and shoved him again.

"Stop."

"Stop being so serious."

"I'll stop being serious when I figure this out."

"Okay," she said, twirling away from him and walking toward the window. "What if the test code snuck onto the production server?"

"How would it *sneak* onto the production server? Does it have little legs? Can it walk across an ethernet cable over to the central memory banks of another computer?"

"I don't know," Danielle said cheerfully. "Can it? You're the expert."

"No. It can't."

He headed back to the bathroom and filled another glass of water.

"So how does it sneak in, then?"

"Who says it sneaks in?" He threw his head back and downed the water in three big gulps. Then he studied his tired eyes in the mirror above the sink.

"I'm saying hypothetically," Danielle replied. "I'm saying, let's assume the test code is sneaky like us. The cops know we're out here somewhere, but they don't know where. We're driving a car they don't know about. We could drive right by them and they'd never know."

"This isn't helpful. Code doesn't drive around in cars."

"Come on, Sean. Work with me."

"Talk sense, then."

She walked toward the bathroom and grabbed him by the shoulders as he came through the door.

"It seems kind of obvious, doesn't it? Sneaking code onto a computer. Can you honestly tell me it's never been done? Isn't there always some way to smuggle a hidden cargo to the place it needs to be?"

"Of course it's been done."

"Give me an example."

"One of the worst hacks in computer history, the SolarWinds hack that compromised just about the entire US government and a big chunk of the Fortune five hundred."

"They snuck the code in?"

"The Russians did that."

"How?"

"The company that made SolarWinds used a weak password on their build server. The Russians guessed the password and snuck some malicious code into the software as it was being compiled. Once it was built and distributed, the bad code infected thousands of servers."

"Why didn't anyone see it?" Danielle asked. "The bad code they snuck in?"

"Because it wasn't there. It wasn't in the code base at all."

"Then how did it get into the final program?"

"It was injected into the main code base at the last second, during the final step of the build."

"How?"

"By the build script. The Russians added a line to the build script to pull in code from this secret, malicious file at the last second, just as it was being fed into the compiler."

"Okay, so did you check for that?"

Sean stood frozen, blinking at her with a look of incomprehension.

"Oh, my God! No. I got so lost in the weeds of the code itself, I didn't think to back up and take a broader view."

"Okay," she said with a triumphant smile. "So, thank you Danielle. See, Sean. This is what I mean about talking things out. Guys think it's a waste of time—"

She turned to watch as he breezed past her to his phone at the little round table.

"But like I said," she continued, "when you have to explain something, it forces you to clarify and you realize..." She saw his eyes focused on the glowing screen, saw him sucked back into his all-consuming investigation. "Oh, now you're going to ignore me again? Now Danielle isn't interesting enough, is she? That's okay, Sean. You go diddle with your phone," she teased. "I'm going to strip off all my clothes and do yoga out in the parking lot."

"Yeah, okay," he said absently.

"Uh-huh," she said, hands on hips. "Nothing I say now registers with you, does it?"

"Yeah, sure." He put his finger to his lips to ask her to be quiet while he focused.

He browsed back through the source-control records until he found the last recorded change to the build script. It was dated January fifth, the same day that the malicious test code had been checked in under Drishti Singh's user account by Ray

Cooper. He was the one to whom she had turned in her laptop. Her name appeared in the log as the person who had created the malicious code. And now her name appeared in the logs as the person who had added a few strange lines to the build script, lines that inserted code from one file into the middle of another file, surreptitiously including the malware in the build.

"That's it," he said. "That's how it gets in to access the grid. He did it just like the Russians did."

He smiled at her. She smiled back and curtsied playfully.

Rubbing the sleep from his eyes, he dug in again and began to trace the flow of data through the program. Without a debugger to help him, he had to trace everything mentally. The work ahead might have taken an hour with his laptop and proper software. Instead, he knew it would take several hours using just his programmer's reason and a small phone screen.

# 54

Anya Lakhani looked up from her desk at the sound of the knock.

"Come in, Carlos."

"You look tired."

"Thanks."

"You said you were digging into some code issue?"

"I'm putting together a briefing now. We'll go through it at today's one o'clock."

"All right. You know the Bureau still thinks it's China."

"I know."

"And the consultants. China all the way."

"Why are you in here, Carlos?"

"I just wanted to pass along a couple of things. One is of interest. The other, not so much."

Espinoza slid some papers out of a manila folder as he approached the desk. She stood to take them.

"What are these?" she asked.

"The first is from the security consultants."

"The ones here in the office? That Empire called in after the breach?"

"Yeah. Their colleagues are inside the Ohio utility right now, doing an audit. No signs of a breach so far, but when one utility is compromised, the others do a check to make sure they're clean. Anyway, no breach there, but they came across some funny code in the automated test suite. No one can make sense of it at this point, but it might relate to the angle you're investigating."

"What's funny about the test code?"

"It contains some encrypted data, and some commands to manipulate the grid. Probably used in simulations, but the auditors flagged it as a code smell, something fishy that deserves a second look."

Anya looked at the papers he had handed her. A half page of summary, in clearly written English, followed by two and half pages of code that might as well have been Greek.

"What's the second thing?" she asked.

Espinoza handed her two more sheets from the folder.

"A note from one of the field-service coordinators. He got a complaint the other night from a veteran technician named Delbert Wright who found some shoddy repair work in a number of substations during routine follow-up inspections. Wright thought maybe one of the out-of-state crews was causing the problems."

"And?"

"And the work at the four substations was done by four different crews. Empire crews, not out-of-staters. Only one guy was on all four teams. Kid named Ben Wood who keeps getting shuffled around because no one wants him in their truck."

"Ben Wood?" When she had interviewed that programmer about Ray Cooper's "little clique," hadn't he mentioned a young field tech named Ben?

"If you can make anything of that," Espinoza said, "add it to your bricfing. I'll see you at one thirty."

# 55

"You have a contact there?"

Sean was fiddling with his phone, trying to click through setup instructions as he drove east on Interstate 64 toward Richmond. Danielle looked numb, exhausted, her glazed eyes staring at the trees rushing by her window.

"Danielle?"

"What time is it?" She turned to look at the dash. "Which one of those dials is the clock?"

"It's ten twenty. Do you have a contact? With the investigators? Didn't someone question you?"

"What are you doing with that phone?"

"Trying to get a new SIM card to work."

"When'd you get a new SIM card?"

"An hour ago. When you were passed out on the motel bed. Who is your contact?"

"Oh, yeah." She pushed herself up in her seat. Her posture straightened momentarily before the fatigue of stress and poor sleep made her slouch again. She unzipped the smaller compartment of her backpack and took out her phone. "It's in here. I'll have to turn it on, or... Um, I have her card somewhere."

"Turn your phone on."

"You sure?"

"Yeah. I want to talk to her. Do you trust this person?"

"I think so."

"Do you think they'll listen to me?"

"I think she will. She told me, um..." Danielle turned and looked out the side window again, trying to will herself awake so she would know how to say this.

"She told you what?"

"She told me to keep an eye on you."

Sean let that sink in for a moment. "You've been watching me? For them?"

"Well, yeah. She said there was some problem with the code and that you were further along in understanding it than they were. She wanted to let you continue."

Again, he took a moment to digest her words. "Why didn't you tell me that?"

"I don't know, Sean. How am I supposed to know how to behave in this situation? I'm trying to hold this balance between trusting you and keeping her as an emergency backup, in case things go wrong. I did what she said—"

"Kept an eye on me?"

"Yeah. Because I didn't know what else to do. What would you have done? Do you have a playbook for how to act when you're abducted?"

"I didn't abduct you."

"Sorry. I know. Do you want me to call her?"

"Yeah. Put her on speaker."

Anya Lakhani answered on the first ring. "Danielle? Are you okay?"

"I'm fine," Danielle said. "Sean wants to talk to you."

"Where are you?"

"On our way to Richmond. Sean wants to talk to you about the code."

"Sean?" said Anya, addressing him directly.

"Hey there. Listen. There's a strange bit of code buried in the tests of the grid-control software."

"You opened a security ticket about it," Anya replied. "With the auditor."

"Yeah, but that didn't go anywhere."

"It did. It went to the head of IT security, who happens to be a good friend of Ray Cooper."

"Right, this is what I wanted to talk about. That test code was pushed into the repository by Ray."

"Probably," Anya said. "Though to all the world, it looks like it was pushed by a former employee named Drishti Singh. She denies any knowledge of it. A team back at Homeland Security has been reviewing the code overnight. It looks malicious, but it can't access the actual control system from where it sits in the test code. Homeland thinks it's the beginning of an attack that the programmer didn't have time to complete."

"He did have time to complete the attack. Go back and take another look at the repository. You'll see Ray also committed a change to the build script on the same day, January fifth, under Drishti's name. The build script merges that test code into the production code in the last second before the code gets compiled. That attack is complete. It's in production now. It's just waiting for a trigger."

Anya was silent for a moment, the only sound from her end was the tapping of keys on a keyboard.

"Can you tell me the name of that file? The build script?"

Sean told her, then added, "From what I can tell, the code that triggers the attack is attached to the monitoring system. Some of the newer components of the grid send a message back to the central station when they're being switched off, so the system can know the difference between a component that went offline due to failure versus one that went offline deliberately, for maintenance or whatnot. Anyway, the trigger for this attack listens for those shutoff messages coming in from the grid.

"The shutoff message includes the identifier of the component being shut off. The trigger code receives the identifier and then encrypts it. When it gets one that matches the encrypted value that Ray buried in the code, the whole attack is set into motion."

"Why is the value encrypted?"

"So if anyone happens to stumble across this code, they'll have no way of knowing which component is the trigger. It took me all night to work this out."

"What happens when the code is triggered?" she asked to the sound of rapid keyboard tapping.

"The system starts to record all the monitoring inputs from all the components on the grid. It does that for fifteen minutes. Mind you, at this point, everything looks good. The grid is operating normally. Then it replays that recording to the main control center, so on their monitors, all the technicians see a view of a healthy, well-functioning system.

"Then, while the observers are blinded, Ray's code gets to work. It ups the voltage coming out of the transformers at every generation center on the grid, and on all the downstream transformers as well. That's more than the lines can handle in hot weather. They begin to melt. But the code is more sinister than that. It also overrides the safety mechanisms on all the software-controlled breakers, relays, and shunts. Those things are supposed to protect the components behind them from damaging power surges. When that protection is disabled, components all down the line are damaged and destroyed. The goal here is to cripple the grid indefinitely. Not just take it down and cause a blackout, but make it almost impossible to repair. This outage will last for months.

"Oh, and if that's not enough for you, it's also going to cause fires. Everywhere. Those melting lines..."

"Okay," said Anya, still typing. "I'm going to have our team look at this and try to verify."

"Excuse me?" Sean said in disbelief. "Shouldn't you take the malicious code offline?"

"And replace it with what?" Anya asked. "Are we supposed to let the whole state go black while we search for a solution?"

"That might be a better option than letting it burn."

"I'm pretty sure that would be a no-go with Empire."

"We don't have time for your people to study the code. I've already studied it. I know what it does."

"How soon will you be here?"

"An hour. Maybe an hour fifteen. Listen, that encrypted bit? The encryption that triggers the attack uses the old bcrypt algorithm. Find someone in IT who has access to the asset database. That lists all the components on Empire's grid. Run all the asset IDs through the bcrypt algorithm and see which one matches the encrypted value in the malicious code. That will tell you which component triggers the bomb.

"Then go look at the project database. That tells where all the work crews are going, which components they're going to have to switch off to do repairs and upgrades. Remember, the code is tripped by a component being manually switched off. The crews have to shut off power on some of the components they're repairing. If you find a project that includes the asset identifier of the triggering component, then you know where and when the attack will occur."

"Got it," Anya said. "I'll get back to you as soon as I can. By the way, I'll tell security to expect you. When you get here, you'll be talking to me and to the FBI agent in charge of the case. Hurry. I'll be alerting Ohio as soon as we hang up."

"Ohio?"

"They have the same time bomb sitting in their system and no one knows it."

"Oh, God," Sean said. "This mess is going to spread?"

"The whole eastern grid is interconnected. We don't know how far it will spread at this point. You want to hear something funny? The guy who has Ray's same job at the Ohio utility, the lead developer in their transmission-and-distribution unit, has a cabin in the mountains just down the road from Ray's."

"Good Lord!" he groaned. "I'll be there as soon as I can."

When he ended the call, Danielle asked if they could stop soon for a bathroom break.

"Yeah," said Sean. "We could use some gas too. Meanwhile—" He handed her his old Android. "Can you figure out how to get that thing to work? It's one of those pay-as-you-go services. The SIM won't activate."

She took the phone and began puzzling through the settings.

# 56

Del Wright glanced back and forth between the road ahead and the paper that his bandaged left hand had pinned against the steering wheel.

"This is a four-person job," he said to the young man in the passenger seat. "And the other two are tied up for at least another hour."

"Doesn't mean we can't start it," Ben Wood replied. The last time Del had seen him was in a hospital, hooked up to an IV. An extreme hangover cure for an extreme hangover made worse by days of sweating beneath a hot summer sun.

"Doesn't make sense for us to start it," Del said. "To start, we gotta cut the breaker. That shuts off power to five thousand homes down the line."

"It doesn't cut power," Ben said. "The juice gets routed to another line. The people don't notice."

"Rerouting strains the other line. That's not good in this heat," Del said. "We ain't gonna strain that line any longer than we have to. We'll wait for the rest of the crew before cutting the breaker."

"Whatever." Ben slouched back in his seat.

"Don't be a smart-ass. Reason you're riding with me today is 'cause none of the other crews want you."

"Reason I'm here today is God's will."

"I see a kid like you," Del said, "I see someone needs direction. A little mentoring won't hurt you, but you gotta listen and stop thinking you already know everything. You hungry?"

"A little bit."

"Mind stopping up ahead?"

"Not at all."

Del nodded. "All right. There's a Sheetz two exits down. We'll take our time. Wait for the second crew before we cut that breaker."

The young man pulled the bill of his cap down, folded his arms across his chest, and shut his eyes. "We'll see," he muttered.

"No," said Del. "I'm the crew chief, and I'm telling you what we're going to do. How long you been with the company, kid?"

"Year and a half."

"And you think that's long enough for you to be calling the shots? I been here twenty-four years."

"We'll see," Ben repeated with sullen defiance.

Del slowed the truck to just under the speed limit. He turned and gave his passenger a swat on the thigh with the back of his hand.

The young man jerked forward and blurted, "Don't touch me! What are you, some kind of fag?"

"Listen, kid. If you want go anywhere in this company, if you want to go anywhere in life, you start by listening and learning. You don't go shooting your mouth off and back-talking when you don't even know what you're saying."

"Don't lecture me, pops. I already got a dad."

"He lecture you?"

"Hell no. That old man doesn't do shit."

"Well, maybe that's your problem. You hung over today?"

"Not enough to stop me working. Just drive. Quit talking at me."

Del brought the truck back up to speed and focused on the road. After a few minutes of silence he said, "You been to the Collier's Ridge substation before?"

"No."

"It's not actually on the ridge. It's in a hollow just behind."

"Do I care?"

"I'm trying to put some information in your head. Like I said, if you want to learn..."

Del gave up. He could see Ben wasn't listening.

They continued in silence toward the exit three miles ahead.

# 57

"Now wait," said the young man in the blue button-down shirt. "Explain this again?"

"I want you to pull a list of all of the grid components from the database—"

"Yeah, okay, I can't do that." He leaned back from his desk in his black mesh chair and gave Anya a smug look.

"Yes, you can," Anya said.

"No. Sorry. That's proprietary information, and it's protected under federal critical energy infrastructure regulations."

"And I'm a federal investigator, invited in by your company's CEO, CTO, chief information security officer, and board of directors. Once you have the data, you're going to run all the component identifiers through the bcrypt algorithm."

"That algorithm is for hashing passwords. Are we trying to crack someone's password?"

"No," said Anya, doing her best to sound patient. "You're going to run all the component identifiers through the bcrypt algorithm until you find one that matches this value." She pointed to the encrypted value on her laptop monitor.

"Why would I do that?" The young man put his hands behind his head and reclined as if he had the upper hand in this exchange. His self-satisfied smile said, The ball's in your court, lady. Explain.

"You're going to do that because I'm telling you to."

"Boy, aren't we serious! Where's your escort, by the way? You don't work here."

She showed him her ID. "I'm an investigator with Homeland Security. I'm my own escort. Now help me out."

"I don't think so," the young man replied skeptically. "This sounds like one of those phishing attacks. You act like it's all urgent so I spill the information before I have time to think through what I'm doing. How do I even know you're an investigator?"

"I just showed you my ID."

"Well, then, where's your warrant?"

"Dammit!" Anya slapped her hand so hard on the desk, the young man jumped. "Pull the data and tell me which identifier matches this one!"

He shook his head, his smug smile returning slowly. "No can do."

"Where's your supervisor?"

"Good question."

"I'll get him to authorize this."

"Good luck."

She turned and left the room. On her way out, she heard him call, "Nice try, lady. Tell the guys in IT I didn't fall for your social-engineering attempt."

# 58

"You want anything?" Danielle asked.

"A Coke." Sean lifted the handle from the pump. "And a hot dog."

"Anything on it?"

"Just ketchup."

He put the nozzle into the tank and started pumping as she walked away. The old Mustang was supposed to take leaded gas. He wondered whether the engine had been rebuilt to accept unleaded. Probably so. Otherwise, the nozzle wouldn't have fit in the tank opening.

He looked at the time on his phone. Ten forty-two. It was already brutally hot, even in the shade by the pumps. The smell of gas fumes, combined with the heat and lack of sleep, made him feel lightheaded. He locked the trigger on the pump handle and stepped away.

He looked toward to store to see if Danielle was at the checkout yet. No. Probably still in the restroom. His mind vaguely registered the familiar face of the big man in the Empire jumpsuit with the dark beard exiting the store with a bag of chips and a quart of orange Gatorade.

Imagine having to work in coveralls today, Sean thought. In this heat! You'd sweat to death in two hours.

The man veered off course, away from the Empire truck parked off to the left and toward Sean himself.

"How's that DR?" Del asked, squinting against the sun. He was just outside the shady covering of the pumps.

"What's that?"

"The Suzuki. It was running rough last time I saw you."

"Oh, yeah. I remember you."

"You had a girl on the back."

"She's inside." Sean pointed toward the store. The gas nozzle clicked and cut the flow of fuel. Sean stepped back toward the car and grabbed the handle. "You were right, by the way."

"About the fuel?"

Sean nodded. "Non-ethanol cleared out the carbs. At least a little bit."

"It'll do that Mustang some good too," Del said. "That's a nice one."

"Thanks."

Del tipped his hat and walked back to the truck.

Sean looked again for Danielle but didn't see her. He replaced the gas cap and went into the store. A young man was leaving the men's room as Sean approached the rear of the chips aisle. He looked familiar. Sean thought a moment before placing him. He was part of the gang that used to go out with Ray after work. Ben something. Surly and full of himself. The guy walked right past him, wiping his hands on a paper towel from the men's room, eyes fixed on the floor, his face hard, focused, determined.

Sean watched him pass, watched him drop the paper towel onto the floor before pushing through the glass doors and walking out into the lot. He was headed for Del's truck.

Sean felt a jolt of energy shoot through him, followed by a sinking feeling of dread. If Ray Cooper wanted to get this done, he would send a trusted lieutenant out on the job, wouldn't he? Ray, who valued loyalty above all else. He changed course, pushed through the door of the women's room and called, "Danielle!"

The young girl washing her hands at the sink jerked her head and looked at him wide eyed and silent.

"Give me a minute," Danielle said. "What are you doing in here anyway? Wait outside."

"We need to leave."

"One minute!"

Someone was tugging at the back of his shirt. He turned and looked at the girl. She was seven years old, maybe six, with earnest black eyes and dark hair parted in the middle.

"Boys go in the other room," she explained solemnly.

"Thank you," Sean said. "Danielle, skip the Coke and food. Come right to the car."

He ran back to the outside in time to see the truck pull out of the lot. It went right. He ran to the end of the lot and watched. A quarter mile down, it turned right again.

He returned to the car, sweaty now from his dash beneath the hot sun. Through the store window, he could see Danielle making her way toward the exit. When she got outside, he honked and waved her on.

"Come on," he yelled. "Run!"

He had the engine running before she got in. She was barely in the seat, her hand still on the handle of the half-open door, when he hit the gas and the car peeled out.

"What the hell, Sean?"

"Buckle up."

He turned right out of the lot.

"Slow down!"

"Call that woman we talked to before. Ask her to find out what work tickets are open today along the stretch of I-64 between Richmond and Charlottesville."

"What's happening?"

"Just call her! Now!"

He swung a hard right where he'd seen the Empire truck turn. Danielle wasn't prepared for it. The turn threw her left, bumping her shoulder into Sean's. The phone flew out of her hand onto the floor at Sean's feet.

"Get that," he said. He scanned the road ahead and saw that it was empty.

"Don't boss me!"

"Just get it!" His eyes instinctively went to the dash, looking for the GPS that would show him what intersections lay ahead on this stretch of two-lane country road. Where the GPS should have been, he saw an old push-button radio.

Danielle leaned over him and picked up the phone. When she straightened up, she asked what was going on.

"Ray's lickspittle."

"What?"

"Ray's little cult boy is out on a job. It might be *the* job. Call Anya."

He had to repeat his instructions about what to ask her.

"And then, here." He pulled his backup phone from his pocket and tossed it into her lap.

"What am I supposed to do with this?"

"Pull up a map. Look for areas of green that aren't labeled. Anything with a dead-end road leading into it."

"What am I looking for?"

"Electrical substations. They're not labeled, but if you see a big patch of green and it's not a park and it has a dead-end road leading into it, tell me."

Danielle called Anya on her phone and pulled up the maps app on Sean's old Android.

# 59

"Ray Cooper is out today," Anya said. She walked quickly down the third-floor hallway, Agent Espinoza keeping pace beside her. "He didn't call in either. That's unusual. I had one of his coworkers call. He doesn't answer."

"Explain again what's going on with Sean Riggs. You said he's coming here?"

"He's coming. And he's as much as admitted he's the one behind the breach. But he has a reason. A good one."

"Doesn't matter," Espinoza said. "He's going to prison."

"It does matter," Anya said. "When it uncovers a far more dangerous attack. And if security had only taken him seriously in the first place... This is it." She pointed to the door at the end of the hall. They entered without knocking. The man with the mustache looked up from his desk, startled.

"Can I help you?"

Espinoza showed his badge, Anya her ID.

"We need a list of all the upgrades and repairs you'll be working on in the coming month. Along with that, we need a list of the identifiers of all components that will be taken offline when those repairs are done. And who supervises that smart-ass developer on the second floor?"

The man blinked a couple of times, looking back and forth between the two intruders.

"Okay, one question at a time."

"First, the work tickets," Anya said. "With component identifiers."

The man turned his questioning eyes to Agent Espinoza, who merely nodded.

"Okay."

"How soon?" Anya asked.

"Fifteen minutes. Twenty max."

"You'll do it?"

"I'll do it myself. Now about the developer, which one are you talking about? I don't know of any smart-asses here at Empire. Not among the developers anyway."

Anya's phone rang. She answered immediately. Danielle repeated the question Sean had instructed her to ask about getting a list of work orders. "We're already on it," she said. "Great minds think alike."

She relayed Danielle's next question to the man at the desk. "Can you flag all the projects along I-64 between Richmond and Charlottesville?"

The man nodded, and she returned her attention to the call. "How are you, Danielle?"

"Um... Stressed?"

# 60

Gravel crunched beneath the tires of the white pickup with the Empire logo. A cloud of dry gray dust kicked up behind it as it approached the top of the ridge. If Del had been less preoccupied with the upcoming task, with the heat, with the throbbing in his bandaged left hand—if he hadn't turned his head to the left to follow the curve of the road, he would have recognized the white GMC pickup parked on the gravelly right shoulder. His passenger recognized it. As they passed, Ben glanced into the empty cab and gave a military-style salute to the driver who wasn't there.

The Empire truck continued over the hundred-foot-high wooded ridge and down the backside. A hundred yards down, an eight-foot-high chain-link fence bearing the Empire logo blocked the road. One sign warned that the site was restricted to authorized personnel. Another showed a man inside a black triangle being knocked backward by a bolt of electricity. *Danger! High Voltage!*

Del pulled up to the card reader by the gate. He rolled down his window and held his employee badge against the black square until the tiny LED light turned green. The high chain-link gate slid slowly from right to left to let him through. After they passed, it slid shut again.

The chain-link, topped by barbed wire, ran around the full perimeter of the facility. A hundred yards farther in, a second chain-link surrounded the substation. Del stopped the truck just outside the inner fence and checked the time on the dash. Eleven fifteen.

He shifted the truck into park and left the engine running. He took off his cap, wiped his forehead, and turned up the AC.

"We just gonna sit here?" Ben asked.

"That's what we're gonna do."

"Why?"

"Wait for the second crew. They got the tools and parts."

"Why not get started now?"

"We already been through this. You want to stand out in that heat? Seems I remember the last time you were out there, you didn't feel too good."

"Neither did you. You were on an IV too."

"All right, then, there's two reasons for us to stay in the AC." Del unscrewed the cap of his Gatorade and took a sip.

"Come on, man. Let's stop fucking around." Ben turned and looked back up the hill toward the rocky outcrop on the wooded ridge. He could see someone moving. Ray's fatigues made him hard to track against the background of brown stone and green trees. A glint of sun coming off the scope of his Winchester 70 as he heaved it off his shoulder told Ben everything was set.

Ray had set up about sixty yards outside the outer fence. Ben and Del were a hundred yards inside it. A hundred sixty yards was an easy shot for a seasoned hunter, but no shot would have to be fired if all went according to plan. All Ben had to do was flip the switch on the breaker. Or let someone else on the crew do it. Ray would be watching through the scope. When it was done, Ray would return quietly to his truck, leave the gravel road, and head west.

Ben had his own plans. His truck was all packed back at home. He had told his girlfriend they'd be taking a trip to the mountains of western North Carolina. That was true. He didn't tell her how long they'd be going. The extra gas cans in the bed of the truck would be more than enough to get them to the cabin.

"Come on," Ben said. "I didn't take this job to sit around on my ass."

"That's not what the other crews tell me. They said you spend half the day with your ass glued to the seat. If you're so anxious to get started, go ahead."

Ben opened his door and hopped out. Del noticed he didn't take any tools. He walked to the gate, held his ID card up to the black box once, twice, three times. The light remained red, and the gate stayed shut.

Ben returned to the truck, took his seat, and said, "Thing's busted."

"You're busted," Del said.

"How's that?"

"You ain't authorized to open that gate. You need a crew chief." Del took a swig of Gatorade. "What were you gonna do when you got in there?"

"Hit the breaker, then do a visual."

Del shook his head as he finished another sip. "Do the visual inspection first. We cut the breaker when the rest of the crew arrives."

"How long's a walk-around take on a station like this?"

"You tell me. You got three buses, surge arresters, switch panels, main breaker. One transformer per line for how many lines?"

"Three."

"Shunts, insulators."

"Insulators don't break."

"Who knows what those storms blew in here? I see branches over by the second bus. Probably blew right off the ridge behind us. A branch hits an insulator, it breaks."

"I'd give it ten minutes for a walk-around," Ben said.

"You couldn't half ass it in ten minutes. I'd give it twenty five."

"How far out is the other crew?"

"Half hour. More if they stop for food."

"So, we'll go in in five," Ben said. "Start the visual."

"Sounds like a plan. But you ain't touching that switch till I say so. In fact, I'll take care of the breaker."

"Suit yourself, old man." Ben leaned back against the seat, tilted his head up, and stared at the ceiling like a bored child who had given up the fight against an unreasonable parent.

Del turned the radio on and flipped through the stations until he found an old Waylon Jennings song.

"You like country?"

"Country's for backwoods redneck fucks."

"Just for that, I'm gonna turn it up."

He cranked the volume and smiled to the lyrics of "Big Mamou." Ben continued to stare at the roof, doing his best to maintain a look of bored indifference as the music grated on his ears.

# 61

"Okay, projects in the coming month along I-64 between Richmond and Charlottesville." Anya and Carlos Espinoza stood behind the desk of the mustachioed man and looked at the screen. The uncooperative young software developer who had refused Anya's earlier requests sat in a chair in front of the desk with his knees together, clutching his closed laptop like a schoolboy holding his lunchbox.

"We have sixty-one matches," the man said. "Mostly small jobs. Line inspections, padmount transformers."

"How many of these tickets are a result of the storm?" Anya asked.

"Most of them, probably. Does it matter?"

Anya turned to Espinoza. "If this code was in place before the storm," she said, "it was probably written to match a work order that existed before the storm."

"You want me to limit the search to tickets created more than three weeks ago?"

"Can you?"

"Sure." The man clicked a box on-screen and changed the date.

"Okay, now we have twelve. These are slightly bigger jobs, including some substation work."

"Can you pull all the component identifiers from all the equipment involved in those jobs?"

"Sure thing. It'll take a minute."

The man focused on his screen, clicked a few times, and then said to the young programmer in front of him, "Jin, I'm going to email you a list of identifiers. You're going to run them through the bcrypt function and tell this nice lady which one is the lottery winner."

Jin raised his index finger to make a point. "Technically, I don't report to you."

"Technically," said Mr. Mustache, "you'll be reporting to the unemployment office if you don't do as I say."

"Okay," Jin said, opening his laptop. "I'll do what you want, but I'm going to write this up and submit a security report."

"That's good protocol, Jin. Let me know if you need help spelling my name." He leaned in and squinted at the monitor. "Oh, boy."

"What?" asked Anya.

"Jin, how long would it take to run a thousand identifiers through bcrypt?"

"About five seconds."

"Okay. It's going to take a lot longer than that to cut and paste all these into an email."

"Why don't I just run the query?" Jin said.

"I thought you'd never ask."

"Can I ask you a question?" Anya was looking at the man behind the desk.

"Of course."

"How hard is it to switch out the software that monitors and manages the live grid? I mean, if there's a problem?"

"It's not like rebooting your laptop or upgrading Microsoft Word. Any software change has to pass formal review, then go through weeks of testing in an isolated test environment. Then it needs several levels of administrative sign-off. It's a rigid process that has to comply with a number of federal regulations. Why?"

"So, there's no chance of swapping out the grid-control software today while the system is running?"

The man laughed. "Do they swap out airplane engines in the middle of a flight?"

# 62

The gravel road ended at a yellow farmhouse behind which stood a brown barn surrounded by rolls of hay. Sean put the Mustang in reverse and cut the wheel sharply, backing off the side of the road before shifting into drive and heading back the way they came.

"You said to look for green spots on the map with dead-end roads," Danielle said.

"Yeah, and we're oh for two."

"There's another one a mile down."

"Does it have a house on it?"

"It doesn't have anything on it. You want to give it a shot?"

"We'll try it. And if we're wrong again, we'll head back to Richmond."

A few minutes later, they were climbing a wooded ridge on a road of gravel. Danielle felt an eerie sense of discomfort as they passed an empty white pickup parked near the top. She couldn't say why, but something made her want to tell Sean to turn around. Leave now. This was a bad place with bad energy. She knew that sinking feeling in the pit of her stomach, that inexplicable gut feeling. Every time she had ignored it in the past, she regretted it.

As they crested the ridge, Sean said, "Bingo!" He pointed ahead at the gate. When they got closer, they could see the Empire logo, the signs warning people to keep out. A hundred yards past the gate, two men exited an Empire truck. The big guy was Del. The other was Ben.

"That's them," Sean said.

"Sean?" Danielle's voice had a plaintive tone. The sinking feeling in her gut was getting worse.

Sean got out of the Mustang, leaving the door open behind him. He walked to the gate, cupped his hands around his mouth, and yelled "Hey!"

The sound of Johnny Cash's "Country Boy" blared back at him from the open doors of the Empire truck.

He watched as Del held his card against the reader at the inner gate. It opened, and Del and Ben walked in.

"Hey!" Louder this time. But not loud enough to be heard over the music.

Sean walked back to the car.

"I feel sick," Danielle groaned.

"God, don't tell me you're pregnant."

"I'm not pregnant, Sean, what the hell?"

"It's just nerves, then."

"No, I swear, something triggered me just now."

"What?"

"I don't know. Is that guy down there the one we ran into when we were on your motorcycle?"

"Good memory."

"He gave you his card, remember? When we were out there on the trail. Why don't you just call him?"

"Holy crap! You're right!"

Sean pulled out his wallet and thumbed past the credit cards to the one piece of paper he could find. Del Wright, Empire Energy.

"Call him." She handed him his phone.

Sean punched in the number and listened. One ring. Two rings. Six rings. Voicemail.

He called again. Same result.

"You think he left his phone in the truck?" Danielle asked.

"I'm going down there."

"How?"

"Climb the fence."

"Over the barbed wire?"

"What other way is there? Give me your phone."

"Why?"

"So I can get that woman from Homeland Security on the line to explain things to her."

"I want my phone."

"Why do you need it?"

"I told you, something is wrong."

"What?"

"I don't know! I'll text you her number."

"Fine."

"What's the number of that phone? Actually, just give it to me. I'll type it in."

"Hurry."

Sean leaned into the car and handed her the phone. As she typed the number, he rummaged through the sports equipment in the back seat. He pushed aside two volleyballs, a net still wrapped in its original packaging, and then pulled a soft plastic bag onto the front seat. Inside he found a dozen volleyball jerseys with vertical stripes of light and dark blue. The colors of the high school team that Sid Miller had coached to the regional finals last year. He pulled half a dozen shirts from the bag and draped them over his arm.

"Here." Danielle handed him the phone.

"Thanks."

Sean ducked out of the car, slid the phone into his back pocket, and climbed the fence. When he reached the top, he draped the shirts over the barbed wire, paused to gather his courage, and then pulled himself over a little too fast. He hung onto the shirts across the top wire for a couple of seconds. The barbs were long enough to go through the fabric and puncture his palms. He was scared to jump, but the pain outweighed the fear. His toes were a few feet above the ground when he let go.

He landed on the other side with a thud. The phone came out of his pocket and smashed onto the gravel beside him. He picked it up without examining it, slid it into his back pocket, and ran down the road toward the gate of the inner fence as a new song blared from the Empire truck. This time, a woman was singing.

Del and Ben were walking a circuit around the substation, Del keeping the young man close, pointing out pieces of equipment and talking.

Danielle stood beside the Mustang and watched. Del and the other person inside the fence didn't see Sean yet.

"I know this song," she muttered.

Sean had almost reached the inner gate. It would be locked when he got there. He would have to run along the fence to where they could see him. He would have to flag them down, get them to come over to the fence and talk to him.

"Ooh, I hate this feeling," Danielle whispered as she held her stomach. "I hate it when I know something is wrong, but I don't know what it is."

Sean was tugging on the inner gate. Danielle muttered, "It's not going to open, stupid. You have to talk to them from the outside. Oh, I feel sick."

She turned away, toward her right, where a subtle movement on a stony outcrop of the ridge above caught her eye. What was that?

The woman's voice coming from the truck below was telling her not to give it up. She knew this song. She knew the song and she felt sick, and something was moving on the ledge of stone that protruded from the hill above.

Something was moving up there and the song was about to get to the line she knew, as the pit of dread in her stomach grew deeper and vaguer and more threatening.

The moving thing on the rock above sent a bright, blinding flash of sunlight into her eyes, and she remembered now where she had seen the white pickup they had passed on their way over the ridge. In the parking lot outside Empire Energy on the day Anya Lakhani had questioned her. She remembered the owner standing beside it as the police car rolled up behind, the man who had glared at her from behind the conference room glass with that disturbing stare, the palpably sick mind looking out through sunken, bloodshot eyes. It was his truck they had passed, his truck parked at the side of the gravel road just over the ridge.

She ran to the gate, cupped her hands around her mouth, and yelled as loud she could, "Sean! Sean!"

From the truck below, Tammy Wynette answered even louder. "Run, Woman, Run!"

# 63

Ray had a good view of her through the Winchester's telescopic sight. The little fertility queen from the Empire offices the other day. How was she mixed up in this? She wasn't with the government. Maybe she had been interviewing for an administrative assistant position. Could that Anya lady not do her job on her own? Did she need someone to help her?

Ray pulled his eye from the sight and blinked. After however many sleepless nights he had now been through, his eyes were bone dry.

It was Donna's fault he couldn't sleep. Donna's fault his eyes burned. Donna might even be ruining his aim. How can you aim when your eyes burn?

She deserved to die a thousand times.

He looked through the scope again. The woman on the road below walked back to the fence. She screamed and screamed and screamed. But when her voice rose up to his perch on the hill, it came through thin and pinched. He would have liked her to put some throat in it. A scream was more satisfying when it carried emotion from deep within. When you could really feel her fear, then it was truly satisfying.

"He can't hear you, you moron," Ray muttered against the stock of his rifle. "Can't you see that? They're not looking at you. None of them are."

He watched as her fingers frantically punched at her phone. She put it to her ear, shifted her weight to her left foot. That made her hip jut out to the right. She had nice hips, he thought. Big, strong hips. She was shaped like an hourglass. Sean Riggs had an hourglass in his car. Was he screwing her? If so, what was wrong with her? Why would she give herself up to that whiny little prick?

He turned his sights down toward the substation. Sean stood outside the inner fence. Del and Ben walked inside, talking.

He panned back to Danielle and watched her remove her phone from her ear and dial again. She looked annoyed. Was she calling Sean? Was he not answering? Perhaps he broke his phone when he jumped down from the fence. Ray had seen him stoop to pick it up off the gravel.

He panned to her left, then to her right. She winced as a glint of sun from the lens of the telescopic sight caught her eye.

"Oh, now you know I'm here," Ray said to no one. "Well good for you. I wouldn't mind having one like you up at the cabin. Start a new brood. God knows from the looks of you, you were built for it."

He pulled the gun back, looked down into the substation. "What the hell are you doing?" he muttered. "Just pull the damn switch already! Why does everyone at this stupid company have to have an hour-long meeting before making a decision?"

He turned and looked back toward the Mustang with his bare eyes now. The fertility queen was leaning into the car. She had a big ass. No one is perfect, Ray thought. Hell, some guys even like them like that.

He watched her lean farther in. She was reaching into the back seat. She found something, pulled back, then leaned down toward the floor in front of the passenger seat.

"What are you up to, Missy?"

He put the sights back on her in time to see her stand. She was holding a backpack. A big, full backpack stuffed with God knows what. She was zipping it shut.

She turned and looked right at him. Right through the scope and into his eyes.

"What's the matter, Missy? Are you scared I'll shoot your boyfriend? Well, maybe I will."

He watched her walk back up the hill, away from the others.

"Where are you going, little woman? Not to the trailhead, I hope. You're not that stupid, are you? Walking into these woods in that bright white shirt? I'll see you coming from a mile away. Lord, it's a wonder any woman on this planet lives past the age of twelve."

He continued to watch her until she was out of sight. Last he saw, she was walking uphill, head bent forward over her phone screen, tapping out a message.

# 64

In the office, the young programmer, Jin, stared quietly at his laptop while Anya, Espinoza, and Mr. Mustache waited quietly around the desk.

"Here!" he exclaimed. "Here's the ID that matches the encrypted data."

He set the laptop on the desk and turned it so they could see.

"That's a breaker," Jin said. "All the identifiers that begin with B-R are breakers."

"Where is it?" Espinoza asked.

"Let me see." Mustache ran his finger down his monitor, scanning the list of component identifiers to see if he could tie this one back to one of the repair jobs Anya had asked about.

"Wouldn't it be faster to just type that into the database?" Espinoza asked.

Anya's phone chimed.

Mustache looked up at Espinoza and smiled. "Good thinking!"

"That breaker is at Collier's Ridge," Anya said.

"How do you—"

She turned her phone to him before he could finish his question. He read the message from Danielle.

colliers ridge rays here hurry PLEASE!!

# 65

Speaking through the fence, Del said, "Come again?"

"You have to stop work on this project," Sean replied.

Ben eyed him with suspicion and hostility.

"We ain't even started," Del said. "How'd you know we were here? How'd you get past that fence back there? You know you're not supposed to be in here."

"Hold on," Sean said. He pulled his phone from his pocket and looked curiously at the cracked screen. "I want you to talk to someone. Do you know this woman from Homeland Security?"

"Homeland Security?" Ben asked. The mention of federal investigators seemed to pique his anger. "What the hell do they have to do with this?" Sean thought he saw a glint of recognition in Ben's eyes. Did Ben remember him from his two outings with Ray's clique during his short stint at Empire?

"Hold on," Sean repeated. He pressed the button that should have lit the screen, but nothing happened.

"Hold on for what?" Ben asked. "We don't take orders from you. You aren't even supposed to be in here. Company fired your sorry ass, remember? Get the hell outta here!"

"He's right," Del said. "You gotta go back up there and—" He looked back toward the Mustang parked outside the gate. "How *did* you get past that fence?"

"Can you call?" Sean asked. "Can you call base and ask about this work ticket?"

"Base?" Ben's voice was full of contempt. "What the hell is base? You think we're on a moon mission here?"

"The office, whatever." The stress of the situation sounded in Sean's voice, which now carried a tinge of desperation. "Just call back and ask them the status of this ticket. Ask if you should stop work."

Del cocked his head. "What's got you all worked up, buddy?"

Sean looked like he was about to tell all, spill the fact right there and then, but a glance at the hard, hateful expression on Ben's face stopped him. He didn't want to say anything in front of Ray's acolyte.

To Del, he said, "Hey, um, can I talk to you out here?"

"Talk in here," Ben said. "Talk to me."

Ignoring him, Del said, "All right."

The three of them began walking back toward the entry gate of the inner fence.

~ ~ ~

Danielle's heart beat furiously as she ascended the hill in the blazing heat. There was no shelter from the sun along this stretch of road. The voice singing behind her now, blasting its lyrics up the wooded hillside, was a man's. She didn't recognize the singer or the song.

The three male figures in the substation below walked along the fence, back toward the inner entry gate. But her back was to them now and she didn't see.

Go back there and try again, she told herself. Warn Sean. Her breath was shaky and shallow, but her feet continued forward as she debated the best course of action.

Go back! Yell louder, said one voice.

You know they can't hear you, said another.

Then use your phone! Call him again.

The calls don't go through. He must have broken his phone when he went over the fence.

Her knees felt weak as she ascended the gravel road. Sweat dripped from her hair, and her mouth was dry with fear. The backpack pressed hot sweat between her shoulder blades and into the base of her spine. Yet, on she went.

Go back, said the voice of doubt. You can't do this. You know you can't.

No. Someone's going to die, she told herself as she crested the hill. Ray's up there with a gun and a scope like he's hunting.

He's hunting humans, and they don't have a chance down there. Someone is going to die, and I can't let that happen.

You're not going to shoot my Sean, you evil bastard. You're not going to shoot those other guys. What if they have families? Do you want to see their children crying over the coffins? Maybe you do. You're a sick man. Anyone can see it just looking at you. You need help.

She was almost at the top of the ridge.

I can't do this, she told herself. I can't shoot a human being. I could barely stand to watch Ronnie kill a deer. But I can't let them die down there either.

She continued down the back side of the ridge toward Ray's truck. There was an opening in the trees just ahead.

She pulled her phone from her pocket and dialed 911 as she turned onto the trail.

"Nine one one, what's your emergency?"

"Active shooter," she said softly, her voice shaking with fear and exertion.

~ ~ ~

"What the hell is the holdup down there?" Ray muttered.

He had Sean Riggs in his sights, moving the crosshairs ever so slightly, aiming now at his mouth, now at his eye.

The three had reached the inner gate. Del and Ben were inside, Sean outside. Del opened the gate and stepped out. His right hand maintained a hold on the gate, keeping it open. The fat bastard was in his way, his broad back blocking a clean shot at Sean Riggs.

Ray took his eye off the site and rubbed his face against his shoulder. The heat made the dryness in his eyes almost unbearable. He looked again through the sight. Del still blocked his shot.

"What the hell are you two jabbering about down there? Move, you fat fuck!" He waved the end of the rifle as if they'd see it and obey his command to separate.

Oh, what the hell, he thought. I invited them both to the club. They both declined. They know where they're going.

Sean's head was visible just above Del's left shoulder. Ray centered the sights on Sean's cheekbone. His eye blinked furiously as he squeezed the trigger.

Sean Riggs turned to point at something as a hole exploded through Del's left shoulder. Del went down, his blood spattered all over Sean's face.

~ ~ ~

"I'm sorry, ma'am," said the emergency operator. "Did you say shooter?"

"Active shooter," Danielle repeated softly. She followed the wooded trail as it turned left, back up toward the top of the ridge she had just crested. The climb became steeper. "I can't talk any louder. He'll hear me."

"Is anyone injured?"

She froze as the sound of a rifle shot rang out.

Go back, the voice inside her head pleaded as the echo of the shot cracked back from a distant hill. Run, woman, run!

"Ma'am?" asked the voice from her phone. "Are you okay?"

"I'm okay," she whispered. "You have my location."

She ended the call and continued forward.

They call you back, she told herself. 911. They call back if you get cut off. She silenced the phone so the ring wouldn't tip Ray off to her location.

Oh, God, she thought. Did he hit one of them? Sean? That big guy? The young one? He's just a kid.

*Go back, Danielle! Turn around!*

She ignored the inner voice, continued cautiously up the hill, remembering everything Ronnie had taught her on their hunting trips. Approach in silence. That was the first rule. She was better at it than he was. Her instinct for stealth had startled Ronnie a dozen times. She had done it to Sean too. Even to Anya in the conference room at Empire when she wasn't even trying.

~ ~ ~

"I hear you back there, Missy," Ray muttered half aloud as his dry red eyes blinked against the blazing sun. "What the hell are they doing down there?"

Del lay face down in the grass. Sean leaned over him.

Okay, Ray thought. Where's Ben? He squinted before being able to make out the third figure.

Ben, you stupid fuck, why are you cowering? You know it's me up here. You don't have to take cover. Look at you! Crawling on the ground like a worm! Get a move on, you dumb bastard!

He fired a second shot into the ground near Ben's waist as a reminder to complete the task. Ben's body convulsed in fear.

"Throw the switch, you idiot!"

Now all three of them were face down. Del motioned weakly to Sean, waving him toward a depression in the ground where he would be harder to hit.

Ray turned from his spot on the rocks and looked back up through the trees on the ridge above him and whispered softly, "Come on down here in your bright, white T-shirt, Missy. You'll be a nice, easy target."

He scanned the tree line for a few seconds, but there was no one there.

~ ~ ~

Crouched behind a stone and peering through the bush in front, she watched him watch her. What had Ronnie said to her on that horrid excursion when he was drunk, when he couldn't fell the deer on the first shot? When he had to follow it and shoot it a second time, and then a third?

He said, "Don't pick up the gun unless you're committed to kill. If you save that decision until it's time to shoot, then you'll sit there debating with yourself and you'll miss your shot. Make up your mind before the gun goes in your hand. Got it?"

She nodded as if he were talking to her there and then.

She looked past Ray, down to the substation where all three men lay flat on the ground. Ray had fired twice. Which ones had he hit?

The dark stain on the back of Del's left shoulder glistened in the sun as it spread. Her heart sank at the thought of having to lie immobile beneath that blazing sun with such a wound. He was probably still alive. He was feeling it, was probably scared, and he couldn't even pick his face up off the ground.

And there was Sean, flattened face down in a depression in the hot grass. When he turned his face toward Ray, she could see it was covered with blood.

Oh, God, she thought. Ray got him. How is he even still moving? How badly is he hurt?

Her first instinct was to reach for her phone, call 911, scream that she needed an ambulance. But she had already called. And how far away was this hollow behind the ridge from—from anything?

The phone was useless. Ray was a hundred feet downhill from her, and he'd hear anything she said. He would turn his gun on her, and that would be the end of it.

She unzipped the big compartment of the backpack as quietly as she could, keeping her eyes on Ray, watching through the bush. Her hand pushed passed the ball she had taken from the back seat of the Mustang, reached down to the bottom of the bag. She wrapped her fingers around the grip and heard Ronnie say again, "Don't pick up the gun unless you're committed to kill."

Yes, I know, she thought.

She watched as Ray turned his attention back to the men below. He was lining up his sights for another shot when the sound of crunching gravel told her a vehicle was coming up the road.

~ ~ ~

Ray heard it too. He turned to his left and watched a county sheriff's car pull up behind the Mustang. For a second, the cruiser just sat there. No one got out.

Ray turned his sights toward the cop car. He couldn't get a view through the passenger window from this angle. But the driver's door would have to open sooner or later, and when it did...

He took his eye off the sight and looked down to the substation. Ben was up on his feet now, walking toward the equipment. That *was* Ben, wasn't it? He blinked twice, looked at the figures lying in the grass outside the fence, and told himself, yes, that was Ben.

Ray watched him walk to a large gray steel box. He picked up the rifle, put the sights on his acolyte to get a better view, watched him pull the breaker switch, watched him turn and give the thumbs-up.

Then he heard the car door open. Ray swung the gun around toward the source of the noise, swung a little too far. The cop came into his sights, then went out. From behind him came the soft sound of a twig snapping.

He muttered quietly, "I know you're back there, Missy."

The cop was bending down now, head inside the driver's window of the Mustang.

"Straighten up, pig," Ray growled softly. "I'll introduce you to the Almighty."

He heard Danielle skitter down the hill behind him, a quick rush through dry leaves on the forest floor that came to an end thirty feet off his right shoulder.

The cop straightened up. The face that appeared above the roof of the Mustang belonged to a woman. He put a bullet through it. The figure dropped and disappeared.

Ray pulled the magazine from the Winchester, quickly loaded in three more cartridges, reattached it, and pulled the bolt.

He turned his sights to the right. In the space between the dark, waxy leaves of a rhododendron he saw spots of bright white. She was down low, lying flat on her belly. He fixed the crosshairs on the brightest spot of white, glaringly lit by a ray of direct sunlight, and fired.

The shot knocked her back at least a foot before the branches of the bush stopped her from going farther. He stood, found another white patch in his sights, and fired again. Again, the bullet knocked her back.

He walked closer. From a distance of ten feet, he spied white again. He raised the rifle to his shoulder and sent a third round into her. Now the white was all gone.

He pulled the magazine from the Winchester and slung the rifle over his shoulder. He walked toward the bush, pulling cartridges from the pocket of his tactical vest and loading them into the magazine as he went.

When he reached the bush, he crouched and pulled back one of the larger branches to have a look.

What was left of her? Just little fragments. Little fragments of white and gray.

Where was her blood? He picked up a stick and poked at one of the fragments. As it turned, he read the dark gray print. Mikasa. What was that? A ball? Yes. A brand-new, bright white volleyball.

Blinking in confusion, he stood and turned back toward the stony outcrop.

"Surprise!" Danielle said softly.

She stood twenty feet in front of him in jeans and a white V-neck T-shirt, both hands on the revolver.

Ray recognized the model. The .22 was joke. Soldiers didn't even bother with such a weapon. It had no stopping power. If an enemy confronted you at this range and your first shot wasn't a kill, you were dead. You could empty the cylinder into your foe, but if he was determined, he would charge right through the barrage. Sure, he might bleed out in half an hour, but that would be half an hour after you were dead.

The .22 was a placebo for women who wanted to feel safe when they walked to their cars after a late night on the job. It was a warning device, a prop they could brandish to make an attacker think twice. It was meant to be wielded but not fired.

Her stance was wrong too. Not fully squared. Weight not far enough forward. She didn't know what she was doing. Probably learned from watching TV shows.

The look of cold determination on her face was a front. A bluff. Her body language told the real story. Her knees were locked. Her shoulders were tense, bunched up toward her ears. She was scared.

Like all women were scared. Like Donna. They pretend at first to truly believe they're your equal. But they're not. Raise a hand and they begin to doubt. Women want to draw you into a mind game. They think they can win if they mess with your head. But as soon as you make it physical, show them your power, they fold.

"Looks like you got yourself a little girly gun there, Missy." Ray took a step toward her. He dropped the rifle magazine and his right hand moved slowly toward the handgun on his belt. "You want to hand it over? Or do you want me to come and take it from you?"

She stood her ground, determined and tense.

His mouth twisted into a smile of contempt, his eyes showed a disregard for his opponent's will that bordered on arrogance. He took another step, his eyes fixed on hers, his hand moving toward the grip of the Sig Sauer on his hip.

Still, she didn't budge.

"Well, Missy?" She was frozen now. Ray recognized her paralysis as a sign of a woman in doubt, a woman about to fold. Another step and he began to chuckle. "What's your decision?"

She shot him in the face.

The bullet he didn't think she had the nerve to fire or the skill to aim struck him directly between the eyes. It carved a tunnel through the middle of his brain, from the front of his skull to the rear. He pitched face-first onto the leafy ground, his lifeless right hand just inches from the pistol he was sure would save him.

Danielle felt a wave of nausea rise from her stomach as she watched thick rivulets of blood flow from his wound onto the dry, brown leaves of the forest floor. She clicked the safety, turned, and ran, her hand covering her mouth.

At the top of the ridge, hyperventilating, she had to stop. Convulsions from her stomach rose into her throat. Her mouth filled with saliva, and then a gushing wave of puke rushed past her lips and through the fingers of her shaking left hand.

She pushed on without waiting to catch her breath. Tears blurred her vision as she stumbled along the winding trail as fast as her feet could move, heading instinctively for the victims in the hollow below.

# 66

"You hear that?" Sean asked.

Del was breathing hard, his face turned sideways toward Sean, palms flat on the ground like he was going to do a push-up. But it was all he could do to breathe. Sean could see the pain and fear in his eyes.

"Hang in there," he said.

"Hear what?" Del grunted.

"That pop up on the ridge."

"Didn't hear it," Del groaned.

"That was a different gun. Maybe a second shooter."

Sean watched Ben hop into the truck, watched Ray's disciple close the driver's door. The passenger door was still open. Ben gunned the truck in reverse, arcing left until the hood pointed toward the gate, then he put it in drive and headed up the hill. The truck's momentum swung the passenger door shut. The vehicle smashed through the chain-link gate, swerved left around the Mustang and the empty patrol car behind it, and disappeared over the ridge in a cloud of dust.

For a moment, the world was quiet. Sean looked at the Mustang outside the gate. Where was Danielle? He prayed she was okay. She would know to hide after she heard the first shot. She would have called 911, and then she would have hidden.

He turned his eyes to the stony outcropping above. It was empty.

That didn't mean anything. The shooter could still be up there, crouched behind a bush or tree.

"Hey," Del grunted. "Get my phone."

"I don't want to get shot."

"Get my phone outta my pocket and call an ambulance."

Sean glanced again at the ridge. He hesitated a second, then crawled toward Del and asked which pocket.

He found the phone, saw the Do Not Disturb icon was active—no wonder Del hadn't answered—then, from the corner of his eye, saw motion on the road above. Danielle was running down the hill toward the broken gate. Her shirt was still white. There was no blood on her jeans. A wave of gratitude swept over him. She hadn't been hit.

Then he watched her turn as if startled. She began walking the other way, back up the road, waving at someone or something farther up, waving them forward. She moved to the side. A police cruiser stopped in a cloud of dust. She leaned in and said something, pointed down toward where Sean and Del lay in the grass below.

She backed away from the car. It weaved around the parked cruiser, past the Mustang, and through the twisted wreckage of the gate. Behind it came another cruiser, and then another. Two ambulances brought up the rear.

Sean wondered what Danielle had said to the cop. And what about the shooter? Where was he? Were the first responders driving into his line of fire?

# 67

Anya reread Danielle's text four times, the one she had tapped out a minute earlier as she left the woods.

> Ray is dead. Two or three more wounded. 911 not here
> yet. HELP!!!

She was in the Empire control center now with Agent Espinoza and Cy Madhi, the director of transmission-and-distribution operations, watching the big monitors that displayed the real-time status of the grid.

Had the switch been pulled, she wondered? Had the plan been set in motion? It didn't look like it. Everything still looked normal. But that was part of the plan, wasn't it? The malware would record normal readings and play them back on the monitors so the grid operators wouldn't know what was really going on.

She called Danielle's phone three times, but got no answer. Danielle had silenced her phone so Ray wouldn't hear it ring when 911 called her back. She hadn't thought to change that since her confrontation with Ray.

Finally, after several tense minutes, Danielle called her.

"He's okay!" She was crying.

"Who's okay?"

"Sean. I thought he'd been shot. His face is all covered with blood. This other guy—oh, I feel so bad for him. He's still on the ground. They're working on him now."

In the background, Anya heard Sean say, "Give me the phone."

"And he shot a cop," Danielle added. "He killed that woman in cold blood. He shot her in the head. For doing her job!"

"Danielle, give me the phone!" Sean's voice was more urgent now.

"Do you know if anyone tripped the breaker?" Anya asked.

"Sorry, what?" She still couldn't think clearly after the strain of what she had just been through. She still felt Ray's red, contemptuous eyes boring into her.

"Is Sean there?" Anya asked.

"He's right—"

Sean took the phone before she could finish her sentence. "It's done," he said. "Ray's little fanboy flipped the switch and the plan is in motion."

"Can you flip it back?"

"It wouldn't matter if we did. As soon as it went off, it triggered the malware. There's nothing in the code that will turn back the clock. Where are you?"

"In the control center."

"Tell them what's going on. They have to shut everything down."

# 68

"Cy?" Anya's tone conveyed the urgency she felt. "We need to cut the power."

Cy Madhi looked annoyed. "We don't just *cut the power*," he mocked. "If you shut it off, the grid collapses."

"I just got a report that the breaker was tripped and—"

"Yeah, I know what you think. Espinoza briefed me, but I don't believe this whole scheme is going to pan out. Has anyone even verified it's in the code?"

"It's in there," Anya said. "Our techs verified what our source said. The build script injects the malicious code at the last second, as the software is being compiled."

"Your source," Cy said skeptically, "is Sean Riggs, whom we fired. His prior employer also fired him. I'm not inclined to take his word on this."

"We verified his findings," Anya protested.

"Maybe you did. But just because the malicious code is in there doesn't mean it's going to work. I'm trying to make sure we don't do anything rash here. Shutting down a statewide grid isn't something you do lightly. It means power goes out to millions of people who are more than tired of living in the dark after those two storms. We're also connected to other states. If we go offline, we destabilize the whole mid-Atlantic and Northeast. We could take down the grid all the way to Chicago. And then there's the problem of restarting it. Do you remember what happened in Texas in 2021? You can't just flip a switch and turn it all back on. A black start requires a huge, coordinated effort and could take days."

"Okay, but do *you* understand?" Anya pleaded. "Do you understand the risk of running this system blind? Your operators won't be seeing the right readings. Everything will look fine from in here, but outside it will all be burning. The lines will be melting. Equipment across the state will be destroyed."

"My job is to keep the system running, not to put everyone in the dark. We'll keep an eye on things."

"But you're not going to see it!"

"Trust me," Cy said. "This is my job. I've been doing it for years." He sat and watched, his eyes moving from monitor to monitor in fixed concentration.

# 69

Del was on his back now, on a gurney, being wheeled across the grass. Two men from the second repair crew, the crew he and Ben had been waiting on before the shooting broke out, walked alongside the medical technicians toward the back of a waiting ambulance.

"How you holding up, Del?"

"Don't crowd him." The EMT turned her back, putting a barrier between Del and his coworkers.

"Been better," Del said, breathing hard. "Felt a thud, hit the ground, and then it started to burn like hell."

"Is he going to make it?" the man asked.

"He'll make it," said the woman. The EMTs were pushing the gurney up into the ambulance now.

"Close that breaker," Del said. "Ben opened it. I told him not to."

His coworker nodded and said he would close it.

Two EMTs stood by the outer gate talking to a sheriff's deputy. They had left the fallen officer in place. A few feet up the road, by the side of the first patrol car, Danielle described what had happened to two other officers. She pointed to the spot from which Ray had fired. Her finger traced a line from the rocky outcropping down to the inner gate, where Del had been hit. Then another line from the rocks to the side of the Mustang, where the first officer lay dead.

"You say you know the man?" asked an officer.

"I didn't know him. I recognized him. He used to work with Sean."

"Ray Cooper," Sean said. "He's under investigation by Homeland Security and the FBI."

"You sure he's dead?" the cop asked.

"I'm sure," Danielle said.

"Can you show us where he is?"

She didn't want to go back up there, didn't want to ever see that man again, but she said yes.

The four of them, Sean, Danielle, and the two armed officers started up the road toward the trailhead.

Down at the substation, Del's coworker closed the breaker and restored the flow of electricity.

"Hell of a thing to have happen at work," he said.

"What do you think it's all about?" his partner asked.

"Who knows. People will shoot anyone these days. Hey, you see that?"

"What?"

"The reading on this line." He tapped the meter beside the breaker.

"One fifteen?"

"It was at ninety-two when I flipped it on."

"Ninety-two thousand volts is about right in this heat."

"So, why'd it jump up to full power?"

The man shrugged. "Give it a minute. If it doesn't go down, we'll call in."

# 70

"Hey, Cy?" The young operations engineer in the khaki slacks and white button-down held a phone to his ear.

"Yeah?"

"Got a call from the crew out at Collier's Ridge. They closed the breaker and the voltage jumped from ninety-two to a hundred fifteen thousand."

"Tell them to keep an eye on it."

Cy and Anya turned their eyes to the monitor on Cy's desk. "I can bring up that substation here," he said. He panned around the map and then zoomed in. "System says it's pushing ninety-two thousand volts, not one fifteen."

"This is what I'm saying," Anya told him calmly. "You're not seeing the right readings. And this might be happening all across the state."

"Hey, Cy?" a woman's voice called from across the room.

Cy looked up.

"PEPCO up in Maryland says our lines are running hot. They're seeing full voltage on the two thirty and five hundred K interconnects. We shouldn't be running anywhere near that in this heat. They want us to dial it down."

"How long can the system run at this level before the lines start to burn?" Anya asked.

"It's not running at that level," Cy replied, pointing to the system map on his monitor. "We're running those lines below capacity, well within the specs for today's heat."

"Okay, but hypothetically," Anya said. "If what the guys at Collier's Ridge and the utility in Maryland say is right, how long can the lines sustain that load?"

"Four minutes. Maybe five." Cy looked back at the young man holding the phone to his ear. "I'm going to cut the breaker at Collier's Ridge from here. Tell them that. Tell them to watch it. I want to know if it goes off."

The young man nodded, and then another voice came from two desks down. "Cy!"

Cy followed the woman's pointing finger up to the monitor that showed customer-reported outages. Clusters of little blue circles began to appear outside Charlottesville, Lynchburg, Roanoke, Newport News.

"The system sensors say there are no outages in those regions," he said to Anya.

"Doesn't that confirm what I'm telling you? Do you think customers are reporting outages that aren't happening? Nothing you're seeing is right. Except that." She pointed back to the map of customer outages, where the little blue bubbles expanded with increasing speed. Danville was out, and now Covington, South Boston, and Manassas.

"Cy?" Another voice now, from the back of the room. "West Virginia and North Carolina say they're going to cut the interconnects if we don't dial down the voltage. I don't know what they're seeing, but it doesn't match what I'm seeing."

"Cut it," Cy said.

"Cut what?"

"Everything," Cy shouted. "Take it all down!"

"Everything?"

"Everything."

The technicians took their seats and began the protocol for shutdown. In seconds, the unexpected disappearance of twenty-one billion watts of power from the eastern grid strained the transmission systems to the north, south, and west. When the voltage frequency dipped to fifty-nine hertz, the emergency safety mechanisms in the other states began shedding load, cutting power to cities and towns. One by one, the other states went black, and an eerie silence descended over the heat-stricken suburbs as tens of millions of air conditioners shut off at once.

Cy shut his eyes and let out a long breath.

"The real work," he told Anya, "starts now. The real work is bringing all this back up."

Anya shook her head. "You'll have to replace the software first. You'll have to roll back to a version you know isn't infected."

"Oh, God," Cy groaned. "I don't even know the procedure for that. That's Ray's job."

# 71

## July 14

"What tipped you off to the code?" asked Agent Espinoza.

In the Richmond office of the FBI, Sean looked around the conference table at a host of unfamiliar faces. Everyone but him wore a suit. The older ones he understood to be supervisors. The younger ones he assumed were field agents. Their badges told him which agencies they came from: FBI, NSA, Homeland Security, Federal Energy Regulatory Commission.

After an outage lasting nearly forty hours, power had been restored five days earlier.

"It just didn't look right," Sean replied. "That code didn't fit in with the rest of the tests. It was issuing commands to a system it wasn't even supposed to be able to reach. It contained encrypted variables. Everything about it was wrong."

"Did you suspect Ray was behind it?"

Sean shook his head. "When I first ran across it, I had no idea who put that code there."

"You understood, though, that when you hacked in, you were in violation of federal law?"

"I knew that. But I had already tried going through the proper channels. That was a dead end."

"Why didn't you contact law enforcement?"

"And tell them what? There's some fishy test code here? Go raid Empire? How far would I have gotten with that? With all the other stuff on your plate, how long would it have taken for you to even start digging into it? Do you think you would have figured it out in time? Before I did?"

"Point taken," Espinoza said. "How did you get the malware into the network in the first place?"

The man from the Federal Energy Regulatory Commission said, "Yes. How?"

The woman from the NSA leaned forward to hear his response.

"That's a whole other story," Sean replied. "You know I was fired once before. From a company that sells supposedly secure routers and firewalls. I did go through the proper channels when I blew the whistle there. I reported the problem to the higher-ups, and when they failed to act, I reported it to federal regulators. Nothing came of that, except that I got fired. And harassed so badly by my former employer, I moved to another town.

"But the problems in those routers were real. They were easy to exploit, if you knew where to look. I adapted an old Chinese malware, one we studied in a cybersecurity course, and I was able to push it through the Empire firewall by exploiting weaknesses I had discovered while working with my former employer.

"Once I was in, it was game on. The malware replicated itself to other machines. The only wrench in the works was the hurricanes. I had to wait until power and internet service came back before I could get the code that was being exfiltrated."

"How did you revive the Chinese malware?" asked the woman from the NSA. "That was a sophisticated piece of work for its day, but it lost its potency once we deciphered it and published its digital signatures. The virus scanners picked it up easily after that. What did you do to get it working again?"

"Computer viruses are like biological viruses. They have a surface that the victim's immune system may or may not recognize, and they have a payload that can be more or less harmful. The Chinese virus had a fundamentally sound design. It just needed some surface alterations to get past the virus scanners, and some updates to its replication and file-stealing payload to cloak its activities better. It's like the flu. You get it one year, and then you're immune to it. The next year, a different strain comes around. You don't have immunity, so you get sick again."

Espinoza turned his attention to Anya Lakhani. "What prompted you to go out to West Virginia?"

"You know. I told you at the time."

"For the record," Espinoza said.

"For the record, I wanted to talk to Ray Cooper so I could rule out the whole Sean Riggs angle as quickly as possible, so we could focus our resources on a more likely culprit. I thought we'd be wasting valuable time if I waited days for Ray to return."

"And the people you found up there?"

"The person," Anya corrected. "Unfriendly. An anti-government type. Armed, belligerent, intimidating. He also happened to work for another electric utility, in a position similar to Ray's. High enough up the ladder to have access to sensitive systems."

The man from FERC cleared his throat. Scanning a page of typed notes, he announced, "We're just a few days into our investigation of the Ohio and Michigan utilities. We've already found evidence of sabotage. Switches, breakers, and shunts that would have protected those grids in a situation like this had been surreptitiously disabled. This was done from the inside by people with a deep knowledge of the grid's topology. Ray's neighbors in West Virginia both had privileged access to the compromised systems. We believe this was an act of conspiracy."

"Neither of Ray's West Virginia buddies is talking," Espinoza said. "All we've established in our interrogations is that they're both hostile to the US government, and both may have ties to extremist groups. Thank you, Anya, for your initiative and impatience in this investigation. If you hadn't been in such a rush to close out an avenue of inquiry that you thought was a dead end, we might all be sitting in the dark now, and for a long time to come."

The debriefing went on for another hour. The man from FERC described the scenario that would have played out had the act of sabotage succeeded. It was every bit as dark as Ray Cooper had imagined. A cybersecurity expert from Homeland Security described the agency's plan for a full postmortem of

Empire's network breach and their coming audit of the security practices of energy utilities across the US.

At the end of the hour, Anya caught Sean on his way out of the room.

"How's Danielle?" she asked.

"Recovering."

"It's hard to shoot someone. That can be traumatic, even when you train for it."

"The whole thing was hard on her."

"Tell her I say hello. Tell her I thank her for being brave and for doing the right thing."

"I will."

He wanted to get out of there, to get back home, to shut himself up in his quiet house with Danielle. To curtain the windows and shut out the world and pull her up against him on the couch and eat popcorn and watch movies and forget for a while all the troubles of the past few weeks.

The woman waiting for him in the hall had other ideas. He tried to pretend he didn't notice the way her eyes had fixed on him. He tried to brush her off when she called his name as he walked by, but she wouldn't be ignored. She grabbed his wrist as he passed, and she said, "You're right, the original Chinese virus was well engineered. We've used it as a template for a number of our own exploits."

"Good for you," Sean said, shaking off her grip. He glanced at her NSA badge as he walked away.

She caught up and walked briskly beside him.

"We want you to walk our team step by step through the process of reviving and augmenting that malware."

"Some other time," Sean said. He picked up his pace, but she stayed right beside him.

"We'll make it worth your while."

"Right now, nothing is worth my while except peace and quiet."

"We have other work for you too."

"I'm not looking for work."

"No, but work will be looking for you after this." She pressed her card into his hand.

Again, he picked up his pace. "I just want to get out of here, okay?"

She slowed and watched him go.

"If we don't hear from you, you'll hear from us," she called.

"Great," Sean muttered sarcastically. But he didn't drop her card into the garbage can by the exit. He put it in his pocket.

# 72

"How's it feeling today?" Carrie asked.

Del sat on the edge of the bed gently draping a sling over his shoulder.

"Still hot and throbbing. The wound is oozing."

"We can change the bandage after breakfast. You want help getting the sling on?"

"Naw. I got it."

Her smile, turning slightly downward at the corners of her mouth, was bittersweet. "That's my Del," she said. "Won't take help from anyone. Can do it all by himself."

"Long as I still can, I will," he said. He groaned as he adjusted the sling. "The part that worries me is how long." He looked his wife in the eye. "You know, I haven't told you how bad the right shoulder really is. Can barely lift it over my head this past year. Now the left one's shot. Literally. And this body's all I got to work with. I've never been one to sit at a desk. I like to be up and around. How am I gonna do my job with two bad shoulders?"

"The doctors say you should get most of your range of motion back. If you do the physical therapy, you'll get your strength back too."

Del nodded. She read in his stoic look the things he would not say. That regaining "most" of his already limited range of motion amounted to an additional handicap. That at age forty-nine, after decades of physical work, he felt the wear in every part of his body. That coming to fatherhood late and having a house full of young children meant he would have to keep bringing in money for years to come. He would be sixty-four when the youngest graduated from high school. He wanted his children to have a chance at a life that wouldn't wear their bodies down. He had no idea how he would pay for their college. He was grateful to his wife for taking this risk with him, for taking the journey of parenthood with no guarantee that it would all work out.

She knew not to ask him whether he would take disability. She knew not to force him to speak aloud the thoughts she could read in his pensive look. Her husband was not the kind to burden others with his troubles. He didn't like to see his children worry. Let them be carefree while life allows. Let hope and imagination flourish in them while they're young.

"Well," he groaned as he stood from the edge of the bed. "Let's get to it."

Carrie watched him cross the room, watched him pass through the door, and then listened to the stairs creak as he slowly made his way down.

"Betcha I can make a pan of eggs one-handed," he called.

What the hell is wrong with this country, she wondered, as she turned to follow him. Our schools have become shooting ranges. Patriots want to burn down the country they claim to love. How can you hold your head up in this world, Del? Sometimes, I don't know where you find the strength.

# 73

## August 4

Sitting on the rear deck of her cousin Sarah's house in Colorado, Donna Cooper shielded her eyes from the morning sun that lit the eastern face of the mountains. Her son, Martin, had started the hike an hour earlier with her cousin's husband and three children. Eight miles up and back on steep terrain. They would be gone till late afternoon. A welcome break for her. And it was heartening to see her son so active and alive in the fresh summer air.

"How's he holding up?" her cousin asked.

Donna moved the papers from her lap to the table—the estate papers from the lawyer in Virginia, the letter from her late husband's life insurance company, the draft of the legal filing to revert to her maiden name.

"Better than me. He said something funny last night. Not funny, but knowing. We were talking about"—she gave her cousin a look that said *you know who*, a name she never wanted to utter again. "I didn't want to push him, but I wanted to get a sense of how he felt about his father's death. He shrugged and said, 'If you dedicate your life to conflict and violence, then don't be surprised if you die by conflict and violence.'

"It floored me, Sarah. I wasn't sure if he was trying to play it cool, trying to deny his feelings. You know he's at that age. He'll be thirteen next month. But I don't think he was playing it cool. When you live with a person like Ray, with this constant feeling of powerlessness, there's a part of you that always wishes he'll get his comeuppance, that one day he'll try to inflict his brutality on the wrong person, and that person will make him pay. Well, he spent his life looking for that person, and I guess he finally found her."

"What about you? You seem... Well, almost too calm."

"If I look calm, it's because I'm making an effort. Martin looks at me all the time, trying to read me. He thinks I don't notice, but I know what he's looking for. He wants some reassurance that things will be okay. I want to give him that, if I can."

"But underneath that," her cousin said. "Are you okay underneath it all?"

Donna shook her head. "I still dream of him every night. I dream I'm back in the house in Virginia. I don't know how I got there, or why, by Ray is furious with me for running away, for taking Martin and abandoning him. I can see the rage building in his eyes. I can feel his anger through every part of my body. It's like this energy his spirit pushes into me. I feel dread and terror in my stomach and in my muscles and bones.

"And then I wake up soaked with sweat, and I tell myself again and again that he's dead, that he can never yell at me, never look at me, never touch me again. But even that's not enough sometimes. Part of me wants him to acknowledge all his wrongs, to apologize, to cry and suffer and beg forgiveness. And I don't even want to forgive him. I want him to plead with God for that."

"Is the counseling helping? The support group?"

"Kind of. I mean, in the sense that—how do I say it? Ray can never acknowledge what he did to us. But they can. The others in the group. They're a testament to what we endured. They lived it like I lived it. And just to be seen and known, to have your experience brought to light and validated, to hear people speak a truth you can't yet put into words, that's a huge step toward recovery.

"But the counselor, I think, is the most helpful. Not because of what she says, but because of who she is. She lived through a marriage like mine, and now she's old and wise and whole and strong. My biggest fear on that long drive across the country was that I could never be whole again, that for the rest of my life, I would feel as low and worthless and hopeless and invisible as I did in the last few years of my marriage.

"I look at normal people—happy, healthy people—and I think, there is no road from here to there. There is no way for someone like me to ever get back to being someone like that."

Donna looked thoughtfully at her cousin, one of those happy, healthy people, to see if she was taking it all in.

"But my counsellor, she did it somehow. I don't know how, and I don't know how I'll do it. But just seeing her, seeing that it's possible, that it *does* happen, that gives me faith. When my mind tells me there's no road back to happiness and light, I think, 'No. There's the evidence right there. *She* is the evidence of the road you cannot see.' And as for Martin..."

She paused and thought a long while, her eyes following a hawk as it glided upward on the invisible breeze of a clear blue morning.

"You know, your parents can really only teach you two things in life. How to be a good person, or how *not* to be a good person. I think he got the lesson. I think he got it deep. Martin is not like his father. He never will be. Of that, I have no doubt."

# 74

August 28

In the brisk, cool breeze coming off the water, they felt the first hint of autumn. Sean and Danielle, nuzzling in heavy cotton sweats and hoodies, swayed gently in a hammock strung between two pine trees at the edge of Moosehead Lake in central Maine. The crisp breeze that cooled these northern woods would not reach Virginia for another month. After a long, sweltering summer, both looked forward to it.

Danielle reflected with a sense of wonder on the course her life had taken over the past nine weeks. Looking back to the day this all began, in a dark, hot grocery store, she marveled and cringed at how bold she had been in pursuit of Sean. *I wasn't chasing some dream guy,* she thought. *I wasn't looking for anything special. I just wanted a break from the boredom of an empty, pointless summer.*

After a seven-day honeymoon phase, the relationship became a trial by fire—on the run from the federal government, being shot at by a psychopath. *If that doesn't put a strain on a couple,* she mused, *what will?* She snuggled in closer, felt the rising of his chest as he breathed, the warmth of his body against the chilly lakeside breeze.

Here among the whispering pines, away from work and phones, social media and instant messaging, away from bills and traffic and the commotion of crowded city streets, she had time to reflect. What was different in her now? What had changed?

She felt more at peace. The restlessness that had driven her to seek new thrills, to pursue Sean that day in the grocery store, had subsided, at least for now. She knew it would return. It was part of her nature, pushed into remission temporarily by an overdose of adrenaline, and she reminded herself to enjoy the quiet while it lasted.

But beneath that lay a deeper change. Confidence, she thought. You never really know how you'll react to a life-and-death challenge until you face one. You imagine some worst-case scenario and how you'd handle it, and you're filled with this awful uncertainty. Will I rise to the occasion, or will fear and doubt get the better of me?

She knew the answer now.

She turned her eyes to Sean, watched him as he stared up through the trees toward the cottony white clouds drifting across the sky. Although he got himself into a mess, he seemed sensible by nature, she thought. His mind was rational, logical. She told herself that if she did get bored again and started seeking out excitement, he would reel her in and keep her out of trouble. We complement each other that way, she thought. My occasional flights of whim, his consistent gravitas. She watched his eyes, wondering what he was thinking.

Sean rubbed his finger across the sharp corner of the card in the pocket of his sweats, the business card the woman from the NSA had given him the day he left the debriefing in Richmond. If we don't hear from you, she warned, you'll hear from us.

Rebecca Strathmore wasn't bluffing. She had pestered him to give her colleagues a full walk-through of how he had crafted his malware exploit. He had ignored her then, and since then had deleted all her voicemails, all her texts, all her emails.

But not without reading or listening to them first. And he hadn't blocked her.

She must have gotten approval from her supervisors to expose as much detail as she had in some of those messages. He wondered whether she was lying about some of the projects she thought he "would be a great fit for." Had the Israelis really found a way to bypass iPhone security without tricking the user into clicking on anything? Were the computers running Iran's nuclear program really unhackable after Stuxnet, even by the NSA?

Had he learned anything about himself through this summer's grueling ordeal? No. It had simply reinforced what his mother had told him since he was a child. "You're destined for a life of trouble, Sean, because you can never let go of a mystery, no matter where it leads."

He sensed that the woman from No Such Agency had already figured that out. The challenges she presented in her messages kept getting more intriguing. And instead of being spooked by her ability to track him, he was impressed. After he and Danielle decided on the spur of the moment to go to Maine, he had received a message from her during the long drive north. "Enjoy the lake."

How did she know?

They really were everywhere, he thought, keeping tabs on whomever they pleased.

But they're not going to get me. They're not going to lure me away from my peace and quiet, from... He kissed Danielle's forehead as it rested on his chest. He stroked her hair as she watched him stare quietly toward the sky.

Thank God for her, he thought. Her light spirit is the perfect counterbalance to my obsessive mind. She doesn't take the world so seriously. She doesn't hold on to things. If I start going off the deep end again, getting too far into some crazy adventure, she can talk me down, bring me back to earth, keep me from getting into too much trouble.

As the sun dropped below the piney hills across the lake, they were both thinking the same thing. No more drama. Savor this season of quiet contentment.

In their cabin just up the hill, electronic bits from the internet seeped into the laptop that idled beside the woodstove they would soon be lighting for warmth. Nobody heard the chime of the incoming email that now sat at the top of Sean's inbox.

> Sean - Becca from The Agency. We've isolated a virus here that sneaks past every packet filter of every known firewall on the market. No one here can figure out how. Up for a challenge? We're offering good money to whoever can crack it. But you'll have to come

into HQ. This one's too dangerous to send out into the wild. Interested?

In her office back in Maryland, Rebecca Strathmore said to the psychological profiler, "Good call to end it with a question. How long do you think it'll be before he bites?"

"Give him a few weeks," the woman said. "He's got a new girlfriend. That'll hold his interest for a while."

"But not forever."

"Not forever, no. Sooner or later, the daily grid reasserts itself. The daily grind gets boring, and some people just can't stand to be bored."

# AFTERWORD

Some of the technical details of the grid failure and computer exploits described in this book come from real events.

In February 2020, Russian hackers managed to slip malicious code into a software update for SolarWinds' Orion application. Orion was deployed to the internal networks of a number of large corporations and critical US government agencies. Once active, the embedded malware reached out to Command and Control (C&C) servers requesting instructions from Russia, asking what its creators wanted it to steal, damage, or take control of.

Because of its high-value targets, its stealth, sophistication, and effectiveness, the SolarWinds hack turned out to be one of the most damaging in US history. The malicious code was able to evade detection for a long time because the hackers employed some of the same tricks described in this book. They didn't drop the malicious code into the main production code base, where other software engineers and security auditors might discover it. They quietly injected it at the last minute into the build server that converted human-readable code into machine-readable programs. Anyone searching Orion's main code base for evidence of malware would never find it.

In the spring of 2024, a San Francisco software engineer named Andres Freund discovered a second and even more insidious hack after a subtle observation of automated tests aroused his interest. The latest version of SSH, a program used to connect to and manage computers around the world, required a few extra milliseconds to secure its connections. Why?

Most programmers wouldn't care, but Freund, having the same relentless curiosity as Sean Riggs, discovered what came to be known as the "XZ Utils backdoor," an exploit that earned a rare ten out of ten on the US government's malware severity scale.

Freund traced the infinitesimal connection delay to some unusually clever code that was injected from an automated test suite into the main program at build time. He published a full description of how the exploit worked and its potentially dire effects just in time to avert a worldwide disaster. The SSH update had been scheduled for release in upcoming versions of the Linux operating system used to run essential services across hundreds of industries. If the exploit had made it into the wild, hackers would have gained control of thousands of critical systems in almost every country on earth.

The mechanism for the power outage described in this novel is based on the Northeast blackout of 2003, the largest in US history, which spread from Ohio to six other states and much of Ontario, knocking out power to more than fifty million people.

The blackout was the result of cascading failures that began with a single overvolted, overheated transmission line sagging in the summer heat near Cleveland, Ohio. When the line dipped low enough to touch a tree branch, it grounded out, sending a surge of power into the earth. A circuit breaker detected the surge, cut power to the line, and routed its current to other lines. The excess current pushed onto those other lines caused them to overheat and sag. They too grounded out when they touched trees or other structures.

The operators in the control room of Ohio's power utility, First Energy, didn't know it at the time, but a bug in their monitoring system prevented them from seeing the alerts that should have lit their monitors as line after line failed and millions lost power. First Energy became aware of the scope of the problem only when calls from other panicked utilities came pouring in. By then, it was too late. The collapse of the Ohio grid brought down Pennsylvania, New York, and a number of other states.

Most of those affected by the 2003 blackout had power restored within forty-eight hours. This was due in part to the huge number of safeguards built into the grid. Breakers, switches, relays, and shunts stop destructive electrical flows from damaging components downstream by cutting them off, or by rerouting the flow of power.

If someone wanted to cause extensive, long-term damage to the grid, they would have to damage or disable these physical safeguards that are spread across thousands of miles of electrical lines. In other words, it would take quite a coordinated conspiracy to inflict the kind of long-term damage Ray and his pals envisioned.

In recent years, however, as the grid has moved toward software-controlled components, cyberattacks have become potentially more destructive. Many components that used to require hands-on access to sabotage can now be manipulated remotely, for good or ill, through the centralized control systems that hackers like to target.

# LIST OF CHARACTERS

<u>Major</u>

**Sean Riggs**—Thirty-two-year-old software engineer with a strong moral conscience and relentless curiosity. Outwardly quiet and unassuming, he doesn't trust the government, corporate executives, or other authorities to do the right thing. He can be reckless and unyielding in his pursuit of knowledge.

**Danielle Duval**—Twenty-eight-year-old digital media strategist living outside Richmond, Virginia. Her optimism, lively, open mind, and impulsiveness mask deep inner strength and resourcefulness, even as they lead her into adventure and trouble.

**Ray Cooper**—Software engineering manager for Empire Energy's transmission-and-distribution systems. Dark, brooding and resentful, he holds a grudge against everyone he can't control, women in particular.

**Del Wright**—Forty-nine-year-old veteran field technician for Empire Energy who has repaired everything from lines to substations. Del's simple, practical outlook and his deep commitment to serving and helping his community put him at odds with Ray.

**Anya Lakhani**—Investigator from Homeland Security, thirty-four-year-old daughter of Indian immigrants. With her agency taking a back seat to the FBI in the investigation of a major cybersecurity breach, her job is to follow up on unpromising leads that more seasoned investigators see as a waste of time. She reports to the task force lead, Carlos Espinoza.

<u>Minor</u>

**Donna Cooper**—Ray Cooper's wife.

**Carrie Wright**—Del's wife. She's as practical and straightforward as he is.

**Ben Wood**—Twenty-four-year-old field technician at Empire Energy, a devoted follower of Ray Cooper.

**Carlos Espinoza**—FBI special agent investigating the hack into Empire Energy's internal computer network.

**Mei Chen**—Security and forensics expert working for the private cybersecurity firm Empire has hired to help investigate the breach of its network. Works with Phil Rudolph, appearing only briefly.

**Phil Rudolph**—Cybersecurity expert working with Mei Chen to help analyze the hack that has compromised Empire's systems.

**Charles Lehrman**—Head of IT security at Empire Energy and another member of Ray's clique.

**Cy Madhi**—Director of operations at Empire's transmission-and-distribution control center. His group monitors and manages the real-time flow of electricity throughout the state power grid. Skeptical, but levelheaded, his even temper balances out Ray's hotheadedness during some of the tenser moments of the hacking investigation.

**Jin**—A young software engineer at Empire Energy who is reluctant to help Anya Lakhani in her investigation.

**Sid Miller**—Sean's next-door neighbor. A high school teacher and sports coach in his midsixties.

**Jerry**—The auto mechanic who wants Sid Miller to retrieve the Mustang from his lot.

**Rebecca Strathmore**—NSA agent and recruiter for government projects.

# ALSO BY ANDREW DIAMOND

## Impala

After four years on the straight and narrow, Russell Fitzpatrick has a boring job, the wrong woman, and an itch for something more. All he needs to get his life going again is a nudge in the wrong direction.

When he receives a cryptic email from a legendary and slightly deranged fellow hacker—his old friend, Charlie, whom he knows to be dead—he tries to tell himself it's none of his concern. But the guy who stalks him across town at night, the two thugs waiting in the alley, and a ruthless FBI agent let him know his days are numbered if he doesn't turn over the money Charlie stole.

The problem is, Russ doesn't have it. As his enemies close in from all sides, Russ slowly unwinds the mystery of his old friend's paranoid mind and finds that Charlie left behind something worth much more than the money. And no one but him is onto it...

A fast-paced page-turner full of suspense, *Impala* has won numerous awards, including:

- Writer's Digest Gold Medal for Genre Fiction (2016)
- Readers' Favorite Gold Medal for Mystery (2017)
- A best of the year nod from IndieReader (2016)
- An Amazon.com Editor's pick for one of the best mystery/thriller titles of September 2016

# Gate 76

Freddy Ferguson #1

A mysterious woman fleeing an unknown terror boards the wrong plane at San Francisco International and disappears into the heart of the country. Freddy Ferguson, a troubled detective with a violent past, believes she's the last living witness to a crime that has captivated the nation.

Sifting through the wreckage of her past, he begins to understand whom she's running from, and why. Now he must track her down before her pursuers can silence her for good.

A modern crime thriller with elements of Raymond Chandler and the classic pulp novels of the 1950s, this character study wrapped in a tale of crime and redemption was named to Kirkus Reviews' Best Books of 2018.


# Kill Romeo

Freddy Ferguson #2

Not since he saw a woman hurry off a jetliner shortly before it exploded in midair (*Gate 76*) has detective and former boxer Freddy Ferguson faced such a deadly puzzle as when he comes across the body of a well-dressed young woman, nameless and unidentifiable, deep in the woods of rural Virginia. In her room at the town inn, she left two mysterious notes hinting at a love gone wrong.

The trail to her killer leads through organized crime, espionage, and the international race for technological supremacy to a seemingly unremarkable man the FBI and CIA have been trying for years to pin down.

# 32 Minutes
Freddy Ferguson #3

A corporate executive vanishes without a trace. His domineering boss wants him back in the office, ASAP.

Did Karl Larsson run off with a mistress? Was he kidnapped? Or had he just walked out once and for all on a life of debt and struggle?

The deeper Freddy Ferguson digs into this one, the less it makes sense. The statements from Larsson's long-suffering wife, from the stoner security guard who was the last to see the man alive, and from the respected reporter known for having the inside scoop just don't add up.

Where is the truth in this most perplexing of cases? Maybe in a slip of the tongue by an arrogant man, or in a dopesick junkie's account of a seemingly random attack. Maybe in the pocket of a man who stalks without fear of being seen, or in the multimillion-dollar transactions of an anonymous shell company.

One thing's for sure, Freddy needs to crack this case before he becomes its next victim.


# The Friday Cage
Claire Chastain #1

Someone new has taken an interest in Claire Chastain. He circles her house when she's alone and follows her on errands across town. He tours her home while she's away, leaving little things disturbingly out of place. He may even be involved in the recent death of her childhood friend.

But who is he? And what does he want?

Claire soon discovers that, like Cary Grant in *North by Northwest*, she's caught up in someone else's dark conspiracy, and she has no choice but to play the game. The only exit from her troubles will be the one she makes, if she's smart enough to figure out when and how to make it.

A suspenseful crime thriller in the tradition of Hitchcock and Ross MacDonald, *The Friday Cage* features an exceptionally tough, sharp-minded protagonist who must do some soul-searching in the midst of her quest to survive.

## The Reisman Case
### Claire Chastain #2

A wealthy business owner asks investigator Claire Chastain to solve a simple case. Is his employee stealing or not?

From the moment she's hired, subtle clues tell her something's wrong: the unbusinesslike business owner, the lingering scent of a woman on the stairs, the rustle in the curtains where someone watches from above.

Claire's gut tells her the case isn't about theft. Her investigation turns up a pathologically anxious suspect, a deeply dysfunctional family, and a murder that she herself appears to have committed.

"If I had known what this case would turn into," she reflects, "I never would have accepted it. No one walks into a burning house."

But she's in it, and she has to find her way out...

## To Hell with Johnny Manic

John Manis, aka Johnny Manic—charming, stylish, impulsive, and reckless—is racked with guilt over the secret he doesn't dare tell. Marilyn Dupree, passionate and volatile, has too much money and the wrong husband. Johnny and Marilyn have a chemistry like nitrogen and glycerin, and that makes Detective Lou Eisenfall very uneasy.

"Poor Lou," Johnny muses as his mind begins to unravel. "There's a madman running around his town, and who knows what he'll do next?"

This riveting tale of deception, murder, and psychological suspense was named one of the best of 2019 by BestThrillers.com.

# Warren Lane

Susan Moore is about to hire the wrong man to investigate her philandering husband, Will. There's something not quite right about that detective, but he's all she has at the moment.

"Warren Lane" drinks too much and has a hard time staying out of trouble. He's just the kind of guy Will's mistress can't resist. And everyone is starting to figure out that Will is hiding a lot more than his affair with a reckless young woman.

# The Sellout

Years of writing thoughtful, heartfelt literary fiction have brought Joe McElwee nothing but poverty and obscurity. Now his blockbuster formulaic thriller, full of mindless action and tired but proven tropes, has him on the verge of wealth and fame.

Not everyone is happy, though. Joe's friend Veronica, a staunch supporter of his honest early work, criticizes him for selling out. Frustrated at his refusal to hear her concerns, she puts a curse on him, forcing him to live as a character inside the novel of an author he despises, best-selling hack Niall Turner, who is the undisputed king of the detective-thriller genre.

McElwee wakes up in nineteen-forties Los Angeles to discover he's entered the Turnerverse, a world marked by two-dimensional characters, outdated stereotypes, gaping plot holes, and poor editing.

Worse yet, he's apparently just committed a murder. In short order, he has to figure out who he is, who his friends and enemies are, and how he fits into a universe that doesn't quite make sense. Along the way, he picks up a beautiful mistress, a femme fatale, an inept assassin, and a sinking sense of shame as he's forced to inhabit the kind of shoddy writing he's now producing.

"I brought you here," Veronica tells him, "to rub your nose in the Turnerverse, so you can see what you're becoming."

Will it be enough to save an honest writer? Or will the lure of wealth and fame be too much for Joe McElwee?

## Wake Up, Wanda Wiley

Hannah Sharpe has been written out of all eighteen of Wanda Wiley's romance novels. A runaway heroine who won't conform to the plots laid out for her, Hannah has been consigned to a realm of fog deep in the recesses of the author's imagination.

Trevor Dunwoody, the protagonist of a macho action thriller that Wanda has regrettably agreed to ghostwrite, is single-minded and obtuse, understanding only what he can beat up, shoot, or screw. Like Hannah, he's a character Wanda doesn't know what to do with. When he appears one day in Hannah's fog world, she can't convince him he's in the wrong story.

Hannah knows she'll be stuck in the limbo of Wanda's subconscious until the writer can find a suitable story to cast her in. But Wanda, trapped in a disastrous relationship with philandering narcissist Dirk Jaworski, is sinking into a deep depression. The pot she smokes to self-medicate impairs her ability to write and thickens the fog of Hannah's timeless isolation.

As Hannah explains her predicament to the thickheaded Trevor, she begins to realize that she knows her author better than her author knows herself. If she can only break out of the limbo of Wanda's subconscious and nudge the writer in the right direction, she can free them both.

But how can Hannah penetrate the fog of her creator's mind from within? The answer is right in front of her in the form of the big, dumb, action-ready tool, Trevor Dunwoody.

# ABOUT THE AUTHOR

Andrew Diamond writes mystery, crime, noir, and an occasional comedy. His books feature cinematic prose, strong characterization, twisting plots, and dark humor. Amazon editors named *Impala* a best of the month mystery, and IndieReader named it to its best of 2016 list. *Impala* also won the Readers' Favorite Gold Medal for Mystery and the 24th Annual Writer's Digest award for genre fiction.

*Gate 76* was named to Kirkus Reviews' Best Books of 2018, while BestThrillers.com selected both *Gate 76* (2018) and *To Hell with Johnny Manic* (2019) to its best of the year list.

You can follow Andrew on Goodreads and at https://adiamond.me.